11/2013

The BRIDE WORE SIZE 12

D0121712

By Meg Cabot

Overbite
Insatiable
Ransom My Heart (with Mia Thermopolis)
Queen of Babble series
Heather Wells series
The Boy series
She Went All the Way
The Princess Diaries series
The Mediator series
The 1–800-WHERE-R-YOU series
All-American Girl series
Nicola and the Viscount
Victoria and the Rogue
Jinx
How to Be Popular
Pants on Fire
Avalon High series
The Airhead series
Allie Finkle's Rules for Girls series
The Abandon series

The BRIDE WORE SIZE 12

MEG CABOT

WILLIAM MORROW

An Imprint of HarperCollins*Publishers*

THE BRIDE WORE SIZE 12. Copyright © 2013 by Meg Cabot, LLC. All
rights reserved. Printed in the United States of America. No part of this
book may be used or reproduced in any manner whatsoever without
written permission except in the case of brief quotations embodied in
critical articles and reviews. For information address HarperCollins Publishers, 10 East 53rd Street, New York, NY 10022.

HarperCollins books may be purchased for educational, business, or
sales promotional use. For information please e-mail the Special Mar-
kets Department at SPsales@harpercollins.com.

Designed by Diahann Sturge

Library of Congress Cataloging-in-Publication Data has been applied for.

ISBN 978-0-06-173479-3

13 14 15 16 17 OV/RRD 10 9 8 7 6 5 4 3 2 1

Acknowledgments

This book could never have been completed without the help and support of many people, including, but not limited to: Beth Ader, Nancy Bender, Jennifer Brown, Michele Jaffe, Ann Larson, Janey Lee, and Rachel Vail. The endlessly amazing people at HarperCollins, especially Carrie Feron, Pamela Spengler-Jaffee, and Nicole Fischer. My agent, Laura J. Langlie. And last but never least, my husband, Benjamin D. Egnatz. But most especially, all of you. You rock! Thanks, as always, for reading.

The pleasure of your company is
requested at the marriage of
Heather Marie Wells
to
Cooper Arthur Cartwright
Saturday, the 28th of September,
at half past two in the afternoon
The Grand Ballroom
The Plaza
Fifth Avenue at
Central Park South
New York, New York

1

Everything's going to work out." That's what I've been saying all month to my fiancé, Cooper. "Everything's going to be great. Wait and see."

Each time I say it, Cooper looks at me in that adorable way he has, one dark eyebrow lifted slightly higher than the other one. He knows exactly what I'm talking about, and it has nothing to do with our upcoming wedding ceremony at the Plaza Hotel in New York City.

"You do know that statistically, more young adults end up in hospital emergency rooms than any other age group?" he points out. "At least for accident-related injuries. And more of them *die* of those injuries than any other age group as well."

When you live with a licensed private detective, you can count on many things. One of them is that sometimes he's going to keep odd hours. Another is that there will be fire-arms in your home.

A third is that occasionally he will trot out random facts you probably never cared to know, like how many registered sex offenders live within a five-mile radius of your home, or that more young people end up in hospital emergency rooms than any other age group.

I glare at him. "So?"

"So it makes sense that in a student population the size of the one at New York College," Cooper says, "you're going to have at least one or two deaths a year."

"Not this year," I say, shaking my head vehemently over our Chinese takeout. Everything we've been eating lately has been delivered in a carton, because with freshman check-in looming, my hours are so long. I'm coming home from work later and later every evening, bone tired from sorting keys and supervising room cleanings. Cooper has a case as well, so his hours haven't been very regular either, although out of respect to his client's privacy, he won't tell me exactly what his duties entail. "This year, everything is going to be differ-ent. No one in Fischer Hall is going to die this year. Not even accidentally."

"How are you going to manage that?" Coop asks, gnawing on a Chinese sparerib. "Bubble wrap all your residents?"

I picture the undergraduate students who live in the resi-dence hall in which I work attempting to navigate the streets of New York City while encased in plastic shipping material. It's a strangely pleasing thought. "Not really feasible. I think they'd object on human rights grounds. Good idea, though."

Now both of Cooper's eyebrows have gone up, and he's looking faintly amused. "Maybe it's better if we can't have kids after all if you think bubble wrapping them is a good idea."

I ignore his sarcasm. "Okay, how about this?" I say. "So long as none of them gets murdered, I'll be happy."

Cooper reaches across the moo shu pork to give my hand a squeeze. "That's one of the many reasons I fell in love with you, Heather. You've never been afraid to dream big."

Yes, this year was going to be different, all right. Totally different from last year, when I first started my job as assistant director of Fischer Residence Hall, and I thought Cooper wasn't attracted to me, and we lost our first student a few weeks into the semester.

This year, Cooper and I were getting married, and we lost our first student before classes even started.

I should have gone with the bubble wrap after all.

2

Welcome to Freshman Orientation Week at Fischer Residence Hall!

New York College and the Department of Housing and Student Affairs is delighted to welcome you to check in one week early in order to help you acclimate to your new home for the coming academic year! Meet your new roommates, your advisers, professors, and deans while becoming familiar with the many services and programs this college has to offer!

Enjoy activities open only to incoming freshmen and transfer students, such as organized trips to some of New York City's top sights, shows, and hot spots, including:

the Statue of Liberty - Ellis Island - Freedom Tower - the Broadway show Wicked- Cake Boss Café - and many, many more!

It's a beautiful day, one of the last of summer. The sky outside my office is clear blue, the temperature a perfect seventy-five degrees.

It's also the first week of freshman orientation at New York College. So far, very little is going right.

"Look," says the attractive woman in tight white jeans who's slid into the chair beside my desk. "It's not like my Kaileigh is spoiled. For spring break last year, she volunteered to build houses in Haiti with Habitat for Humanity.

She lived in a tent with no running water. She knows how to rough it."

I keep a polite smile plastered on my face. "So what exactly is Kaileigh's problem with her room, Mrs. Harris?"

"Oh, it's not her room." Mrs. Harris has to raise her voice to be heard over the drilling. Carl, the building engineer, is perched on a ladder near the office photocopier, doing what we're telling the student staff is the last of some "minor electrical repair work" left over from the renovation the building received over the summer.

When the students discover what Carl is really doing—installing the wiring for a set of security monitors on which my boss, Lisa, and I will be able to watch everything that occurs in the fifteenth-floor hallway—they'll probably launch a protest over the invasion of their privacy, even though it's being done for their protection.

"It's Kaileigh's room*mate*," Mrs. Harris goes on.

I nod sympathetically before launching into a speech I've given so many times I occasionally feel like one of those performing robots at Disney World's Country Bear Jamboree, only not quite as cuddly:

"You know, Mrs. Harris, an important part of the college experience is meeting new people, some of whom might come from cultures other than your own—"

Mrs. Harris cuts me off. "Oh, I know all about that. We read the orientation material you people sent us over the summer. But there are limits to what someone can be expected to put up with."

"What's Kaileigh's problem with her roommate?"

"Oh, my Kaileigh isn't one to complain," Mrs. Harris says,

her skillfully made-up eyes widening at the idea of Kaileigh ever doing anything remotely wrong. "She doesn't even know I'm here. A problem with Ameera—that's the name of Kaileigh's roommate—was the last thing we were expecting. Those two girls have been texting and Skyping back and forth all summer, ever since they found out they were assigned together, and everything seemed fine. I assumed they were going to be BFFs, best friends forever, you know?"

I'm aware of what BFF stands for, but I only smile encouragingly.

"It wasn't until this week, when Ameera and Kaileigh actually started *living* together, that we realized—"

Mrs. Harris bites her bottom lip and glances down at her perfectly manicured nails and tastefully jeweled fingers, hesitant to continue. A father standing directly behind Mrs. Harris—not her husband—keeps glancing at his gold watch. A Rolex, of course. Few New York College students request financial aid . . . or if they do, they aren't the types to have their parents do their complaining for them.

"*What?*" I'm as impatient with Mrs. Harris as the guy with the Rolex, only for different reasons. "What did you realize about your daughter's roommate?"

"Well . . . I don't know any other way to put this," Mrs. Harris says. "Ameera is . . . well, she . . . she's . . . she's a *slut*."

The parents in line behind Mrs. Harris look shocked. Carl, on top of his ladder, drops his drill.

I'm a little stunned myself.

Mrs. Harris appears uncomfortable, but doesn't ask to speak somewhere more private, which is good, since the door to Lisa's office is closed, and the conference room down the hall is being used as a headquarters for the surveillance team that's monitoring our new VIR (Very Important Resident) twenty-four hours a day, seven days a week.

"Uh," I say, struggling to remember what section in the New York College Student Housing Guide covers "slut." Oh, yeah. None. "Maybe we should—"

"I'm not trying to be judgmental," Mrs. Harris hurries to assure me (and Carl, since it's clear, as he hurries down the ladder to fetch his drill, that he's paying rapt attention. A slut in Fischer Hall? This is the best news he's heard all day). "It's the simple truth. Kaileigh's been telling us about it all week. Ameera has only slept in the room once since she checked in. *Once.* And according to Kaileigh and her suite mates, it's a different boy every night . . . and once even a girl!"

Carl stumbles on his way back to the ladder. A slutty *bisexual?* His expression is one of complete and utter joy.

Mrs. Harris is too caught up in her narration to notice.

"How well can Ameera know any of these people? She's only been in the city a week, like my Kaileigh. They both arrived the first day of Freshman Orientation. I guess I don't have to tell you how disturbing I find all of this."

I'm too astonished to say anything in reply. There is a large candy dish on my desk, but instead of being filled with candy, it's filled with brightly wrapped condoms from the student health center. All year students waiting for the elevator dart into my office to plunge their hands into the candy bowl, snatching up free condoms by the fistful.

This is how I combat the problem of frisky co-eds. They're going to play, so why should they have to pay a lifetime for it?

Mrs. Harris doesn't seem aware of the candy bowl, however, or that my attitude about teen sex is different from hers, since she goes on, "And apparently Ameera didn't bother coming home at all this morning."

I'm finally able to find my voice.

"Well, that was thoughtful of her. She's probably aware of how much the odd hours she's been keeping have disturbed your daughter, and wanted to allow her the chance to sleep in." I pray this is the truth and that Ameera isn't lying dead in a Dumpster in an alley somewhere.

She most likely isn't. Most likely she's curled in a hot hipster's Brooklyn loft bed, enjoying some postcoital languor and her first latte of the day. I wish we could change places. Except that my hot dude of choice lives around the corner, not in Brooklyn, and would no sooner own a loft bed than a nose ring.

"You know, Mrs. Harris," I go on, "here at New York College we encourage students to explore who they are in ways they might not have been able to while living at home, and sometimes that means exploring who they are . . . um . . . sexually . . ."

"But every night this week, with as many people?" Mrs. Harris is having none of my soothing administrative psychobabble. "That is simply unacceptable. They told me at that desk in the lobby that this is the place to come if students need their rooms changed."

"It is," Gold Rolex says. He's as fully engaged in our conversation as Carl, and almost as excited by it. "That's why I'm here too. My son was assigned to that dorm across the park, what's it called? Oh, yeah. Wasser Hall. He's miserable over there. Apparently Fischer Hall is the 'cool' place to live."

Gold Rolex makes quotation marks in the air with his fingers when he says the word "cool," and laughs at the absurdity of one building being "cooler" than another. A number of the parents in line behind him laugh along with him.

If only they knew just how absurd the idea of Fischer Hall being the "cool place to live" really is.

"At least your kid's in the right building," Gold Watch tells Mrs. Harris. "I gotta get mine on some kind of Room Change Wait List in order for him to be able to move in here."

A lot of murmuring goes on in the line behind him. Apparently many of the parents have heard of this list. That's why they're here too. It's essential that they get their kids into Fischer Hall, the "cool place to live."

Especially now that they've heard about Ameera, I'm sure.

I can hardly believe it. If you'd told me a year ago—even a *week* ago—that there'd be a line out my office door of parents waiting to get their kids on a wait list to get into Fischer Hall, I'd have said you were nuts.

But here it is, happening right in front of my eyes. The line snakes out the residence hall director's office, then disappears down the hallway, which is as noisy and crowded as my office, since it's situated directly opposite the elevators to Fischer Hall's upper floors.

No wonder most of the parents look as if they, like me, are beginning to get a headache. They're all wearing expressions of impatience—some, of bitter resignation—and some look outright annoyed.

I can understand why. It's nearly noon. I'm sure I'm not the only one who's eager for lunch (although I'm probably the only one feeling that way because according to my

At-A-Glance desk calendar, I'm having lunch with my extremely attractive private detective boyfriend and our very exclusive—and outrageously expensive—wedding planner).

At least I have the satisfaction of knowing all the hard work my staff and I put in over the summer—not to mention the tremendous amount of money the college poured into the Fischer Hall renovation—has paid off . . . maybe a little *too* well. I almost wish Lisa or even our graduate assistant Sarah was around so I could ask them to pinch me to make sure I'm not dreaming.

But there's only Carl, and no way am I asking Carl to pinch me. I just know when he related the story to all the guys in the break room downstairs it would somehow get twisted into something pervy, like me showing him my boobs.

"Right," Mrs. Harris says, brightening at Rolex Watch's mention of the Room Change Wait List. "That's what Kaileigh needs, a room change. In a just world I think *Ameera* should be the one to have to move—"

Where does Mrs. Harris want me to move her? I wonder. Fischer Hall has a number of "exploration floors" this year, reserved for students who wish to immerse themselves in the major they're studying, such as French Floor, Deutsches Haus, and "Artistic Craft," but none reserved for "Aspiring Sluts."

"—but I'm sure there's some kind of bias rule against that," Mrs. Harris goes on bitterly, "so I want Kaileigh moved, right away."

Of course, before Kaileigh catches any of Ameera's cooties.

I sigh, wishing fervently that Lisa were available to field this one, because I'm afraid I'm going to say something rude.

"Do you have any single rooms available?" Mrs. Harris asks, raising her white designer purse and opening it to draw out her checkbook. "I'll pay the difference in cost. All I want is for my Kaileigh to be happy."

"Uh," I say, keeping control of my temper with an effort. "We do have single rooms, but they're only available to the resident assistant staff, seniors, and individuals with special needs."

And "slut bashing" your roommate does not qualify as a special need, I keep myself from adding, with an effort. *Except for my need to want to bash you over the head.*

Instead, I reach for an innocuous black binder I keep on a shelf beside my desk and say, "I can put your daughter on the Room Change Wait List, but I think it's a little premature for that . . ."

My voice trails off as I become aware that everyone in the room seems to have inhaled. At first I'm not sure why.

Then I see that they're all staring at the label on the front of the binder I'm holding—*Room Change Wait List*—like it's the Ark of the Covenant, or something.

"That's it," I hear someone farther down the line whisper. "The *list*."

It's all beginning to come back to me . . . what it's like to be popular. People used to line up like this in front of me fifteen years ago, but it was to get my autograph after playing a sold-out concert (back in the days when I was number one on the pop record charts), not to get their kid's name on a waiting list to move into the residence hall where I work.

"Then," I say, lowering the binder and doing my Country

Bear Jamboree automaton imitation again, "if Kaileigh still feels uncomfortable, she can come down here and fill out a room change request form, and as soon as a space becomes available through the wait list, we'll contact you. I mean, Kaileigh. But right now Fischer Hall is filled to capacity."

There is a surprisingly loud groan, not just from Mrs. Harris, but from everyone standing in line behind her.

I decide it's better not to tell them that the wait list of students clamoring to live in Fischer Hall is already over five hundred students long, and that the chances of Kaileigh—or any other student—receiving a room change is zero.

"Worked here for twenty years, and I never thought I'd see this," I hear Carl mutter under his breath. "People lining up to move into this dump? What is the world coming to?"

I've only worked in Fischer Hall for a year, but I feel the same way. Not that I consider Fischer Hall a dump.

Still, I'm trying to act like a professional, so I don't agree with him . . . out loud, anyway.

"I don't understand," Mrs. Harris says. "I'm here. I've waited all this time. Why can't I just fill out the form for Kaileigh?"

"Well, even though I know you'd never do anything against Kaileigh's wishes," I say tactfully, "I've had family members—and roommates—request that students be moved from rooms in which the resident was in fact perfectly happy." Exactly the way spurned lovers sometimes call the electric company and try to get their ex's power shut off, out of sheer spite. "So that's why I need Kaileigh—and any other student who wants a room change," I add, loudly enough for all the other parents to hear, "to come here and fill out the paperwork him or herself."

Not unexpectedly, Mrs. Harris and all the other parents who've been waiting in line for so long groan again.

Seeing Mrs. Harris's mutinous expression, I hurry to add, before she can interrupt, "Kaileigh hasn't even tried talking to Ameera about the problem yet, has she? Or their RA?"

Mrs. Harris rolls her eyes. "The RA? You mean that girl Jasmine, who lives down the hall? I've been knocking on her door all morning, but she's not there. I don't see why you hired her. My Kaileigh would do a much better job of making herself available."

"Kaileigh's a freshman," I point out, trying not to let her dig at our student staff—most of whom are new to the building, just like Kaileigh—irritate me, and go on, "Resident assistants have to be juniors or seniors. Look, I'm sure this whole thing between your daughter and her roommate will have blown over by the time classes start and the girls have to buckle down and start studying. In the meantime, if Kaileigh—or anyone else—really does feel the situation is untenable, they're welcome to come down here and schedule an appointment with the hall director, or look at this list and see if there's someone on it with whom they might want to swap rooms."

While Mrs. Harris continues to fume—she's a parent who feels all of her daughter's decisions need to be made for her—I notice a few faces in the line suddenly appear much more cheerful. But those faces all belong to students.

Not the typical sweatshirt-and-Ugg-wearing students I normally see in my office, however. The girls are rocking sparkly eye shadow, tons of bangles, sky-high platform heels, and miniskirts. The boys are even more carefully styled than the girls, sporting pressed oxford-cloth shirts, skinny jeans, and pastel scarves (tossed around necks thinner than my upper arms). They're making me feel as if I showed up to work today underdressed in my dark jeans, white button-up blouse, and flats.

These kids want to make an impression on someone . . . and it isn't me. I highly doubt it's any of these parents either.

I have a pretty good idea who it is, though.

One of the students, a blonde in extremely high heels, leans forward and calls, "Hey. Hey!" to get Mrs. Harris's attention.

When Mrs. Harris glances at her, the girl says, "Hi, I'm Isabel. I got assigned to Wasser Hall, the building across the park where that guy's son lives." She points at Gold Rolex, who blushes from the attention. "Anyway, I'll *totally* swap rooms with your daughter. I wouldn't mind living with a slut . . . especially one who's never home. In fact, I'd *love* that. I'll live with anyone so long as I can be in Fischer Hall . . . and near *him*."

The boys and girls all titter excitedly. They know exactly who the *him* is that she's referring to, even if Mrs. Harris looks blank.

I knew it. It isn't the makeover Fischer Hall received, or the reality show that was filmed here over the summer featuring two very well-known celebrities, my ex-boyfriend and future brother-in-law, Jordan Cartwright, and his wife, Tania Trace (though the show is in "postproduction" and won't air until after Christmas), or even all our hard work that's catapulted the building to such heights of popularity.

It's our Very Important Resident (for whom Carl's installing the security monitors, and the surveillance crew has been stationed down the hall). Word about him has spread faster than I ever imagined . . . not surprisingly, since he hasn't kept a very low profile, despite his insistence on being called by his self-chosen "American" name instead of the one his parents gave him.

I wonder which was the biggest tip-off to his fellow students: the newly installed security cameras in the lobby and our office, as well as on the fifteenth-floor hallway and exterior ledges outside his windows? Or the fact that he's the only student in the history of New York College ever to be assigned an entire suite to himself, two bedrooms and one bathroom for one person?

Or is it the chauffeured white Escalade that's parked outside the building twenty-four hours a day, available for his personal use any time of day or night?

Or perhaps it's his constantly updated social media networking feed (over a million followers and growing), shots of him playing competitive tennis, riding horses in the desert, skydiving onto his own personal yacht, even dancing in nightclubs with the locals, to the frustration of his diligent yet exhausted bodyguards and now the entire New York College housing staff?

It couldn't possibly be his father's $500 million donation to the college, a donation so large—only after his son was admitted—that it became front-page news in every paper in the city?

Clearly all of this has done nothing to lower our VIR's profile.

But it's done *everything* to boost Fischer Hall's reputation as *the* place to live.

Mrs. Harris, however, has no idea about any of this.

"Oh, no," Mrs. Harris says, in some confusion, to Isabel's offer. "That's just it. Kaileigh would never want to move out of Fischer Hall. She adores all the people she's met since she's moved in here, especially the girls in the room next door, her suite mates, Chantelle and Nishi. And she'd never *request* a room change." Mrs. Harris darts a nervous look in my direction. "That's why I'm here to do it for her. She wouldn't want to hurt Ameera's feelings. Kaileigh's got such a tender heart, you see."

I hear a snort from behind Mrs. Harris, though it doesn't come from the direction of the students. I see that a wild-haired young woman in overalls has entered the office, a teacup and saucer balanced carefully in her hands.

"Excuse me," apologizes Sarah, looking genuinely contrite when she sees that her derisive snigger at the words "tender heart" was overheard. She's the graduate student assigned to assist the Fischer Hall director's office, and she knows she isn't supposed to smirk at the parents. "I was . . . I was just—" She's at a loss for words.

"Taking that tea in to Ms. Wu?" I ask, rescuing her. "Go ahead." I nod at the hall director's closed office door. "She's been waiting for it."

"Sorry that took me so long." Sarah quickly opens the door to Lisa's office, allowing me a glimpse of my boss, miserably resting her head on top of her desk, as Sarah goes in. "The line in the caf was unbelievable. Here you go, Lise. This will make you feel better—"

A soft moan escapes from Lisa before the door closes behind Sarah.

Mrs. Harris stares after the younger girl, apparently having missed the snort at her expense.

"If the hall director is in," the older woman says, a calculated expression on her face, "perhaps I'd be better off speaking with her about getting Kaileigh a room change, since she's in charge. My husband and I leave here to go back to Ohio on Saturday, and if Kaileigh's going to move, it will have to be soon. She can't possibly cart all her own things, she'll need our help. As I said, I'm really quite worried about Ameera's lifestyle. My Kaileigh was looking forward to having a real roommate this year, not someone who—"

"I'm sorry." I cut her off, though I use my sweetest tone. "The hall director isn't feeling well. She has a stomach bug. You wouldn't want to spoil the rest of your trip to New York by catching it."

Mrs. Harris looks alarmed. "Oh, no. Certainly not."

In the hallway outside, the elevator doors ding, and the noise level increases noticeably as residents rush to get off the car while others rush to cram themselves, and their plastic bins of belongings, on. Fischer Hall was constructed in the mid-1800s, so the lobby floor is made of marble, the ceilings all nearly twelve feet high (twenty in the cafeteria), with chandeliers that sparkle with the very same crystals they did in the days of Henry James (though they've now been retrofitted with energy-saving bulbs instead of real candles).

Therefore the noise during any period of high foot traffic (such as lunch and dinnertime) can get to be a little much, thanks to the voices of so many high-spirited young people mingling together at once, not to mention the pinging of the electronic scanner as they slide their ID cards through it to gain access to the building, and the bark of Pete, behind the security desk, telling everyone to "Slow down, it's not a race," and "Have your ID card ready or you're not going anywhere, no way, no how," on top of the constant dinging of the elevator doors as they open and close.

But the noise in the hallway increases to a level I've rarely heard before, and it doesn't take long to figure out why when I hear Isabel and her friends whisper excitedly, "Oh my God, he's coming this way! It's . . ."

A second later, a tall, dark-haired boy dressed in skinny jeans and a camouflage-print sports jacket—shoulder seams nearly bursting against its owner's sizable muscles; sleeves pushed casually to elbows to reveal a dazzling diamond-and-platinum watch—strides into my office, followed by a retinue of young women and hulking bodyguards.

"*Prince Rashid,*" breathes Isabel and her friends, starstruck.

"Please," His Highness Crown Prince Rashid Ashraf bin Zayed Faisal says, with a wink and a modest tip of his fedora, followed by a slow smile that reveals all of his perfectly white, even teeth. "In this country I go by my American name, Shiraz. Because like the wine, I'm best served chilled."

3

Falcons, Ferraris, and a Big Fat Inheritance: Just a Day in the Life for Rascally Rashid of Qalif

What's Crown Prince Rashid Ashraf bin Zayed Faisal got that you don't have? Everything.

A competitive tennis player whose father boasts the largest fortune in the Middle East, Prince Rashid never walks. Why should he when he can take one of his gold-rimmed Escalades?

Twenty-one, Rashid's already earned his country's only gold medal in the Summer Olympics, but that's not enough for "Shiraz." No, now he wants to try to earn a college degree in the good ol' U.S. of A., right here at New York College.

Don't worry though, fellow peasants, the *Express* is on the case. We'll keep you apprised of all his daily dealings, and let you know if we see him in the dining hall eating spaghetti and meatballs like us proletarians.

New York College Express, your daily student news blog

The door to the hall director's office is thrown open. Sarah takes one glimpse at "Shiraz," his biceps nearly bursting out of his camo sports coat, and looks as if she might follow our boss's example and lose her breakfast.

"You have *got* to be kidding me," she says.

"Well, hey there, pretty lady." The prince lowers his dark, sooty lashes and flashes an even more dazzling smile, the one that's caused the press to dub him "Rascally Rashid."

The smile has no effect on Sarah.

"What do *you* want?" she growls.

"Me?" The prince seems surprised by her hostility. "I don't want anything."

"Then why are you here?"

"Sarah," I say in a warning tone, worried about the suspicious looks Rashid's bodyguards are giving her.

While it's true that most of the New York College community has welcomed Rashid with open arms, a small minority hasn't been particularly thrilled by the young prince's enrollment, despite the massive donation his father—His Highness General Sheikh Mohammed bin Zayed Faisal, crown prince and deputy supreme commander of the armed forces of Qalif—made to New York College's School of Arts and Sciences.

This dislike could have something to do with the fact that Prince Rashid is rumored to have scored pretty dismally on the SATs, well below the already minimal average required for admission to New York College.

But it probably has more to do with the fact that Qalif, though famous for its beautiful beaches and architecture—and prodigious oil production—does not allow freedom of the press or religious expression, and its government (led by Prince Rashid's father) is said to repress women, homosexuals, and the poor.

At a supersecret administrative staff meeting—to which

Sarah hadn't been invited because she's only a graduate student, not a full-time employee—we'd been told that there've been threats on the young prince's life, some of which may have come from members of the New York College community, who are calling the money Rashid's father donated to the school "blood money," and the school's president, Phillip Allington, "a traitor to his country" for having accepted it.

Fortunately, protecting visiting royalty falls under the responsibility of the U.S. State Department (thank God; the last thing we need is Pete from campus security thinking it's his duty to keep the heir to the throne to Qalif safe, in addition to forcing all seven hundred of our residents to sign in their guests to the building), so they've set up their office in our conference room.

But all that really means is that if Sarah doesn't watch out, she's going to find herself getting arrested by the U.S. Bureau of Diplomatic Security . . . if one of Prince Rashid's bodyguards doesn't kill her first.

"I'm here with her." Rashid points at a young woman who's gotten off the elevator along with him.

"Of course you are," Sarah says with an unpleasant laugh. "You know in this country, unlike yours, Your Highness, women are not legally required to walk behind men."

Prince Rashid looks even more surprised, and a little hurt.

"Miss." The larger of the two bodyguards narrows his coal-black eyes at Sarah. "Do you have a problem with the prince?"

"No," Sarah says. "I have a problem with his entire *country*, starting with the way his people treat my people, and by people I mean the people of Israel—"

As the bodyguard takes a step toward Sarah, I rise from

my desk, certain that an international incident is about to occur right in the Fischer Hall director's office.

But Rashid raises a hand to calm his security man, saying something in swift Arabic that ends with, "So chill out, okay, Hamad?"

Hamad doesn't look very chill, however. His broad shoulders beneath his impeccably cut charcoal suit jacket are tense. I can't help noticing a subtle bump in the side of his suit jacket beneath the left arm that I know from living with a private detective indicates a firearm.

Before I have time to feel nervous about this, however, I hear a gasp.

"Mom?" cries the girl who's followed Rashid into my office.

Mrs. Harris pops up from my office chair.

"Kaileigh?" Mrs. Harris cries. "Oh, my goodness, it's you! Sweetheart, you didn't tell me you were going out."

Kaileigh—she of the tender heart—says woodenly, "Shiraz and Nishi and Chantelle and I were going to go grab some lunch. Why are you in the hall director's office?"

"Oh, I was just, uh, er . . ." Mrs. Harris's face turns the color of my That's Hot pink nail polish.

"Your mom stopped in to ask me a question about the, um . . . Parent Parting." I rush to Mrs. Harris's rescue, grabbing a flyer from the top of the pile on my desk. "The final farewell ceremony is Saturday at three in the Winer Sports Complex, Mrs. Harris. We highly recommend you and your husband attend. It's going to be a beautiful way for the two of you to say good-bye to your daughter until you see her again at Parents Weekend in October."

I'm quoting directly from the flyer. In the opinion of

many of my coworkers as well as myself, the Parent Parting is a joke . . . though considering the way some parents—including Mrs. Harris—seem to think their tenderhearted darlings can't cope without them, it's probably not a bad idea. According to administrators at other schools, some parents have begun renting apartments near their children's dorms so they can "help" their sons and daughters transition through their first semester.

This "help" includes showing up at their child's instructors' office hours and demanding that the professors give the child better grades.

So holding a candlelit "parent-parting" ceremony at the end of orientation week isn't simply a nice thing to do. It's becoming a necessity on many campuses.

It's the fact that attendance is mandatory for administrative staff that I find a bit irksome. I have errands to run on the weekend, not to mention a wedding to plan. Plus, *I'm* not going to have any problem parting with the parents. I can't really relate to these modern day, ultra-involved parents who want to do everything for their kids. Maybe that's because my own parents were the exact opposite . . . they couldn't have cared less what happened to me.

Well, except during the days when I was making tons of money for them, of course. But—at least so far as Mom was concerned—it was only the money she cared about. That's why she took off with all of it.

If only I'd known then what I do now. I'd have had a very different kind of Parent Parting ceremony with her.

"Oh," Mrs. Harris says, taking the flyer from me. "Thank you. Yes, this is, er, exactly what I wanted to know."

Behind her, Gold Rolex looks perplexed. "I thought you were here for the same reason as the rest of us, to sign your daughter up for the—"

"It's so nice that you're going to lunch with your new friends, Kaileigh," Mrs. Harris interrupts him hastily. "But Daddy and I were going to take you out to lunch today in Chinatown. Remember?"

A look of annoyance flashes across Kaileigh's pretty face, which she just as quickly squelches.

"That's okay, Mom," she says. "You guys don't leave until Saturday. We can grab lunch together in Chinatown another time."

Mrs. Harris looks as hurt as if her daughter has stabbed her in the heart.

"Oh," she says. "Well, let me call Daddy now. He and I can join you and your friends. It won't take a minute, he's over at Best Buy getting you that new printer you said you wanted, so he isn't far."

Mrs. Harris is busy digging through her purse for her phone, so she misses the eye roll her daughter shares with her suite mates.

"It's okay, Mom," Kaileigh says again. "Really. You and Daddy and I have had *every meal this week* together. Maybe we can skip this one so I can hang out with my friends."

"No, no, it's cool," Rashid says, digging into the pocket of his sports coat for his own cell phone. "I'd love for Mr. and Mrs. H to join us—"

Kaileigh glares at him. "That won't be necessary, Shiraz. The reservation you made was only for *four*."

"Five," Rashid corrects her, his thumb moving over the

screen of his phone. "Don't forget Ameera. I'll call Drew. He can get us a bigger table."

"So sweet," I overhear one of the boys in line murmur with a sigh. "He's even nice to old people!"

Sarah looks furious. She doesn't want to find out something nice about the prince.

Kaileigh doesn't look too happy either, but for other reasons. She's dressed exactly like her suite mates and the girls standing in line to put themselves on the Fischer Hall Room Change Wait List—like someone who's ready to go out, but definitely *not* with her parents. Her long hair has been perfectly straightened, dozens of shiny gold bangles dangle from each wrist, and her miniskirt hits at the most flattering place on her slim thighs.

Rashid is similarly well coiffed. If he's conscious of the excited stares he's receiving from the students in line, he doesn't show it. He's probably used to it, being the Prince Harry of Middle Eastern royalty.

"You have a reservation?" Mrs. Harris looks bewildered. "You're not going to the cafeteria?"

"No, Mom," Kaileigh says, exasperated. "Shiraz got us a table at Nobu. It's only supposed to have, like, the best sushi in the *entire world*."

Carl, up on his ladder, nods. "It really does. Try the blackened sea bass. You won't regret it."

"But . . ." Mrs. Harris glances from Rashid to his bodyguards then back to her daughter. "We got Kaileigh the nineteen-meals-per-week plan so she could eat in the dining halls here on campus. I'm sure all of your parents are paying for the same thing." Mrs. Harris shoots her daughter's friends a disapproving look. "None of those meals are refundable. Are they, Ms. Wells?"

Put on the spot, I shake my head . . . though I highly doubt the son of the crowned head of one of the wealthiest countries in the world (according to *Forbes* magazine) cares very much about getting his money back for any uneaten meals on his dining plan.

"Mom, it's not going to kill anyone if we skip a meal in the cafeteria now and then." Kaileigh grimaces at her friends, as if to say, *My mom's so embarrassing, right?* "I actually only stopped in here on our way out because I can't find my RA and there's something wrong with my roommate."

"Ameera is back?" Mrs. Harris sounds surprised.

"Yeah," Kaileigh says. "After I hung up from talking to you this morning, I took a shower, and when I got out, Ameera was in her bed. Only she—"

The door to Lisa's office immediately opens.

"What's wrong with her?" Lisa barks at Kaileigh.

Kaileigh's eyes widen. I don't blame her. Not only is Lisa quite a sight in her current state, resembling an Asian version of Fantine during her death scene in *Les Misérables*, minus the shaved head, but she also appears to have come out of nowhere, possessed with powers of precognition.

"My roommate?" Kaileigh asks. "She . . . she won't wake up."

4

Room Change Request

Name: _____
ID#: _____
Sex: ___ M ___ F ___ Gender Neutral
E-mail: _____
Cell phone: _____
Where do you currently live? _____
_____

What kind of change are you interested
in making? _____
_____

Reason for room change request.
Please check all that apply:
___ Not getting along with roommate
___ Wish for less expensive housing option
___ Wish to move closer to campus
___ Other (explain in space below)
_____
_____

By signing, I agree that I wish to be
offered a room change by the New York
College Housing Office.
X _____

W hat room are you in?" My boss's pallid face peers through the crack between her door and the jamb, but her voice has all the force of a whip.

Looking a little shocked, Kaileigh replies automatically, "Room fourteen-twelve."

"Heather," Lisa barks. "Call the RA for—"

"—the fourteenth floor. I'm on it."

I pull out the list I typed out myself of all the emergency numbers for the building, including all the new resident assistants. I used to consider the fact that I'd shrunk this list down to a wallet-size card (that I'd then laminated) pretty high-tech until one of the new RAs—the RA for the fourteenth floor, as a matter of fact, Jasmine—asked in a snarky tone, "Is it okay if I throw this away after I input the numbers into my smartphone?"

Imagine the nerve, implying that the list I'd worked so hard to make (because, of course, I'd distributed tiny laminated wallet-size copies to everyone) was disposable!

When Jasmine drops her smartphone in a rain puddle as she's escorting some student to the hospital (and no matter what anyone says, this *does* sometimes happen), how will she know who to call from the emergency room pay phone to come relieve her?

Good luck with that, Jasmine.

Lisa opens her office door even farther, and a small brown-and-white projectile bursts out from behind her legs, then begins to run excitedly around the room, sniffing everyone's shoes. Both of Prince Rashid's bodyguards reach inside their jackets for their sidearms.

"It's a dog!" I cry as I dial. "Tricky, come here. You guys, it's a Jack Russell terrier, not a threat."

The dog races over to me for one of the treats I keep for such emergencies—although they've never before involved weapons—while Hamad and his partner relax, but not without reproachful looks in my boss's direction.

Lisa doesn't even notice.

"Is Ameera breathing?" Lisa asks Kaileigh, who is still round-eyed with astonishment over how Lisa knows about her roommate's situation.

There's actually a good explanation: a long metal grate a few inches from the ceiling that separates Lisa's office from the one in which my desk sits. The grate allegedly provides "light and ventilation to employees in the outer office," since the outer office has no windows.

But what it actually does is allow us to snoop on each other's conversations.

It doesn't hurt, however, to let the students think we're psychic (they never notice the grate), so we don't bother disabusing them of the notion.

"I think she was breathing." Kaileigh, unlike everyone else, is staring at Lisa instead of the dog, whose entire backside is quivering in ecstasy as I pass him treats one-handed, the other hand still gripping the phone. "How would I know?"

"Had she vomited in the bed?" Lisa demands. "Were her lips blue?"

"Of course she was breathing," says Kaileigh's suite mate Chantelle. "I mean, why wouldn't she be breathing? She's just, like, hungover."

"We didn't check the color of her lips, though. She had the covers pulled up over her head. We just shook her and she wouldn't wake up." Nishi's squatted down in front of the dog and is scratching his ears, to his delight. "Oh my God, he's *so* cute. What's his name?"

"Tricky." I hang up the handset. To Lisa, I say, "Voice mail. Jasmine's not answering."

Lisa looks worried, and not only about Ameera. Jasmine isn't the RA on duty, but all student employees are supposed to be "available" during orientation week. The fact that Jasmine isn't answering her phone (especially since it's the hall director's office calling) is troubling.

Then again, it's only the first week of school. Jasmine will learn . . . especially after Lisa Wu gets through with her at the next staff meeting.

"I told you," Mrs. Harris says, looking triumphant. "She's not there."

"I'll phone the front desk to have the RA on duty go check on Ameera," I say, ignoring Mrs. Harris as I dial, "and also Jasmine."

"No need," Sarah says quickly. "I'll go." She turns to face Kaileigh, who seems to be the only one who's concerned about her roommate . . . or maybe she's still freaked out about Lisa's apparent mind-reading abilities. "I'm the graduate housing assistant for this building. It's my job, along with Ms. Wu and Ms. Wells, to help assist in matters like this."

One might assume Sarah's superciliousness stems from an anxiety to make up for her earlier faux pas with Kaileigh's mother—and possibly for the attitude she pulled with Prince Rashid—but the truth is, she basically lives for moments like this, since she's studying for her master's degree in psychology.

On her way out the door, Sarah says over her shoulder, "Lisa, why don't you go upstairs and get back in bed? Heather and I have things under control."

Like Sarah's, the hall director's position is live-in. Lisa receives free room and board—a one-bedroom apartment on the sixteenth floor that she shares with her husband, Cory, and of course, Tricky—in addition to a salary that isn't much more than mine, but I have to pay my own rent.

Or I would if I didn't live rent-free on a floor of my landlord's brownstone in exchange for doing his bookkeeping . . . or at least I did until we became romantically involved. I still do his bookkeeping, but now I live rent-free in the entire brownstone.

"Ms. Wu." Mrs. Harris sees her opportunity for an impromptu meeting with someone in charge—even though the person in charge looks like death warmed over—and jumps in before Lisa can disappear on her. "Perhaps you and I should speak privately—"

Lisa shakes her head as if everyone's voices sound like irritating flies buzzing around her ears.

"Not now," she says.

Mrs. Harris looks taken aback. "But—"

"I said *not now.*"

Rolex Watch has taken a step forward to speak with me, but hearing Lisa's tone, he takes a quick step back again.

"Gavin, it's me," I say when the student worker manning the reception desk in the lobby picks up. "Can you please grab the master key for the fourteenth floor? Sarah's going to be up in a minute to borrow it. And have you seen Jasmine anywhere?"

"Who's Jasmine?"

Gavin's one of my most reliable work-study employees, but only for showing up when he says he's going to—and sometimes even when he's least expected, but also most needed.

Unfortunately, he's not necessarily the best at paying attention when he's actually doing his work-study job, which is working at Fischer Hall's hub, the front desk where residents go to receive their mail and packages, report problems, and borrow keys if they've locked themselves out of their rooms. Gavin aspires to a career in filmmaking, not hospitality, and it shows.

I sigh. "Jasmine's one of the new RAs, Gavin. Remember? She works on the fourteenth floor. You met her at the student staff icebreaker last weekend."

"Whatevs." This is Gavin's favorite word. "There were like five girls named Jasmine at that thing. Is she the hot Asian Jasmine who's premed? Or the hot Indian Jasmine who's prelaw? Or is she the hot white Jasmine who's studying communications? Or—"

"Don't you have a girlfriend, Gavin?" I interrupt.

"Of course I do," he says. "Jamie's the hottest girl in this dorm, I mean residence hall. After you, of course, Heather. But that doesn't mean all the Jasmines who live here aren't hot too. You see, I'm a man who appreciates women. Women of all races, sizes"—he lowers his voice suggestively—"and ages too, if you get my meaning, Heather."

I swallow. "You know what, Gavin, I do. Just give Sarah the master key for the fourteenth floor when she gets up there, please."

"Oh, here she is," Gavin says in his normal voice. I hear the rattle of the metal cabinet in which we lock all the master keys—except the building master, which is kept in a box in the bottom drawer of Lisa's desk—then Sarah's voice, in the background saying "Thanks, Gavin."

"Good," I say, when Gavin comes back on the line. "Now

do me a favor and beep the RA on duty?" I'm looking at the schedule pinned to the bulletin board next to my desk. "It's Howard Chen. Tell him to get up to fourteen-twelve and meet Sarah for a possibly sick student."

"Okay, I will," Gavin says, sounding skeptical, "but he isn't going to like it."

"What do you mean, he isn't going to like it? I don't care if he doesn't like it, it's his job, he doesn't have a choice."

"I know," Gavin says. "I'm just saying, I had to call old Howard a little while ago about a lockout, and Howard was pretty pissed about it. He says he isn't feeling too hot."

I glance at Lisa, then lower my voice to hiss, "Well, tell Howard from me that he can suck it up. He gets free room and board for the entire year but only has to be on duty a couple of days a month. Lisa has the stomach flu, has to be here nine to five every day, be on duty in the building at night, and yet *she* still made it to work."

"There seems to be a lot of that flu thing going around with RAs today," Gavin says obliquely, and hangs up.

"Excuse me."

The second my receiver hits the phone cradle, Rolex Watch is on me like cream cheese on a bagel.

"I'm sorry, I can see you've got a lot going on right now, and I really hate to bother you, but what about that Room Change Wait List you mentioned?"

Fed up, I pull open my bottom desk drawer and grab a stack of bright orange forms.

"Here," I say. "Give your son one of these."

A small riot ensues as the line surges forward, hands eagerly grabbing to take a form.

I realize I probably should have handed them out sooner, but when a building has been known as Death Dorm as long as Fischer Hall has, it takes a while to adjust to the fact that it's suddenly gotten to be a place where people actually want to live.

"Here you go, miss," Rolex Watch says a few minutes later, handing his completed form back to me, seeming to feel no compunction about doing so, even though I'd explained just moments before that only residents were to fill them out. "And can I ask just one more thing—"

Anything to get rid of him. "Go ahead."

He lowers his voice. "I'm sure you get this all the time, but has anyone ever told you that you look just like Heather Wells the pop singer?"

He seems so sincere, his plump face beaming, that I realize he isn't putting me on. He genuinely has no idea. I don't keep a nameplate or anything like that on my desk.

"No," I say with a smile, taking the form from his fingers. "No one's ever told me that before. But thank you. I'll take it as a compliment."

"Oh, it is," he assures me. "Such a pretty girl. My daughter loved Heather Wells. She has all her CDs. Still plays them too, sometimes. There was that one song—" He can't seem to think of the name.

" 'Sugar Rush'?"

"That's the one! So catchy. Oh, darn. Now I'm going to be humming it all day."

I nod. "Hard to get it out of your head."

"Oh, well," he says with a sheepish grin. "Thank you. I

knew when people told me New Yorkers were mean that they were all lying. I haven't met a mean one yet."

I smile at him. "We aren't all bad."

Soon my office has emptied—except for Mrs. Harris and her daughter and her suite mates, and of course the prince and his bodyguards.

"Is there anything I can do to help?" the prince is asking, looking regally worried.

"You can go to your lunch," Lisa says stiffly. "This is none of your concern."

"I'm afraid it is," the prince says. "I'm acquainted with the young lady in question. She's very . . . amiable."

I notice Chantelle and Nishi exchange glances as they kneel beside Tricky, who is basking in their attention. *Amiable!* they mouth to another in delight. They can't get enough of the prince's good looks and royal manners.

I'm probably the only one in the room who immediately thinks, *Acquainted with the young lady in question?* She hasn't slept in her room a single night all week. Just how acquainted with Ameera is the prince?

"Could my car be of service?" he asks. "It's quite roomy. Perhaps it could help transport the young lady to the hospital?"

"That's what we have ambulances for," Lisa says coldly. She isn't impressed with his princely ways any more than Sarah was. "We'll call one if we need one." She seems to realize how mean she sounds, and adds, in a gentler tone, "I appreciate the offer, but it's our job to handle these kinds of situations. You don't need to get involved . . . Shiraz."

"I can't say I'm surprised about any of this." It may not

have surprised Mrs. Harris, but she seems to be relishing the drama. "I knew when you said Ameera didn't come home last night, Kaileigh, that something like this was going to happen—"

"But we don't actually know that anything's happened, do we?" Lisa interrupts, sounding mean again. She's weaving a little on her feet, as if the industrial carpeting is swaying before her eyes, but manages to stay erect. "So let's reserve judgment until we do, okay?"

"Yeah, Mom," Kaileigh says, narrowing her eyes at her mother.

"But I really don't think Kaileigh should have to put up with this kind of stress, especially when classes start." Mrs. Harris is like Tricky when he's got hold of one of his treats. She isn't going to let go, no matter what. "What's all this worrying going to do to her grades?"

"Mom," Kaileigh says sharply. "I'm fine. What's the big deal? Ameera partied a little too hard last night, and now she's—wait." Kaileigh narrows her eyes at her mother. "Is *that* why you're in here? You came down to complain about Ameera? Oh my God, I can't believe you. I happen to like my room, Mom, *and* my roommates. I'm in college now. Why can't you let me live my own life?"

"Excuse me," Lisa says, a greenish tint having suddenly overtaken her. She darts back into her office, slamming the door closed behind her. Thanks to the metal grate, we can hear all too clearly why she needed to be excused.

"Poor thing," Carl comments from the top of his ladder, making a tsk-tsking sound with his tongue. "Lots of people coming down with that stomach flu. My guys had to snake two toilets this morning. Everybody, wash your hands." Carl wags his drill with grandfatherly emphasis. "That's the only way to keep it from spreading."

Everyone looks down at their hands, including the prince's bodyguards. Even Shiraz looks as if he's lost some of his self-proclaimed chill.

"Well," he says, beginning to back out the door, "if I can't be of any use here, I'd best be going. No offense, but I can't afford to get sick right now. I've got tickets to the U.S. Open this weekend. Not playing, just as a spectator—" Seeing the looks his bodyguards exchange, he adds, in a deeper, mock-serious tone, "Plus with the course load I'm going to be taking, I know Father would want me to stay healthy for my studies . . ."

"We'll go with you," Nishi says, reluctantly releasing Tricky and climbing to her feet. "There's no reason we need to stick around, right? You'll take care of Ameera if anything is wrong?"

"Nothing's wrong with Ameera," I assure her, "but of course we'll take care of her if anything is."

Is it my (overactive) imagination, or does the prince look as relieved to hear this as the girls?

"Thanks," Kaileigh says, smiling at me gratefully. The look she throws her mother, however, is the opposite of grateful. "I'll call you and Daddy later, Mother," she adds icily.

"Good-bye, Mrs. Harris, Miss Wells, sir," the prince says, with polite nods to Kaileigh's mother, me, and even Carl, who salutes back with his drill. "I hope you feel better," he calls to Lisa through the metal grate. Her only response is a groan.

Whatever else they might say about the heir to the throne of Qalif, he's unfailingly polite. He and Kaileigh and the rest of their entourage begin to file out of my office, just as a tall, devastatingly handsome man with thick dark hair and piercing blue eyes comes striding in.

Whenever Cooper Cartwright enters a room, I'm always amazed that the sight of him doesn't cause every other woman in the vicinity to swoon, the way I feel like doing. Maybe they're just better at hiding the shattering effect his rugged masculinity has on them. Mrs. Harris barely even glances in his direction, which I find completely perplexing, since he seems to emanate testosterone in his nonskinny jeans and unclingy sports coat in a way Prince Rashid never could.

Then again, we all know how Mrs. Harris feels about sex, so I guess it's no wonder.

Cooper watches the prince and his entourage without comment until, after they're gone, he asks, "His Royal Highness, the VIR, I take it?"

"He prefers to be called Shiraz," I correct Cooper. "Because he's best served chilled."

"It's nice to know he's assimilating," Cooper says drily, lowering himself onto the visitors' couch.

Only Tricky greets Cooper the way I believe he should be greeted . . . and would greet him myself if we weren't surrounded by observers. The dog throws himself onto the couch, lays his paws upon Cooper's chest, and enthusiastically begins lapping Cooper's five o'clock shadow (even though it's lunchtime) with his tongue.

"Whoa," Cooper says, attempting unsuccessfully to fight off the dog's advances. "I'm happy to see you too, Trix, but

I can tell one of us didn't brush his teeth this morning, and it wasn't me."

Mrs. Harris, still failing to notice my fiancé, says to me, "Kaileigh's father is on his way over. He says for the money we're paying—over fifty thousand dollars a year—Kaileigh should have a roommate who is serious about her studies."

I raise my eyebrows. "Mrs. Harris, I already told you we don't have any other rooms—"

"That's why we want to speak to someone in charge." She nods at Lisa's closed office door. "Not Miss Wu. Her supervisor. The director of housing."

"Mrs. Harris," I say, in a tone I can't keep from becoming sharp. "I'll be happy to direct you to the Housing Office, where you can make an appointment with Dr. Stanley Jessup, the director of housing, but before I do, keep in mind that I'll be calling his office myself to tell him that your daughter stood in front of me just five minutes ago and said she liked her room and her roommates and requested that you allow her to live her own life."

Mrs. Harris's face turns pink. I've called her bluff, and she knows it. Cooper, meanwhile, is smiling into Tricky's fur. He loves it when I get bossy with the parents. He says it turns him on. I hope he can control himself until we get outside the building and into a taxi to the Plaza, where we'll be meeting our extremely hard-to-get-an-appointment-with wedding planner.

"Kaileigh was admitted to New York College," I go on, "one of the best colleges in the country"—"best" is a leap; but it's certainly one of the most expensive—"because she's clearly very intelligent. As a parent, you need to start trusting her to handle her own problems, and let her make her own decisions. I personally think they'll be great ones, not only because she's attending a fine school and at eighteen is now a legal adult, but because she was raised by a fantastic mom. *You*, Mrs. Harris. Kaileigh's going to do great in college because she had *you* as a role model. You gave her the wings she needs to fly. Now, why don't you let her spread them?"

At the end of this long speech—which, I have to admit, I got out of a greeting card and I've delivered approximately four times already this week—I give Mrs. Harris my most dazzling smile, the one that Cooper says knocks his socks off. I've noticed that it frequently knocks his pants off as well.

Unfortunately—or fortunately, since we're in an office setting—this time it does neither. Mrs. Harris keeps both her pants and socks on as well.

But she does look touched.

"Oh," she says, reaching into her purse and pulling out a tissue with which she dabs at the corners of her eyes. "That's so nice of you to say. Her father and I have tried so hard with her. She has a younger brother, you know, and let's just say we won't be allowing *him* to go to Haiti to build houses for Habitat for Humanity, even though it's such a worthy cause, because he simply hasn't shown the same kind of responsibility that Kaileigh has. But then they say boys don't mature as quickly as—"

Mercifully, my office phone rings before she can go on much longer. I see on the caller ID that it's Sarah.

"I'm so sorry," I say apologetically to Mrs. Harris. "I have to get this. Maybe we could talk another time?"

Mrs. Harris nods her understanding and mouths *Thank*

you so much for everything as I pick up the receiver and say, "Hello, Fischer Hall director's office, how may I help you?"

"I know you know it's me," Sarah says. Her voice sounds weirdly congested. "Is Kaileigh's mom still sitting there?"

"Yes, this is Heather Wells," I say, smiling brightly at Mrs. Harris as she waves from my office door on her way out.

"Oh, crap," Sarah says. "I can't believe she's still there. It's bad, Heather. Really, really bad."

I keep the smile plastered on my face, but shift my glance to Cooper now that Mrs. Harris is finally gone. He's scratching Tricky's ears, but when he sees my expression, his fingers still, his gaze locking on mine.

"Really?" I ask. Even though Mrs. Harris is gone, I keep my tone businesslike. There are still people milling around outside the door. "How bad?"

"It's not fair," Sarah says. She's crying now. "Classes haven't even started yet, Heather. Classes haven't even started yet."

Behind me, I hear Lisa's office door open. This time I don't think it's because of anything she's overheard, because I've kept my end of the conversation so neutral.

I think my new boss might actually have some kind of extrasensory perception.

"Heather?" Lisa asks in a soft voice. "What is it? Is that Sarah?"

I nod, picking up a pen and lowering my gaze to the At-A-Glance calendar on my desk. Slowly, I begin to cross out *Lunch w/ Coop and Perry*. Lunch with the outrageously exclusive and expensive wedding planner is definitely canceled.

"Sarah," I say into the phone. "Take a deep breath. Whatever it is, we'll handle it—"

"I don't understand it." Sarah is babbling into the phone. "I just saw her at dinner last night. She was fine. We had falafel. We had freaking falafel together last night in the caf. How can she be dead?"

I knit my brows. Sarah isn't making any sense. "You ate dinner with Kaileigh's roommate Ameera last night in the cafeteria?"

"No!" Sarah cries with a sob. "Not Ameera! Ameera is fine, we checked on her, she's fine, just hungover or something. I'm talking about Jasmine, the fourteenth-floor RA. You told me to look in on her, so when we knocked and she didn't answer her door, we keyed into her room to make sure she was all right, because I could hear music playing. Why would she have left her music on if she wasn't in the room? Well, she's here, but she isn't all right. She's dead, Heather. She's dead!"

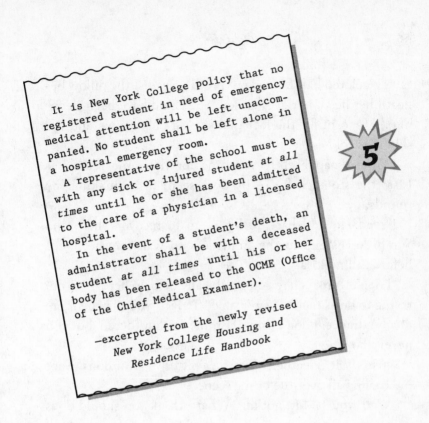

5

Lisa insisted she come upstairs and sit with Jasmine's body, but I had my doubts this was the wisest course of action.

"You're sick, Lise," I say when I call downstairs to report my findings. Sarah is a mess when I arrive, and the RA on duty, Howard Chen, is nowhere to be seen. That's because— I soon discover—he's in the trash chute room down the hall, throwing up.

Howard isn't vomiting because of the sight that met him and Sarah in room 1416, though. Jasmine looks perfectly peaceful in her white tank top and green terry shorts, her

tawny-colored hair fanned out prettily against the pillow beneath her head, her eyes closed. She could have been sleeping . . . except for the fact that she isn't breathing, and her
skin is as cold as ice.

Howard's apparently vomiting for the same reason as
Lisa: the stomach flu really does seem to be making the
rounds.

I send Howard back to his room to recover, then send
Sarah downstairs to the front desk to wait for the police
before calling Lisa.

"I don't think you're going to be any help up here," I go on,
trying to be as tactful as possible. "In fact, you may be more
of a hindrance. I don't think Jasmine was murdered, but you
never know."

"Just say it, Heather," Lisa says bitterly. "You don't want
me barfing all over the crime scene."

"Well, you said it, not me. What I think you should do is
go home and get in bed. I'll call the Housing Office and tell
Dr. Jessup what's happened. Although he's probably going
to want you to call Jasmine's parents."

Lisa's voice cracks. "Oh God, Heather."

"I know. But you knew Jasmine better than anyone, since
she went through RA training with you. The news will be
best coming from you. I know it's going to suck, but . . ."

Jasmine has framed photos by the side of her bed. She has
her arms around a happy-looking older couple—no doubt
Mom and Dad—and a panting golden retriever. They appear
to be camping.

I have to look away. I have no such photos of myself with
my parents. We never had pets when I was growing up. My

mom said it was too hard to take them on the road when I was touring.

Then Mom left. So.

"I understand. It's just . . ." Lisa's voice cracks again. "She was so young."

"I know," I say again, looking around Jasmine's room, anywhere but at the family photo and Jasmine's pretty face. She *had* been young . . . and so full of promise.

Jasmine had painted the walls of her room a cheerful powder blue—painting your room is a housing violation, unless you paint the walls white again before you move out—and covered them with cutouts of white clouds and photos of women she'd admired . . . mostly TV journalists like Diane Sawyer and Katie Couric.

That's when I remember what Gavin had asked over the phone a little earlier:

Is she the hot white Jasmine who's studying communications?

She was.

Only now her dream of being the next Diane Sawyer is never going to come true.Something pricks at the corners of my eyes—tears, I realize. I turn my back on Jasmine and her room and lift the blinds. We aren't supposed to touch anything in the deceased's room, since it could be a crime scene, but I have to look at *something* that isn't going to make me cry.

I can't believe the only real contact I ever had with Jasmine was her snarky comment about my emergency phone list. I'd kind of disliked her for it.

Now I'll never have a chance for another interaction with her, because she's dead. The least I can do is try to figure out why, even though that isn't part of my job description.

It isn't *not* part of my job description, though, which is to assist the hall director in all matters pertaining to the smooth functioning of the building. Certainly figuring out how Jasmine died would fall under that category.

I concentrate on Jasmine's view—which is spectacular—of the busy streets and rooftops of the West Village. Between the treetops I occasionally catch a glimpse of the Hudson River.

So many of the kids who come to New York College arrive with dreams of making it big in Manhattan, having spent their youth watching *Sex and the City* reruns or reading *The Amazing Spider-Man*. Something had happened to cut Jasmine down dead before she ever had a chance of living out her dream, however.

What was it?

Lisa is wondering the same thing.

"How could something like this happen, Heather? Our first week, before classes have even started?"

"I don't know," I say, relieved my tears aren't affecting my voice. "If it helps, whatever happened to her"—brain aneurysm? drugs? poisoned apple?—"I don't see any signs that she suffered."

"It doesn't help," Lisa says gloomily into the phone.

"Yeah," I say. It never does. "Look, Lisa, this is bad, but it isn't as bad as it could be. You could say something to her parents like that Jasmine died during the happiest, most exciting time of her life. She got the RA job . . . she was a role model to so many people—"

Lisa makes a gagging noise, and I realize I've made her throw up. Literally.

"Yeah," I say. "I know. Cheesy. Look, you sound like you're getting worse. Go to bed. I'll call Dr. Jessup."

"No," Lisa says weakly. "I'll do it. Then I'm coming up there. The police are going to want to talk to me—"

"Lisa, don't be ridiculous. The police aren't even here yet. I mean it. Go home. Get in bed. This is a horrible tragedy, but it's going to be all right." I steal a glance at Jasmine, then look back out the window at the river and lower my voice—which is ridiculous, since Jasmine can't hear me—and say, "Jasmine was an RA, but she was new to the building, and she didn't work here for very long. None of us really knew her."

"Heather!" Lisa cries. "How can you—?"

"Because it's true. She didn't really know us either, or most of her residents, since the majority of the students on her floor are upperclassmen, so most of them haven't even checked in yet. They won't get here until next weekend. Classes don't start until after Labor Day."

Jasmine's floor is one of the highest in the building, which means it's one of the most desirable (this is why the prince was assigned to a suite just above it).

"Most of the rooms on the upper floors were chosen in last year's room selection lottery by upperclassmen before you—or Jasmine—ever even got here," I go on, "which means only a few of the rooms on Jasmine's floor were left to assign to incoming freshmen and transfer students. Since orientation week is only for new students, first year and transfer, most of the upperclassmen don't choose to arrive until the weekend before classes begin."

"True," Lisa says hesitantly.

"So this is sad, but not as sad as if it happened in the middle of the year. The only people on her floor right now, really, are Kaileigh and Ameera and those other girls. You'll pull someone in off the RA wait list to replace Jasmine, and the majority of kids won't even know there was a death in the building, because it happened before they got here."

"Heather!" Lisa says with a gasp.

"I said it was sad. I didn't say it was fair. We have to be practical about it."

"This job has hardened you," Lisa says, not unkindly. "What if Jasmine died of what *I* have? What if I gave it to her? What if it's some kind of deadly—"

"She didn't," I say flatly. "I already checked her trash can and toilet. There's no vomit. And Howard Chen has what you have too, and he's not dead."

"Oh, great." This is Lisa's first student death—although we'd come close before—and the stress in her voice is almost palpable. "Wait. I just thought of something. The prince. You don't think there's a connection, do you, between Jasmine dying and the prince?"

"I don't see how there could be," I say.

"He clearly knows her residents."

"I know, but no one said anything about Jasmine not answering her door to go to Nobu, just Ameera."

But the coincidence—a VIR about whom there'd been death threats, and then a death in the room on the floor below his? It was going to be too big for some people (particularly the media) to ignore, and Lisa knew it.

"Okay," Lisa says firmly. "That's it. I'm coming up there right now."

That's when I hear a deep voice—familiar and resonant—through Lisa's phone.

"You aren't going anywhere except where Heather said, home, to bed."

"Cooper?" Lisa sounds startled. "Oh my God, you're still here?"

My thought, exactly.

"Of course I'm still here," he says. "I'm supposed to be having lunch with my bride-to-be, remember?"

"Oh, Cooper," Lisa cries. "Of course. I'm so sorry—"

"You're going to be sorrier," I hear him say, "if you don't take care of yourself now, and get sicker later."

"But," I hear Lisa protest weakly.

"No 'buts,'" Cooper says. "You're going back to bed even if I have to carry you there."

"You can't lift me," I hear Lisa say, but there's uncertainty in her voice.

"What are you talking about?" Cooper sounds offended. "I carry Heather to bed every night. How do you think I maintain this buff physique?"

Lisa probably would have laughed if the situation hadn't been so bleak.

I, on the other hand, frown. Cooper does have a buff physique, but he doesn't carry me to bed *every* night. There'd just been that one night when I'd had a few too many grapefruit and vodkas and we'd started horsing around—

"Okay, okay," I hear Lisa say. "I'm going. But first let me—"

"Oh my God, go home before my fiancé has to sling you over his shoulder King Kong style," I practically shout into the phone.

Lisa gives in, says good-bye, and hangs up. I hang up too, but only to go and sit on the bed opposite Jasmine's to make another phone call, careful not to touch anything, or shed any of my DNA, or look in the direction of the dead girl lying opposite me.

All RAs are assigned a single room, but these contain enough furniture for a double, since Fischer Hall lacks storage space. What the RA chooses to do with his or her extra furniture isn't any of our concern, so long as it's back in the room by the time he or she has moved out.

Jasmine had chosen to use both of her beds, one as a couch for visitors to lounge on, and the other for sleeping. I'm sitting on the one she'd reserved for visitors. The other bed is the one on which Jasmine lies, very, very dead.

"Gavin?" I say, when the person on the other end of the phone picks up.

"Hey, Heather," he says. He sounds a lot more subdued than when we'd spoken earlier. "Sarah told me. Bummer."

Only Gavin would call a girl dying in the prime of her life a "bummer."

"Yes," I say. "It is, indeed, a bummer. Have the police shown up yet?"

"No. I heard there's a subway fire over at the Christopher Street station. You know they never show up for a dead body if there are live people they have a chance of saving. You guys shouldn't have said Jasmine's dead. You should have said she's dying. Then they'd come faster."

I sigh at the truth of this. "Is Sarah there?"

"She's here," he says, not sounding too thrilled about it.

"She's, like, crying all over the magazines I was saving to read later."

"Gavin," I say. "You're not supposed to read other people's magazines. You're supposed to put them in the mailboxes of the people to whom they are addressed."

"I know," Gavin says. "But there's been another death in the building, and the new issue of *Entertainment Weekly* just arrived. I need something to calm my nerves."

I look at the fluffy white clouds Jasmine painted on the ceiling. "Fine. Listen, Gavin. Can you do me a favor?"

"For you? Anything."

"Good. I need you to get out the emergency phone list—"

It's his turn to sigh.

"—and text all RAs that there's going to be an emergency staff meeting today at six in the second-floor library. Oh, and then can you put a sign on the door of the second-floor library that it's going to be closed for a meeting at six? We're going to have to break the news to them about Jasmine."

Gavin says, "Intense. I'll do it, but if you'd let me set up a group text on your phone, you could do it yourself next time."

"I sincerely hope there isn't going to be a next time, Gavin. And I don't think my phone knows how to do that."

"Your phone knows how to do it," Gavin says, sounding amused. "*You* don't. Look, I get a break in an hour. Why don't you let me take you to lunch in the caf, and I'll set up the group text for you."

"Gavin," I say, with practiced patience. "I'm engaged. You got an invitation to my wedding, remember? You RSVP'd that you're coming . . . with your girlfriend."

"Yeah, but you're not married yet. There's still a chance for me. I'm pretty sure I can win you over with my advanced technological know-how, which is vastly superior to your fiancé's, or he'd have shown you how to group text, or even text, period, something I've noticed you seem to have a little trouble with. Not that it bothers me. It only makes you even more adorable."

"Gavin," I say, with a glance at Jasmine. "This is a highly inappropriate time for you to be hitting on me. Not that there's ever an appropriate time to hit on your boss. Besides, what about Jamie? She's a lovely girl, who is also *your age*."

"I know," he says. "But I met you first. Anyway, Jamie knows how I feel about you. We have an arrangement. You're my freebie."

"Your what?"

"My celebrity freebie. If I ever get a chance with you, Jamie says it's okay to take it. Her celebrity freebie is Robert Downey Jr., but she says she only wants him if he's in his *Iron Man* suit, so I don't think that one is going to happen."

"How nice," I say. "Please will you just send the group text?"

"Okay, but I don't know how many of those RAs are going to show up because of the *flu*."

"Gavin, why do you keep saying it that way?"

"What way?"

"As if they don't really have the flu."

"I ain't saying nothing," Gavin says. "I ain't no narc."

"Gavin," I say. "You grew up in the suburbs and now attend

a major private nonsectarian American college in New York City. It doesn't sound natural when you use double negatives."

"Harsh," Gavin responds.

A knock sounds on Jasmine's door.

"I have to go," I say, getting up to answer it. "Send the group text. And tell them if I hear about any RA faking sick, there's going to be major trouble."

"Oh, trust me," Gavin says. "They ain't faking." He hangs up.

So do I, then open Jasmine's door. I expect to see men and women in blue from the Sixth Precinct standing in the hallway.

But that's not who it is.

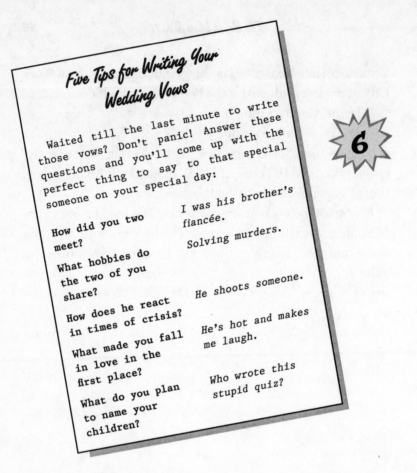

Five Tips for Writing Your Wedding Vows

Waited till the last minute to write those vows? Don't panic! Answer these questions and you'll come up with the perfect thing to say to that special someone on your special day:

How did you two meet?

I was his brother's fiancée.

What hobbies do the two of you share?

Solving murders.

How does he react in times of crisis?

He shoots someone.

What made you fall in love in the first place?

He's hot and makes me laugh.

What do you plan to name your children?

Who wrote this stupid quiz?

6

I got your boss to her apartment," Cooper says gruffly by way of greeting. He immediately fills the small room with his strong masculine energy. "And that dog of hers too. I left her on her couch with her phone and a couple of bottles of ginger ale. You should call her husband to let him know how sick she is. I doubt she's told him."

He goes straight to Jasmine's bed to peer down at the dead girl. "Christ, Heather. Are they getting younger or are we getting older? This one looks like she's barely twelve years old. Are you sure she isn't sleeping?"

"I'm sure," I say. "Cooper, thanks for coming up to check on me, but the police are going to get here any minute. You're probably getting DNA all over the place. And you know not everyone on campus likes you as much as I do, especially since you shot that guy over the summer."

He looks hurt. "I got named Hot Stud of the Week by *New York College Express*, the daily student news blog, for doing that."

"I know," I say sympathetically. "And while they and *I* personally appreciated it very much, especially since you saved my life, I still think you'd better go. There's that anti-gun-violence group on campus. They complain anytime anyone uses a gun, even against someone who deserves it."

He ignores me, looking around Jasmine's room. "Any sign that someone was in here last night when she died?"

I shake my head. "Sarah says everything was exactly like this when she arrived—and I want to keep it that way, so don't touch anything."

He gives me a sour look. "Who do you think you're dealing with here? This is what I do for a living."

"I thought you make your living sneaking into hotel rooms and planting hidden cameras to take pictures of people cheating on their spouses."

"Well, that too," he says, with a shrug of his big shoulders.

"Everything was exactly like this except that her computer was on—" I point to a laptop on Jasmine's desk. "It was playing a song list set on repeat. Sarah switched it off in order to call the office, so she could hear me. That's it."

Cooper walks over to the desk, leaning down to look at the computer. "Weird that someone would have music playing when they're trying to fall asleep."

"Weird for you," I say. "You live in your own multimillion-dollar brownstone. Try living in a noisy dorm, especially on a floor with a lot of new students across the hall, away from home for the first time. Lots of people in that situation can't sleep *without* music playing. It drowns out all the ambient noise. These walls are thick, but not that thick. Cooper, what are you doing?"

He's taken one of his ubiquitous handkerchiefs from his pocket and hit the return key on the computer keyboard. He always carries a neatly folded bandana (preferably in blue) somewhere on his person, a trick he picked up from one of his many formerly incarcerated friends. Keeps you from leaving fingerprints, he says.

"Just checking to see the last thing she was doing on the computer before she went to bed, besides listening to iTunes." He squints down at the keyboard, then the screen. "Twitter," he says with some disgust.

Cooper refuses to participate in any form of social networking. He doesn't have a Web site advertising his private investigation business. His clients come from lawyers he knows, word of mouth, and a discreet listing in—of all things—the phone book. He seems to have all the work he can handle, though, proof that not everyone turns to the Internet for their professional needs.

"What a shocker, a college student using Twitter," I say sarcastically. "Now, come on, you know if the cops find you here they're going to blame me for messing up their crime scene . . . if her death turns out to be murder."

He pokes around a little more on her computer. "She wasn't logged on," he says. "To Twitter. It's just the whaddayoucallit, home page. What was her Twitter handle?"

"How would I know?"

He looks around. "Where's her phone?"

I follow his gaze. "I don't know."

"Do you have her phone number? We could call her phone."

"Of course I have her number," I say, pulling out my phone and—a little proudly—the wallet-size list of emergency numbers I'd made. "But why is it so important we find her phone?"

"Because then we can find the last person she was talking to. It's possible that person could give us a little insight into how she died."

"Or we could just wait for the OCME to tell us." I'm dialing. "And don't you have a case of your own you're supposed to be working on?"

"It's insurance fraud, a little less pressing than this," Cooper says. "No dead bodies are involved."

"Oh." I hold my cell phone away from my ear. "That's weird. Jasmine's phone is ringing in my ear, but not in her room. And now it's gone to voice mail."

"Her phone's not in here," Cooper says, looking around the room.

"Of course it's here," I say, looking around as well. "She must have it on vibrate."

The clothes Jasmine had worn the day before are in a heap on the floor beside her bathroom door. I walk over to the pile and begin to feel through the pockets of her jeans.

"What young person do you know who doesn't take her phone to bed with her?" Cooper points at Jasmine's nightstand, which sits beneath her wide casement window, between the two beds. "It should be right there. But it's gone."

"It's not gone," I say. Look, her wallet's here." I hold it up. "Cash, credit cards, ID, everything still inside. Even her keys." I jingle them. "So she wasn't robbed. Who would steal her phone and not her cash? There's a hundred bucks in this wallet. And that laptop over there is top of the line. It's not like someone broke in here—there's no sign the door's been tampered with. Who would take her phone but not her laptop and cash?"

Cooper shakes his head, unconvinced. "Then where *is* her phone?"

I eye Jasmine's body. "Probably there." I point.

Cooper's gaze follows the direction of my finger, which is aimed at her bedclothes, tangled around the bottom of her legs. He takes a quick step backward.

"No way," he says.

"Well, you're the one who thinks all young people take their phones to bed with them," I say. "Where else is it going to be? Except maybe under her."

"Well, *I'm* not going to look," Cooper declares. "You do it."

"*I'm* not doing it," I say. "That's disturbing the dead. It's my job to make sure no one messes with her . . . including me."

"But how else are we going to know whether or not it's there?"

"*We* aren't going to know," I say firmly, beginning to shove him toward the door. "The OCME will find it, if it's there. The only thing either of us *has* to do is leave, meaning you, before the cops get here and arrest you for disturbing a potential crime scene. Go do your job, and I'll do mine."

"Fine," he says, tugging on his shirt, which I've caused to become untucked with all my shoving. "I will. You don't have to get so huffy about it. Just because your case is more interesting than mine—"

"This isn't a *case*, Cooper. It's a resident in my building who died, and it's tragic, but you yourself reminded me just the other day that more young adults end up in hospital emergency rooms than any other age group . . . and more of them *die* in those emergency rooms than any other age group too. So I guess it's natural that we might lose someone, even this early in the year. But you can't leap to the conclusion that there was foul play involved, because we don't know yet—"

Cooper turns by the door somewhere in the middle of this long speech to put his hands on my shoulders. When I'm finished, he says, "Heather. Heather, I know, okay? I'm sorry. I'm so sorry this happened, and I'm sorry to have upset you. That's the last thing I'd ever want to do. I only wanted to help. I promise I'll stay out of it from now on, if that's what you want. I'll go home and call Perry to cancel our lunch appointment. Okay?"

I groan. I'd forgotten all about our meeting with the wedding planner.

"Oh God. We're never going to be able to get another appointment with her after canceling like this. You know how she is."

It's only because of a sudden cancellation (the bride left the groom for his brother) and Cooper's father pulling a few strings to get us moved up the waiting list (apparently you can do this if you're the CEO of a large recording company) that we managed to get a wedding booked at the Plaza at all. Perry, our wedding planner, can't stop reminding us how fortunate we are, because it's rare that any size wedding— let alone one as large as ours—is "thrown together at the last minute" in New York City like this. Apparently by "thrown together at the last minute" she means had tens of thousands of our own dollars—many of which are going to her— poured into it weeks in advance.

Sometimes I want to punch Perry in the throat.

"I think we have a fairly good excuse for canceling," Cooper says soothingly. "So you let me handle Perry. You take care of the situation here."

The weight of his strong hands on my shoulders—not to mention his deep voice—has a soothing effect, and for the first time since I entered the room to find Jasmine lying there—maybe for the first time since her resident's mother Mrs. Harris took a seat next to my desk—I begin to feel calm.

I wrap my own arms around Cooper's waist, comforted, as always, by his warmth, and the smell of the fabric softener we use, mixed with his own innate Cooperish scent.

"I'm sorry I snapped," I say. "It seems horrible to say under these circumstances, but I was really looking forward to going over the seating arrangements with you."

"Not horrible," he says. "Human. And another one of the many reasons I love you."

He kisses me, then, almost as abruptly as he appeared, he slips out the door to room 1416 and disappears down the back staircase, well before the elevator doors open and several uniformed officers from the Sixth Precinct show up, looking around questioningly.

"Down here," I call, raising an arm.

It's a good thing Cooper isn't here, I think, or he'd comment on how the cops look as young as Jasmine.

At that very moment the door to room 1412 opens, and a pale brown, inquisitive face, framed by a mass of dark curling hair peers out, first at me, then at the approaching police officers.

"What's going on?" the girl asks drowsily.

"Nothing," I say, noting that the handmade tag on her door—in construction paper cut into the same cloud shapes as the ones on Jasmine's ceiling—has the names Chantelle, Nishi, Kaileigh, and Ameera written on it in sparkly silver cursive. "Go back to bed."

The girl doesn't listen. Even washed free of makeup, her eyes are huge and dark and beautiful.

"Why are there police here?" she asks in a sleep-roughened voice. She has a British accent. "Has something happened?"

"Nothing for you to worry about, miss." The first officer is a gangly young man, the leather of his gun belt creaking noisily as he strides toward us. "We got it under control. Go on back inside your room."

It's too late. By now the girl is standing in the middle of the hallway in her cream-colored slip and flowered silk dressing gown, her brown feet bare, her hair a riotous ebony halo around her slim shoulders. She wears no jewelry except for a single gold chain around her neck, from which dangles a pair of interlocked silver rings, which jingle softly when she walks.

I know that all the other residents of room 1412—Chantelle, Nishi, and Kaileigh—are out to lunch at Nobu with Prince Rashid. This girl, then, must be Ameera, the one Kaileigh's mother described as "a slut."

I'm not sure what a slut is supposed to look like, but to me, Ameera looks more like an angel. I remember what Prince Rashid said, about Ameera being "amiable." She seems like the kind of girl a prince—or any boy—would find amiable indeed.

Her gaze travels past me, into Jasmine's room.

"That's where my RA, Jasmine, lives," she says, fully awake now. "Is she there? Jasmine?" Ameera darts toward the door I've foolishly left opened behind me. "Jasmine?"

I manage to catch her around the waist—she's slim as a child, and doesn't weigh much more than one. One of the female officers darts forward to help me, but Ameera is much stronger than she looks. She manages to drag both myself and the female officer a few steps into Jasmine's room . . . enough so that she sees her RA's dead body on the bed.

That's when Ameera begins to scream.

It's a long, long time before she stops.

Fischer Hall Casino Night

Do you like to GAMBLE?
$ Blackjack $ Roulette $ Texas Hold'Em $
Ready for a night of revelry
on a romantic riverboat ride
around Manhattan Island?

Then come to Fischer Hall's Freshman
Orientation Casino Night!
Win chips that can be cashed in
for New York College loot!
$$$$
Buses leave outside the building
at **5:00 P.M. SHARP**
Be there or be
LEFT OUT FOREVER

7

One thing I did not expect when I took on the job as assistant resident hall director of Fischer Hall was that I was going to get to know so many investigators from the NYC Office of the Chief Medical Examiner on a first-name basis.

But thanks to there having been so many sudden deaths in the building over the past year, that's exactly what's happened.

"Hi, Heather," says Eva, the MLI (medicolegal investigator) who shows up to examine Jasmine. "How's it going? Oh, hey, thanks for the wedding invitation. Is it all right if I bring my mother as my plus one? She's so damned excited about going to a real celebrity wedding, *and* she's never been to a wedding at the Plaza before. Plus, you know the chances of *my* ever getting married at this point are slim to none—Mom says I scare guys off with all these tattoos—so you'd be doing me a real solid."

"Oh," I say, surprised to hear this . . . not that Eva wants to bring her mother to my wedding, but because these are not exactly the first words I expect to hear someone say as they're walking into the room of a deceased twenty-year-old. "Sure."

Also, I don't recall inviting Eva to my wedding.

But this isn't the most pressing concern on my mind at the moment.

The Housing Office has kicked into crisis mode, sending all its best people over to Fischer Hall to "deal with" the situation, including the on-staff psychologist, Dr. Flynn, and grief counselor, Dr. Gillian Kilgore.

It's Gillian who—along with a nurse from Student Health Services—gets Ameera calmed down. She turns out to be way beyond my help. Every time she looked at me—and the female police officer—after we removed her from Jasmine's room, all she seemed to able to see was the face of her dead RA.

That made her start weeping again, burying her head in her hands so that her long dark hair fell over her face.

It took two young male police officers to drag Ameera out of room 1416 and back into her own room. Afterward, they sat her down and explained that we'd found Jasmine that way—none of us had *done* it to her.

I don't think she believed us, though.

"But she was *fine* at the party last night," Ameera kept saying through her tears. Because of her English accent, she pronounced it *pahty*. "She was fine!"

"What party?" I asked, bewildered.

This only set Ameera off into a fresh fit of hysterics, for some reason.

So I'd gone back into Jasmine's room, reflecting that I'd made a new discovery:

It's sometimes preferable to sit with the corpse of a student than to be in the company of a live one.

Maybe Lisa's right: this job *has* hardened me. What a depressing thought for a girl who's supposed to be getting married in a month.

I tried not to dwell on this, however.

Death certificates can't be issued for anyone who dies suddenly (and unattended by a physician) in New York State unless that body has first been seen by an MLI (then brought to the Office of the Chief Medical Examiner—OCME).

Due to budget cuts, however, there are only a few MLIs assigned to each borough, so depending on how many deaths occur in the city on a given day, it can take anywhere from forty-five minutes to eight hours (sometimes more) for an investigator to show up after a death has been reported.

It took almost four hours for an MLI to show up to examine Jasmine.

Normally this would have meant my spending the afternoon hanging around with a bunch of yawning cops and uptight administrators.

But that's not how things turned out this time. Because

this time, Fischer Hall is housing a VIR, and the deceased lived one floor below him. And one of the first phone calls Dr. Jessup makes after learning about Jasmine's death appears to have been to Prince Rashid's special protection team, and they, in turn, have taken over the investigation.

"ID, please." Special Agent Richard Lancaster, who looks devastatingly handsome in his dark suit and tie (not that I've noticed, since I'm a happily engaged woman), steps in front of the door to Jasmine's room and holds out an intimidatingly large hand.

At least, it intimidates me. Medicolegal Investigator Eva Kovalenko, not so much. She looks as offended as if the agent asked to see something much more intimate than a mere ID.

"Who the hell are you," Eva demands, "and what are you doing at my crime scene?"

"*Potential* crime scene," Special Agent Lancaster corrects her.

"Who asked you?" Eva looks even more offended.

I don't blame Special Agent Lancaster for not realizing who Eva is. With her spiky bleached-blond hair, eyebrow rings, and yellow-rose-of-Texas neck tattoo (the only tattoo that peeks out from beneath her clothes, as she's wearing a long-sleeved coroner's jacket. I've seen her in short sleeves, and know she has plenty more), Eva looks more like a student than an employee of the OCME.

Still, her attitude isn't helping much.

"Uh, Eva," I say. "This is Special Agent Lancaster. He works for the State Department—"

"Bureau of Diplomatic Security," the agent elaborates

woodenly. "It's the security and law enforcement arm of the U.S. State Department."

"Who the hell died?" Eva demands. "The shah of Iran?"

"Uh, no," I say. "It's a student."

"The kid of the shah of Iran?"

"Ma'am," Special Agent Lancaster says in a slow, impassive tone to Eva, "I'm going to need your full name and also the name of your supervisor—"

"My supervisor is the chief medical examiner," Eva says, whipping a business card out from the pocket of her coat before jostling Special Agent Lancaster aside (and nearly running over his size-twelve feet with her wheelie bag). "Now get the hell out of my way so I can do my job."

Special Agent Lancaster looks a little startled. He'd had no trouble at all running off the cops from the Sixth Precinct (although they were still in the building. They'd merely retreated downstairs to the dining hall to drink coffee, which Magda, the cafeteria's extremely popular head cashier and one of my best friends, had been only too delighted to offer to them for free), not to mention everyone who'd shown up from the Housing Office, who were now gathered downstairs in the second-floor library, holding their crisis resolution meeting, which I had to admit I was a little relieved not to be attending.

But the agent was going to have his hands full with Eva, and I could tell he knew it. I saw him touch the wireless communication piece in his ear, then begin speaking softly to someone, most likely in the bureau's makeshift headquarters in the first-floor conference room. He was probably calling for reinforcements.

"So, um, this is the deceased," I say to Eva, stepping past the special agent and into room 1416, then pointing Eva in the direction of Jasmine's body, though of course she'd have had a hard time missing it. It was the only corpse in the immediate vicinity.

"Her name is Jasmine Albright," I say to Eva. "She's twenty, a junior. Sarah, our grad assistant, said she had dinner with Jasmine last night—they both had falafel—and Jasmine was fine. Then we tried to reach her this morning and she didn't pick up. That's all I know."

I don't mention the thing Ameera had said, about Jasmine having been at a *pahty* the night before. None of us—at least those of us who'd been there at the time—had been able to get another word out of her about it. Hopefully Drs. Flynn or Kilgore had better luck, but so far I haven't heard anything.

Eva mutters a curse word as she looks Jasmine over while simultaneously taking a pair of latex gloves from the kit she carries with her—literally a wheelie bag filled with tools used for collecting postmortem evidence.

"Sorry about this, Heather," Eva says sympathetically. "I couldn't believe it when I got the address. I was like, *Noooo. Not Death Dorm again!*"

"Thanks," I say. I'm as used to Eva's quirks as I am to her spiked blond hair and tattoos. Contrary to popular belief, medical examiners are usually quite cheerful, though not surprisingly a bit prone to gallows humor, since they spend the majority of their time around dead people.

"What's up with the suit, though?" Eva asks, flashing a look of annoyance at Special Agent Lancaster. "This girl have rich parents or something?"

"Not that I know of," I say. "He's here because we have a Very Important Resident who lives—"

"Ms. Wells," Special Agent Lancaster snaps, pausing his phone conversation. "The reason for my presence here is on a need-to-know basis, and Ms. Kovalenko does *not* need to. It has nothing to do with this girl's unfortunate death."

Eva looks at me questioningly. I shrug. "As far as I know," I say, "it doesn't."

"Well," she says, her lips forming a hard line. "Ramon and I will be the judge of that, won't we . . . if he ever finds a place to park the van. What's going on out there in front of the building, anyway?"

"What do you mean?"

"There are all these buses parked outside, and kids getting onto them."

Suddenly I remember.

"Oh God." I put a hand to my mouth. "Casino Night." I'd totally forgotten.

"*What* night?" Eva asks.

"Casino Night." I shake my head. "It's part of orientation week for the new students. All the kids are being taken on a harbor cruise around Manhattan for mocktails and gambling. Not real gambling, of course, there's no cash involved, they win prizes like New York College sweatshirts and other swag."

Eva shakes her head. "Things have certainly changed from when I went to college. We thought it was cool when they gave us free hot dogs to grill over a hibachi in the quad. Now you people take them on cruises around Manhattan."

"Well," I say. "Hibachis aren't allowed anymore, because they're considered a fire hazard."

Eva rolls her eyes. "Of course. We wouldn't want any of them learning a skill that might actually come in handy someday, such as barbecuing, would we?" She throws Special Agent Lancaster a narrow-eyed glance. "When my boy Ramon gets here you'll let him through, right, 007? Or are you going to shoot him?"

Special Agent Lancaster eyes her. Is it my imagination, or is he smiling a little? If so, it would be a first.

"That depends," he says drily. "Your boy Ramon have ID?"

"No," Eva replies sarcastically. "He likes to roam around the city with body bags and a gurney for fun."

I've sunk down onto the bed opposite Jasmine's body, feeling a little queasy, and hope it's because of the situation—or the tuna salad sandwich I hastily grabbed for lunch from the dining hall—and not because I've picked up Lisa's flu. It's close to five o'clock, and all I want to do is go home, crawl into bed, and stay there, preferably with my dog, Cooper, some popcorn, the remote, and a large alcoholic beverage. Maybe not in that order.

"Looks like you lucked out this time." Eva's conversational tone rouses me from my fantasy of a vodka-and-cheese-popcorn-soaked *Say Yes to the Dress* marathon. "No blood spatter or body fluids for your housekeeping crew to have to clean up. God, we couldn't believe how many messy ones you guys had last year. Those girls in the elevator shafts? Oh, and the head in the pot in the cafeteria? Man, that one took the prize."

"I'd have preferred not to be eligible for that contest, especially not this year," I say weakly. "It's freshman orientation week right now."

"I see what you mean." Eva is raising the dead girl's eyelids to examine her pupils. "It's kind of early to say what the cause of death is without tox screens, but I don't see any sign of trauma. You find any prescription pill bottles lying around?"

I'm not surprised by the question. Prescription drug overdose, we were told at an incredibly boring drug-and-alcohol-awareness training session over the summer, is one of the leading causes of death for young adults (after accidents). Someone dies of a prescription pill overdose every nineteen minutes in this country.

"No." Surprisingly, it's Special Agent Lancaster who replies. "There's a bottle of Tylenol in her medicine cabinet." He nods toward 1416's bathroom. Unlike many residence halls, all rooms in Fischer Hall have private baths. The building once housed floor-through apartments for some of Manhattan's wealthiest socialites. Few of the architectural details of those days remain (except in the lobby and cafeteria, which used to be a ballroom), but residents don't have to go down the hallway to shower. "But it still has the protective seal on it."

Eva nods as if this is what she expects to hear. She's feeling the victim's jaw. "She's been dead at least twelve hours. Probably passed away last night sometime around . . . I'm going to say three in the morning. She have any preexisting conditions that you knew of?"

"Asthma, according to her student file." I'd grabbed it on my way upstairs, then skimmed it during the elevator ride to the fourteenth floor.

Special Agent Lancaster says, "Her inhaler is over there

on the dresser. It seems like it's plenty close enough for her to grab."

"And it's practically full," I say, then blush, not having meant to let that slip. We weren't supposed to have touched anything, but the inhaler is something I found after Cooper left and, because his paranoia about Jasmine's missing cell phone had made me suspicious, I'd lifted it—using Jasmine's discarded shirt from the day before—and given it a shake.

Eva doesn't notice. She picks up the inhaler and gives it a shake herself, then drops it into an evidence bag.

"We'll take a look at it," she says, marking something down on her clipboard. "You know, people don't take asthma as seriously as they should. About nine people a day die from it. It's one of this country's most common and costly diseases. She could have had an asthma attack brought on by a reaction to an allergen. Speaking of," she adds, "my mom thinks she's allergic to gluten. She's not, of course. But I'm putting up with it to keep the peace. So if you guys could serve some gluten-free stuff at your wedding, that would be great. Not necessarily a whole separate gluten-free cake, but like some fresh fruit, or whatever."

"Um," I say. "Okay. I'll have the wedding planner make sure the caterer knows."

Not that I mind that Eva and her mother are coming to my wedding, but I wonder again how they got an invitation. I know I didn't put them on my list. Granted, my list is pretty lame—it has fewer than fifty people on it, most of whom work either for New York College or the NYPD. From my family, there is only my father and his sister. I haven't spoken to my mother in over a decade. Even if I had her address—

which I don't—no way would I have invited her. Weddings are supposed to be occasions for joy, not psychodrama.

So while the addition of a cool punk medical examiner and her mom at my wedding is definitely a plus, I'd still like to know how it happened. Did Cooper add Eva and her plus one because he felt sorry for me, as there are so many more people (at least three hundred) on his side?

It's all very baffling, but again, not something I have time to figure out just now.

"And there's no sign of, um, vomit in her toilet or trash can," I volunteer. "So I don't think she had that stomach flu so many people have."

Eva looks at me like I'm nuts. "What stomach flu?"

"You know," I say. I'm still sitting on Jasmine's visitors' bed, looking at the posters she'd hung on her walls. "That stomach flu that's going around." Then I gasp. "Oh God! Casino Night . . . if there's a virus or whatever going around, won't they *all* get it if they're confined to a small space, like on a boat? I saw on *Voyage to Death* that that happened on the *Queen Mary 2*. The entire ship got the norovirus, a thousand passengers or something, even crew members. The toilets got clogged from everyone's vomit."

Eva glances at me in amusement. "If I understand it correctly, this cruise your residents are going on is only around the island of Manhattan, not the Caribbean. They'll be home in a few hours, so I think they'll be all right. And anyway, I haven't heard of any stomach flu going around." She looks over at Special Agent Lancaster. "Have you heard about any stomach flu going around?"

Special Agent Lancaster shakes his head. "None of my

people have it." Then he touches his earpiece. "My people are asking, by the way, how much longer you're going to be."

"As long as it takes, 007," Eva says. "Why, do you have a train to catch and then derail for Her Majesty?"

"I'm not MI6," Special Agent Lancaster says, flushing a little. "I thought I explained. I'm Diplomatic Security, with the—"

"State Department, yes, yes," Eva says, impatiently. "So you said. So is that a passport in your pocket, or are you just glad to see me?"

Special Agent Lancaster frowns and turns away, but I see the back of his neck turning red.

"No one has a sense of humor anymore," Eva mutters. I'm not sure she notices that the agent is blushing.

There's a loud rattle from the hallway as the doors to the service elevator open.

"Finally," Eva says. "It's Ramon."

Ramon is Eva's partner from the OCME, finally arriving with the body bag and gurney.

"Hey, Ramon," Eva calls out as Special Agent Lancaster stops him and demands to see ID. "Check out the guy in the hallway. He's a real-life James Bond."

Ramon looks perplexed, but shows his ID. "How are you doing, sir?" he asks Special Agent Lancaster.

"Peachy," says the agent, and waves Ramon into the room.

"Have you heard about some flu that's going around?" Eva asks him.

"It's too early in the fall for the flu," Ramon says matter-of-factly. He has a white paper sack balanced on top of the gurney. An extremely pleasant—and familiar—odor enters the room along with him. "Hey, Heather," he says to me. "Sorry about your loss." To Eva, he says, "Hey, boss, guess what I stopped for since I had to drive around for so long looking for a parking space, and we got stuck with that crispy critter over on the West Side Highway and didn't have time for lunch today?"

Eva's expression brightens as she recognizes the logo on the sack. "Murray's? Oh, Ramon, you're too good to me."

"You know it's policy never to stop in this neighborhood without getting sandwiches from Murray's."

Eva leaps up to look inside the sack while Ramon wheels the gurney to the side of Jasmine's bed, then goes to look down at the body. I rise to join him.

"So young," he says sadly, crossing himself. "My wife and I have a girl her age. Seems like such a waste."

"Yeah." There doesn't seem to be much else to say.

"At least there's no blood this time," he points out. "You had it bad last year. Remember the girl in the pot?"

"I try not to," I say.

"Sorry. What's with the suit?" Ramon whispers, nodding at Special Agent Lancaster.

"VIR," I say, glancing back down at Jasmine. "Very Important Resident."

"Her?" he asks, sounding surprised.

"No," I say. "Upstairs. Son of someone important. There've been death threats."

"She looks like she died in her sleep," Ramon says. "Not like anyone killed her."

"I know," I say. "I guess it's protocol, or something."

"Oh," he says. "Well, I wanted to tell you, thank you very

much for the wedding invitation. My wife and I will be very honored to attend."

I look back at him. I didn't send Ramon an invitation to my wedding. "Great," I say. "See you there."

He nods somberly. "Well. Guess I better get to it. Hey, boss," he calls to Eva. "Time to tag and bag."

Eva, who was unable to resist taking a bite of Smokey Joe—I recognize the scent, as I've had it many times myself: smoked mozzarella, marinated sun-dried tomatoes, and balsamic vinaigrette and basil on crisply baked focaccia—looks up guiltily.

"Sorry," she mumbles with her mouth full, then wipes her lips with practiced skill so that the crumbs fall directly into the Murray's bag and not onto Jasmine's floor. "Just a sec."

In the hallway, Special Agent Lancaster rolls his eyes, but otherwise chooses to pretend he hasn't noticed anything amiss.

I move out of the way so that Eva and Ramon can get to work, admiring as always the tender movements with which they prepare the deceased for transport.

It's only when they have Jasmine zipped up and on the gurney and I go to her bed to straighten her sheets—even though we're not supposed to, but it can't matter anymore; I want her room to look nice for her parents when they come—that I realize that Cooper was right all along:

Jasmine's smartphone is missing.

All Pain and No Gain for the President of the Pansies

Rumors are flying that the faculty and staff of New York College are set to approve a vote of no confidence in Phillip Allington, the school's sixteenth president. If such a vote occurs, it will be another embarrassing setback for a man who's already had a great many in a very short period of time.

"His emphasis on athletics, along with raises and perks for a few top employees, is more appropriate for a state university than a private college," one staff member is quoted as saying.

Staff and faculty have also criticized Allington's managerial style, claiming he is motivated by a desire to get the school basketball team's Division I status reinstated (it was revoked after a decades-old cheating scandal), and not by academic goals.

"Why else would he be accepting money from a known misogynistic, homophobic, anti-Semite like the leader of Qalif, General Sheikh Mohammed bin Zayed Sultan Faisal?" asked the staff member.

Phone calls to the president's office asking for a response to this question were still unanswered by press time.

New York College Express,
your daily student news blog

Maybe she loaned it to someone," Patty says.

"Yes, Patty," I reply, taking a sip from my glass of white wine. "Because young girls often loan their cell phones to other people."

"Wait." Patty, one of my oldest and dearest friends, frowns. "Are you being sarcastic?"

"Of course she is." Cooper lowers his wineglass. "That's why they're called *personal* mobile devices. Unless Jasmine lost it—which seems like it would be an odd coincidence—someone took it. The question is, who? And why?"

We're gathered around a well-used wooden table in the middle of Cooper's—and soon to be mine—back deck, enjoying the remnants of a late supper Cooper has prepared (lemon-and-herb chicken, roasted new potatoes, and a Boston lettuce salad tossed in a mustard vinaigrette). Our friends Patty and Frank brought the wine, and gelato for dessert.

Even though the surprise dinner party is supposed to get my mind off the grim day I'd had at work, it's hard to think of anything else, especially since no one seems to be able to talk about anything else.

Or maybe because the brownstone (left to Cooper by his eccentric grandfather Arthur Cartwright) is just a block or two from Fischer Hall. I can actually see the back of the building from the wrought-iron chair in which I'm sitting.

I'm trying not to look up. I'm trying to enjoy the company of my friends, allowing the wine and conversation to wash away the unpleasantness of the day, basking in the glow of the flickering flames of the citronella candles, the twinkling of the party globe string lights Cooper's hung across the deck's arbor.

But I can't help it. I look up.

"We all know what happened to her phone," Patty's husband, Frank, is saying. He drops his voice to a mock-dramatic tone. "The *murderer* took it. Because the victim took a photo of him as he was choking the life from her, recording her own death, and he had to get rid of the evidence."

"Okay," I say. "First, never do that voice again. You're scaring your child." I point at Frank and Patty's son, Indiana, sitting on the deck floor, noisily bashing one of his metal Tonka trucks into another. "And second, there's no evidence she was murdered. Eva, the MLI, thinks it was probably asthma."

Patty snorts. "That kid isn't scared of anything. And who dies of *asthma?*"

"Nine people a day," I say knowingly, taking another sip of my white wine and trying not to notice that I can see Lisa Wu's husband, Cory—identifiable to me by the white blob of his shirt and thin stripe of his tie—moving rapidly from their kitchen through their living room to their bedroom, way up in their apartment on Fischer Hall's sixteenth floor. He's probably bringing Lisa tea to settle her stomach. "It's one of this country's most common and costly diseases."

Patty stares at me. "Whoa. And to think, I knew you when you didn't even have your GED. Look at you now, all 'one of this country's most common and costly diseases.'"

"I'm taking Critical Thinking this semester," I inform her.

"It's a four-credit course required by everyone going for their bachelor's degree at the New York College School of Continuing Education."

"I would think New York College would just give you the damn degree already," Patty says, "considering you've caught like ten murderers on their campus since you started working for them."

"Ten's an exaggeration," I say modestly, dropping my gaze from Lisa's apartment. There's Gavin at his desk in his window a few floors below. I can tell by the blue glow that he's at his computer, probably working on his screenplay. This latest one is about zombies. "And I had a little help."

I smile sweetly at Cooper, but he doesn't notice since he's busy frowning down at Indy, who is now attempting to ram one of his trucks into my dog Lucy's paws. Lucy, looking frightened, gets up and moves to the safety provided by the wrought-iron legs of Cooper's chair. Neither Frank nor Patty notices their son's behavior.

Frank and Patty's little boy, Indiana, can be pretty sweet when he wants to be, but he's at that age when he can also be a handful. Like now, as the doorbell rings shrilly. Indy jumps up, shrieking "I'll get it!" and tears into the house.

"Frank," Patty says calmly. She's too far advanced in her second pregnancy to leap after her first child, although even when not pregnant, Patty has never been much of a leaper. A dancer by profession—which is how we met, when she performed backup for me onstage during my Sugar Rush tour—she's graceful, but has always been more sinuous than energetic. "Get him before he destroys something."

"I'll do it," Cooper says, carefully scooting back his chair so as not to injure Lucy. "I have to see who it is anyway."

"My child." Frank lays his napkin on the table with a sigh and follows Cooper. "My responsibility." Though I know the truth, that Frank is fascinated by Cooper's career, and is really following him to see if he can learn some new trick of the private detection trade.

I don't ask anything stupid like *Who could that be at this hour?* because I'm used to Cooper having late-night visitors, most of whom are what Cooper describes as work "colleagues." They all have nicknames like "Sammy the Schnozz" or "Virgin Hal." I've stopped asking what these names mean (in the case of the Sammy the Schnozz, it's obvious. His nose is extremely large and has been broken and badly reset many times. In the case of Virgin Hal, I'm not sure I want to know).

I've noticed that many of them are on Cooper's invitation list. "I owe them" is all Cooper will mutter when I ask about it, and I'm pretty sure he isn't referring to the poker night he sometimes hosts. I mentioned that I look forward to his introducing one nicknamed "The Real Bum Farto" to his mother, and Cooper only smiled mysteriously.

"So," I say to Patty when the guys are gone, hoping to steer the conversation away from Jasmine's death, though this will be difficult, since Patty's sitting directly opposite and below the window of 1416, Jasmine's room. The window is dark.

As soon as Jasmine's parents come to get her things— which I, and probably Sarah, will help them pack up—a new RA, chosen by Lisa from the waiting list, will move in. Only then will I be able to see a light in room 1416's window again when I look up.

"Have you found out yet if the new baby is a boy or a girl?"

"Hell no," Patty says, breaking off a piece of dark chocolate from the bar she and Frank brought to go with the gelato. "If I find out it's another boy, I won't push, I swear to God."

"Aw, come on, Patty," I say. "You don't mean that."

Patty makes owl eyes at me. "Oh, yes I do. Just wait until you have a baby, then you'll know. You need all the energy you've got to push the little bugger out. And why would I push if I know at the end all I'm going to get is another little hell demon like Indy, whose only goal in life is to flush all my jewelry down the toilet? Don't get me wrong, I love my son, and there's nothing I wouldn't do for him, but this next one better be a little girl."

"Here, Patty," I say, passing her a plate left over from the appetizer course. "Have a little cheese to go with your *whine*."

Patty laughs, then stops abruptly and looks at me with wide, guilt-stricken eyes.

"Oh God, Heather," she says, biting her lower lip. "I'm sorry. I didn't mean—when I said that just now, about wait until you have a baby, I completely forgot about your, uh . . ."

"Inability to get pregnant due to severe uterine scarring thanks to endometriosis?" I lower the cheese platter I'm still holding. "It's okay, Patty. I guess Cooper and I will have to experience the wonders of parenthood through your children. And of course all the kids in the dorm where I work."

Patty doesn't look comforted. "Oh, Heather, you're making light of it, but I know it really hurt when you found out. Isn't there anything the doctors can do?"

"Of course there is," I say, "and if we wanted a child that desperately, we'd be exploring those options, and others, like adoption or foster care. But neither of us feels an overwhelming urge right now to reproduce *or* be a parent. We're happy with the way things are. Why? Do we seem sad to you?"

Patty shakes her head until her long crystal earrings sway. "No," she says. She lifts her napkin to dab at the corners of her eyes, which have gone shiny in the light from the candle flames. "No, not at all. You seem happier than I've ever seen you—and we've known each other since we were kids, or close enough. And obviously Cooper's over the moon—well, he's always been crazy about you. I knew he was in love with you from the moment you two met—"

"Oh, come on," I interrupt, thrilled by her words but certain she's only saying them to please me.

"I'm serious! He could never look at anyone but you if you were in the room, and that hasn't changed. The other girls and I used to laugh about it. I mean, you were going out with his little brother, so it wasn't like he could make a move or anything. But the minute you and Jordan broke up, none of us were surprised that Cooper was there to the rescue, offering you a place to live—"

"—in exchange for doing his bookkeeping," I point out.

"Oh, please," Patty says. "Like the man couldn't afford to hire a bookkeeper. You're not *that* good with numbers. He had designs on you the whole time. I'm so happy for you, Heather, really." She reaches out across the table to grasp my hand and squeeze. "So happy for you I can *almost* forgive you for letting those bratty little twin sisters of his be bridesmaids."

"Oh, come on," I say again. "You're matron of honor. Why can't you let Jessica and Nicole have their moment in the spotlight too?"

"Because they're spoiled little troublemakers," Patty replies, releasing my hand to dab at her eyes again. She isn't crying anymore, she's indignant. "Did you know one of them—I can't keep their names straight, but the chubby one who thinks she can write songs—"

I hear footsteps and voices in the kitchen behind me. Patty hears them too, and her gaze flicks past me—she's sitting facing the glassed-in kitchen addition, whereas I'm looking out toward the yard—and I see her expression change from one of annoyance to wide-eyed alarm.

I turn in my chair to see who Cooper has let inside the house, but not before I recognize one of the voices. My blood goes cold in my veins, despite the warm evening air.

"What are you talking about?" A trim, middle-aged woman dressed in a cream-colored pantsuit is asking Cooper as she clip-clops behind him in a pair of high heels. "She'll be delighted to see me."

"I wouldn't be so sure," Cooper says. His voice is as cold as the wine in my glass. He's leading the woman past the kitchen table and toward the open door to the back deck, his expression grim, while Frank follows behind them both, Indiana squirming in his arms.

"Oh, don't be ridiculous," the woman says. She has an expertly coiffed auburn bob and a tastefully made-up face, a filmy cream-colored scarf thrown around her throat, probably more for dramatic effect than to hide whatever the ravages of time have done to her neck—she was always a fan of plastic surgery. "She wants to see me. I'm here because she invited me."

Patty's hand closes around my wrist. Her fingers feel as cold as my blood has gone.

"That's what I wanted to tell you," she whispers. Like mine, Patty's gaze is glued to the woman in the kitchen. "Your future sister-in-law, the do-gooder—"

"Nicole," I say, through lips gone numb with shock.

"Yeah. She told me at our last fitting—the one you couldn't come to because you had that emergency drug-and-alcohol-awareness training session—that she felt bad because there were so many more people on the groom's side than the bride's. So she got some kid from where you work to swipe your Rolodex, and your dad to cough up an address book I guess he copied from you a while back, and then she went through them both and added a whole bunch of people to the bride's side."

I feel a swooping sensation in the pit of my stomach, and it isn't the good kind, the kind I get when Cooper comes walking into the room and I realize all over again how handsome he looks and how lucky I am that he chose me (of course, he's lucky I chose him too). It's the bad kind of swooping, the kind that means *Warning, warning, get out now.*

This is what I get, I think to myself. This is what I get for being too busy at work to pay attention to my wedding, and leaving it all up to Perry. Who, Cooper informed me earlier, hadn't been too pleased about the fact that we'd canceled lunch. She'd stressed how busy and important she is, and implied her schedule is so tight, we might not get another appointment with her before our actual wedding day.

A day I can now see is going to be a disaster.

"Jessica and Magda and I told Nicole she shouldn't have done it," Patty goes on rapidly, "that you'd invited everyone you wanted to, but she said that it would be a nice surprise, and that your dad and Cooper approved them all, but now I'm guessing—"

"She didn't tell anybody," I say. My throat has gone as dry as sand, but I can't move a muscle to reach for my wineglass. "Except my dad, I'll bet, who's been hoping for a reconciliation between us two for a long time."

The woman standing inside the glass addition sees Patty and me sitting beneath the string of party globes and claps her hands dramatically.

"There she is!" she cries. "There's my girl!"

Then she rushes through the open screen door and out onto the deck to embrace me, nearly choking me in a thick cloud of Chanel perfume, a scent I've only ever associated with her, and not in a good way.

"Hi, Mom," I say.

I don't want to look like a big white lightbulb
I don't want to shine too bright
I don't want to look like a marshmallow
I only want you to hold me tight

"Wedding Gown,"
written by Heather Wells

9

Uh, honey," Frank says to Patty from the doorway. "We need to get going now."

"In a minute."

Patty's gaze is riveted on my mother, who has taken a seat in the chair Cooper had vacated to answer the door.

Lucy, usually friendly to strangers (she's a wonderful companion, but the world's worst watchdog), slinks out from beneath the chair and goes inside. Perhaps she, like Patty, suspects that fireworks are about to go off. Unlike Patty, however, Lucy has the sense to get out of the blast range.

"I didn't mean to interrupt your little party," my mother says, looking down at the detritus of our meal. "I'm so glad you learned how to cook, Heather. That's a skill every bride should have."

"I didn't," I say coldly. "Cooper made it. What are you doing here, Mom?"

"Patty, we really need to leave," Frank says, his tone more urgent than before. "It's past Indy's bedtime."

Frank's son is wriggling in his arms, crying to be put down, pointing in the direction Lucy has gone. He wants to run over my dog's feet with his trucks some more.

"What do you mean, what am I doing here?" my mother asks. "You're the one getting married. You sent me an invitation!"

She opens her arms wide, and silver bangles jangle on both her slim wrists. She's wearing quite a bit of jewelry. Rings on almost every finger, long silver chains and pendants around her neck, and a diamond stud in each earlobe that peeks out beneath her red hair—hair that was frosty blond the last time I'd seen her.

"And can I just say, I approve," Mom goes on, dropping her arms with a smile. "I always liked Cooper. He's so much more stable than Jordan. I never wanted to tell you while you two were dating, of course, Heather, but I always thought Jordan was a little bit of a putz."

My mother winks companionably at Cooper, who has taken up a defensive stance, leaning against the deck railing, his arms folded across his chest. He's watching my mother like she's a suspect in one of his cases, and at any moment he's going to tackle her to the ground.

"No offense to your brother, of course, Cooper," Mom adds.

"No offense taken, Janet," Cooper replies.

"Oh, please," my mother says with a wave of her hand, causing the silver bangles to jingle again. "We're practically family. Call me Mom."

"I'd rather not," Cooper says politely.

His tone is so dangerously devoid of emotion that I glance at him, and find that his blue-eyed gaze is fastened on me. I can almost feel the protective waves radiating from him.

I know if Cooper had had his way, he never would have let my mother in the house. There's got to be a good explanation for why he did.

"I didn't send you an invitation to my wedding, Mom," I say. "There was a mix-up. And even if I *had* sent you an invitation, that doesn't explain why you've shown up here now, at nine o'clock at night, a whole month before the ceremony."

"A mix-up?" Mom looks shocked. She does shocked very well because she's had so much work done on her face, her eyebrows seem frozen into semisurprised arches. "But when I called your father, he said—"

"I don't care what Dad said," I interrupt her. "You know perfectly well he's been on a redemption jag since he got out of jail. He's all about making amends. Plus, he's still gaga for you. He'd tell you anything you wanted to hear."

"Oh, Heather." My mother looks down modestly, then rearranges her scarf so that more of her necklaces show. "You know that isn't true. Your father and I split up long ago. It has to be twenty years now. You have to give up hoping that we're ever going to get back together—"

"Trust me," I say. "I'm not entertaining any such thoughts. Where's Ricardo?"

"Ricardo?" My mother's gaze skitters away, as if my former manager—with whom she fled the U.S., along with all the money in our joint account—might be hiding somewhere in the shadows of our backyard. "Oh, he's back in Buenos Aires, I suppose. He and I had a bit of a falling-out."

Things are suddenly becoming clearer.

"You mean he dumped you," I say. "And took what was left of my money with him?"

"Oh, Heather," Mom says again, this time in an irritated tone, her gaze skittering back toward me. "Why do you always assume the worst in people?"

"Gee, Mom, I don't know. Look at the role models I had in my life."

My mother shakes her head, her auburn bob shimmering under the party globes. "You know better than to talk that way, especially at the dining table. I didn't raise you to be such a poor hostess. The least you could do is offer me a glass of wine. It's been a long flight, and I'm really quite thirsty."

"You just got off the plane?" I cry in astonishment. "From *Argentina*?"

"Her bags are in the foyer," Cooper points out. "All ten of them. Louis Vuitton."

Now I know why he let her in. My mother has never traveled light. Even Cooper—who knows better than anyone how much I despise Janet Wells—wouldn't leave a middle-aged woman fresh off the plane from Argentina standing on his stoop with ten Louis Vuitton bags, especially at night, a block from Washington Square Park, where the late-night drug-dealing trade is brisk (if for the most part nonviolent).

"I didn't realize New York City had gotten so popular as a fall tourist destination," my mom says, giving Patty a dazzling smile for handing her a glass full of wine—Patty's own, but from which Patty hadn't sipped, being pregnant. She says she only "likes looking at it."

"But there are literally no hotel rooms available right now. Even the Washington Square Hotel, which I don't remember as being particularly luxurious from the days when you and I used to stay there, Heather, is booked solid. And it's three hundred dollars a night!"

"Those hotels aren't filled with tourists," I say to her acidly. "They're filled with concerned parents here to drop their kids off at New York College, the place where I work and go to school now on tuition remission because *you* stole all my savings—"

"Oh, honey," my mother says, looking vaguely amused as she sets down her wineglass to lay a hand on mine. "You aren't still mad about *that*, are you? Because you have to know it isn't healthy to hold on to old grudges. Those kinds of feelings will eat away at you over time and cause you to have a stroke or heart attack if you don't let them go. I'm not saying I was the perfect mother. Sure, I might have done some things I'm not proud of. But I was under a heck of a lot of pressure, raising you all by myself while your father was in jail for not keeping track of our taxes. I did the best I could under pretty lousy conditions, let me tell you. And keep in mind you loved it out there on that stage. You took to performing like a fish takes to water."

I glare at her. "And you and Ricardo took all the money I earned for it like a couple of sharks."

"But you're doing all right now, aren't you?" she asks. "You have a beautiful home, and lovely friends, and this marvelous man here who loves you and wants to marry you. That's so much more than many people have. You should really learn to count your blessings, Heather."

She flips my hand over and holds it toward the flame of the nearest citronella candle, causing the sapphire at the center of the cluster of diamonds in the engagement ring Cooper gave me to glow with the same blue intensity as his eyes.

"Ho-ho!" my mother cries. "That's quite a rock. I guess you're doing very well indeed. So what are you complaining about? It's only money, Heather. You're starting your new married life, so why not use this opportunity to forget the past and let bygones be bygones? Don't you think that's healthier than holding on to old grudges?"

I'm so stunned, I can't summon a reply—at least not out loud. Plenty flash through my head. *Only money? You think this is only about the money?* I want to ask her.

What about everything else she took from me? Because when she took that money—my money, money I could have used to go to college, or help pay for my own kids' college, if I ever have any—she also took my future, and my career, and my pride, and in very short order after that, my boyfriend, Jordan, my home, my life, and, yes, my hope. My hope that there was justice and fairness in the world. My own mother took that from me.

And yes, everything's turned out fine—better than fine—but not thanks to her. Because there's one thing she took from me that I will never get back, and that's a mother I could trust, one who loved me. Janet Wells certainly didn't.

Because she didn't merely steal from me: she abandoned me. Dad left because he had to. She left because she *wanted* to.

How can she not see the difference?

But I can't say any of those things to her. I can't even seem to move. I'm frozen stiff, as cold and unmoving as poor Jasmine Albright, whose body I sat with all afternoon.

Cooper, on the other hand, moves very quickly, pushing away from the deck railing as if he's about to lunge at her. Frank steps into his path, still holding his son, saying urgently, "Don't, man. It's not worth it."

My mother is blinking bewilderedly at all of us.

"What?" she asks. "What did I say? Oh, good heavens. You can't still be upset about the money. That was so long ago! And it wasn't only Heather's money. I was Heather's agent, and Ricardo was her manager. We *earned* that money—"

"Ten percent," I say, finally finding my voice. "That was your cut. Ten percent, not *all* of it."

"Oh, honestly, Heather," Mom says, taking a sip of her wine. "I'm not saying what I did was right, because of course it wasn't. I made poor choices. But you were still a child. Ricardo and I were adults, with adult issues. You know Ricardo had a gambling problem. There were criminals—*real* criminals, with guns, wearing very thick gold chains—after him. What was I supposed to do, let him die?"

"No, but you didn't have to go with him."

"But I loved him! Would you leave Cooper if gold-chain-wearing thugs were after him?"

"Of course not," I say. "I would stay and help him fight."

"Against men with *guns*?"

"Heather's been to the range with me a few times this

summer," Cooper says mildly. He's looking calmer. "She's a pretty good shot."

"Of paper targets," I say modestly.

"What I find interesting, Janet," Cooper says, "is that for someone so convinced she didn't do anything so wrong, you were awfully careful to wait until the statute of limitations had run out before you returned to the United States . . . five years, with an additional five years while the prosecutor sought, unsuccessfully, to locate you for extradition. That sounds about right, doesn't it, for a class-B felony—grand larceny in the first degree—for New York State?"

My mother chokes a little on the mouthful of wine she's just swallowed. "Don't . . . don't be ridiculous. I told you, I came back to be with Heather during this important time in her life. And I don't know why the money is still such an issue with her; she could always have earned more if she'd simply laid off the hot fudge sundaes and hadn't been so insistent on singing all those silly songs she wrote herself—"

It's Patty who interrupts, which is surprising since she's normally the most easygoing of creatures, slow to take offense.

But that's the thing about people like my friend Patty . . . and maybe me. When we do form a grudge, we hold it for years, and then like a kettle left to simmer on a back burner, before you know it, we've burned the house down.

"Frank is right," Patty says, getting up from her chair. "We have to go now. Janet, where can we drop you? We brought our car. It's parked out front. We'll be happy to take you anywhere you want to go."

"Go?" my mother echoes, looking as shocked as if someone swapped her pinot grigio for a merlot. "But I told you, I have nowhere to go—"

"You were resourceful enough to find your way from Buenos Aires to my door," I say sweetly. "I'm sure you'll manage."

"Frank, honey," Patty says, getting up, "why don't you go put Indy in his car seat while Cooper puts Janet's suitcases in the trunk. It's a Range Rover," she explains to my mother, "so there should be *more* than enough room for you and all your bags."

"Great idea," Cooper says before my mother can utter another word. He strides from the deck, Frank following him, still looking a little confused, his son slung over one shoulder.

Frank isn't the only one who looks confused.

"But I thought I told you," my mother is saying, "I couldn't get a hotel reservation. I'm sure Heather and Cooper don't mind if I stay here. They seem to have more than enough room, and I'm family. I don't expect special treatment. They'll hardly know I'm here."

"That isn't the—" I begin with irritation, but Patty cuts me off.

"Oh, I don't think that would be a very good idea, Janet." Patty steps toward my mother and leans down to take away her wineglass. "You know the old saying about in-laws: If you want a loving relationship with them, put them in a hotel when they come to visit."

"But I just told you," my mother cries, leaping to her feet. "I couldn't *find* a hotel room."

"Oh, Cooper will be able to take care of that," Patty says,

placing an arm around my mom's shoulder. "He's a private detective, you know. A lot of people in this town owe him favors. Don't they, Heather?"

"A ton," I say. "In fact, some of his clients *are* hotels. We'll find you a room somewhere. I can't promise you the St. Regis, of course, but it won't necessarily be a youth hostel, either."

My mother purses her lips. Patty's been steering her gently toward the kitchen, and in its less than flattering light Mom's face no longer looks quite as unlined as it did in the glow from the candles and party globes.

"No hotels," she says in a hard voice that sounds more like the one I remember from my childhood and teen years than the pseudo-sophisticated one she's using in front of my friends.

I raise my eyebrows. *My* mother doesn't want to stay in a hotel? Mom always loved hotel living when we were on tour, the room service, the maid service, the bright lights in the lobby, the bar . . .

Especially the bar, since that's where she could have her assignations with Ricardo.

Things have really changed if Mom's turning down an offer to stay in a hotel.

"If I can't stay with Heather, I'd rather stay with my ex-husband," she says, with a sniff. "Alan invited me, but I would have preferred—well, never mind that now."

Circumstances might have changed for Mom, but that doesn't mean she has.

"Fine," I say. "You go stay with Dad. He'll be delighted to have you. See you later, Mom."

Then I go to the screen door and hold it open for her so that she can go inside the house, into the kitchen, down the hall, and out the front door, down the stoop, across the sidewalk, and into Frank and Patty's car, away from me, hopefully for another ten years or longer.

Before she goes, my mother looks at me with an expression I don't recognize, because I've never seen it on her face before. Disappointment, maybe. It couldn't possibly be guilt or remorse. My mother isn't capable of feelings like those, or she'd never have done the terrible things she did to me in the first place.

"Good-bye, Heather," Mom says, still wearing the odd expression.

And then she leaves.

10

Welcome to Fischer Dining Hall!

New York College is proud to present its new sustainable and healthy eating initiative at Fischer Hall. Fischer Dining Hall supports local growers by serving a selection of seasonal, locally grown fruits and vegetables (whenever possible). The fish we serve is harvested using sustainable farming methods and we serve only cage-free eggs (unless otherwise noted).

Monday–Friday: 7:30 A.M.–8:00 P.M.
Saturday: 11:00 A.M.–8:00 P.M.
Sunday: Closed

Fischer Dining Hall features Magda Diego, voted "Most Popular Employee" by *New York College Express,* your daily student news blog

I'm in the Fischer Hall cafeteria the next morning preparing my traditional A.M. pick-me-up of hot chocolate mixed with coffee and a generous dollop of whipped cream when Magda approaches me.

"Heather," she says. *"Amiga.* I heard. The dead girl. Your mother. You are not having a very good week, are you?"

"It could be worse," I say. "At least I still have my ravishing good looks."

Magda grins and gives me a mock punch in the arm. "You'll always have those."

Magda's wearing the dining system's mandatory new uniform, a light green lab coat with the words "Made Fresh Daily!" stitched over the left breast. The uniforms used to be pink, which flattered Magda's bleached-blond hair and dark eyebrows. The green isn't doing anyone on the dining staff any favors, but it goes with the health and wellness program the food service company is trying to convince the students it's offering—though to be honest, the food hasn't really changed, only the presentation.

Fortunately Magda's boss, Gerald, can't dictate what she does with the rest of her appearance, so Magda's pinned a towering cascade of artificial blond ringlets to the top of her head, painted her long nails metallic gold (encrusted with glitter), and thrust her feet into a pair of matching metallic-gold kitten heels.

"Come," she says, opening her arms. "Time for a hug."

I set down my morning pick-me-up and let Magda hug me, even though I'm not really a hugger, unless of course the hug is from Cooper.

Magda's hugs are pretty special, though. She's soft, like butter, and smells of something exotically fruity. I was reading a magazine once while getting a pedicure and happened upon an ad featuring a sample of a celebrity fragrance, and realized I was smelling Magda. Magda smells exactly like Beyoncé.

"Thanks, Magda," I say as she squeezes me tight. "But everything's going to be all right."

"I know it is," Magda says, releasing me. "I wanted to make sure you know it is too. Jimmy!" She screams the name of one of the guys behind the hot serving line, startling him.

It's virtually empty in the dining hall before ten during orientation week. "Heather's here. Where is that bagel I asked you to save her?"

"Oh, Magda," I say, embarrassed. "I can get one myself."

"No, you can't," she says, patting my shoulder. "There was a rush on bagels earlier, see?" She points at the bagel basket over by the breakfast buffet, next to the cutting board where the butter, jams, and cream cheeses are kept on ice. "Some group of orientation kids, going to the Cloisters for the day. But I made sure Jimmy saved you one. He's got it. *Jimmy!*"

Jimmy, who was in the middle of a text conversation on his cell phone, puts the device away and snaps to it, slicing a bagel he's been hiding for me and putting it into the conveyer-belt toaster. Magda is only in charge of the ID scanner at the door, but she's ruled the dining hall like a queen for years.

"Thanks, Mags," I say to her, truly thankful as I eye what had formerly been the waffle bar but is now the Fischer Hall "fresh fruit spa water bar" (today's options are watermelon or orange). "But hold the bacon, will you, Jimmy? I've got my final dress fitting on Friday," I explain apologetically. "I'm trying to stay relatively the same size I was when they measured me for it. If I burst the seams due to all the stress eating I've been doing lately, they'll have to start over, and they'll never finish by next month."

"Hold the bacon, Jimmy," Magda yells at Jimmy, who shoots her an annoyed look because he heard me the first time and has already gone back to his texting.

"Thanks, Jimmy," I say, watching as my bagel is carried along the toaster's fiery red bars. "Maybe I'll have something healthy along with my carbs," I say to Magda. "Some grapes or something."

Magda raises a skeptical eyebrow. "Grapes are nice, I guess."

We stroll toward the salad bar, which, in the updated cafeteria, is featured front and center. The menu now offers more vegan and gluten-free options, which is lovely for those students who enjoy eating vegan and gluten-free, but horrible for people like me, who enjoy meat and gluten, preferably together in sandwich form with mayonnaise.

"I heard the girl died from asthma," Magda says.

"That's what the medical investigator thinks it could have been," I say. "She won't know until after she gets the tox screens."

"Poor little movie star," Magda says, shaking her head.

Magda refers to all Fischer Hall residents as movie stars, because once, long before I started working there, a scene from one of the *Teenage Mutant Ninja Turtle* movies was shot in the building's penthouse, and many of the residents were cast as extras, gazing up from Washington Square Park in amazement as either Donatello or Raphael performed amazing feats of turtle daring high above their heads.

Magda was a teenager herself at the time, newly emigrated from the Dominican Republic, but it left an indelible impression on her . . . that in America, anything can happen. A scene from a movie could even be shot at your place of work, and you could become a movie star . . . or at least a tiny blob in a crowd scene in a movie about teenage mutant turtles who are also ninjas.

Maybe that's why every day since she's dressed for work as

if a film director might come walking in and cast her in his next picture. You just never knew.

"How'd you hear about my mom?" I ask Magda as I steal a couple of grapes from the artfully arranged bunches by the "Fruitopia."

"Patty texted me last night," Magda says, fishing her smartphone from the pocket of her uniform and waving it at me. Her phone, like the rest of her, is covered in metallic-gold spangles. "She texted all the bridesmaids. She was so angry with that little sister of Cooper's—Nicole—for what she did, inviting your mother like that. I told her when I found out she was doing it, sending those extra invitations, I said, 'Don't do it. Heather won't like it.' But she kept saying, 'Oh, no, she will. Heather has so few people coming to the wedding, and my brother has so many. It will be a nice surprise. My dad will pay for it.' I thought, well, maybe she *will* like it. But inviting your mother like that? I couldn't imagine that would be a nice surprise."

"No," I say, chewing a grape. "It really wasn't."

"You know, Nicole is lucky we live here in the United States, because back where I come from, if a woman did something like that to another woman—especially the bride of her brother—"

Magda makes a slashing motion beneath her chin, accompanied by a sound like oxygen being sucked from a windpipe. A nearby student, preparing a healthy fruit salad for herself, looks a little frightened.

"That's it," Magda goes on. "That woman is dead. Because someone will have killed her. I can find someone to do it for you, if you want. Don't tell Pete"—Pete is Magda's boy-friend, an ex-cop who is now one of Fischer Hall's best se-curity officers—"but I have a lot of friends who will do that kind of thing. For Heather Wells, they'd do it for free. You know how popular your records were in my country. Still are," she adds, loyally.

"Well," I say, after taking a quick sip of my breakfast bev-erage, which I feel I need after Magda's somewhat dramatic performance as well as her offer. "I'm flattered. Thanks, but I don't think that will be necessary. Cooper's handling it on his own."

I'd come out of the bathroom the night before after using my rotating facial brush—I'd been told if I used it every night, by my wedding day my skin would be glowing—to find Cooper on his cell phone with his little sister.

"That's it, Nicole," he was saying, appearing to be finishing up a volatile conversation. "This whole thing is your fault. You had no right. No, I don't care why you did it. No, an apology won't help. Didn't you hear what I said? *You made her cry.* So you are dead to me. Stop calling. Corpses can't dial phones."

Then he hung up.

I raised my eyebrows.

"I didn't cry," I'd said.

Cooper had swung around, startled to see me in my fuzzy pink robe and slippers, with my face glowing from the bris-tles of the rotating facial brush.

"Christ," he said. "I didn't know you were there."

"I can see that," I said. "But I didn't cry. And you don't

have to be so mean to Nicole. She thought she was doing a good thing. A mother-and-child reunion, like in the Paul Simon song."

"Yeah, well, I just gave her a new song," Cooper growled. "Since she loves writing them so much, now she can write about a big brother who's going to bury his sister if she doesn't correct her egregious mistake."

I hadn't been able to keep from smiling. Cooper's family may not have had any felons in it, like mine, but it did have its own drama, like his twin sisters, whose conception came as something of a late-in-life surprise to his mother. Jessica and Nicole were sent off to boarding school at an early age to get them off their parents' hands, but now, newly graduated from college, they were back home and as incorrigible as prepubescents.

I preferred them over my mother, however.

"You can't bury her," I said, sinking down onto the side of the bed. "She isn't dead. That's a terrible thing to say at a time when a girl really is gone. Think how Jasmine's parents must be feeling. They really are going to have to bury their daughter."

"All I care about is how *you* feel," Cooper said, sitting beside me and wrapping a strong arm around my shoulders. "What happened tonight never should have happened. I'm sorrier than I can say that it did. Let me make it up to you."

"Okay. Stop being so mean to your sister." I leaned into him. His warmth was reassuring, as was the steady thump of his heart against my arm.

"That isn't quite what I meant by 'let me make it up to you.'"

"Why? It's what I want. And why did you tell Nicole that I cried? I didn't cry."

"Yes, you did," he said. "You had the water running so you thought I couldn't hear you, but I did."

"Oh." I stared down at my toes, embarrassed. I'd gotten a new pedicure for check-in, That's Hot pink. It looked good.

Jasmine had had a pedicure too. Powder blue, like her walls.

"I figured you wanted to be alone," Cooper said, "or you wouldn't have sat crying in your bathtub, you'd have come out and cried dainty tears on my strong manly chest."

"I didn't expect to start crying," I said. "My mother just makes me so mad."

What she really made me was sad—sad that I didn't have a mother who loved me the way Kaileigh Harris's mother loved her, so much that she couldn't let her go, not even to have lunch without her, which wasn't exactly healthy, but at least it showed she cared.

But I was afraid I might start crying again if I admitted this out loud, and I didn't want to start crying again, especially after I'd finally gotten control of myself.

"I know she does. Your mother makes me mad too," Cooper admitted. "So does my sister. I don't want anyone interfering with what's supposed to be our day, and I don't want anyone making you unhappy." He took a deep breath, then added, all in a rush, "That's why I'm going to tail your mother while she's here in town."

"What?" I stared at him. "Cooper, *have you lost your mind?*"

"Probably. But it's the only way I can think of to make sure she's here for the reason she says she is, to see you, and not to run some kind of scam that might end up hurting you—"

"Cooper, no." I shook my head. "You already have a case. A *paying* case. The best way to deal with people like my mom is to ignore them."

"I didn't say I was going to *talk* to her. I'm only going to tail her. Just a little." He held his thumb and index finger an inch apart. "Heather, come on, you have to admit it's a little odd. Why is she here now, a month before the wedding? And what's the deal with her not wanting to stay in a hotel?"

I sighed. I had to admit he was right. These were both questions I'd wondered myself. "And honestly, look at it from my perspective," he went on. "I'm a detective. What kind of boyfriend would I be if I didn't detect the person who's making the girl I love most in the world so unhappy?"

This went straight to my heart.

"My mother doesn't have the power to make me unhappy anymore," I said. "Not unless I let her. And I'm not going to let her this time, Cooper. I'm *not*."

But even as I said it, tears filled my eyes again.

Cooper's arm tightened around my shoulders, and he placed his other arm around me as well.

"I know you aren't," he said. "But in the meantime, whether you like it or not, I'm going to do what I can to make sure that she doesn't have another opportunity to make you unhappy. Tonight was unfortunate—I should never have let her inside the house, but—"

"I know," I said, lifting my hand to stroke his cheek. "She caught you off guard. She had all those bags, and she'd sent the cab away, and she pulled her defenseless, poor-little-me act. That's what she was always good at, you know: manipulating people. That's the real reason I couldn't make it in the music business without her. I was never very good at manipulating."

Cooper lifted one of my hands and kissed it tenderly. "But you're good at something more useful: being able to tell when someone's trying to manipulate you. And, of course, being incredibly, irresistibly gorgeous."

He'd kissed me then, deeply, and for a long time we didn't talk at all. We were too busy doing other things, our bodies having sunk back against the bed. Owen, the cat I'd adopted from a former boss, watched the whole time from the top of the dresser, his eyes half closed. It was difficult to tell if he approved. In general, I'm guessing he did.

I didn't tell Magda this part, however. Or the part about how Cooper was going to have my mother tailed. Only the part about Cooper declaring his sister dead to him.

"He wants to kick Nicole out of the wedding," I say, strolling back toward Jimmy's counter, where he's put my bagel, lightly toasted, on a plate. "Thanks, Jimmy."

"He might as well let me have her killed, then," Magda says. "Because she's going to want to die. Being your bridesmaid is the best thing that ever happened to that girl. She told me. She said, 'This is the best thing that's ever happened to me.' And you know, I believe her. I don't think she has any friends. Nicole told me she never had a boyfriend. She told me during the last bridesmaid gown fitting that she's a virgin."

"She *is*?" I'm surprised, and yet somehow not surprised at the same time.

"She says so." Magda walks me toward the condiment bar, where they keep the cream cheese. "But she plans to correct this at your wedding. She thinks there'll be a lot of—what did she call them again? Oh, right—eligible bachelors there."

"Wow." I can't help thinking of Cooper's friend Virgin Hal. Is he really a virgin? I wonder. Would he and Nicole hit it off? He's kind of goofy. But then, Nicole, who has been known to break into self-written songs about tasting her own menstrual blood, is no prize either.

"Heather."

I turn to see Julio Juarez, Fischer Hall's head housekeeper, approaching me, looking as if he feels embarrassed about disturbing me while I'm preparing my breakfast, which of course I should have had before I left for work. But I'm running a little late due to all the excitement—some of it welcome—from the night before.

"Good morning, Julio," I say. "Do you want a bagel? I know someone who can hook you up." I wink at Jimmy, who doesn't notice due to texting.

"Oh, no, thank you, Heather," Julio says, looking even more embarrassed. Julio takes his job very seriously, ironing his brown uniform very carefully every morning before work and never allowing a speck of grime to remain on the lobby's marble floors for longer than an hour. He is quick to fetch me when residents scratch graffiti into the brass elevator fittings with their keys or leave soda cans to stain the felt of the billiard table in the game room, hoping, as he does, that I will be able to catch the miscreants and bill them for their crimes. His pride in and love for Fischer Hall are immense.

"I heard about the girl who died," Julio says, his brown eyes sad. "I am wondering if her parents will be needing boxes for her things. In the basement I have many boxes from the check-in. We were going to throw them out on trash day, but if you want, I will save some good ones for the girl's parents."

"Oh, Julio," I say, suddenly no longer hungry for my bagel. "That's a really nice thought. I don't know when her parents are coming for her things, but it will probably be soon. So yes, please pick out some nice boxes and set them aside for Jasmine's family."

Julio's eyes look more cheerful. Everyone likes to do something to help when there's been a death in the building.

"Okay," he says. "I will save some boxes. Now, what do I do about the trash on fifteen?"

"Trash on fifteen?" I echo.

"Yes," he says. "Every morning the trash chute room on the fifteenth floor is filled with trash. Too much trash. No one is putting it down the chute."

Each floor on Fischer Hall, like most prewar buildings in Manhattan, has a room where residents can take their garbage. They're supposed to sort it into separate cans for recycling, then stuff the nonrecycling down a chute for disposal. In olden times, the chute went to an incinerator, but those had long since been eliminated because of air-quality issues. Now the chutes lead to a massive compacter in the basement.

"Can you tell who's doing it?" I ask, knowing the answer before the words are even out of my mouth.

"The prince," Julio and Magda say at the same time.

"A prince isn't going to take out his own garbage," Magda says. Her eyes have lit up. She completely adores the idea that a prince lives in Fischer Hall. It's as exciting to her as the fact that a movie was once filmed here, and that a reality TV show was shot here over the summer starring her favorite female pop star, Tania Trace (she is always polite enough to add, "Except for you, Heather"). "How would a prince know how to take out his garbage? He's always had butlers to do it, in the palace!"

"Well, he's taking the garbage out of his room," I say. "He's just not sorting it or stuffing it down the chute. Right, Julio?"

Julio shakes his head in disbelief. "Right. And there's a *lot* of it. Every morning since he moved in. So much. I've never seen so much garbage. The bags are tied very neat, but there's so much, and I have to sort through them myself. It's a lot of extra work."

"What's in them?" I ask, curiosity getting the better of me. I've never had the chance to sort through a prince's garbage.

"Cups," Julio replies promptly. "Many, many plastic cups. And bottles. Mostly tequila. Good tequila. Some vodka. Much champagne. And some wine."

"Shiraz," I say, shaking my head. "A royal alcoholic."

"Although he *is* twenty-one," Magda points out.

When I eye her incredulously, she says, "What? I read it in *Us Weekly*. He had his royal birthday bash in London. Usher performed at it."

I try not to look impressed.

"He's obviously throwing parties in his room, Magda," I say. "He's not drinking all that booze by himself. And if he's having parties, that's a problem. This is freshman orientation week. He can't be serving alcohol to minors."

Magda looks prim. "You don't *know* he's doing that."

I remember what Cooper said about my ability to tell when someone is manipulating me.

"No," I say. "But I've got a pretty good feeling." I look at Julio and smile. "Don't worry. I'll get to the bottom of this."

He smiles back. "Thank you, Heather. Oh, and thank you for the wedding invitation. My wife, Anna, is very excited."

"Oh," I say, keeping my smile in place. "Great! See you later."

As Julio hurries away to continue his battle against dirt, Magda looks at me.

"You invited Julio to your wedding?" she asks in astonishment. "Did you invite Jimmy too?"

"No, I didn't invite Jimmy," I say, my smile vanishing. "I didn't invite Julio either. Nicole did. I didn't want *that* many people from work coming. I invited you, obviously, and Pete, and Lisa and her husband, Cory, and Tom Snelling and his boyfriend, Steven"—Tom was a former Fischer Hall director, now director of Waverly Hall—"and Sarah and Gavin, and Muffy Fowler, of course." Muffy's the head of New York College's media relations. "I was trying to keep the numbers manageable, at least on my side. But you know what?" I add with sudden emotion. "Maybe what Nicole did wasn't such a bad thing, after all. I *want* the people I see every day around me at my wedding."

"Tell me you still feel that way," Magda says drily, "when Carl shows up with the inflatable doll he keeps in his locker downstairs as his plus one."

Diamonds are forever
That's what all the ads say
But what do ads know
About love and what makes it stay?

"Diamonds,"
written by Heather Wells

I'm surprised to find the Fischer Hall director's office open and Lisa Wu already at her desk.

I'm even more surprised to find her eating a breakfast burrito supreme, looking surprisingly perky compared to yesterday.

"Oh my God," she says with her mouth full when she sees me. "I was worried you weren't going to come in today."

"Oh my God," I say back to her. "I was worried *you* weren't going to come in today."

"I think it was only a twenty-four-hour bug," she says, after she swallows. The burrito is almost bigger than her head. "I feel fine this morning. Some of the RAs at the meeting last night, though—oh my God. They were hurting puppies. You do not want to catch this thing, whatever it is."

"I'll be careful to wash my hands," I solemnly assure her.

Lisa Wu is a petite girl, six years younger than I am despite being my boss, with long black hair that she sometimes pulls back in a scrunchie (despite my objections) because she's too busy to fuss with it.

Today she's taken care to style it, no doubt because there's been a student death in the building. She's dressed in a more businesslike fashion than I've ever seen her, in navy-blue slacks and a white knit short-sleeved sweater. Instead of the flip-flops she normally wears, she's put on black loafers. There's no sign of Tricky, her dog. I assume she's left him upstairs because there'll be college bigwigs lurking around, and it wouldn't be considered professional to have her Jack Russell terrier bouncing up to them, wagging his tail.

"Hey, Magda told me about your mom," she says. "I'm so sorry that happened to you."

Word travels fast when one of your bridesmaids is in charge of the place where everyone gets their breakfast.

"It's okay," I say. "How are *you* holding up, besides the flu? How did calling Jasmine's parents go? And the meeting with the RAs—besides their being sick?"

"Ugh," she says, collapsing against the back of her chair. "Horrible, naturally. Jasmine's parents are in shock. They'll be driving in from New Jersey this afternoon to meet with us, and with the coroner's office. I think they're expecting answers. Hopefully by then someone will have one. As for the staff . . . well, Jasmine was new, but she was pretty pop-

ular. Mostly people's reactions were the same as Jasmine's
parents: disbelief. I think when the medical examiner gets
back with the results, saying *how* she died, there can be a
little closure, and the staff will get over it."

I nod and murmur, "Sure," because I know it's what Lisa
needs to hear, not because I believe it. The word "closure"
gets tossed around a lot by people in helping professions
and on shows like *CSI* and *Law & Order,* but there's rarely
any actual closure when someone young dies, even of natural causes. The death seems so wrong and unnecessary and
senseless. There will never be any closure. Jasmine's family
and friends will move forward, but they'll never "get over
it." They aren't supposed to. That's why it's called a loss.

I've laid my bagel and coffee drink on my desk and sat
down, more or less joining Lisa for breakfast, though we're
in separate offices. I swivel my chair around to look at her
through her office door.

"I don't know how you've done this so many times," Lisa
says mournfully. "I really don't. I feel like I've been kicked
all over my body by a horse. Especially in the boobs." She
reaches up to illustrate, rubbing them.

"That's an interesting reaction to a student death," I remark.
"I can't say I've ever had that one before."

Lisa shrugs. "Well, I slept like a log last night. Cory said
I snored."

"It's probably all the stress," I say. "And the flu, leaving
your body. Is that Tabasco sauce or ketchup on that burrito?"

"Both," she says, shoveling more of it into her mouth.
"Anyway, we're going to have a long day ahead of us. That
Fowler woman—"

"Muffy," I say. "Head of media relations."

"Whatever. She thinks it's in our best interest to keep Jasmine's death out of the press because of Prince Rashid and the animosity toward him on the part of some in the college community."

"Gee," I say, sarcastically. "You think?"

"So we can't send out a mass text to the residents saying one of the RAs died, even though I understand that's what the college does under normal circumstances. We can't even advertise that there'll be grief counselors available if anyone feels the need to see one, though Dr. Flynn and Dr. Kilgore are going to be here all day, for any residents or staff who want to talk about what happened. That includes you, by the way."

I turn my head, my mouth full of bagel, to stare at her. "*Me?* Why would *I* need to talk to anyone?"

"Heather, you sat with a young girl's dead body *all day* yesterday," Lisa says. "Then you went home and your mom, who abandoned you a decade ago, dropped by unannounced. I think there's a possibility you might need to talk to a mental health specialist. There's no shame in it, you know. Cory and I saw a shrink before we got married. We still go sometimes. It's fun."

"Fun?" I can't stop staring at her. "How is telling some shrink your darkest secrets *fun?*"

"That's not the fun part," Lisa says. "It's that the shrinks sometimes point out that stuff you didn't think was that important probably really *is* important, and after it's been pointed out, you realize all these ways you've been sabotaging your own life. Like maybe you do have some issues about your mom abandoning you when you were in your late teens, even though you think you're over it, and that's what makes you feel so overprotective of the kids who live here, who are also in their late teens."

"Of course I have issues about my mom," I say, maybe a little more defensively than I mean to. "I don't need a shrink to point that out. I'm totally envious of people who have loving relationships with their mothers. I'll never have that. But that doesn't mean I'm *overprotective* of the kids who live here. I'm only doing my job. It's not my fault they keep getting themselves killed."

"Okay, okay," Lisa says, wadding up the tin foil her burrito had been wrapped in—amazingly, she'd eaten the whole thing. She must have been pretty hungry after throwing up so much the day before—and shooting a perfect three-pointer into the trash basket. "Forget I ever mentioned it. Anyway, we have a meeting set up this afternoon with a candidate for Jasmine's position who Dr. Jessup swears will be perfect."

"Wow," I say. "That was fast."

"Well, we need to get the ball rolling on finding a replacement. The sooner we find a good match, the sooner the staff can begin to heal. And Dr. Jessup says this candidate is a winner. The only reason he didn't make the original cut was because he applied late. He's a little bit older, a transfer student from New Mexico, Dave something or other."

"Okay," I say. "Well, good, I look forward to meeting Dave something or other."

"Ha," Lisa says. "You're funny. He's coming at two. Jasmine's parents will be meeting with us—and Dr. Jessup and Dr. Flynn—a little later. Maybe by then the coroner's office will know how Jasmine died."

The phone on her desk begins to ring.

"And so it begins," she says, and lifts the receiver. "Hello, Fischer Hall director's office, Lisa Wu speaking."

I finish my bagel while I listen to her say "Uh-huh" and "Yes, I understand" to whoever is on the other end of the phone, probably not even conscious the whole time that she keeps tugging at her bra like it isn't fitting correctly.

Do I need therapy? I wonder. Maybe what I need is some time off. Not for my honeymoon—I'm already getting that. Cooper and I are going to Italy—but now, right now, so I can deal with all this wedding crap and maybe my mom. (Not that Lisa's right. My issues with my mom aren't psychological. They're purely practical.)

I suspect Cooper might be right, and that whatever has brought Mom back to the United States has nothing to do with me, despite her claim that she's here to help with my wedding. It's probably a good idea for him to find out why she's really here, before the actual reason blows up in my face, as things concerning my mother have a tendency to do.

Patty's right, too. This place should give me an honorary degree. I've already mastered the art of critical thinking. And what about all the criminals I've caught on campus?

This reminds me of Prince Rashid's extracurricular activities, so after I've finished my bagel and returned the plate to the dining hall, I stop by the security desk on my way back to my office.

"Hey, Pete," I say casually. "Looking forward to seeing you out of that uniform and in a suit at my wedding, Magda looking hot on your arm."

Pete doesn't fall for it.

"Whaddaya want, Heather?" he asks. He's gotten portlier than he'd like to be since he started dating Magda, and his daughter, Nancy, who is something of a math and science prodigy though she's still only in junior high, had explained to him that if his LDL cholesterol got any "lousier," he'd probably have a heart attack. He needed to up his HDL, or "happy" cholesterol, she'd explained, and stop eating all the free donuts Magda kept sneaking him from the caf.

So lately Magda has been bringing him free carrot sticks. This has not put him in a very good mood.

"I want to see the sign-in logs for the past few nights," I say.

All residents are required to sign in each of their guests, who are supposed to show picture ID before entering the building, ID they then leave with the security guard during their stay.

"Particularly for Prince Rashid," I go on. "Also, can you roll back any video you have on the hallway outside his room during the evening?"

"Can I roll back any video I have on the hallway outside his room during the evening?" Pete echoes, in a rude imitation of my voice. He makes it much higher-pitched and Valley Girlish than I believe I sound. "Why should I? Do you know how hard it is to work these fricking things?"

He gestures at the stack of video monitors in front of him, which has grown much larger since Prince Rashid moved into the building.

"I barely know how to work my kid's Xbox," Pete complains, "and you're asking me to play back something—"

"I'll buy you lunch," I say. "Not from the caf. From wherever you want. A sandwich from Murray's. Dumplings from Suzie's. A slice from Joe's Pizza . . ."

His gaze flicks toward the cafeteria doors. This early in the morning, the week before classes have begun, there's no one but us two in the lobby, and the student worker behind the desk, who happens to be Gavin, dressed in his pajamas and dozing. He's desperate to earn as much money as he can before school starts so he can buy, he explained to me in excruciatingly boring detail, some kind of camera, with which he intends to film the greatest American horror story ever told.

It was at that point that I'd stopped listening and gave him all the hours at the desk that he wanted. No one else had volunteered, so it worked out great for both of us.

"Choza Taqueria?" Pete asks. "And you won't tell Magda? Because she's been ratting me out to my kid every time I eat anything over four hundred calories."

"Of course I won't tell Magda," I say. "Choza Taqueria it is."

Pete hands me the sign-in logs and begins to fiddle with the monitors. "I don't know if I'll be able to find anything," he says. "I think these things record back over themselves after twenty-four hours."

"Just do your best," I say.

I don't know what I expected to find in the sign-in logs, but certainly not what I end up finding: a big fat zero. Prince Rashid's signature is nowhere. I wonder if the prince is even required to sign in his guests, or if he has some kind of special privileges we don't know about, passed down to him from the president's office. I wouldn't be surprised.

Kaileigh Harris, on the other hand, seems to have had numerous guests: she's signed in her mother and father three to four times a day, poor thing. Other residents have signed in their parents multiple times a day as well.

I never went to college, of course—until now—but I can't see either of my parents expressing the slightest interest in coming to visit me if I'd gone, unless somehow I'd been earning money for them on campus. Then I'm sure they'd both have come to visit me a lot, maybe even as often as Kaileigh's mom and dad.

Scanning the sheet from the night Jasmine died, I see that she signed in no one. No guests—at least from outside the building.

"Pete," I ask, looking up from the log, "does our VIR get special sign-in privileges? I can't find any trace of his signature on these logs, but Julio tells me he's been partying every night."

"He don't got any special privileges with me," Pete says, his gaze still on the monitor. "I don't know about any of the other guards. On the other hand—"

He crooks a finger at me. I circle around to the back of the desk. He's found the footage I'm looking for, and all for the price of a few tacos.

There, on the grainy black-and-white video surveillance tape, are a number of young people walking down the fifteenth-floor hallway toward room 1512—Prince Rashid's room. They look happy and smiling.

And many of them are extremely familiar.

"Wait a minute," I say, stunned by what I'm seeing. "What night is this?"

Pete squints at the numbers on the bottom of the screen. "Monday. No, wait. Tuesday. Yeah, Tuesday. Night before last."

The night Jasmine died.

12

**New York College
Alcohol Policy**

Residents of New York College residence halls are required to abide by all New York State and New York College regulations regarding the use of alcohol. These rules specify that persons under twenty-one years of age are prohibited from possessing and/or consuming any alcoholic beverage while on New York College property.

In residence halls, persons under the age of twenty-one are in violation of the New York College alcohol policy if found to be in the presence of alcohol. Any resident over the age of twenty-one found to have given and/or purchased alcohol for residents under the age of twenty-one will also be found in violation of that policy, and subject to appropriate sanctions and/or punitive action.

No," Lisa says. Her face has turned slightly green, as if the burrito she had for breakfast is coming back up. "It isn't possible."

"It's right there on the monitor," I say. "You can go down to Pete's desk and see for yourself."

"Oh," Lisa says, swallowing hard. "I believe you. It's just that—"

"Or Gavin can tell you about it. Can't you, Gavin?"

I turn to Gavin, whom I've dragged to the hall director's office, hanging a "Closed—Back in Five Minutes" sign on the front desk, and another one that says PLEASE KNOCK! on the door to our office, which I've closed and locked so we won't be disturbed, though it's doubtful any residents will drop by so early in the morning.

Parents, on the other hand, are another story.

Gavin's sitting in a chair across from Lisa's, looking miserable. And not only because he's been hauled into his boss's office before ten in the morning, wearing only the Goofy slippers his mother gave him, a moth-eaten New York College T-shirt, and a pair of plaid flannel pajama bottoms, but because he's been caught in a lie he can't get out of.

Only he doesn't consider it a lie.

"I told you before, I ain't no narc," he says, folding his arms across his chest. His protest, however, sounds weak.

"Gavin," I say. "I am seconds—literally seconds—away from calling Detective Canavan down at the Sixth Precinct, and you know how disappointed he was in you the last time he was in this office. Do you really want to go through that again?"

Gavin looks sullenly down at his floppy-eared slippers. "No, ma'am."

"Then tell Lisa what you know about all the RAs being so sick."

"It wasn't *all* of them," he says, raising his tousle-haired head. "Mostly the new ones. Look, do I really have to—"

"Why were they sick, Gavin?" Lisa's voice has gone cold as ice. "Are you saying it wasn't the flu, like I had?"

"Uh, no, ma'am." Gavin looks back down at his slippers. "They were just hungover."

"Hungover?" Lisa's eyes flare like firecrackers. "What do you mean they were hungover?"

"Because they'd been up partying all night in room fifteen-twelve with Sexy Sheikh," Gavin explains. "I mean, Prince Rashid."

Lisa's face pales. She's shaking her head the way Tricky does when he has a flea. *No. No, no, no.*

"It has to have been the same party Ameera was talking about," I say to her. "Remember, I told you. She said Jasmine seemed fine during the party. It must have been a party at Prince Rashid's. Jasmine's on the tape. I saw her in the hallway, going into the prince's room with the others."

Lisa is still shaking her head, not because she doesn't believe me, but because she's so angry. I can see the tips of her ears turning red, a sure sign that she's upset.

Silence fills Lisa's small office. Outside the two wide windows that look onto the street, I can hear the rapid footsteps on the sidewalk of people who are late to work, and the sound of a car pulling into that rarest of all commodities in Manhattan—a parking spot.

"Who . . ." Lisa says to Gavin, after she's had a chance to control her breathing. "Who from the RA staff has been to the parties in Rashid's room? I want names. All of them."

She's lifted a pen. Now she holds it poised over a New York College notepad on her desk.

"Oh, man," Gavin says, lifting his gaze to the ceiling. "Come *on*. Don't do this to me! This is *not* cool."

"You want to know what's not cool, Gavin," Lisa says, sounding angrier than I've ever heard her. "A young woman on my staff was found dead yesterday morning, and last night when I asked her peers if any of them had seen her the night before, not a single one of them volunteered that they'd been to a party with her, a party in *my* building, information that might actually help the coroner determine the cause of her death. They sat there and lied to my face about it. So if you know anything about it, start talking, or by God, Gavin, you can start looking for a new place to live."

Gavin's eyes widen perceptibly. Without skipping another beat, he begins coughing up names. "Howard Chen. And both the other Jasmines."

Lisa writes *Howard Chen, Jasmine Singh, Jasmine Tsai* on her notepad.

"Christopher Mintz," Gavin goes on. "And that Josh guy, the one who always wears a Yankees baseball cap."

Joshua Dungarden, Lisa writes. I notice her hand trembling, but she keeps a firm grip on the pen.

"Stephanie, from the fourth floor."

Stephanie Moody, Lisa writes.

"That Ryan guy. Oh, and that one with the long nose and glasses."

Lisa stops writing and glares at Gavin. "Excuse me?"

"You know." Gavin points at his nose. "The girl with the glasses."

"Megan Malarty?"

"Yeah, that one. Oh, and the guy with the Justin Bieber hair."

"I saw him on the tape too," I say. "Kyle."

Lisa writes down *Megan Malarty* and *Kyle Cheeseman* on the notepad.

"Is that all?" I ask Gavin.

He nods, then hesitates. "Oh, well, except Jasmine. Jasmine—well, Dead Jasmine. She was there too." He looks from Lisa to me and then back again, apologetic. "Sorry to call her Dead Jasmine, but I can't remember her last name. There are so many Jasmines. I guess it was a popular name the year they were all born, or something."

"It's all right, Gavin," Lisa says, distracted. "Albright. Her last name was Albright."

Lisa runs her pen quickly down the list. I know what she's doing.

Counting.

"Gavin," I say while Lisa is occupied. "How do you know all these RAs were at the party the night Jasmine died? I didn't recognize this many on the video. Were you there?"

Gavin hesitates, looking out Lisa's windows as if he's contemplating throwing himself from them.

Unfortunately for him, the windows are covered in wrought-iron bars. Not to keep people in but, since we're on the first floor and this is New York City, to keep thieves out.

"Gavin, it's okay, you're not going to get in trouble," I explain. "You're over twenty-one, and so is the prince. He didn't do anything illegal serving *you* alcohol, or the RAs who were twenty-one and older."

Though for the ones who were drinking while on duty, it's a different story. And since Ameera—who is a freshman and only eighteen—was apparently at the party, the presence of *any* of the RAs in Rashid's room while he was serving alcohol is problematic. In New York College residence halls, it's a violation of the student code of conduct for anyone under the age of twenty-one to be found in possession of alcohol, and a further violation of policy for those over the age of twenty-one to serve alcohol to residents under the legal drinking age.

It's no wonder none of the RAs admitted the truth to Lisa. Their mere presence in room 1512 the night before Jasmine's death was a violation of their employment contract with New York College.

"Of course I wasn't there," Gavin says, his arms still folded across his chest, but now more out of disgust than defensiveness. "He invited me, but how could I go? Somebody's got to man the front desk, am I right, and make sure folks are getting their toilet paper and trash bags and billiard cues? Jamie and I have been splitting the night shifts to make a little extra cash. Besides, we don't go in for that kind of stuff. Alcohol's not my thing. *You* of all people should know that, Heather."

I do, actually. To commemorate his twenty-first birthday, Gavin had gotten it into his head to consume twenty-one shots. This decision had landed him—and me, beside him, as his appointed administrative hand-holder—in the emergency room.

"I haven't touched a drop since then," he says, with a touch of sanctimoniousness. "Well, except the occasional beer now and then," he adds, when I raise an eyebrow. "You know I love my PBR." Pabst Blue Ribbon, official beer of the screenplay-writing hipster. "Mostly I only smoke weed."

When Lisa sends him a chastising look over her notepad, he cries, raising both hands, "It's medicinal, honest, for my ADHD! From California. It's completely legal there."

"So how do you know the prince's guest list so intimately," I ask, thinking it's a good time to change the subject, "if you've never attended any of his little soirees?"

"Because people keep bragging about how bangin' they are," Gavin says. "What do you think I do when I'm sitting up there at that desk?"

"You're supposed to be sorting and distributing the mail," I say. "Not to mention handing out the toilet paper and trash bags and billiard cues."

"I *listen*," Gavin says. "Only by listening to people's speech patterns can a writer ever hope to craft truly convincing dialogue. That's how Tarantino does it. So that's what I do while I'm sorting the mail. I *listen*. You know how those RAs are always hanging out behind the desk—even though they aren't supposed to? Well, that stupid sheikh and his parties are all they ever talk about. It's Midnight at the Oasis up there in his room, man. They all know his daddy's a sultan . . . a nomad known to all . . . fifty girls to attend him."

"So they jump to his beck and call," I murmur before I can stop myself.

"*Exactly*," Gavin says, leaning forward in his chair to point at me excitedly. "God, I *love* you! *No one* my age gets that reference! Why aren't you marrying *me*?"

Lisa taps the list she's made with her pen, drawing our attention. "What are you two talking about?"

"Nothing," I say quickly. "Gavin, no one *my* age gets that reference. And I told you before, it's too late. I'm in love with Cooper Cartwright."

"It's not too late," Gavin insists. "You can still call it off.

When *Teen Zombie Apocalypse* is a hit, I'll be able to support you."

"Thanks for the offer, but I like my job, as well as my current choice of husband."

Gavin looks sulkily down at his slippers. "Your loss," he mumbles.

"This is more than half the RA staff," Lisa says, gazing down at the list in front of her. "And it's not *mostly* the new staff. It's *all* the new staff. The only ones who aren't here, if Gavin is correct, are Davinia, Rajiv, Tina, and Jean, the RAs who worked here over the summer."

"Yeah," Gavin says, with a nod. "They're cool. They're not going to fall under the spell of some foreign prince tennis champ smooth talker who knows how to mix a caipirinha and wears skinny jeans."

"Gavin." Lisa blinks at him. "Thanks for the help. You should probably get back to the front desk now."

"Oh, thank God," he says, leaping from the chair and hurrying from the office. After he's pulled open the door, he pauses uncertainly, his Goofy-slippered foot on the stop. "You want this open or closed?"

The outside door to the hall director's office—leading to the main office, where my desk sits, along with Sarah's desk, the RAs' staff mailboxes, and the photocopier—is never closed, except after five.

But we can't run the risk of anyone overhearing us, especially anyone from the prince's surveillance team, who are stationed down the hall.

"Closed," Lisa and I say in unison.

Gavin nods and releases the doorstop, allowing the door to swing shut behind him.

I glance at Lisa, who's lost any appearance of health. She looks almost as ill as she had yesterday.

"I wish I could fire all of them," she says through gritted teeth, staring down at the list of names on her notepad.

"Oh, Lisa." I can't think of anything else to say.

"I can't, of course," she says bitterly. "There are proper channels you have to go through, even to terminate the employment of a student worker. But I wish I could. It's not like I'm the one who hired any of them."

This is true. The new RAs were selected over the summer by Simon Hague, the hall director assigned to supervise Fischer Hall during the interim before Lisa was hired. Simon had made a lot of questionable choices during that time, so I'm not particularly surprised the students he hired have turned out to be less than reliable.

"Heather, they lied to me," Lisa goes on miserably. "They sat at that meeting last night—which was about Jasmine, who *died*—and lied to my face, commiserating with me about having the flu, pretending they had the same thing I did. None of them had the same thing I did. They were freaking hungover because they'd been out all night partying with a resident, *in my hall. My hall.*"

"Lisa," I begin, but she isn't finished.

"After one of them died—*died*—those stupid little shits still chose to save their own skins rather than tell me the truth. I wouldn't have punished them if they'd come clean. Everyone makes mistakes. But they didn't have the common decency to tell me the truth about something this important? Heather, we have an entire academic year ahead of us. How am I supposed to trust them? They lied about a *dead girl*, someone who was supposed to be their friend. They all lied, straight to my face."

When Lisa looks up, not only are the tips of her ears red, but her eyes are filled with tears. I instantly recognize the look of hurt and betrayal on her face.

It's exactly how I've been feeling for ten years about my mother.

"Oh, Lisa," I say. I slip out of my chair and go to lean over her desk to hug her. "I'm sorry. I'm so, so sorry."

Lisa hugs me back, stifling a sob.

"I know I should really be trying to view this as a professional advocate for students' rights to grow and develop individually and collectively," she says in a choked voice, "but I can't, because I kind of hate my job so much right now."

"It's okay," I say, patting her on the back. "I kind of hate my job right now too."

Guess you could say
I'm here to stay
I'm still believing
From you I'm never leaving

I know they say that I'm naïve
That's okay with me
It's been a long long road
But with you I wanna get old

"The Long Road,"
written by Heather Wells

13

So," Lisa says, after she's composed herself. "What do you think I should do?"

"Well," I say, going back to my desk. "I'm going to guess that the whole thing yesterday with Special Agent Lancaster had to do with the fact that Prince Rashid's people already knew that Jasmine Albright had been to his party. That's why they were so careful to keep the cops away."

Lisa pauses in shock while noisily blowing her nose. "Oh God. Of course. You know what I bet? I bet that weirdo prince roofied all the drinks."

Surprised that someone has suggested something even creepier than I could imagine, I say, "Okay, let's not get ahead of ourselves" as I pick up my phone. "But I'm going to give Eva over at the medical examiner's office a call to let her know there was some illicit partying going on—"

"If they think I'm not sending that rotten royal a disciplinary letter," I hear Lisa muttering behind her computer screen, "just because his daddy's rich and donated a ton of money to this school, they're crazy. I'm hitting him with every sanction in the book. And I'm putting every single one of those RAs who was at his party on probation. One more strike and they're out."

"Can you do that?" I ask curiously. "I thought it was three strikes and you're out."

"Why not? I already have to hire one new one to replace Jasmine. What difference does nine more make?"

"Um," I say. "Kind of a lot." The resident assistants count on their employment with the college for free room and board for the year. Without it . . . well, without it, they'll suddenly have to find an affordable place to live for the fall and spring semesters. And in downtown New York City, that's no easy task.

And finding and training nine new RAs, for all Lisa's bravado, isn't going to be easy, either.

"Well," Lisa says primly. "That's something they should have thought about before they decided to drink with freshmen in *my building*. I wish I could fire them without putting them on probation first, but that would be a violation of their employment contract. So probation is what they get."

Lisa's on fire this morning, I think to myself as I flip

through my Rolodex for Eva's number. She should get a twenty-four-hour flu more often.

"Hi, Eva?" I say, when I hear a grumpy voice at the end of the line say something very quickly that may, or may not, be, "OCME."

"Hold on. I'll go see if I can find her." I hear footsteps walk away from the phone and the grumpy voice yell, *"Eva! You left your phone in the locker room again!"*

As I'm holding, a key rattles in the lock to the director's office door, and Sarah comes trundling in, holding her backpack, a can of Coke, a paper bag with oily food stains on the sides, and her laptop.

"Why is this door closed?" she demands.

As usual, Sarah appears to have rolled out of bed and come directly downstairs for work without bathing, although she clearly stopped in the caf for breakfast. The aroma from the bag indicates that she too has opted for the dining hall's less than healthy options, most likely a bacon-egg-and-cheddar sandwich. She has her wildly frizzing hair pulled back into a single clip and is wearing her ubiquitous overalls, though at least she appears to have changed into a fresh T-shirt.

"What are you guys doing?" she asks, throwing an aggravated look at me and Lisa as she heads to her desk, where she dumps her breakfast, beverage, backpack, and laptop. "Why isn't the office open? It's nearly nine-thirty. What's the matter with you two? God, never mind, have you seen this morning's *New York College Express*, the daily student news blog?"

"I'm on hold with the medical examiner," I say, pointing to the receiver.

"I'm putting all the RAs on probation," Lisa calls from

her office. "No, wait, not all of them. Just the new ones who aren't already dead."

Sarah ignores us. She doesn't think we're serious.

"Check it out." She opens her laptop and, sitting in her office chair, begins scooting toward me. "It's another one about Rascally Rashid."

"Let me guess," I say. "Is it about how he's been throwing wild blowout parties in his room every night since he's checked in?"

Sarah stops midscoot.

"What? No. How could he have been doing that? We'd have heard about it. He'd have been written up."

"Not if all the RAs were on his guest list," Lisa calls from her office. "Which they were."

"The *RAs* have been going to parties in Prince Rashid's room?" Sarah's mouth falls open.

"Howard Chen didn't have the flu," Lisa calls. "He was just hungover."

Sarah's mouth snaps shut, and her eyes flash. "I rubbed his back while he puked, and he was just hungover? That little shit."

There's a fumbling sound from the other end of the phone, and then I hear Eva's voice, sounding a little breathless and none too happy. "Hello? Who is this?"

"Eva," I say quickly. "Sorry to disturb you, it's Heather Wells from Fischer Hall."

"Oh." Eva doesn't sound pleased to hear me. "Hey, Heather. Look, the M.E. hasn't even gotten to your dead girl yet, things are so backed up around here—"

"No, no," I say. "That's fine. I only wanted to let you know we found out a couple of things about her activities the night before she died."

Rapidly, I fill Eva in about the party Jasmine attended in Prince Rashid's room.

"So were they sick because they were hungover," Eva asks in a much more interested tone when I'm finished, "or because they ingested something at the party that might have been a toxin? And because our vic was an asthmatic, and had a weakened immune system, it ended up killing her?"

I hadn't considered this. "I don't know."

"Of course you don't know. See, this information about the party would have been helpful to know yesterday." Now Eva sounds irritated. "That way we could have done things a little differently."

"Believe me," I say. "I know."

"Get the trash bags your housekeeper says he found outside the kid's room," Eva says. "The ones with the cups. And any bags you can find containing vomit from the other victims who allegedly had the flu would be superhelpful."

I wrinkle my nose. "I'll see what I can do, but that was yesterday's trash. It went out already. Our trash pickup days are Thursdays and—"

"Holy Christ," Eva says. "We'll just have to run a tox screen for everything under the goddamn sun and it's going to take a month. Meanwhile, her parents will be screaming at us, wanting to know why it's taking so long, because on TV the M.E.s get their tox screens back from the lab in three hours."

"If it's any consolation," I say, lowering my voice while glancing over at Lisa, who's still fiddling with her bra straps as she speaks with whomever she's got on the phone, "my boss really did have the flu. It was the twenty-four-hour kind and she's better now, but still kind of sore, especially her boobs. Moody too."

There's a beat before Eva says, "Your boss is the one who just got married, right?"

"Uh," I say. "Right."

"Yeah. There's no such thing as a twenty-four-hour stomach flu that leaves your boobs sore. Breast tenderness, moodiness, nausea, and vomiting are all early signs of pregnancy. Tell your boss to take an e.p.t. And call me back if you find out anything else about Jasmine."

I hear a click, and then the line goes dead.

I stare at the receiver in stunned silence for a moment. Lisa? Pregnant? But that's impossible. Lisa doesn't want kids. It's one of the first things she ever told me. She and her husband, Cory, both come from huge families and have tons of nieces and nephews. They're sick of kids. Tricky, their dog, is enough.

"Well, that's done." Lisa, in her office, hangs up the phone. "I've left a message with Dr. Jessup that I'm putting all my RAs on probation."

"Wait." Sarah rises from her desk chair and goes to stand in front of the door to Lisa's office. "You were *serious* about that?"

"Not all of them," Lisa corrects herself. "Only the ones who were drinking while in the presence of residents under the age of twenty-one. One more strike and they're out."

"Lisa," Sarah says, astonished. "You can't do that. The *entire* staff?"

"It's my building," Lisa says. "I can do whatever I want."

Maybe Eva's right. Maybe Lisa *is* pregnant, and doesn't know it. But how is that possible? She'd have to know, right? How could someone not know she's pregnant?

"No," Sarah says. "You can't. If they screw up, how are we going to replace them? We're going to have to train—wait, how many are there?"

"Nine," Lisa says. "Ten including Jasmine Albright."

"*Ten* RAs?" Sarah shakes her head, her frizzy ponytail flying. "How are we going to replace and train *ten* people?"

"Don't be so negative," I say. "Maybe they won't violate their probation."

Sarah looks at me like I'm crazy. "Have you *met* any of them?"

Lisa shrugs. "It's going to be a challenge. But it will be better than having lying sneaks who are under a prince's thumb working on our staff."

There's an entire TV series called *I Didn't Know I Was Pregnant* about women who didn't know they were pregnant and then suddenly gave birth while in the grocery store or on a camping trip. It's one of my favorite shows. I love to watch it late at night after Cooper's fallen asleep so he won't know I watch such dumb TV programs.

But how could my own boss not know she's pregnant? She has a master's degree. It's impossible.

"Listen, I completely agree that what those guys did was terrible, but I think you should only give them a warning," Sarah says. "I don't think we should be rocking the boat too hard around here. That's what I've been trying to tell you guys. Not only is a girl dead, but this morning, on *New York College Express*—"

"It's *my* building," Lisa says, folding her arms over her chest, but careful—I note—to avoid touching the nipple area. "I think I should be able to discipline my staff the way I see fit. And if I feel that I need an entirely new RA staff—or *mostly* new RA staff—for the good of the hall, then you need to support me, Sarah."

"I do," Sarah says. "You know I do. But I'm pretty sure you're going to want to show staff solidarity, especially after you read this."

She darts back to her desk, retrieves her laptop, then opens it up and hands it to Lisa. I get up to scan it over her shoulder. As I do, my heart sinks.

Living the Suite Life, the blog post's title reads. *Rascally Rashid Has Two Double Rooms to Himself in Fischer Hall.*

Uh-oh.

Living the Suite Life:
Rascally Rashid Has Two Double Rooms to Himself in Fischer Hall

Did you apply to live in Fischer Hall, the hottest dorm on campus (where the upcoming new reality show *Jordan Loves Tania* was filmed), but get assigned to that pit of suck, Wasser Hall, instead? Well, maybe if Crown Prince Rashid of Qalif hadn't been assigned to four spaces in Fischer Hall instead of one, there might have been some left over for you. But we're guessing your dad didn't donate an estimated $500 million to the college the way the prince's did.

Word has it that Rascally Rashid is living it up royal—blue blood style in room 1512, a suite that would normally house four students, but this year has been reassigned as a single fit for a king, complete with a private Jacuzzi tub, wet bar, water bed, and home theater.

Our Fischer Hall insider says the prince is generous about sharing, though, entertaining regularly in his room(s). Those interested in a royal audience need only contact the Fischer Hall director's office, where someone will be happy to put them in touch with Rashid's not-so-secret security detail, located in a conference room down the hall.

New York College Express, your daily student news blog

This is bad." The director of housing, Dr. Jessup, is sitting on an expensive leather chair in President Allington's office, jiggling his right leg. "This is very, very bad."

"We know the piece in the *Express* was bad, Stan," I say. I'm sitting beside him at the vast, shiny conference table, which I can feel shaking because of the force of his jiggling. "But you know what's worse?"

"Don't say that a girl died in your building yesterday."

Dr. Jessup's got a fake smile plastered across his tanned face—I can tell he played a lot of golf over the summer—and is speaking from the side of his mouth as President Allington's assistant moves around the shiny mahogany-and-glass conference table, making sure we have enough cream and finger sandwiches.

"I *am* going to say it. A girl died in our building yesterday." I don't bother to lower my voice. "And we're being dragged up to the president's office just because something about our VIR got posted online. That's not only worse, it's a waste of time."

It doesn't matter if I lower my voice. No one's going to overhear me, least of all President Allington. His office is as wide as the Fischer Hall penthouse, and on an even higher floor on a building on the south side of Washington Square Park. It appears to have been decorated by someone with a fondness for black leather furniture and dark wood paneling. Floor-to-ceiling windows on two sides look out across SoHo and Fifth Avenue, while full-length portraits of the president and his wife, Eleanor, scowl down at us from beside a couple of potted palms.

The president's desk—where he's currently consulting with media relations expert Muffy Fowler and some of the college's expert legal team—is approximately the size of a Gap checkout counter and seems a thousand miles away.

It's intimidating enough to make a person want to throw up . . .

. . . which one person, namely my boss, Lisa, is already doing down the hall in the ladies' room.

"No," Dr. Jessup says to me, still speaking out of the corner of his mouth. "That girl's death, while doubtlessly tragic, does not financially impact our department in any way. That Twitter or Tweet or twat or whatever it was from the *Express*, does. *That's* why this is worse. Not because these people are bureaucratic nimrods whose thumbs are up their asses." He smiles beatifically at President Allington's assistant, who is laying out a silver coffee and tea service. "Those sandwiches look simply lovely, Gloria."

Gloria smiles back. "Why, thank you, Stan," she says with a flirtatious wink before walking away.

"It was a blog post," I tell Dr. Jessup, though I don't know why I bother, since his gaze is on Gloria's departing legs. "And how does it financially impact our department?"

"We were supposed to keep the prince's room assignment a *secret*," Dr. Jessup hisses. "The fact that he has twenty-four-hour security, and where those security personnel are based, is supposed to be a *secret*. How the hell did the *Express* find out about it? The president's going to cut off our funding over this. And he's been very generous with our funding lately. Where do you think we got the money to upgrade your building this past summer? From this office. I was hoping to renovate your friend Tom's building, Waverly Hall, next. Did you know those boys in the frat houses only have one working elevator? And it hasn't been upgraded since 1995. But I bet I can kiss that money good-bye now."

He smiles at one of the guys from Legal who comes over to snag a finger sandwich. "How you doing, Bill?" Dr. Jessup asks chummily.

"Oh, you know," Bill says, chewing. "Can't complain. Hey, I played Maidstone over the weekend. Birdied the sixth hole."

"Did you really, you old bastard?" Dr. Jessup asks. "Guess they've lowered their standards."

Both men guffaw at Dr. Jessup's joke while I sit there feeling guilty in spite of the fact that I had nothing to do with leaking the information about Prince Rashid to the New York College student news blog. I know how much Tom loves Waverly Hall, and would have appreciated a new elevator.

"You know, Prince Rashid himself could have leaked the information," I say to Dr. Jessup after Bill walks away. "He hasn't exactly been Mr. Subtle. I counted over fifty people going into that party he had the night Jasmine died. Any one of them could have tattled to the *Express*."

"But only someone from your staff could have known about the location of the security detail," Dr. Jessup says. "The guy can't be stupid enough to have been bragging to his party guests about that."

Dr. Jessup has a point. Rashid is followed everywhere he goes by two armed bodyguards. He has to be aware he's received death threats. He may have nicknamed himself after a dry red table wine, but that doesn't mean he's stupid.

"Oh my God." Lisa returns from the ladies' room and collapses into the expensive black leather chair beside mine. "Sorry I was gone for so long. Did I miss anything? Ooo, are those cucumber? My favorite."

She leans over and picks up a tiny sandwich from one of the platters President Allington's assistant has left in front of us, then pops it into her mouth and begins chewing delightedly. When her gaze meets mine, she asks, "What?" with her mouth full. "Do I have something on my face?"

"No. You must be feeling better," I say, in a neutral tone.

"Oh, I am," she says, and pours herself a cup of tea. "I'm starving. I think that was just some of the leftover flu virus before. Or queasiness from the elevator ride. That thing goes so fast. Thirty floors is a lot."

"Right," I say, still in the neutral tone.

Is this really how it's going to go? I wonder. The girl who can't have kids is going to have to point out to the girl who doesn't want them that she's maybe—possibly even likely—pregnant?

"Well, hey there, y'all."

Muffy Fowler has strolled over to join us at the conference table. She's wearing a wide smile and a cream-colored skirt and peplum jacket, with matching cream-colored shoes. Beside her is the president of the college, a gray-haired man dressed in a somber business suit (who, I happen to know, since he and his wife live in the penthouse of Fischer Hall, feels more comfortable in a sweatsuit, preferably in the school colors of blue and gold).

Behind the president are a number of men I don't know, along with one I do . . . Special Agent Lancaster. He's wearing his seemingly habitual scowl, dark suit and tie, and earpiece.

"Thanks so much for coming, Stan," Muffy says, reaching out her hand to grasp Dr. Jessup's as he rises to greet her. The smile she gives me is distantly polite, even though we know each other well. The smile says, *Up here in the president's office, we're going to act like we don't know each other at all, okay? After work, over drinks, we'll kick off our high heels and eviscerate these people behind their backs.*

Except that I'm wearing flats with my dark stretch cords and equally stretchy black tunic blouse. I didn't know I was going to have a meeting in the president's office today.

Muffy introduces Lisa and me to the newcomers, whose names and titles I fail to catch. It doesn't matter, because I wouldn't have remembered them anyway. They're all men in business suits who look exactly the same, have the same kind of nonsense titles—executive vice chancellor for the general council; senior executive of the board of trustees; chairman of global affairs—and, if the *New York College Express* is to be trusted, receive the same kind of enormous bonuses.

They're here, Muffy explains, to "troubleshoot this here itty-bitty little thing." In times of crisis, Muffy's southern drawl becomes more pronounced.

"How about y'all take a seat now, and let's get right to business," Muffy says as she tucks her cream-colored skirt beneath her in a ladylike manner. We all do as she suggested and take a seat, with the exception of Special Agent Lancaster, who declares he'd prefer to stand. I suppose if he sat down, the stick up his butt would lodge so deeply into his brain that he would instantly expire, and then we'd have another corpse on our hands, so it's just as well.

"So," Muffy says. Her lipstick is a very bright red, as are her fingernails. "I'm sure y'all know why y'all are here—"

"Yes," I say. "A girl in our building died yesterday."

"Another one?" President Allington cries in surprise. A bite of egg salad sandwich falls out of his mouth and tumbles down the front of his blue-and-gold tie. "Jesus Christ!"

Gloria comes rushing over with a napkin to sponge the mayonnaise stains off his tie while the rest of us politely avert our gazes.

"Er, yes, Phillip," Muffy says. "Remember, I told you? She died yesterday, of asthma."

"Who the hell dies of asthma?" President Allington wants to know.

"Nine people a day," I volunteer. "It's one of this country's most common and costly diseases."

"Jesus Christ," President Allington says again, this time less loudly. "Who knew?"

"Yes," Muffy says, trying to take back control of her meeting. "Well, sad as that is, it's not what we're here to talk about. This is about the piece that appeared on *New York College Express* this morning. As y'all know, we've gone to great strides to keep that information out of the press—"

"I know, Muffy," Dr. Jessup says apologetically, "and I just want to assure you that a lot of the particulars in that piece were pure lies."

"Right," Lisa says. "That kid does *not* have a water bed. His people asked if he could have a water bed, but we said no, right, Heather? Heather?"

"True," I say, startled. I'd been distracted by the finger sandwiches. "Water beds are restricted in residence halls."

"Really?" Bill asks. "Why?"

"Because the weight from the water could cause the bed to fall through the floor, endangering the residents below."

I can't help noticing that Lisa, President Allington, and I are the only ones touching the finger sandwiches. I think about putting back the one I've just taken, but Lisa is right: they're really good. Plus the one I've snagged is salmon. Everyone knows salmon is good for you. It's filled with omega-3 fatty acids, which are excellent for brain health.

"The prince doesn't have a Jacuzzi either," I add quickly, just so people don't think I'm not paying attention. "The plumbing in Fischer Hall is so old, there's no way it would support a Jacuzzi. So both those things weren't true. I don't know about the wet bar or home theater."

"He's got both of those," Special Agent Lancaster confirms.

"Hot damn," Bill says. "That kid's living the dream."

"Okay," Muffy says, sounding a little frustrated. "Those things aren't really the issue here. The issue we're concerned with is who gave the *Express* the information about the location of the prince's security surveillance team. We have good reason to believe it was a member of your staff, Lisa."

Lisa's face goes whiter that Muffy's skirt. "Who" is the only word that comes out of Lisa's mouth. I get the feeling that she doesn't risk saying more. Also that she's probably regretting the cucumber sandwich.

"Well, that's the dang problem," Muffy says. "We just don't know for sure. We think the *Express* knows, but of course they're claiming freedom of the press and all that fiddle-faddle."

I cannot believe that Muffy just called the First Amendment fiddle-faddle. Fiddle Faddle is a delicious candy-coated popcorn snack food. It has nothing to do with the Bill of Rights.

"But since this is a private institution and the *Express* is funded by donors," Muffy continues in a more cheerful tone, "we had the school's IT department pull all their communication records, didn't we, Charlie?"

Charlie, a balding man in glasses who is sitting across the conference table, laughs diabolically. "We sure did!"

Dr. Jessup has begun to perspire visibly. "And what precisely did the IT department discover?"

Charlie opens an expensive leather briefcase that's been sitting at his feet, then pulls out a file and reads from it.

"Someone with a New York College campus IP address has been sending e-mails to the *New York College Express* for some time. The techs haven't been able to trace precisely who it is, but they have been able to pin down that it's someone from the west side of Washington Square Park. There's only one building owned by New York College on the west side of Washington Square, and that building," Charlie concludes dramatically, "is Fischer Hall."

To quote President Allington, *Jesus Christ*.

"Excuse me," Lisa says, and throws a hand over her mouth as she darts from the room.

I have the nice dress
White froth princess
But I might lose
With the shoes
Buckle strap
Pump or sandal
Won't hide from them
That I'm a scandal

"Might Lose with the Shoes,"
written by Heather Wells

15

Everyone's gaze follows Lisa as she flees for the ladies' room.

"Is she all right?" Gloria, President Allington's assistant, asks in concern. "Shall I go after her?"

"No, she's fine," I say. "She's getting over the flu."

Now everyone's gaze flies to the pile of finger sandwiches, into which Lisa had been digging energetically.

"I don't think she's in the contagious phase anymore," I add quickly.

"Well, that's good," Bill says, leaning in for a roast beef and honey mustard on a croissant. "These things sure are tasty."

"I think we can move on without her," Muffy says, sounding impatient again. "Heather, do you know of anyone on your staff who has a reason to feel disgruntled about the prince, or the country of Qalif, or the college?"

"No," I say, determined not to mention Sarah. "Prince Rashid seems popular and well liked. People are lining up out my door—literally—for a chance to move into the building so they can be near him. And not to kill him, to party with him. To be totally honest, his partying is getting to be a bit of a problem. Lisa was going to send him a disciplinary letter about it today, as a matter of fact, because—"

"If I may," Dr. Jessup interrupts quickly. "She hadn't cleared that through me. Just because the boy enjoys a social gathering is no reason to discipline him."

"Heck," Bill says, licking his fingers. "If we spent all our time writing disciplinary letters to every boy in this school who likes to party, we'd never have time to party ourselves!"

All the men, with the exception of Special Agent Lancaster, laugh at Bill's hilarious joke.

"Actually we have first-year students on camera going into the prince's room, where alcohol is being served," I say when they're done laughing, with a glance at Special Agent Lancaster. "I imagine you're aware of this, right?"

Special Agent Lancaster shakes his head, but not in denial. "The bureau doesn't comment on the behavior of those we're protecting. We only provide for their safety."

I narrow my eyes at him for giving such a wishy-washy response, then continue: "Well, it's a violation of the student code of conduct for residents over the age of twenty-one to provide alcohol to students who haven't yet reached the legal drinking age, and that's exactly what Prince Rashid is doing. I understand that in his homeland, the drinking laws might be more lax, but here in the U.S.—"

For the first time ever, I hear Special Agent Lancaster laugh. It's a sarcastic laugh, more of a single *Ha!* of derision. But it's still a laugh, and draws everyone's attention, including mine.

"Pardon me," the agent says, the stoic mask of professionalism falling back into place. "I only meant to observe that in the prince's homeland, consumption of alcohol of any kind is illegal, and the penalty for being found with it is imprisonment and fifty lashes."

"Holy crap!" Bill cries, choking a little on his eighth sandwich. Not that I'm counting, except that he's bogarting all the egg salad and salmons, which are my favorite. "People still use the lash?"

"The penalty for premarital sex in Qalif," Special Agent Lancaster observes casually, "is beheading, so the lash is quite mild in comparison."

"Oh my," purrs Muffy, looking at Special Agent Lancaster from beneath her eyelashes. "How atrocious."

I know Muffy well enough to tell that she likes what she sees. Muffy has recently gotten out of a long-term relationship—well, long term for her—with a professor ex-boyfriend of mine, Tad, who turned out to be a little too vegan for Muffy's taste.

It appears that a special agent for the U.S. State Department who has intimate knowledge of the human rights violations of the country of Qalif might be a little . . . meatier for Muffy.

"Isn't Fischer Hall where that girl lives?" one of the men

whose name I didn't catch asks. "The one who was dating that fellow who was head of the GSC?"

My amusement over Muffy's flirting with Special Agent Lancaster quickly dies when I realize they're talking about Sarah.

"GSC?" President Allington looks bewildered.

"Graduate Student Collective," Charlie, the guy with the file folder, says. He pulls a small laptop from his briefcase and opens it. "You remember, they were the ones whining last year for better wages and benefits or some silliness."

I've never been to a meeting in the president's office before, but now that I'm here, I can't believe this is what goes on. I'm constantly hearing how there's no money in the budget for things we need—security cameras in the second-floor library, or pens, for instance—but there appears to be plenty of money for finger sandwiches.

Then people sit around eating them while bad-mouthing excellent employees like Sarah, who works so hard for the school. She wasn't whining when she went on strike last year. She was hoping to improve conditions for many hard-working staff members like herself.

"I think I know who you're talking about," I say, "and—"

"The GSC is planning on joining the faculty in the up-coming no-confidence vote on the president," Charlie goes on, as if I hadn't spoken.

"Hey," President Allington says, offended. "Why doesn't the faculty have confidence in me?"

"We explained this to you already, Phil," Muffy says in a tired voice. "They're a little miffed about the money you accepted from Prince Rashid's father . . . and maybe a few other donors who might not have the most stellar reputations."

"Who cares where the money comes from if we do good things with it?" the president demands. "What else am I supposed to do? It's not like this school's got an endowment, like the Ivy Leagues. We gotta take whatever money we can get. If that means letting in dumb rich kids who've got parents who can pay their tuition—and some who can donate extra—well, then, by God, I'm going to do it. I'm trying to educate young people here!"

"We understand that, Phil," Muffy says in a soothing tone. "But you can't blame the faculty, let alone the students, for objecting when they find out their shiny new classrooms have been paid for with money donated by murderers, misogynists, and anti-Semites."

"Now hold on there," a businessman in a yellow power tie cries, almost spilling his coffee in his haste to put it down. "That's not what we're doing."

"Isn't it?" Muffy asks sweetly. "Do you remember what all those college kids did back in the eighties when they found out their schools held financial investments in South Africa?"

Dr. Jessup dutifully holds up his hand as if we're in a classroom, but Muffy doesn't call on him.

"They set up little ol' tent villages outside the administration buildings, demanding divestment and an end to apartheid," she goes on. "I was only a little girl myself when that happened, but even I remember it was not a pretty sight."

"But we're not invested in Qalif," Yellow Power Tie says in exasperation.

"Aren't we?" I ask. "The heir to its throne is living in one of our residence halls. We've taken half a billion dollars from his father. I could see how that might be enough to anger some people."

"Like that girl in the GSC," Charlie says. "What was her name?"

"That's not who I meant," I say hastily. "Sarah's our office's grad student assistant, and while she's no fan of Qalif, I can personally guarantee that she isn't the leak." At least, I hope I can. "Sarah loves New York College, just like she loves Fischer Hall and its residents. She would do anything to protect them. She's the one who brought the piece in *The Express* on Prince Rashid to our attention this morning."

"That doesn't mean she didn't write it," Yellow Power Tie says with a bitter laugh. "If she showed it to you, it's probably because she *is* the leak. Leaks can never wait to show off their handiwork."

I glare at him. This is a classic example of how wars get started, I think, because some blowhard sitting in an ivory tower, high above the commoners, starts spouting off about something of which he knows nothing.

"No," Muffy says, coming to my (and Sarah's) defense. "Heather's right. I know Sarah. She might not agree with the school's politics, but she wouldn't do anything to endanger her residents."

"But we know the leak is coming from somewhere in your building!" Charlie cries. "Who else could it be? I thought only the freshman and transfer students had checked in this week. What would any of them care about where we're getting our donations? They're still feeling lucky to have been admitted here at all."

He has a point.

"It's possible it could be someone else on the staff," I admit. "Someone besides Sarah. There are a lot of new resident assistants this year, and some of them haven't exercised the best judgment. They were all at Prince Rashid's party, for example. One of them died afterward, and the rest of them didn't even admit to us that they'd been there themselves, or that they'd seen her there. We caught them on the video monitors. Lisa's planning on putting them on probation to teach them a lesson."

There are a few seconds of silence as the men—and Muffy and Gloria, who is just coming in with a plate of fresh-baked chocolate chip cookies—digest this. Then Bill says, "Well, heck. Skip the probation. Why not fire them?"

Charlie closes his briefcase with a snap. "Sounds good to me."

"The damage is already done," Muffy says musingly, "but if one of them is the leak, termination would eliminate the problem. They've already violated their employment contract once, and proved they can't be trusted."

"Agreed." Yellow Power Tie lifts his coffee cup again, clearly in a celebratory mood. "But before they move out, we'll have to make sure they sign confidentiality agreements that they won't discuss anything they've seen inside the building, or they'll be expelled."

A guy in a blue tie begins making a note on his smartphone. "I'll have Legal write something up. Should have it ready to be placed in their mailboxes by five o'clock. That way," he adds with a diabolical grin, "when their parents start calling our offices to bitch and moan about having to start paying their room and board, we'll all have gone home."

"I like it," says the president, rubbing his hands together with glee. "How about one of those cookies, Gloria? They smell amazing."

Gloria beams and walks toward him. "Fresh baked, the way you like them, Phil."

"Wait," I say. My heart is pounding in my chest. "I said it's possible *one* of them might be the leak. You can't kick *all* of them out of the building . . . especially not without any warning!"

"We just did," says Charlie with a shrug.

I feel a rush of emotions . . . mainly concern and worry for Fischer Hall. What will happen to the building if we fire nine members of the student staff, then have to replace them all— and train their replacements—a week before classes start?

It's going to be a nightmare . . . almost as bad as the nightmare of losing an RA to natural causes.

I'd known there'd be repercussions from what I'd seen on the security tape, but that this would be one of them had never occurred to me.

"Now, hold on here a minute." Dr. Jessup looks uncomfortable. "I don't mean to be the bad guy here, and I agree these RAs screwed up and need to be disciplined. But they're still students. We can't throw them out onto the street. They were promised room and board for the academic year."

"They fucked up, Stan," Bill says, munching on a cookie. "When you fuck up, shit gets real."

"We don't even know for sure any of them is the leak," I

say, grasping at straws. "We can't punish all of them for what one of them *may* have done."

"Really?" The guy in the blue tie presses send on his phone and smiles at me. "Seems to me they all bit from the forbidden fruit by going to the prince's party. Now they gotta pay the price, like Adam and Eve."

Lisa comes hurrying back into the room, looking flushed but much better than she had earlier, and takes her seat.

"I'm so sorry," she says brightly. "What did I miss?"

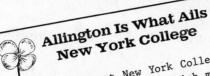

Allington Is What Ails New York College

For students at New York College, tuition keeps creeping up, which means we have to take on more debt to pay the bills. Yet our college president, Phillip Allington, who owns a $4.5 million home in the Hamptons, lives rent-free in a luxury penthouse at the top of Fischer Hall. And his son drives around in a convertible Mercedes and is a co-owner of the nightclub Epiphany (try the mojito, by the way, it's delish).

Something stinks in Greenwich Village and we here at the *Express* say its name is Allington.

All week long, this blog will be reporting on how your tuition dollars may be going to fund the Allingtons' extravagant lifestyle. Our first report is called "Who Pays for Mrs. Allington's Birds?," a hard-hitting exposé on the exotic birds belonging to the wife of our college president, and how much she might be spending on them.

New York College Express,
your daily student news blog

16

Lisa cries the whole way back to our office.

"I'm sorry," she says between sobs as we walk through Washington Square Park, dodging black squirrels, tourists, and young nannies pushing baby strollers. "I don't know what's wrong with me. I don't even necessarily disagree with them. Those RAs are such rotten shits. They deserve to be kicked out. I just c-can't stop crying. Like I can't seem to stop puking."

"Yeah," I say. "About that . . ."

I have a hand on her arm and am steering her through the crowds—it's another beautiful warm fall day, and the park is packed—since I'm not sure she can see through her tears. No one pays any attention to crazy Asian girls walking through the park crying because there are so many other distracting things to look at, such as the barefoot guitar players, overturned-plastic-can drummers, incense sellers, proselytizers, and cute dogs.

"Is there any chance you could be pregnant?" I ask.

Lisa stops walking in the middle of the park, or as close to the middle as we can get without walking directly into the huge fountain, the jets of which are shooting twenty feet into the air.

"What did you say?" Lisa demands. She isn't crying anymore.

"I'm sorry. I didn't mean to blurt it out like that. I probably should have saved this conversation for when we get back to the office, only I'm not going back to the office now. I'm going to make sure you get there, then I have to go run an errand—"

"Heather!" The tips of Lisa's ears begin to turn red.

"It's a work-related errand," I say. "Don't worry. But even if I went back to the office with you, you know we hardly ever have any privacy there. I just talked to Sarah"—I wave my cell phone in front of her—"and she says there's another line of parents out the door—including Kaileigh's mom, who's heard about Jasmine being dead. She isn't too happy that her daughter is not only assigned to a floor with a dead RA, but that her roommate Ameera is now weeping all the time instead of out sleeping around. Plus you have that RA candidate arriving at two, and Jasmine's parents scheduled to arrive at three, plus nine RAs to fire. When are we going to have another chance to talk about this? I'm guessing this is my only opportunity."

"To ask me if I'm *pregnant?*" Lisa's eyebrows have shot up to their limits.

"You're showing a lot of the early symptoms," I explain, having to raise my voice to be heard over a guy who has come strolling by playing the bagpipes. "Breast tenderness, moodiness, nausea, vomiting. I could be totally wrong, but Eva thinks—"

"*Eva?*" Lisa's voice too rises. The bagpiper, who is wearing a kilt, has decided to stand near us. He's gathered a small crowd of admirers. "You told the *medicolegal investigator* that I've been moody lately? And that *my boobs hurt?* For God's sake, Heather!"

"Well, you clearly don't have the flu, because you're fine right now," I point out. "Except for the crying. When's the last time you had your period?"

"When's the last time you had yours?" she fires back, outraged.

"Three years ago," I say. "I'm on continuous birth control pills for my endometriosis. Lisa, even if I weren't on the pill, I couldn't get pregnant. I have no idea what it's like to be pregnant, and I doubt I ever will. I know it's none of my business if you are, but I sit in the office outside yours all day, five days a week, so I know you pretty well. And if you *are* pregnant, I just want to make sure you know it, and take care of yourself."

Lisa turns sober. "Oh, Heather," she says, and reaches out

to squeeze one of my arms. "Of course. I'm so sorry. Things have been so crazy lately. Honestly, I can't even remember when I last had my period."

The bagpiper ends his dirge on her last words, so that everyone nearby hears her shout "I can't even remember when I last had my period" and looks over at us with varying degrees of pity, confusion, and amusement.

Lisa lifts her free hand to her now pale face. "Oh my God," she says, and tightens her grip on my arm, then begins dragging me around the opposite end of the fountain, away from the bagpiper and his audience. "Oh my God. I can't believe I just did that."

"It's okay," I say. "I don't think anyone heard you."

"Are you kidding me? They *all* heard me. Oh, *crap*."

Her face pales even further. I'm not sure why until I turn my head in the direction she's looking. Moving swiftly toward us is a large crowd of people, some of whom look familiar—

And no wonder, since they're residents of Fischer Hall.

"Hi, Lisa!" Jasmine Tsai calls, waving cheerfully as she steers a group of her residents across the park. "Hi, Heather! Hey, you guys," she informs her residents, who are clearly all first-years. "That's the director of Fischer Hall, Lisa, and the assistant director, Heather Wells. Say hi."

The residents—the majority of whom are overexcited girls dressed to meet boys, under the auspices of taking a walking tour of the campus—all squeal and wave. "Hi, Lisa! Hi, Heather!"

Lisa and I wave lamely back, noticing that there are a few boys trailing along behind the group, but not the kind of boys the girls on the tour appear to be interested in.

"Hi, Lisa. Hi, Heather," Howard Chen and Christopher Mintz call sheepishly.

"Hi, you guys," I call back, and give them a thumbs-up. "Looking good! Way to show your school spirit."

Neither boy waves back. I can hardly blame them.

"Oh God," Lisa says, when they're out of earshot. "They heard me. They totally heard me. Now the whole dorm knows I might be pregnant."

"No," I say. "They didn't hear you." They probably did. "Anyway, what do you mean, you can't remember when you had your last period?"

"I don't know." Lisa turns to stride quickly toward Fischer Hall, looming before us on the west side of the park like the elegant—if slightly battered—brick lady that she is. "The truth is, it's been so busy, what with my wedding and then starting this job and moving in, then everything we went through when they were filming that reality show in the building, then RA training and check-in. I've barely had a minute to myself. I must have had it in June. I'm almost sure I had it in July—"

"Lisa," I say, having to jog a little to keep up with her rapid steps. "It's almost September."

"Oh my God." She looks like someone punched her in the stomach. "Oh my God. How could this happen to me? I'm the hall director. I'm supposed to be a role model. How could I let this happen?"

"You don't know that anything's happened yet," I say. Except that quite a lot has happened. A member of her staff is dead, and most of the rest of them are about to be fired. I don't feel I need to belabor this point, however. "You're probably only late because of the stress of check-in. But it's better to know, right? Why don't you go to the drugstore right now, get an early pregnancy test, then go up to your apartment and take it before you go back to work?"

I turn her bodily so that instead of facing Fischer Hall, she's facing the dog run, behind which (a block away, on Bleecker Street) the nearest pharmacy is located.

"If you want me to go with you," I say, noticing that her knees have locked and she's not budging, "I will."

"What?" Lisa asks in surprise. She's begun to move again, thankfully in the direction of the drugstore. "No. I'm an adult, I can go to the pharmacy by myself, thank you. Besides, I thought you said you had an errand to run."

"I do, a quick one. I'll be back in ten minutes."

"Fine," Lisa says. She's trudging as if her feet are encased in cement blocks. "See you then."

I turn around and head for a horrifically designed building once described as a "miracle of modern architecture," but which really is just a spiky tower of windows and black metal triangles, called the Gottlieb Student Center. As I stride toward it, I pull out my cell phone and return one of the many messages Cooper has left.

"Hey," I say. "It's me."

"Jesus," he says. "I thought you died. Where have you been?"

"Having finger sandwiches with the president of New York College and his millionaire cronies," I say. "One of them birdied the sixth hole at Maidstone last weekend."

"I put a guy in a headlock in a bar in Jersey City last weekend," Cooper says. "Where's my finger sandwich?"

"I'll have a finger sandwich for you when I get home, big boy," I say, lowering my voice to a sexy growl.

Cooper sounds surprised, but delightedly so. "Whoa. Is that a promise?"

"Uh . . ." I was actually joking. I'm not even sure what a finger sandwich is, in sexual terms. Is it a thing? I realize it must be and I've promised to do something in bed with my husband-to-be I have no idea how to do. I'm going to have to Google it. This is what I get for getting carried away on the phone with my fiancé during working hours. "Definitely. Anyway, what's up?"

"Oh, not a whole lot," he says. "Nicole's only called me seven times begging me to forgive her. Your mother's left three messages back at the house for you, your dad's left one, and Perry the wedding planner refuses to call back to reschedule our lunch from yesterday. I think she's trying to teach us a lesson for canceling on her. She's incredibly important and sought after, you know."

"Damn," I say, forgetting about the finger sandwich. "We need to go over those seating charts, especially in light of the fact that your sister's invited an additional—how many people? Do you even know?"

"Nicole says no more than twenty, but I'm guessing she's afraid to fess up to the real number."

My smartphone chirps. I look down at the screen and see that Eva from the OCME is trying to get through to me.

"Cooper, let me call you back," I say. "I've got the medical examiner's office on the line."

"Don't forget your promise," he says in a sexy voice before hanging up.

Maybe his voice wasn't purposely sexy, I think to myself as I press to accept Eva's call. It sort of always sounds that way.

"Eva, hi," I say, crossing the street along with a crowd of excited freshmen, a few parents, and some orientation leaders in blue-and-gold "Welcome to NYC!" T-shirts. "What's up?"

"Hey, Heather." Eva sounds a bit friendlier than she had before, though no less harassed. She's still all business. "So I wanted to give you a heads-up. Your dead girl must be somebody pretty important—or connected to somebody pretty important. They just completed the autopsy."

"No way. I thought you said—"

"That we're completely backed up? Yeah, we are. We got bodies in here that have been waiting for autopsy since the weekend before last. But the chief got a call. A few calls, actually."

"I take it they weren't only from the victim's parents."

"No way," Eva says with a snort. "State Department."

It's my turn to snort. "How funny. Special Agent Lancaster just got through telling me the bureau's only job is to provide for the safety of those they are protecting."

"Oh?" Eva's voice turns casual. "You've seen Special Agent Lancaster today? How is he?"

I've hurried up the steps to the student building and am flashing my staff ID at the security guard at the entrance. He nods and allows me through the gate. "Special Agent Lancaster seemed just fine, Eva. Why, do you miss him?"

"That jackass?" Eva sounds indignant. "No! He's so not my type. He looks like he goes home every night and listens to podcasts about the rise of the Aryan Nation while polishing his gun."

"I think you're being a little hard on him," I say, fighting my way through the crowds of students to the elevator, "but whatever. What's the news on the autopsy?"

"Oh," Eva says. "So I told the chief what you said to me this morning about the party the vic was at the night before she died. Even if we put a rush on the tox screens, it will still be a few days before we get the results—better than a few weeks, though. Hey, what'd you hear about the trash from the party the vic went to? Get anything?"

"I don't know yet, I've been away from the office almost all day. As soon as I hear anything, I'll let you know."

"Okay. Anyway, they looked a little closer at your vic during the postmortem because of your info and also, I'll be honest, because of all the pressure they were getting from upstairs. And guess what they found."

I've pressed the up button for the elevator. "I have no idea."

"Nothing. No sign of sexual assault, no sign of overdose, no sign of obvious trauma. The vic was in perfect health . . . except for one thing, which the chief wouldn't even really have looked for if you hadn't said anything."

"Really? What?"

"Teeth imprints. And you'll never guess where. *Inside the victim's upper lip.*"

I stand in front of the elevator bank, pressing my smartphone as hard as I can to my ear, since it's difficult to hear with all the noise from the students. The Gottlieb Student Center, in addition to being an architectural blight on the south side of Washington Square, houses many of New York College's student clubs, the student government, and a dining center that offers selections from such culinary luminaries as Pizza Hut and Burger King, making it one of the campus's most popular eateries. This is why the student center is always packed and why the wait for an elevator can sometimes be as long as the wait for an elevator in Fischer Hall.

I can tell that Eva is expecting some kind of reaction from me, but I have no idea what, since I don't understand what she's talking about. Tooth imprints inside the victim's upper lip? How could someone die from that?

"I don't understand," I finally admit.

"Heather," Eva says, in a tone that suggests she believes I'm a little slow. "Jasmine didn't die of an asthma attack. Well, the asthma certainly helped speed things up, but we're listing the manner of death as homicide."

"Wait," I say. A group of musical theater students nearby me have burst into a chorus of "Magic to Do" from *Pippin*, which I'm sure they find charming but I'm finding extremely annoying since I can barely hear Eva. I stick a finger in my nonphone ear. *"What?"*

"We see this kind of thing a lot, almost exclusively in women and children. Someone of superior strength holds a hand over the victim's lips and nose until she stops breathing. If they hold it there hard enough, it can cause lacerations inside the victim's mouth. The teeth imprints were Jasmine's own as she struggled to open her mouth, trying to breathe."

The elevator doors slide open in front of me, and a flood of students comes pouring out. I'm buffeted by the tide, but can't move out of the way because I'm too stunned by what I've just heard. Behind me, the musical theater majors are still insisting that they've got magic to do.

"You mean—"

"That's right," Eva says. "Jasmine was suffocated to death."

17

I knock on the open door beside the sign that reads NYC EXPRESS. It's a single office in a hallway on the fourth floor of the Gottlieb Student Center. Unlike the lobby of the building, the fourth floor, which is carpeted in New York College blue and gold, is not at all crowded.

I used to do a lot of media and press tours back in my "Sugar Rush" days. As far as press rooms go, the one for the *New York College Express* is not very impressive, housing only four desks containing a few computers and a single phone.

Then again, as the sign says, they're a poor, student-run organization.

There is only one person inside the office, a boy wearing jeans and a blue New York College hoodie. He's typing on a laptop in front of one of the building's massive floor-to-ceiling windows, which is covered in crooked blinds that have seen better days.

The boy doesn't answer my knock. I soon see that that's because he's wearing earbuds. I enter the office—which is mostly devoid of human activity, but filled with empty pizza boxes and soda containers—and tap his shoulder.

The boy jumps, startled, and pulls out the earbuds, allowing them to dangle from a thin white cord down his chest.

"Oh, shit, you scared me," he says, leaping from his chair. His smile is crooked and charming. He's a white boy with adorably mussed dark hair. He clearly belongs to the Gavin McGoren why-bother-showering-before-work? school of thought. "Can I help you?"

"Yes, I think you can," I say, looking around for a place to sit. It's impossible to find one that isn't covered in empty food containers. "You know if you don't take the trash out once in a while, you'll get mice in here, right?"

"Oh, we already have one," the boy says, hastily pulling some pizza boxes off a chair for me. "Well, it could be a baby rat. I can't really tell which it is. Anyway, I named him Algernon. He's supercute. I don't have the heart to let them set up traps for him. He's the only other living being I see in here most days, since the rest of the staff hasn't come back to the city from break yet. Al's my only IRL friend until classes start."

"IRL?" I use a clean napkin to carefully brush crumbs from the seat of the chair he's offered me. Mice—or baby rats—mean droppings, and no matter how cute Algernon might be, droppings mean disease, which means hospitalization, which means my wedding will be even more of a disaster than it already is.

"In real life." The boy sits back down in his chair and studies me. "I'm sorry, have we met? You look familiar."

"I don't know," I say vaguely. In real life? This boy's "real life" seems to consist of sitting by himself in an untidy office, churning out copy for a student news blog, with only a mouse—or baby rat—as a companion. I feel sorry for him, but he seems completely cheerful about it. "Do you ever eat in any of the dining halls?"

He points at me, then snaps his fingers. "That's it! You're Heather Wells! You're totally famous. I knew I'd seen you before." He lifts his laptop and begins to type. "You interested in doing an interview? Our readers would totally love it. I could set you up with one of our entertainment bloggers when they get back to campus. I know just the one, she's a *huge* fan of old crappy pop music—"

"Uh, maybe," I say, trying not to feel offended. Old crappy pop music? The pop music I performed wasn't that crappy. And thirty isn't that old . . . although maybe it is to a twenty-year-old. "I'm actually here to talk to you about something school-related. What's your name?"

"Oh, sorry. Cam. Cameron Ripley. I'm the editor in chief." He narrows his hazel eyes at me. "Hey, you work in Death Dorm—I mean, Fischer Hall—now, don't you? This isn't about the piece I ran this morning, is it? The one about the prince? I'm sorry, but I know that story was solid. I have confirmation that he lives in your building. The admin's been all over me about my source for that piece, which is *not* cool. We may be student run and online only, but we're still journalists and we do not have to tell them shit about our—"

"It's not about that," I interrupt. "Well, it's peripherally about that. I wanted to see if you'd be interested in a swap."

He eyes me suspiciously. "What kind of swap?"

"Of information." I cross my legs—which isn't as sexy as it sounds since I'm wearing cords, but a girl does what she can. "I have information you might be interested in. And you have information I might be interested in. Maybe we could work something out."

"I don't know," Cam says. He continues to eye me like I'm the enemy. The cords are definitely working against me. Also, I might be a little too old for him, despite the whole cougar thing I've apparently got going with Gavin. "We don't usually work that way. And while a piece on you would be interesting, it wouldn't be *that* interesting. No offense, but most of my readers have probably never heard of you. Britney Spears, yeah, but you? You haven't put out an album in a really—"

"The information isn't about me," I interrupt, beginning to feel annoyed with this kid. Despite the fact that he's nice to mice, he's kind of a pill.

I'm not even really sure why I'm doing what I'm about to do. I know I could get in big trouble—lose my job, even—for doing it.

But something's been bothering me ever since I heard

Charlie in President Allington's office say that "the leak" had been traced back to an IP address in Fischer Hall. It isn't only that I want to prove who the leak *isn't*—Sarah.

I need to find out who it *is*. Although ever since Eva's phone call, I have a sneaking suspicion that I already know.

"It's about Fischer Hall," I explain. "You know there was a student death there yesterday."

He nearly drops his laptop. *"What?"*

I shrug and uncross my legs, beginning to get up from my chair. "But since you're not interested in making a deal—"

"No, wait." Cam leans forward to block my exit from the office. "I'm interested! I'm totally interested. Who died?"

I sink back into my chair, recrossing my legs. "I'm risking my job just being here. Why should I tell you what I know without getting something in return?"

"I totally understand," Cam says. He leaps up to close the door to the office. The minute he does so, the smell of stale pizza and other, less pleasant odors begin to become much more noticeable. "Look, I can't promise anything, but—"

"I can't promise anything either," I say. "Except another exclusive about the prince."

He grabs his laptop, his gaze blazing eagerly. "You're kidding me. Something else, in addition to info about the kid who croaked?"

Shame surges over me. I have a sudden urge to throw open the door and flee the room, to get as far as possible from Cameron Ripley and his smelly office and pet baby rat.

But then I remind myself that he's a journalist. It's his responsibility to report the news, no matter how heartbreaking, in as much detail as possible (while hopefully leaving the victim with some dignity) so that the public can be alerted to the danger and the perpetrator hopefully brought to justice.

He's only doing his job, exactly like I'm only doing mine. Maybe we've gotten a little hardened by some of the things we've seen IRL.

"Yes, both," I say, after swallowing. "A girl was found dead in her room in Fischer Hall yesterday morning. The night before, she was seen at a party on the floor above, in Prince Rashid's room."

Cam is typing so quickly his fingers appear to be flying over his keyboard. "Holy shit," he says, grinning, his gaze on his screen. "This is amazing. This is the best scoop we've gotten in ages. Names, though. I need names!"

"Not until you give *me* a name."

He glances up from the screen, confused. "What? How can I give you a name? This is the first I'm hearing about any of this. You're telling *me* about it."

"I want the name of your source on the Prince Rashid stories you've been printing," I say. "Then I'll give you the name of the dead girl, and anything else you want, including a story so explosive, it's going to rock this campus to its core. But the people it concerns most directly aren't going know about it until five o'clock today. So you'll have to hold off posting it until then."

Cam's face goes slack with astonishment—then tightens with excitement. "Five o'clock today? What is it? Does it have to do with the faculty's vote of no confidence on the president? That's it, isn't it?"

I wag a finger at him. "Nuh-uh. I'm not telling you until you tell me. And remember—you're not using my name in any of this. I'm an 'inside source.'"

"Of course," Cam says. He's so anxious for the story, he's abandoned all journalistic integrity, rushing back to his desk to hit the keyboard on the desktop computer. "I have it right here . . . uh . . . someplace. But I'm just warning you, those tips were always sent via direct message from a Twitter account, I think. Yeah. Here it is." He reads from screen. "ResLifeGirl. Sorry, no name. Will that work? Is it enough?"

"Yes," I say grimly. "It's enough."

It's exactly what I suspected. I don't need a name. I have all the information I need.

Twitter, Cooper had said in disgust when he'd opened Jasmine's laptop the day we'd found her dead, because Cooper can't stand social media.

But it turns out to have its uses. Like sending anonymous tips to student news blogs.

ResLife is probably short for "residence life," which is the programming and counseling aspect of the Housing Office that Lisa, Sarah, and resident assistants specialize and train in (as opposed to the administrative and facility side, which is more my line of work: room assignments and flooded bathrooms).

Often people don't know it, but when they look back at the experiences they enjoyed in their dorm during their college years, those were their "res life" experiences.

Only a female RA (or someone working in a hall director's office) would choose ResLifeGirl as a screen name.

"When's the last time ResLifeGirl contacted you?" I ask.

Cam studies the screen. "Uh . . . hmm. That's weird."

"What's weird?"

"She's been in contact daily this last week, but since the day before yesterday . . . nothing."

This actually makes perfect sense. Last week all the RAs were required to move in to help with preparation for freshman check-in. We'd obviously filled them in at that time about our incoming VIR. And ResLifeGirl wouldn't have had time to log in with her screen name the night of Prince Rashid's party, because she'd been busy.

Busy getting murdered.

That was when the communications major—who'd admired female news journalists like Katie Couric and Diane Sawyer, and so would have gotten a certain thrill out of leaking secrets to the college's student-run news blog—had her smartphone stolen, and her voice physically stifled by a hand that had ended up robbing her of her breath as well.

Despite the fact that the closed door to the office has made it warm and stuffy, I feel a chill.

Jasmine had been ResLifeGirl, the *New York College Express* tipster. It seemed reasonable to believe she'd gotten killed for it.

Only by whom? And for what? Had she seen something at Rashid's party? Had it been something she'd been about to share with the world via Twitter, something someone didn't want shared, so they'd silenced her . . . permanently?

The penalty for premarital sex in Qalif is beheading, I remembered Special Agent Lancaster saying. *So the lash is quite mild in comparison.*

Oh, come on. This isn't Qalif. It's Greenwich Village, for God's sake.

"Did ResLifeGirl ever do any writing for you?" I ask Cameron.

"No," Cam says, scooting his chair away from the desk. "No way. I'm not answering any more questions. I gave you what you wanted; now it's my turn. Who died? And how? And what's happening at five o'clock?"

"Okay," I say. "The dead girl is Jasmine Albright. She was twenty, a junior, and an RA in Fischer Hall, fourteenth floor."

He's on his laptop again, and never stops typing the entire time I'm speaking. It's clear that he didn't know Jasmine. I'm not sure if this is a relief to me, or worse, somehow.

"An RA? Fourteenth floor—that's one floor below Rascally Rashid's!"

There's no moss gathering on Cameron. "Right. I told you the victim went to a party in his room the night she died."

Now he stops typing and stares at me. "You're telling me an *RA* died after a party in the prince's room? What killed her?"

"I'll be able to tell you the cause of death after five o'clock today," I say, "but only if you hold the second part of this story until then." This is a lie. I have no intention of telling him the cause—or manner—of Jasmine's death. "I can tell you that there was no sign of an overdose, or alcohol poisoning, or anything like that. The victim did have asthma, though."

Cam makes a disappointed face. "She died of *asthma*?"

"I didn't say that. I said she *had* asthma."

Cameron looks less disappointed, and more like someone who's stumbled across an exciting mystery. Of course, he didn't know the victim, so it doesn't matter to him how Jasmine died. He's just looking for a story that will bring his blog a lot of hits.

"Okay, so she had asthma, but didn't die from it." He keeps typing. "What's the deal with the five o'clock thing?"

"Well," I say. "She wasn't the only RA at Prince Rashid's party."

Cameron smirks. "What an ass-kisser. You know the best way not to get caught throwing a rager is to invite the RAs. So what are their names?"

"That's the part of the story you can't print until five o'clock."

Cameron shakes his head, confused. "Why? What happens at five o'clock?"

I lift my purse from the floor and shoulder it. "At five o'clock today, all the RAs from Fischer Hall who were at Prince Rashid's party are going to receive notices that their employment with the New York College Housing Office has been terminated."

"What?" Cameron jerks his fingers from his keyboard as if they've been singed.

I nod. "You heard me. And don't worry, I'm sure you'll be hearing from all those RAs about the injustice of what's happening to them as soon as they get their letters. You'll have their names soon enough. Just keep in mind that they were asked by their employer—my boss—if they'd seen Jasmine the night before she died, and they all said no. They lied to save their own skins, even though if they'd told the truth, it might have helped the investigation into Jasmine's death. It's too late now. But you did *not* hear any of this from me."

"No worries." Cameron shakes his head in disbelief as he turns back to his keyboard. "Heather, do you even realize how huge this is? Not only is a girl dead, and a bunch of RAs are getting fired, but it all happened because of a party being given by the heir to the throne of Qalif, whose father donated *five hundred million dollars* to New York College. This story could get picked up by the print media." His tone has turned reverential. "It could make CNN."

"Let's not get ahead of ourselves," I remark drily. "You know what I would do if I were you? Not that I'm telling you how to do your job."

He shakes his head again, this time in answer to my question. "No, what?"

"I'd try to get in touch with ResLifeGirl. Maybe she could tell you more about what happened at that party."

"Hey," he says, nodding. "That's a good idea."

So he hasn't yet figured out that ResLifeGirl was Jasmine.

"Also, you should ask the facilities office of this building for a live trap," I say as I open the office door. "Then you can catch Algernon and let him go out in the park. I know it's nice to have a friend in real life and everything," I add, "but he'll be happier there, and then you'll have a slimmer chance of catching the hantavirus, which is spread by mouse droppings. It can make people really sick. People even die from it."

Cam looks up from his keyboard.

"Is that what killed Jasmine Albright?" he asks excitedly. "Hantavirus? I know Death Dorm—I mean Fischer Hall—is an old building. Are you stating there's a mouse infestation in it, causing people to die? Because that would make insanely good copy."

I roll my eyes. "No, Cam," I say. "And if I were saying that, *I* wouldn't be stating anything, remember? Because this is all coming from an 'inside source.'"

"Right, right," he says, putting his earbuds back in. "Don't worry, I got you covered. No names." Then he begins typing away, lost in his cyberlife.

I pull the door closed behind me on my way out, deciding that maybe it's better Cameron keeps Algernon around after all. He seems to need the company, even if the company is only a baby rat.

There's the dress mess
There's the veil travail
There's the guest guess
Might as well as bail

"The Whole Shebang,"
written by Heather Wells

18

You did *what?*" Cooper's voice cracks on the word "what."

"Well, *I* knew the leak wasn't Sarah, but how else was I going to prove it to everyone in the president's office?"

I'm walking swiftly across the park toward Fischer Hall, anxious to get back to work, my cell phone pressed to my ear. I'm late for Lisa's interview with the new RA candidate. Not that she needs my help, necessarily, but she wasn't in the best condition when I last saw her.

"It's not your job to prove Sarah isn't the leak," Cooper says. "Sarah's a big girl. She can take care of herself."

"Of course she can. But they already fired more than half the staff," I say. "I couldn't let Sarah be next. I had to find out who the leak really was. I figured if I offered to swap intel with the editor of the *Express*—"

"Swap intel with the editor of the *Express?*" Cooper interrupts, sounding weirdly echo-y, as if he's in a tunnel or something. But I can still hear the incredulity in his voice. "Heather, are you listening to yourself?"

"Whatever, it worked. And now we know the reason Jasmine was killed was because she had information that someone didn't want her spreading, probably on her phone that you kept pointing out was missing."

"*We* know no such thing," Cooper says. "And don't sound so proud of yourself, because if it *is* true, you just put yourself—not to mention the staff of the *Express*—in serious danger."

"Aw," I say, my ponytail swinging behind me as I hurry through the crowded park. "Are you worried about me? That's so sweet. I know I should be offended, because I'm a feminist, and the whole overprotective boyfriend thing is so *Twilight*, but whatever, I love it, keep it coming."

"Heather, I'm not joking." He sounds irritated. "Whatever it was Jasmine found out, recorded on her phone, and was apparently ready to Tweet to the world was worth killing her for. And that means it will be worth killing whoever uncovers the truth about it."

"But I didn't tell the *Express* about it. How could I? I don't know what it is that Jasmine found out. Whoever killed her did it before she got a chance to spill the beans. They have no idea we know Jasmine's the leak, or even that there was anything *to* leak. So why would I, or anyone who works for the *Express*, be in danger?"

"Because we're not talking about a girl killed in a lovers' quarrel. We're talking about a young woman who was murdered because of something to do with the heir to the throne of one of the richest countries in the world. Are you sure no one you know saw you come out of the student center? There's no one following you?"

"No one even follows the drag queen version of me on Twitter." I oblige him, however, by looking around. It's still a gorgeous day. The sun is brightly shining, and I've had to lower my sunglasses to protect my eyes from the glare. "Why would anyone bother to follow me in real life?"

My voice dries up in my throat as I see one of Prince Rashid's bodyguards—the one he calls Hamad—strolling along, eating a soft pretzel he evidently purchased from a street vendor, not five yards behind me. Like me, he's wearing sunglasses, but it's unmistakably him. No one else in the park is wearing a dark business suit with a matching dark shirt, tie, and earpiece.

"Heather?" Cooper asks. "Can you hear me?"

His voice startles me. I jump and turn quickly back around, hoping Hamad hasn't noticed that I've seen him.

"Yes," I say. "Sorry. Bad connection." No way am I telling him that he's right, and I am being followed . . . if that's actually what's happening. Maybe Hamad simply enjoys New York street vendor pretzels and ran out for a quick snack on his break from bodyguard duties. Pretzels are delicious, after all. "Where are you, anyway? You're not tailing my mother, are you?"

"Of course not," Cooper says. "You asked me not to. And I'd never do anything you asked me not to do. "

I snort sarcastically at this. "Right." Fischer Hall is straight ahead. I can see the large blue-and-gold New York College flag hanging above the front door, snapping in the fresh breeze. Home will always be where Cooper is, but Fischer Hall is a close second. I increase my pace. "Just wondering, you sound a little far away."

"Only physically, baby," he says. "My heart's always with you. I'll be home in time for dinner . . . which I assume will be finger sandwiches."

I try to summon up a laugh at his joke, but I'm feeling a little dispirited because Hamad truly does appear to be following me.

Of course he is. He works in Fischer Hall too. I'm over-reacting.

"Ha," I say. "Okay, great. See you then."

"Heather," Cooper says. "Call Canavan over at the Sixth Precinct. Tell him everything you just told me. He may have his hands tied because of the State Department, but I think you should keep him in the loop."

"Right," I say. I've begun to walk so rapidly, anxious to get away from my shadow, that I've reached Washington Square West—at the exact same time, I notice, as Hamad. He's finished his pretzel and has raised his sunglasses so he can glare at me, much like the way he'd glared at Sarah the other day in the office . . . like he'd very much like to draw his sidearm and shoot.

We both stand at the edge of the park. There's a line of taxicabs and buses that we must allow to go roaring past before we can cross the street to Fischer Hall. While we wait, Hamad stares at me in a manner I can only describe as extremely hostile, his dark eyes like twin black bullet holes.

"So I'll see you when you get home," I say into the phone to Cooper, my gaze still on Hamad.

"Wait," Cooper says. "You're calling Canavan now, right?"

"I sure am. Just like you're not tailing my mom. Bye now." I turn off my phone before Cooper can say another word. I don't need to be distracted by my boyfriend's sexy voice as I'm about to be killed on the street by the bodyguard of the son of a foreign dictator.

"Hello," I say pleasantly to Hamad as I slip my phone back into my purse. "Have a nice lunch?"

Hamad doesn't respond, except to continue to glare at me.

"I saw that you were enjoying a pretzel," I say. "Those are a New York City specialty. We're quite well known for our soft pretzels. Did you have mustard on yours? I find the mustard really brings out the salt in a pleasantly tangy way."

Hamad doesn't say anything. He merely crumples up the napkin the pretzel vendor had given him with his lunch and tosses it without a word into my face. My *face*.

Then he steps into the middle of Washington Square West, though the traffic there is still flowing steadily. A taxicab comes screeching to a halt barely a foot before striking him, and the New York cabby—who happens to be Punjabi—leans out his window to scream at Hamad, "Hey! What's the matter with you? You want to get yourself killed? Wait for the light, you idiot!"

Hamad continues haughtily the rest of the way across the street, not seeming to care that he's become the focus of attention of so many people, including a number of blue-and-gold-shirted orientation leaders outside of Fischer Hall, attempting to gather their flocks of first-year students in order to take them to various afternoon outings.

I lean down to lift the crumpled napkin he's thrown in my face.

"Hey," I call to him, dangling the napkin between my index finger and thumb. "Littering is prohibited in New York City. It's punishable by a fine of up to two hundred and fifty dollars! So please use a trash receptacle next time." I walk a few steps to a nearby metal trash can and toss the napkin inside it. "See? It's not that difficult."

Before entering Fischer Hall, Hamad hurls me a look of such pure and utter contempt that, for a moment, it's as if the sun has gone behind the clouds.

A chill goes down my spine that's not unlike the one I felt in Cam Ripley's office. Maybe I *did* make a mistake going to the student union after all.

"Heather?" one of the orientation leaders asks me with concern when the traffic slows down enough for me to cross the street. "Are you all right? Was something going on between you and that guy?"

"Oh, no," I say breezily. Though truthfully, I don't feel particularly breezy inside. "We were just fooling around."

"It didn't look like he was fooling," she says.

I smile in what I hope is a reassuring manner and go inside, where there is no sign of Hamad. He probably already took an elevator to the fifteenth floor.

Hamad is from another country that has very different customs than ours, I tell myself. Maybe in Qalif it's an insult for a woman to comment on a man's condiment preferences.

Or maybe Hamad is a cold-blooded killer and wanted to let me know in no uncertain terms that I'm his next victim.

Either way, it probably isn't such a bad idea to make that call to Detective Canavan, like Cooper suggested, and mention the incident.

It's busy in the lobby, as it always is after lunch. The residents who've slept in are finally up and around, and their more ambitious peers are on to their afternoon activities, as are (unfortunately) their parents.

"Everything okay?" I ask Pete as I approach the security desk.

"Depends on who you ask," he answers with a shrug.

"What does that mean?"

"You'll see," he says, and smirks as he bites into the tacos I bought for him (well, I paid for, he ordered) from Choza Taqueria on MacDougal.

My heart sinks. "I'm going to find something waiting for me in my office that I'm not going to like, aren't I?"

He stops smirking and looks surprised. "No, you're gonna like it. Almost as much as I like these tacos—which is a lot."

I'm not certain I believe him. Pete might think I'd like finding my mother in my office, but he'd be very wrong.

"Great," I say.

But when I walk into my office, what I find *is* a pleasant surprise. There's an enormous floral arrangement sitting in a crystal vase on my desk, and it's not one of those chintzy FTD ones either, all carnations and baby's breath, but gorgeous hydrangeas, hyacinths, roses, and some blooms I can't even identify, they're so foreign and rare. Every single bloom is pure white, the bouquet perfectly arranged to fit the expensive square-shaped vase it's been delivered in. The flowers fill the office with their exotic scent.

Sarah is sitting at her desk, flowerless. The door to Lisa's office is closed.

"Nice, right?" Sarah says, when she sees my face light up at the sight of the overflowing vase of blossoms. "Guess you've got a fan."

Cooper! I think immediately. He's the only person I know who would do something so thoughtful—and classy. He knows how much it hurt, having my mother show up like she did last night. That, plus having a student death in the building—when I'd sworn to myself that this year was going to be different—has really thrown me for a loop.

This is exactly the kind of thing he'd do to cheer me up . . . especially after upsetting me by saying all that nonsense about how he was going to tail her.

"Oh," I say softly, reaching out to gently touch one delicate, ivory petal. "He didn't have to go to all this trouble."

"He really didn't," Sarah says, taking a big bite of the burger she's grabbed from the caf and is eating at her desk. "But then," she adds, with her mouth full, "that's the kind of guy he is, isn't he?"

I lean forward to sniff a rose. Heaven, especially after experiencing so much dark unpleasantness outside the building just now with Prince Rashid's bodyguard. "I'm so lucky."

"You are," Sarah agrees. "We all are, really. So, so lucky to have him in our lives."

There's something slightly off about her tone.

"Wait," I say, lifting my nose from the flowers and stiffening. "These are from Cooper, right?"

"Ha." Sarah cackles. "You wish. Open the card."

There's an ivory note card tucked amid the dark green leaves. I reach for it.

From the Desk of
His Royal Highness Prince
Rashid Ashraf bin Zayed Sultan Faisal

FOR MS. WELLS, WITH MY DEEPEST
SYMPATHIES FOR YOUR LOSS. I WAS
SO SORRY TO HEAR WHAT YOU WENT
THROUGH YESTERDAY. PLEASE LET ME
KNOW IF THERE'S ANYTHING MY STAFF
OR I CAN DO FOR YOU DURING THIS
TERRIBLE TIME.

YOURS VERY TRULY,
Rashid

19

I turn to stare at Sarah in disbelief. "These flowers are from *Prince Rashid?*"

"Or Shiraz." Sarah rolls her eyes. "Whichever he's calling himself this week."

"But—" I stare at the arrangement. "They're so . . . *nice.*"

"Well, his dad has billions of dollars," Sarah reminds me with more than a hint of sarcasm in her tone. "I'm sure he can afford a decent florist."

Of course she's right.

"That's not what I mean," I say. "I'm surprised by the gesture. It's kind of mature. And what's written in the card is so nice."

Sarah snorts as she wipes ketchup from the side of her mouth with a napkin. "He probably didn't even write it. I bet there's a palace publicist or secretary who does all his press."

I stare at the card. Except for the prince's title and formal name, which is engraved, the rest is written in somewhat cramped block print, in black ink, by someone clearly better used to texting—or maybe the more manly art of falconry.

"How did you know they're from Prince Rashid?" I ask Sarah.

"Because he's been down here twice to check if you got them," she says. "The florist only delivered them ten minutes ago. There's a bouquet for Lisa too, but she's been locked inside the office with the new RA candidate since before I got back from Disbursements, so she hasn't seen it. I had them keep it up at the front desk since there's no room in here for two gigantic vases of flowers. I think I'm getting an allergy attack from yours alone."

I look down at the handwriting on the card. I want to believe that Rashid wrote the message himself, but it seems unlikely. Then again, it's on Qalif royal letterhead, with the name Rashid signed with a flourish and everything. Forgetting that Sarah is sitting across from me, I do the unthinkable and lick the signature.

"Oh my God," Sarah cries, watching me. "What are you doing?"

"Look." I show her the card. "The ink is smeared."

"So?" Sarah cries.

"So that's how you can tell if someone really signed something themselves, or if it was typed, or printed with a stamp. If it smears, they signed it themselves with a pen. It's an old music business trick to use a stamp to sign head shots because they make you sign so many of them. Or just reproduce the head shot with an autograph already printed on it, not personalized." I look more closely at the card. "Someone really handwrote this."

"Yes, of course someone did," Sarah says, still sounding disgusted. "I already told you, his secretary or publicist."

"Wouldn't you hire someone with less crappy handwriting to be your secretary if you were going to have them pretend to be you?"

"What does it matter whether or not he wrote it?" Sarah demands. "It doesn't change anything. Jasmine's still dead, Rashid's still a jerk, and Kaileigh's mom is still stalking you. She was by here a million times while you and Lisa were out. Here are your messages." She rises to slam a handful of slips of paper on my desk. "Where were you guys, anyway? I tried calling but neither of you would pick up."

I sit down and begin to sort through the "While You Were Out" messages, careful to keep my tone neutral. It's clear Sarah knows nothing of the fate that's about to befall the RAs. "Lisa didn't say?"

"I told you, she's been locked in her office since before I got back from Disbursements." Sarah lowers her voice to a whisper, nodding at Lisa's closed door. "It says on her calendar that she has the interview with that new RA candidate right now."

"Right," I say to Sarah. "We had a meeting up in the president's office about Jasmine."

Sarah rolls her eyes. "What a waste of time *that* must have been."

"Yeah," I say. "It was."

I don't dare tell her the truth about what happened during the meeting. When she finds out that all nine of our new RAs are being fired, she's going to explode with righteous indignation. She's young enough—and despite her gruff demeanor, tenderhearted enough—that she'll side with the student workers, and probably even attempt to help them lodge a formal protest.

Nor do I dare call Detective Canavan, as I promised Cooper I would, since Sarah will eavesdrop on the conversation, and overhear that Jasmine's cause of death wasn't natural, something I'd prefer to keep secret as long as possible. I could slip out to call the detective on my cell, but I'm still feeling a little shaken by my run-in with Prince Rashid's bodyguard. At least with my backside planted firmly in my office chair I know Hamad can't sneak up behind me.

Instead, I bend over my messages. One of them is from Julio. He's written only two words—*No trash*—but I understand exactly what he means. As I'd expected, Eva's request for DNA analysis had come too late. All the trash from Rashid's party has already been put out and picked up at the curb by DSNY, the Department of Sanitation, New York City. Julio and his crew are extremely thorough.

"Did Mrs. Harris say what she wanted?" I ask Sarah. There are three messages from the front desk saying that Kaileigh's mother needs me to call her. Both the "Urgent" and "ASAP" boxes are checked.

A concerned mom is the last person I feel like speaking

with at the moment. I hesitate to even pick up my office phone. I can see the red light flashing ominously. She's probably left me voice messages as well.

"What else?" Sarah asks. "She's upset her kid's RA is dead, and she wants Kaileigh to have a room change."

Sarah is making quick work of her cheeseburger, which looks—and smells—like a particularly good one. My stomach rumbles. It seems like it's been a long time since the finger sandwiches in the president's office.

"I told Mrs. Harris yesterday that only Kaileigh can fill out the paperwork to request a room change," I say.

"Yeah, well, according to Mrs. Harris, Kaileigh's roommate Ameera saw their RA's dead body, and now Kaileigh is too emotionally caught up in her roommate's trauma over that horrible experience to be asked to do something as mundane as fill out paperwork," Sarah says.

"Are you serious?" I ask. "Does Kaileigh even want to move out? Or is her mother still trying to make her move out?"

"Who knows? Apparently, Mr. Harris is going to be contacting their attorney to get Kaileigh out of her housing contract because we're so incompetent we allowed someone to die down the hall from Kaileigh's room, so we can expect to be hearing from him soon."

"Oh God," I say, and lay my head on my desk. "I wish it had been me who died, and not Jasmine."

"Well, that's a psychologically unhealthy statement to make," Sarah says primly. I can hear her licking ketchup off her fingers. "Especially from someone who's about to get married. Isn't this supposed to be the happiest time of your life?"

"That's what people tell me," I say.

My head still on my desk, I lift one of the many messages from the pile. It was taken by Gavin, from my mother. *Please call*, it says. *Urgent.*

Oh God.

"Anyway," Sarah goes on, "the Harrises aren't wrong about Ameera. I saw her going in to see Dr. Flynn this morning. She was crying about as much as she was yesterday. It's hard to believe such a skinny little body could hold that many tears. Maybe that's why the prince sent her flowers too."

I lift my head from the desk to stare at her. "What do you mean?"

"What do you mean, what do I mean? I mean Prince Rashid sent Ameera flowers too. I saw them at the front desk when I had the florist drop Lisa's off there." Sarah looks a little uncomfortable. "I have to admit I was being a little nosy checking who they were for. I thought they might be for me because, after all, I'm the one who discovered the body. If anyone should get flowers, it should be me. But *no*, no one ever thinks to send the graduate assistant flowers, only the pretty girl and the hall director and her—"

"Why would Rashid send *Ameera* flowers?" I interrupt, asking the question of myself more than of Sarah.

"How should I know?" she replies. "I assumed he was only sending them to you and Lisa to suck up because he knows he's been busted for throwing that party."

"But it's not like Lisa can discipline him," I say. "The college would never let her, considering how much money his father's donated. So he didn't *have* to send us flowers. And he certainly didn't have to send them to Ameera."

"No," Sarah admits reluctantly. "But Ameera's gorgeous. And she's sad. He's probably hitting on her while she's in an emotionally weakened state because he wants to get in her pants."

I glare at her.

Sarah's right, of course. It's likely Rashid sent Lisa and me the flowers out of guilt because he—or one of his employees—is somehow responsible for Jasmine's death, and Ameera the flowers because she's hot.

Still, I can't shake the memory of Rashid's face the day before in our office when he'd heard Ameera was ill, how his dark eyebrows had knit with concern. That concern hadn't seemed fake. He'd forgotten all about his glamorous lunch reservation at Nobu, even offering the use of his chauffeur-driven Escalade to transport her to the hospital.

Maybe I'm a romantic fool, but any boy willing to do that can't be *all* bad . . . or thinking solely about getting into a girl's pants.

"You don't think there's the slightest possibility," I say to Sarah, "that he might have done it out of genuine decency—"

Sarah rolls her eyes. "Really, Heather? After everything you've been through, you *still* think there are decent guys out there? And that *Prince Rashid* might be one of them? Prince *Rashid?*"

"Well . . ." I say. "Okay, it was bad that he threw that party, but he isn't from this country, and he was only trying to make friends—"

"Oh my God, you're so naïve. But it's not totally your fault. You didn't really have a normal childhood—" Now Sarah has launched into her psychologist's tone. "And you got the

last decent guy. And Cooper's a total exception to the rule."
She thoughtfully chews a french fry. "Well, Tom Snelling is
decent too, but he's gay, so he doesn't count. There are definitely no decent *heterosexual* guys left."

Even though I know it stems from her having been disappointed in love, I find Sarah's jadedness a little annoying.

"What about Cory, Lisa's husband?" I ask.

"He works in *investment banking*." Sarah gives a mock
shudder. "And anyway, we hardly ever see him. The jury is
still out on him."

"What about Gavin?"

Sarah throws me a sarcastic look.

"Okay, he still has some growing up to do," I admit, "but
under our tutelage—"

"Face it, Heather: guys are scum."

It's kind of ironic that as she says this, Kyle Cheeseman,
one of the new RAs—the one with the Justin Bieber hair,
who also wears jeans that droop so low below his waistline
that I'm able to read the band on his underwear, especially
since his shirt is completely unbuttoned, revealing his hair-
less chest and stone-hard abs—saunters off the elevator and
into the office to check his staff mailbox (all the RAs are
required to do so at least twice a day).

"Hey, sexy ladies," Kyle says. "Wow, Heather, nice flowers."

"I believe I've told you to stop calling us sexy ladies, Kyle,"
Sarah snaps from her desk. "We're your supervisors."

"Whoa," Kyle says. "Never mind. You aren't sexy. You're
both mad pimpin'."

Behind Kyle is Rajiv—who'd worked as an RA last year
and also through the summer—and Howard Chen, looking

considerably healthier than when I'd last seen him vomiting into the fourteenth-floor trash chute the day before.

"It's physically impossible for us to be pimps," Sarah says. "Pimps are men who control prostitutes, taking a large portion of their earnings in return for providing them with their clients. Do either Heather or I resemble men who procure clients for prostitutes to you?"

"No." Howard Chen looks furious on behalf of both Sarah and me. "What is wrong with you, Kyle?" Howard is wearing a hoodie from Harvard, where his parents wish he'd gone. They'd had to settle for Howard's safety school, New York College, instead.

"Shut up, Howard," Kyle says. "Jesus Christ, I was only trying to pay them a compliment!"

"Kyle," Rajiv says calmly. "Has anyone ever told you before that you're an imbecile? Why is your shirt unbuttoned? Are you expecting to be mobbed by Beliebers later?"

Kyle pouts. He's felt inside his staff mailbox, which I knew without a glance would be empty. The termination letters won't be delivered until just before five o'clock so the president and his cronies can arrange to be long gone when the RAs receive them, and therefore not have to field their—or more likely, their parents'—complaints.

"How about simply asking us how our day is going," Sarah says. "That's the customary way of greeting one's coworkers."

Kyle looks a little lost, but asks gamely, "How is your day going?," swallowing so hard I can see his Adam's apple bob.

I'm starting to wonder if maybe Sarah is right: could it be that there aren't any decent guys left?

As if on cue, the door to Lisa's office is thrown open, and she stands there with a clipboard in hand, looking paler than usual, some of her dark hair slipping out of the clip into which she's attempted to tuck it, but otherwise seeming like her normal self.

"Hi, guys," she says, moving aside to make room for someone who's been inside her office to pass through the doorway. "I'd like you to meet our newest staff member, Dave Fernandez."

As soon as Sarah lays eyes on Dave Fernandez, who waves amiably in the general direction of everyone in the office, she begins to choke on the fry she's just swallowed.

I don't blame her.

"Dave will be moving onto the fourteenth floor," Lisa goes on, ignoring Sarah's sputters, "just as soon as Jasmine's room becomes available."

"Hi," Dave says. His voice is deeply melodic, his manner easygoing. "Lisa's told me a lot of nice things about you guys, and Jasmine too. Wish I could have known her. Sorry to be meeting all of you under these circumstances, but I'm glad to have the privilege, just the same."

He's several years older than the other boys—older than Sarah, and possibly even Lisa—which might explain his self-assured nonchalance, but I think there's something more than that. I can't quite put my finger on what it is, though. Possibly it's the fact that he's wearing well-scuffed cowboy boots beneath his jeans. Cowboy boots, in New York City! His underwear isn't showing either, and he's wearing a shirt that's properly buttoned.

He still manages to look cool, however. So cool that in

comparison to him, Kyle looks like a middle schooler. Maybe it's because the cowboy boots give Dave an extra couple inches in height over everyone else in the room.

"It's great to have you here, Dave," I say. "I'm Heather Wells, assistant hall director. When you figure out what day you're moving in, let me know. I can make sure the room is clean and ready for you."

Dave nods in my direction. "Thanks, Heather," he says with a smile.

Sarah has swigged some water from her New York College stainless-steel water bottle to wash down the fry, and now she nearly gags on it. I suspect that's because Dave's smile is so dazzling and his biceps so defined, they put even Prince Rashid's to shame.

Sarah very badly wants to introduce herself to him, but she can't quite seem to get the words out.

"Unh," Sarah says.

"I need someone to show Dave over to the Housing Office so we can get his paperwork in order," Lisa says. "Anyone care to volunteer?"

"Gurk," Sarah chokes, eagerly waving an arm to volunteer. "Murg."

"Not you, Sarah," Lisa says. "I need you to stay here."

Dave's dark eyebrows lower with concern. "You all right over there, Sarah?"

"Oh, um," Sarah says. She chokes some more, her face turning a delicate shade of magenta. "Yes, thanks, I just, ahem, swallowed wrong."

"I hate when that happens," Dave says with another one of his amazing smiles.

"Howard, Kyle, would one of you mind?" Lisa asks.

Kyle whips out his cell phone and glances at it. "Ooo, can't, Lisa, I'm late to meet my trainer."

"I c-can't either, Lisa," Howard stammers. "I have to study."

Lisa frowns at Howard. "Classes haven't started yet, Howard."

"I'm t-trying to get a head start on my reading," Howard says. "I'm premed, remember?"

Lisa gives Howard an odd look, but it doesn't matter. There are plenty of other volunteers.

"I'll do it," Rajiv says. "I'm heading in that direction anyway."

"No, no," Sarah says, leaping up from behind her desk. "Really, I don't mind doing it. I'm free."

"You aren't free, Sarah," Lisa says, looking annoyed. "I'm expecting Jasmine's parents within the hour. I need you here."

Sarah looks crushed but, never one to shirk her duty, says, "Of course. Well, nice to meet you, Dave." Having recovered from her embarrassing drooling incident, she thrusts her hand toward the new hire. "I'm Sarah Rosenberg, the building GA."

"Hi, Sarah Rosenberg, the building GA," Dave says, thrusting out his own strong brown hand. "Pleased to make your acquaintance."

It's only when his fingers end up dangling about twelve inches higher than Sarah's that I take a closer look at Dave's face and realize the truth.

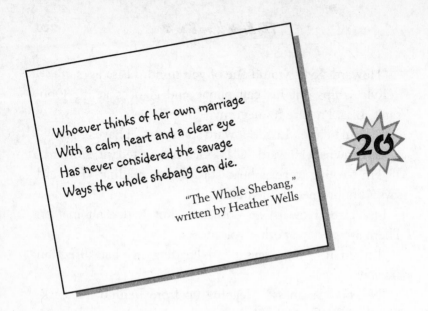

Whoever thinks of her own marriage
With a calm heart and a clear eye
Has never considered the savage
Ways the whole shebang can die.

"The Whole Shebang,"
written by Heather Wells

20

Sarah's incredulous. "You hired a *blind* RA?"

We're standing in Lisa's office. Kyle and Howard have left, as has Rajiv. He's gone to escort Dave to the Housing Office to get his paperwork completed, though at first Dave protested that he didn't need an escort.

"I've already taken a tour of the campus," he'd said cheerfully. "The Housing Office is straight across the park, then another two blocks straight from there, then it's the first door to the right, on the corner."

It was a strange way to put it (to a sighted person), but he was completely correct.

"I'm headed to the bookstore," Rajiv had said, "which is in the same direction, but two doors down. Might as well go together."

Rajiv seemed fascinated by the sight of the collapsible white cane Dave suddenly produced from his backpack, unfolded, then slashed about like a cowboy with a whip (we all backed away to avoid getting hit). I got the feeling Rajiv wanted to see Dave swinging that thing through the park. I wanted to too.

"What if I did hire a blind RA?" Lisa demands, folding her arms across her chest, then wincing and dropping them to her sides again. It was obvious—to me, anyway—that her nipples were still sore. "I never expected *you*, of all people, Sarah, to be so close-minded. Dave may be limited visually, but he makes up for it by being far from limited mentally."

Sarah's mouth sags open. "I didn't mean—I just meant, how is he going to . . . ?"

" . . . do the job for which he's been hired?" Lisa finishes for her. "This is only a guess, but I'm thinking he's going to do it better than either Howard or Kyle."

"And he's *literally* going to do it blind," I point out.

Neither Lisa nor Sarah smiles at my little joke. I'm not surprised. Many of my finest witticisms go unappreciated.

"Dave may no longer be able to drive, or make out people's facial expressions, or even tell what kind of food he's feeding his cat," Lisa goes on, "but during my interview with him, it was obvious to me that he sees a lot more than most sighted people. It might interest you to know that he served in the military over in Afghanistan. His vision problems are the result of head trauma from a roadside bomb."

I can't help inhaling sharply. "Oh, how terrible." Sarah's mouth sags even further.

"But according to his application," Lisa says, tapping the manila file on her desk, "he's already learned how to read braille. He's decided to go back to school to get his master's degree in computer science, and none of the people who recommended him for the RA position believe his lack of sight will stand in his way. His parents are deceased, so he's here on a full academic scholarship, which means he's also a work-study student."

As soon as I hear the words "work-study student," I pounce. Work-study students are like gold, because 35 percent of what they earn working for us comes out of the college's budget, not the building's individual budget. That leaves me more money to buy fun things, such as snacks and soda for staff parties . . . although technically I'm not supposed to be using money from the budget to purchase these kinds of items.

But after seeing the orgy of finger sandwiches in the president's office, I'm going to be buying all the pizza and Diet Coke for the staff—what's left of it—our budget can afford.

"We could give him a work-study position at the front desk," I say. "There are always night and early-morning shifts open. Classes will be starting soon, and as much as Gavin might disagree, he can't work twenty-four/seven—"

"That's what I was thinking," Lisa says with a smile at me. "Dave says he has this thing, some kind of label maker that prints things in braille."

"Perfect," I say, thinking of my emergency contact list. It would look even more brilliant shrunk down to pocket size in braille. "Working the desk will be a big change after dodging IEDs in Afghanistan, but it pays, and we definitely need the help."

"I don't think Dave's going to mind," Lisa says. "He says he's ready to make a completely new start, he and Itchy, his cat."

I hear a whimper from Sarah's direction. When I glance at her, I'm surprised to see that her face has crumpled.

"Sarah," I ask in alarm. "What's wrong?"

Lisa frowns at her. "Sarah, I know residents aren't allowed to have pets in the building, but I told Dave we'd make an exception for Itchy because it's a therapy cat. My understanding is that the animal has really helped him through his recovery—"

"God!" Sarah cries. Tears are beginning to trickle down her face. It's a repeat performance of yesterday, only this time there's no dead body in sight. "What kind of person do you think I am? I'm not upset because you're bending the rules for his cat! I think it's incredibly sweet that he has a cat. I think it's incredibly sweet that you—oh, Lisa!"

Sarah raises her arms, and to my surprise—and Lisa's too, evidently, judging from her stunned expression—throws her arms around Lisa's neck, embracing her in what looks to me like a stranglehold of a hug.

"This is just . . . You're just . . . This is all just so *great*," Sarah sobs into Lisa's neck. "This is *exactly* what the staff needs after everything that's happened with Jasmine. Someone like Dave. Thank you. *Thank you*."

"Oh," Lisa says, her eyes widening at me over Sarah's broad shoulder. "Um. Okay. Well, I wouldn't thank me yet, Sarah. I haven't told you the bad news."

"I don't care," Sarah says, still clinging to Lisa. "I don't

---

care, I don't care. I'm so happy right now. I'm so happy someone like Dave's going to be joining our staff."

"I bet you are," I say. "I saw you checking out his biceps. Guess there are some decent guys left after all, huh, Sarah?"

"Shut up, Heather," Sarah says, but happily, without a trace of her usual rancor. "You're such a great person, Lisa. I'm serious. I know I usually have a bad attitude, and I may come off as kind of bitchy sometimes"—sometimes?—"but I want you to know that I genuinely love this job, and I genuinely love you." She lifts her head and looks over at me. "Both of you. For real. You're my best friends. Well, my only friends, really. But I want to make sure you know it."

"Okay," Lisa says, patting Sarah on the back. "That's great, Sarah. We feel the same way about you. Don't we, Heather?"

"You know," I can't help pointing out, "we don't even know for sure that Dave's heterosexual. He could have a girlfriend. You're kind of just assuming—"

"*Don't we, Heather?*" Lisa says again, through gritted teeth.

"Yes, Sarah," I say, patting her on the back the way Lisa had. "We both love you too."

"Great," Lisa says, prying Sarah's grip from her neck. "But you and I are still going to have to have a little chat about some other stuff that's going on around here, Sarah. Stuff I don't think you're going to like very much. But first I have to have a talk with Heather really fast. Could you give us some privacy for a few minutes? Like I said, Jasmine's parents should be here soon, so knock on my door when they show up. And please take that dirty plate back to the cafeteria, it's stinking up the entire office. I've asked you before not to eat at your desk. Bagels in the morning are one thing, but cheeseburgers are disgusting."

"Of course," Sarah says, practically floating.

Lisa pauses as she's about to close the door to her office with me inside. "Where did those flowers come from?" she asks, noticing the bouquet on my desk.

"Prince Rashid had them delivered," Sarah replies. She's in such a good mood now, she doesn't make any disparaging remarks about the repressive regime in Qalif, or large flowers being overcompensation by men concerned about the size of their genitalia. "He sent some to you too, Lisa. They're up at the desk. Want me to get them and bring them back for you?"

"Ugh, no," Lisa says, swinging the door closed. "The smell is making me sick."

As soon as the door is shut, Lisa sinks down into her office chair, pulls open a desk drawer, and brings out a little white plastic wand. "Take a look at this," she says to me grimly.

I examine the wand, which Lisa lays on the top of her desk. It's clearly a wand from a pregnancy test. I recognize it from having seen them on TV and in the movies.

"Oh," I say, attempting to sound casual. "So you did the test already?"

"Of course I did the test already," Lisa says miserably. "I did six of them. I bought three of the kind that come two in a pack." She pulls more of the wands from her desk drawer and lays them out on top of her desk, quite close to Dave's file. "They're supposed to be ninety-nine percent accurate, and they all say the same thing."

"You peed on all those?" I ask, my eyes widening.

"Of course I peed on them," Lisa says. "That's how you find out if you're pregnant." She widens her own eyes at me. "Oh my God. Have you never done a pregnancy test before?"

"Well, no," I admit. "I told you, I've got chronic endometriosis. I couldn't get pregnant without medical intervention even if I never used birth control, and I've never not used birth control, so how am I going to get pregnant?" I remind myself never to touch that area of Lisa's desk again, at least not until I've borrowed some cleansing liquid from Julio and thoroughly disinfected it. Not that I think Lisa is carrying any diseases, but honestly, used pregnancy tests are way more revolting than Sarah eating cheeseburgers at her desk. "So what do they say?"

"They say I'm pregnant!" Lisa cries. "See the plus sign? That means pregnant. Super-duper pregnant. Six times six pregnant." She flops against the back of her office chair. "I have a dead RA, nine who are about to be fired, and a baby. Whoop-de-do! I'm the luckiest residence hall director in the world."

I find myself needing to sit down. I sink into one of the hard-backed chairs to the side of Lisa's desk.

After the information Eva had given me, I'd suspected Lisa was pregnant, of course, but I hadn't fully believed it. Now that the truth is glaringly obvious, I'm having a hard time processing it.

But not as hard a time as Lisa.

"Heather, what am I going to do?" she asks, leaning forward to drop her head onto her desk. "This is so not how things were supposed to go. I just started this job. I have a building to run. I can't have a baby!"

"Well," I say carefully. "If you decide to keep it, I'm sure we can work something out. You bring your dog to work all the time. Why not a baby?"

Lisa, her head still on her desk, lets out a sarcastic snort. "Babies aren't dogs, Heather, in case you never noticed."

"Still, babies are pretty small," I go on, every bit as carefully. "We could probably fit yours in the bottom drawer of that file cabinet over there. No one will ever even notice."

Lisa raises her head. Her face is tear-streaked. "Cory's going to notice," she says, pulling a tissue from the box on one corner of her desk. "We had an agreement: no kids."

"Well, sorry," I say, "but if Cory was that antichildren, he should have done a little bit more to make sure you two didn't have any."

She frowns. "What do you mean?"

"He could have had a vasectomy."

Lisa gasps. "Heather!"

"Why not? It's a simple procedure that only takes half an hour to perform, and doctors do close to half a million of them every year in the U.S. alone." I watch way too much of the Discovery Channel. "So why did Cory never get one? Do you think it might be because he's secretly undecided on the subject of kids?"

Lisa stares at me, her mouth slightly ajar.

"Oh God, Heather. I never even thought of that. Do you really think that's true?"

I shrug. "How should I know? But I think before you make any decisions about this, you and Cory need to have a long talk. And you need to visit your gynecologist too. Six plus signs probably mean you really are pregnant," I say, waving my hand at her white wands, "but you never know. And remember, it's *your* body. Whatever you decide to do is up to *you*."

Lisa's shoulders slump. "That's just it," she says. "I don't know what to do. I feel so awful telling you all this, because I know how badly you want a baby and can't have one, and here I am, never having wanted one, pregnant by mistake, like some dumb teenager on MTV."

"Hey," I say, reaching out to squeeze one of her hands. "It's not like that. If I really wanted a kid, there are steps I could take. I'm just not any more ready to jump on the baby train than you are. But I'll be here for you, no matter what. More important, I think Cory will be too. He completely adores you."

Lisa's gaze softens as she glances at a framed photo on her desk of her and Cory on their wedding day, holding Tricky, their ring bearer. "You think so?"

"I *know* so." I give her hand a final squeeze, then release it. "It's pretty obvious from the way he looks at you. Every time I see you guys together, his face is all goopy and smiley. He really, really loves you."

The tips of Lisa's ears turn red as she flushes, but this time from pleasure, not rage. "Goopy?" she echoes with a little laugh. "That's not even a real word."

"But you know what I'm talking about. That look guys get on their faces when the person they love is around . . . like they can't believe anyone that amazing would ever fall for someone like them. That's Cory, with you. It's like he thinks he's won the lottery or something. You two are going to be okay, no matter what."

"You're exaggerating to make me feel better," Lisa says, but she's smiling as she lifts the wedding photo on her desk and gazes down at it. "I do know the look you mean, though. It *is* kind of goopy. And he's so great around our nieces and nephews. I always kind of suspected he secretly wanted a kid of his own . . . Oh, but, Heather, what if we have this baby and he turns out to be a serial killer?"

"What if you have this baby and *she* turns out to be a genius who finds the cure for cancer?" I hold my arms out wide. "Lisa, the fact is, you and Cory *aren't* teenagers on MTV. You're happily married college-educated adults with great, stable jobs and a kick-ass apartment in Greenwich Village for which you don't even pay rent, in a building assistant-directed by *me*. You're going to make *incredible* parents."

Lisa's flush of pleasure increases. "I hate you so much right now for making this all sound so reasonable. How are Cory and I going to backpack around Peru with a baby?"

"Leave the baby here in the file cabinet. I told you, I'll watch her. Only from nine to five, though, then Gavin will have to take her."

Lisa bursts into laughter.

There's a knock on the door. "You guys?" Sarah asks hesitantly. "Can I come in?"

"Yes, of course, Sarah," Lisa says, hastily dabbing the tissue to her eyes to wipe away evidence of her tears.

Sarah opens the door, popping her head inside.

"First," she says in a low, intense voice, "Jasmine's parents are here. Dr. Flynn already met them at the front desk and has escorted them to the second-floor library. Second, I could hear almost every word the two of you were saying in here." She points at the grate above the doorway. "And I just want you to know, Lisa, all that stuff they say online about the abortion pill isn't true. My friend Natasha said when she took it, she hardly had any cramping."

Lisa drops her wedding photo.

Fortunately, my reflexes are lightning quick, and I save the frame from being smashed against the floor.

"Dammit, Sarah," I say, setting the photo back on Lisa's desk. "What did I tell you about eavesdropping?"

"Whatever," Sarah says, looking bored. "But also, Lisa, if you decide to forgo the pills, I'm an excellent babysitter. Newborns seriously love me. It's why I'm considering going into child psychology."

Lisa's face has gone ashen. She looks like she's about to start throwing up again. "Sarah," she says. "If you tell *anyone* about this—"

Sarah puffs out her chest, offended. "I'm insulted you'd even suggest such a thing. I totally understand your ambivalent feelings toward parenthood, Lisa. You don't want to lose your autonomy, but you also want to be the best mother you can be. Your concerns are completely natural. Also, hormones are raging through your body, so you need to consider that as well."

"That's not the—oh my God. Forget it." Lisa sweeps her pregnancy test wands back into her desk drawer, closes it, then rises to her feet.

"Heather and I are going upstairs to meet with the Albrights," she says, throwing back her shoulders. "Sarah, at five o'clock today all the new RAs are going to receive letters from the president's office informing them that their employment with the Housing Office has been terminated and that they have until Sunday afternoon to find alternative lodgings."

Sarah's face falls. *"What?"* she cries. "You can't be serious."

"I'm serious as a heart attack," Lisa says. "I suggest you not be here at five o'clock, and also that if any of the terminated RAs contact you, you do not engage. Your own employment is none too secure thanks to the continued leaks about Prince Rashid to the *New York College Express.*"

Now Sarah looks stricken. "You can't think *I'm* the one leaking information about him to the—"

"Heather and I don't," Lisa says stiffly. "But a lot of people do, thanks to your past history and your very vocal opinions about Qalif. So if you value your job, I suggest you start keeping your mouth shut, and lay low."

Sarah nods wordlessly, her eyes shiny with unshed tears.

"I'm glad you understand," Lisa says in a slightly more sympathetic tone. To me, she says, "Come on, Heather."

But we've hardly gone two steps when an all-too-familiar voice sounds from the doorway to the main office.

"Ms. Wells! There you are. Where have you been all day? I must have left you a dozen messages. Why haven't you returned any of my calls?"

Mrs. Harris, Kaileigh's mother, comes bustling in, then plops her backside into the visitors' chair in front of my desk, balancing her large designer handbag on her knees and peering out from behind the enormous bouquet Rashid sent me.

"Of course I understand how busy you all must be after the tragedy." She lowers her voice dramatically as she says the word "tragedy." "But I really must speak to you about

Kaileigh's roommate situation. It's gotten a thousand times worse since I spoke to you yesterday. I hope you got the message I left that Mr. Harris is consulting our lawyer back home in Ohio. That's how bad things have gotten. He didn't even want me to come here, but I said I'm sure we didn't have to stoop to litigation, as you seem like a reasonable person."

"Okay, Mrs. Harris," I call to her from Lisa's office. "Thanks. I'll be with you in just a second."

I duck back into Lisa's office to whisper, "Lisa, you go on upstairs to meet with the Albrights. Sarah, you go home. I'll handle Mrs. Harris."

Lisa glances at the clock hanging on the office wall. The little hand is already on five, and the big hand is inching perilously close to twelve. At any moment the letters from the president's office will be delivered to the RAs, and all hell will be breaking loose.

"Are you sure?" Lisa asks, chewing her lower lip uncertainly.

I nod. "I've been shot at before by homicidal maniacs. I think I can handle an angry mother."

What Is New York College Doing with Your Tuition Money?

We all know that tuition is going up at New York College at the same time that large donations from certain Middle Eastern countries are said to be flowing in. What is the college doing with all our money?

Rumor has it that plans have been submitted to the city by New York College to build a state-of-the art fitness center (possibly for the president's beloved Pansy basketball players).

The new fitness center—estimated to cost over $300 million—will feature, among other things, an indoor sand volleyball court, a forty-foot climbing wall, ten racquetball and squash courts, an indoor Olympic-size pool, steam rooms, saunas, four performance studios, twenty thousand pounds of free weights, three yoga studios, two hundred pieces of cardio equipment, and four full-size tennis courts on the roof.

Thank goodness the college is spending all this money on a gym and not on new lab equipment or recruiting better professors, because I enrolled at New York College to get ripped abs, not an education!

New York College Express,
your daily student news blog

21

I'd just finished talking to Mrs. Harris—who doesn't have much of anything new to say, except that she really, really wants her daughter, Kaileigh, to be moved from room 1412 because now Ameera, instead of "slutting it up," is spending all her time weeping—and was typing a letter, when I got a call from the front desk.

It's Gavin.

"Hey," he says. "Some dude just dropped off a bunch of official-looking letters for the RAs. They're from the president's office."

"So?"

"Well," Gavin says. He sounds nervous. "I put them in their regular mailboxes instead of bringing them back to the office to go in their staff mailboxes."

"That's okay," I say.

Dear Ameera, I'm typing. *This letter is to inform you that a mandatory meeting has been scheduled for you in the Fischer Hall director's office tomorrow at 9:00* A.M.

"Well," Gavin says. "You know that Megan chick with the long nose?"

"Gavin, you know better than to call women chicks."

"Sorry. That Megan woman? She opened her letter. And now she's crying and calling her parents on her cell phone in the middle of the lobby, saying she's been fired from her RA position."

This is a nightmare. It has to be. Maybe I'll wake up soon and be in Italy, on my honeymoon with Cooper, and I'll tell him about it and we'll laugh over mimosas.

Probably not though.

"And?"

"Well, I thought you should know about it," Gavin says.

"Thanks, Gavin," I say. I've started another letter. It says the exact same thing as Ameera's letter, but begins *Dear Rashid*.

That's because the other thing Mrs. Harris complained about is that the prince is spending too much time around her daughter's room.

"Every time I'm in there," she said, "it seems like he's knocking on the door, asking what the girls are doing, if the girls want to go out, if the girls want to come up to his room to watch a movie or play with his Xbox or if Ameera got his flowers. Did you know he sent her flowers, exactly like the ones you have here?" She swatted at the flowers the prince sent me, because the bouquet really is quite large, and was getting in her way as she tried to speak to me. "I asked Kaileigh if the prince sent *her* flowers, because you know she was quite badly shocked by the death of her RA too. But *no*, he didn't bother. Only Ameera. But Ameera won't even see him. Every time the prince comes over, Ameera pulls the covers over her head and refuses to even look at him. Well, you and I are adult women, Ms. Wells, *we* know what's going on there."

I'd stared at her in confusion. "We do?"

"Of course we do," Mrs. Harris said. "I'm sure the prince heard what kind of girl Ameera is, and she's playing hard to get. That's why he's sending *her* flowers, and not my Kaileigh. My Kaileigh would never think of doing those kinds of things, not even with a prince, even if he *did* take her and her suite mates to that fancy sushi restaurant for lunch. Because that's all it was, lunch. Kaileigh assured me of that."

I'm not sure Mrs. Harris is right about any of her theories, but I *am* sure that if I can get Ameera and Rashid in the same room—my office—at the same time, I might get some kind of explanation out of them as to what's going on, and that could (hopefully) lead to a clue as to what Jasmine saw the night she was killed, and maybe even a clue as to why she was killed and who killed her.

It's a long shot, but so far it's looking like the only shot I have.

Failure to attend this meeting will result in disciplinary action, I type. *If you have any questions, please contact Heather Wells, Fischer Hall assistant director.*

"Oh, crap." Gavin's voice distracts me on the phone. "That Christopher Mintz guy just got his letter. So did Joshua Dungarden. Oh, shit." He's snickering into the receiver. "He's crying! He's crying! Like a little kid!"

"Gavin," I say severely. "Hang up the phone. But wait, before you do—" I think of my own two letters sitting on the printer. Somehow I have to get them up to the desk so they can be delivered to Ameera and Rashid's mailboxes. Also, somehow I have to get out of the building and home, and I have to do all this without going through the lobby and running into all these crying kids. And also keep those kids from coming back here and trashing this office after I leave, something disgruntled ex-employees have been known to do.

"Can you come back here and pick up two letters I need delivered? And also have Pete turn off the alarm on the side doors so I can leave through them? And then call Carl and have him change the locks to the residence hall director's office, and make sure to give the new keys only to Lisa, Sarah, and me?"

There's a long pause before Gavin says, "For you, my lady, I would clip the wings of a dragon."

I hesitate. "Does that mean you'll call Carl, and the rest of the stuff I asked you to do?"

He heaves a gusty sigh. "Yes. That means I'll call Carl, and the rest of the stuff you asked me to do."

"Great! Thanks."

I hang up, wondering how Sarah could ever have discounted Gavin as one of the decent guys. He's definitely a little weird, but extremely decent.

After he comes back to get the letters for Ameera and Rashid, assures me Pete's turned off the alarm on the emergency side exit that the president occasionally uses as an entrance for party guests when he entertains in the penthouse upstairs, and that Carl's on his way to change the lock to the outside door to the office (the RAs don't have keys to Lisa's office, so that's all right), I shut off the lights and slip away, just as indignant sobs can be heard floating down the hallway toward me.

I know it's cowardly, but after such a long day, I can't handle any more drama. I duck out the side exit, slamming the door securely closed behind me, then see, through the heavy security glass, Carl heading down the hallway toward the office with his toolbox, several of the fired RAs trailing behind him, furious expressions on their tearstained faces.

I've escaped in the nick of time.

Handing someone a letter of termination at the stroke of
five and then fleeing the office is a pretty cowardly act, but
it happens fairly often. The most common day to fire people
is Friday, due to the (mistaken) belief that they'll spend the
weekend calming down, when this is not, in fact, the case.
They can't even use those two days to look for a new job,
because who's hiring on weekends?

This is why it's better to fire people in the middle of the
day, and give them lots of support, than to do it the way
President Allington chose to.

But then, not everyone makes the best choices, and the
choices the Fischer Hall RAs made that led to their being
fired hadn't been very good either. So maybe they and President Allington deserve each other.

Of course, I'm no better, slinking off the way I do. My
shoulders sagging in relief, I turn to begin strolling down the
sidewalk, enjoying the feel of the late-afternoon sun on my
face and the sound of birds tweeting in the trees that line the
quiet side street, happy I still have *my* job.

Unfortunately my calm is short-lived, since I've only gone
a few steps before I realize I've come face-to-face with my
nemesis from earlier in the afternoon: Hamad.

He's holding open the door of the prince's pure-white Escalade as Rashid prepares to step into it. Both the prince and
his bodyguard are staring at me, one with utter hatred and
the other in surprise.

"Miss Wells." The prince lowers his foot from the frame
of the Escalade and quickly crosses the sidewalk toward me.
"Good afternoon. I'm so glad to see you. How are you? Are
you well?"

Confused by his solicitousness—and wary of his body-guard's stony-eyed glare—I take a quick, stumbling step backward.

"I'm fine, thanks. Just heading home. Don't want to be late for my subway, so if you'll excuse me—"

I'm lying, of course. I live only a block away. And how can someone be late for the subway? New York City subways run constantly.

But how's the royal prince of Qalif going to know this? Besides, I don't want any of the newly fired RAs to see me out here on the street, and I definitely don't want to spend any more time than I have to in the company of the extremely unpleasant, woman-hating Hamad.

Or maybe Hamad doesn't hate all women. Maybe he only hates me.

"Please," Rashid says. Today he's wearing a white blazer, instead of a camo-colored one, and poppy-red skinny jeans. He must think this is what American girls find stylish, but he resembles a barber's pole. He gestures toward his tricked-out chariot. "Let us drive you home. You must be tired after having been through so much unpleasantness. Did you receive the flowers I sent you?"

I can't help taking yet another step away from him. My plan isn't working.

"Yes, I got the flowers," I say. "Thank you, they're beautiful. But no thanks for the ride. You're obviously on your way somewhere. I wouldn't want you to go to any trouble." I also don't want him to know where I live, or that I lied about having to take the train.

"Please, it's no trouble," Rashid says. "A lady like you is too beautiful to ride the subway, Miss Wells. The trains in this country are filled with dirty miscreants. We insist that you allow us to escort you safely home."

"No, really," I say, though I enjoy hearing that I'm too beautiful to ride the subway. I have to be sure to tell this to Cooper. "I'll be fine—"

My wrist is suddenly seized in a grip of iron, right below the Bakelite bangle I'm wearing. I look up to see Hamad's fiery gaze burning down at me.

"Did you not hear the prince?" he asks. "We insist that you allow us to escort you."

The next thing I know, the prince's bodyguard is pulling me forcibly toward the car.

"Hamad," the prince says, followed by a stream of words in Arabic. His tone sounds alarmed—for my welfare, I hope.

But he could be alarmed that Hamad is being so obvious about kidnapping me, especially in broad daylight, with so many people around, most of whom are staring at us curiously, no doubt wondering why the dark-haired guy in the suit and shoulder holster is trying to drag the nice blond lady into his car.

I don't want to have to break out my self-defense moves. It will make things awkward with the president's office, I'll bet, if I jam an elbow into Hamad's solar plexus or rake my nails down his face. Sadly I have on flats, so grinding a high heel into the small bones of his foot isn't really an option, but I can still deliver a solid kick to one of his shins. According to Cooper (who's been schooling me), this is supposed to be one of the most painful blows you can deliver to an opponent, aside from the obvious knee-to-groin, which most trained fighters learn to guard against.

Before I have a chance to do any of these things, however, an extremely familiar—and mightily welcome—sound fills my ears: the siren from an NYPD patrol car.

It only has to give a single whoop before I find myself liberated, Hamad releasing me so quickly I nearly lose my footing. The prince puts a gentle hand to my elbow to help balance me.

"Are you all right?" he asks, concerned.

No, of course I'm not all right, and what kind of weirdos are you employing? is what I want to say, but I don't get a chance (and probably wouldn't have said, anyway), since a beige Crown Victoria with a single flashing light on the dashboard pulls up in front of the Escalade, and an older man with a thick head of steel-gray hair—and an equally thick gray mustache—leans out the driver's-side window, an unlit cigar dangling from his hand.

"You out winning friends and influencing people, as usual, Wells?"

It's my old friend from the Sixth Precinct, Detective Canavan.

"Something like that," I mutter, yanking my elbow from Rashid's grip. I head instinctively toward the Vic, massaging my wrist.

"Officer," Rashid says, following me toward the car. What is *with* these people? "I'm so sorry. We were offering Miss Wells a ride home, and my associate got a bit carried away."

"Is that what you call it?"

Detective Canavan is wearing aviator-style sunglasses, the

lenses mirrored, making it impossible to see his eyes. I'm able to see the way his shaggy gray eyebrows are raised in skepticism over the gold-rimmed frames, however.

"You know where Miss Wells lives?" Canavan asks.

"Well, no," the prince admits. "But I was hoping to spare her a train ride."

"A train ride," Detective Canavan says drily. "Of course."

In the passenger seat beside the detective, a younger, heavier-set man, also dressed in plain clothes says, "But, Sarge, I thought you said Ms. Wells lives right around the—"

"Turner, remember what we discussed? When I need your opinion, I will ask for it." Canavan puts the unlit cigar in his mouth. "Wells," he says to me. "This is your lucky day. You got multiple grown men"—he eyes Rashid—" . . . well, semigrown men, anyway—vying for the chance to drive you home and spare you a train ride. Who's it gonna be, me or these mutts?"

The prince raises his own eyebrows, which are neither shaggy nor gray. "I beg your pardon?" He's not used to being called a mutt, which is police slang for a generally unpleasant individual.

"Gosh, Detective," I say, batting my eyelashes. "You know I'm the kind of girl who can never resist an invitation to ride in a real undercover police car."

I grab the handle to the rear passenger door and slide into the Vic, my heart still thumping at my narrow escape.

Canavan looks at the prince and says conversationally, "Kid, don't take it personally. She's got a thing for cops. In fact, she's marrying a PI in a few weeks."

"PI?" I hear Rashid echo. Between "mutts" and "PI," his head is probably spinning.

It could be my imagination, but as I settle into the back of the unmarked patrol car and slip on my seat belt, I notice Hamad's gaze seeming to burn into me.

Maybe it's not my imagination, though. A second later, the bodyguard steps off the curb and strides toward the car, thrusting an index finger passionately in Rashid's direction.

"Mutt? *Mutt?* Do you have any idea to whom you are speaking?" he demands of Detective Canavan. "This man is the Crown Prince Rashid Ashraf bin Zayed Sultan Faisal, the most sovereign heir to the kingdom of Qalif, and you will address him with the respect he—"

"Aw, zip it," Detective Canavan growls, and puts his foot on the gas pedal at the same time as he lays his finger on the control button of his window, closing it on Hamad's temper tantrum.

The Crown Vic slides smoothly out into the traffic on Washington Square West, leaving the bodyguard behind, shaking his fist at us in anger.

"Nice to see you're still doing such a swell job with customer service at the dorm there, Wells," Canavan observes. "Probably going to win employee of the year. Or what's that thing they give you administrators? A crocus award?"

"Pansy. And in case it wasn't clear, that was the crown prince of Qalif," I say. "His dad, General Sheikh Mohammed bin Zayed Sultan Faisal, donated five hundred million bucks to the school."

"Oh, well, la-di-da," Canavan says, holding his cigar out

like it's a teacup, one pinkie raised. "What the hell was all that back there?"

"It looked like the A-rab was trying to stuff her into the Escalade," Turner says helpfully, "and she didn't want to go. Probably going to force her into one of those sex-slave rings, or a harem, like in that Liam Neeson movie *Taken*."

"Once again, when one of your brilliant insights is needed, Turner, I will ask for it," Canavan declares, "but not before. I was asking the girl."

"Sorry, Sarge," Turner mumbles.

"I'm not entirely sure what that was about," I admit. "It could have been simple overzealousness, or it could have been something more. I want you to know, though, that I had the situation completely under control."

Canavan's only reply is a grunt that he somehow manages to fill with skepticism.

"I did," I insist.

"Sure you did, Wells."

"Whatever," I say. "So how did you happen to come driving by? It seems a little coincidental."

"It wasn't. Your boyfriend, Cartwright, called me and said I was going to hear from you, but that if I didn't, I should go check on you, since you were probably in trouble. Given that we at the New York City Police Department have nothing better to do all day but jump at the command of every two-bit private eye in town, I hightailed it over here to save your ass, as I am wont to do on what is becoming a regular basis. And what do I find, but that you are, indeed, in trouble. You, Wells, are what we in the force like to call a shitkicker.

If there's any shit around, I always seem to find you in the middle, kicking it."

I'm torn between righteous indignation over Detective Canavan calling Cooper a two-bit private eye, me a shit-kicker, and the idea that I'd need rescuing in the first place.

Although the overwhelming sensation I'm feeling is waves of love toward Cooper for having done such a dopey, masculine, wonderful thing like call in the cavalry to come rescue me when he himself couldn't be there to do the job. I fish in my purse for my cell phone, pull it out, discover that I've left it turned off all afternoon, turn it back on, and text Cooper:

So you called Canavan to come rescue me? You're going to get a lot more than a finger sandwich when you get home. Love you, you big lug.

I push send before I remember I still don't know what a finger sandwich is (sexually).

"First of all," I say to Canavan, from the backseat, "I am perfectly capable of looking out for myself. Secondly—"

"It's a good thing we came looking for you," Canavan's seemingly irrepressible trainee interrupts. "We almost had another body on our hands."

"Turner," Canavan says, in a warning tone.

"Oh, come on," I say. "Hamad wasn't actually trying to kill me. The prince wouldn't have allowed it. I don't think so, anyway. And besides, I was ready to give that guy my patented Heather Wells chop to the shins—"

"I didn't mean you, Miss Wells," Turner interrupts again. "I meant the kid from the student center, what's his name, again, Sarge? Ripley something or other?"

I feel a cold grip on my spine. "*Cameron Ripley*, the editor of the *New York College Express*? He's *dead*?"

"Dammit, probie," Canavan grumbles. "How many times do I have to tell you to keep your fat yap shut?"

"Sorry, Sarge." Turner looks guilty-faced.

"*What are you two talking about?*" I demand, my heart in my throat.

"Cartwright told us about the little visit you paid to Ripley earlier today, and the tip you gave him, about how the last person who leaked intel about the prince to the school paper ended up dead," Canavan explains. "So we contacted campus security, told them they might want to keep an eye on the kid. Unfortunately, the rent-a-cop got there a little late. Kid had already been strangled. Sorry, Wells. Like I said, you're a shitkicker."

An invitation to a wedding
invokes more trouble
than a summons to a police court.

William Feather

22

I feel a sudden urge to vomit, even though it's been hours since I had anything to eat, and then it was only tiny pieces of bread with delicate slices of salmon between them.

"Stop the car," I say, reaching woozily for the door handle. "I need to get out now."

It's only when the door won't open that I remember I'm in a police car, even if it's an unmarked one. Of course the door won't open.

The backseat of police cars is for suspects.

"What's going on here?" I demand. "Am I under arrest? I

didn't hurt that boy. What happened to him wasn't my fault!"

Except that it was. Cooper tried to warn me.

Now Cameron Ripley is dead, and his only friend in the world, a baby rat, will die of starvation because no one else will be kindhearted enough to leave slices of pizza lying around for him.

"What's wrong with you?" Canavan notices my frenzied attempts to escape in his rearview mirror. "I said the kid was strangled, not dead. He's up at Mount Sinai. He's in serious, but stable, condition."

I quit pounding on the door handle and sink back against the seat, my heart slowing its riotous beating.

"Oh," I say, relief pouring over me. "Well, why didn't you say that?"

"I did," Canavan says crankily. "Strangled doesn't mean dead. Did I say dead? No, I did not. Kid had a cord wrapped around his neck pretty tightly, cutting off his windpipe, so he's not going to be doing any swallowing—much less talking—for a while, but he's going to be all right eventually. Now why don't you tell me just what in the hell is going on over there at that lunatic asylum where you work. Your husband-to-be wasn't too clear when he called. But that's probably because he seemed to think you were in mortal danger, and he's stuck somewhere in traffic uptown."

This only partly explains why Cooper hasn't called *me* in so long, I think, pulling out my cell phone again and checking it for a return text.

Nothing. But this isn't so unusual, I assure myself. Cooper would never talk or text on a cell phone while driving.

Still, you'd think someone convinced I'm in "mortal

danger" would have texted, or even left a voice mail, earlier in the day to that effect.

Quickly I fill in the detective on the addition of Prince Rashid to Fischer Hall's student population, and the subsequent death of Jasmine Albright, and the determination by the U.S. State Department that the investigation into the case be handled by them, and not the NYPD.

"Can they do that?" asks Detective Turner, Canavan's newly assigned, much younger, and much less cynical "probie" (detective-in-training, still under probation).

"They can do whatever they want," Canavan mutters as he drives. "It's the government."

"But they can't possibly argue that *Cameron*'s attempted murder falls under the purview of the State Department," I say. "Prince Rashid's room isn't anywhere near the student center. And they can't know why someone wanted him dead, unless they've figured out, like we did, that Jasmine was the leak. Have they?"

"Do I look like a guy who's got connections with the U.S. State Department?" Detective Canavan demands. With his half-chewed cigar hanging from one side of his mouth, he looks more like a guy who's got connections with the Mob.

"What did Cameron say he saw when you questioned him?" I ask.

"Didn't you hear what I said?" Canavan sounds annoyed. "That kid's not going to be talking for a month. His windpipe was practically severed. Whoever strangled him knew what they were doing. The hospital's got him so doped up on painkillers, you could ask him if the sky is green and he'd write YES! on the dry-erase board they've given him to com-

municate. Nobody's going to get anything useful out of that
kid for days."

"Well, what about the security guard?" I ask. "Did the security guard see anyone fleeing the premises when he found
Cameron?"

"Fleeing the premises?" Detective Canavan echoes sarcastically. "Have you been watching *Castle* again?"

"It's a reasonable question," I say. "And *Castle*'s a very
good show."

"When Security Officer Wynona Perez—it was a female
guard—exited the elevator to the student center's fourth
floor," Detective Turner says, reading from notes he'd evidently taken on his iPhone, "she found the door to the *New
York College Express* ajar, and the victim, Cameron Ripley,
on the floor, apparently having been dragged from his
desk chair by his headphones, the cord to which had been
wrapped around his neck twice and tightened until he lost
consciousness. The offices of the *Express* had been ransacked,
pizza boxes and empty soda containers thrown across every
surface—"

"Uh," I interrupt. "The offices weren't ransacked. That's
how they looked when I was there. Cameron's a student . . .
and a writer. That's how writers are." Private eyes are too,
but I don't feel that admitting this will add anything to the
investigation.

"Oh," Turner says, looking dubious, and continues, "So
Perez unloosened the cord and performed CPR, requesting
emergency services via radio, which responded to the student center approximately five minutes later, three forty-five
today—"

"Turner," Canavan interrupts in a bored voice. "What have I told you about using that thing for note taking? What are you going to do when there's a real emergency in this city and you can't access any of your data because your wireless service has crashed because it exceeded its bandwidth?"

Turner looks confused. "That can happen?"

Canavan digs his notepad from his belt. "You know what's never gonna exceed its bandwidth? Paper. And what have I told you about sharing incident reports with suspects?"

"Not to," Turner says shamefacedly.

I gasp. "*Suspect?* You think *I* tried to kill that boy? I thought you said you came by to pick me up because Cooper was worried about me. I thought you said you were here to *protect* me."

"Well," Canavan says with a shrug. "That, and because you're one of only two people caught on the hallway security monitors going into that kid's office today, besides him."

I'm flabbergasted.

"So you *are* arresting me? Who's the other person? Why aren't you arresting him? Or her?"

"We're having a little trouble identifying the other person," Canavan admits. "Due to the fact that the security tapes are not in our possession."

"What do you mean, the security tapes aren't in your possession? Who possesses them?"

"They were confiscated from the college security office about a half hour ago by someone named Lancaster."

Hearing the name, I begin to fume. "He's with the—"

"—State Department," Detective Canavan finishes along with me.

"So they *do* know about Jasmine being the leak," I say, then chew my bottom lip nervously. I'd chew on my thumbnail, but I only have a month till I get married, not enough time for it to grow back, though my future sister-in-law Tania assures me I can get gel nails that will look almost completely natural.

Surely, I tell myself, it isn't my fault Cameron was attacked. Cooper had to have been wrong about someone following me into the offices of the *Express*. I hadn't seen anyone I'd recognized . . . except, of course, Hamad.

But it couldn't have been Hamad, since I'd seen him going into Fischer Hall shortly before I had . . . unless, of course, he'd doubled back and attempted to kill Cameron.

If Hamad had been the killer, wouldn't he be skilled enough in assassination techniques to have stuck around to make sure he finished the job?

Except who else could have reason not only to suffocate Jasmine, but attempt to choke the life out of the editor of the college's daily news blog?

One of the first principles of criminology—which will be my major at New York College (if I ever get through all my prerequisites and am allowed to begin taking classes in my major)—is that crimes are committed for very few reasons: Financial or material gain (greed) is a major one. Passion, such as anger, jealousy, lust, or love, is also way up there, along with a desire to cover up another crime.

Whenever a crime is committed, a good detective always asks herself one question:

"Who benefits?" I ask, a little more loudly than I'd intended to.

"No shouting from the backseat," Canavan snaps. "The no-yapping rule goes for you too, Wells, as well as Turner here. Can't you see I'm driving? Why I haven't put in for retirement is beyond me. I could be home barbecuing a nice juicy steak in my backyard right now if it weren't for you two yahoos."

"I'm serious," I say. Detective Canavan loves his job, and he knows it, even if training newbies and "rescuing" the girlfriends of private eyes aren't his favorite things to do. "We've failed to ask ourselves the crucial question of criminal investigation: who benefits from the death of Jasmine Albright?"

"Aw, jeez," Canavan says, rolling his eyes behind his aviators. "*Castle* again?"

"Whoever killed Jasmine—and meant to kill Cam—benefited by silencing them about something only they knew," I continue, ignoring him.

Detective Turner likes this game.

"It had to be something about the prince," he says. "And most likely something that happened the night of the big party. Right?"

"Right," I say. "Only *what*? Who would benefit most from keeping that secret?"

"The prince!" Turner cries.

"Jesus, Mary, and Joseph," Canavan mutters.

"I think so too," I say. "And the prince's bodyguard Hamad—the one you saw grab me—clearly feels highly protective of the prince. If Rashid were to be shamed in some way—like being kicked out of school for having drugs, or something—the bodyguard would definitely have a lot to lose . . . not only his cushy career, but maybe even his life, if he were ever to go back to Qalif. They have people executed there for things we take for granted, like fornication."

Turner looks confused. "What's that?"

"Premarital sex. So Hamad would benefit big-time from hushing up any scandal concerning the prince."

"We need to find out if it's that Hamad guy on that security tape from the student center," Turner says.

"Totally," I agree. "Or we need to find Jasmine's phone, which has been missing since the night she was killed. Because I'm guessing whatever happened the night of the party that the killer wants to cover up, she recorded it, and was going to send it to the *Express*, but never got the chance, because the killer stopped her."

"Maybe," Turner says excitedly, "that A-rab guy and the prince are lovers, and the girl filmed them having a homosexual interlude at the party, and the A-rab wants to keep it quiet so he and the prince can continue their shocking affair of the flesh."

Both Canavan and I turn our heads to look at him. Turner goes slightly red around the collar of his shirt.

"What?" he asks. "I saw that in a movie once."

"I'll bet you did," Canavan says darkly.

"If fornication is against the law in their country, you can bet homosexuality is too," Turner goes on excitedly. "Sarge, we'd better bring that Hamad guy in for questioning right away. I think Ms. Wells is right, there's something hinky about him."

"Turner." Canavan tightens his grip on the steering wheel as he fights for patience. "Need I remind you that in this country, homosexuality is not a crime?" His voice rises in volume with each word. "And we are not going to cause an international incident by bringing in the bodyguard of the heir to the throne of Qalif for questioning without one shred of evidence against him because a half-assed probie like you thinks there's something *hinky* about him."

Turner begins to mutter something apologetic when Detective Canavan suddenly cries, "Shit on a cracker!" and slams on the brakes.

At first I think he's reacting to a brilliant insight he's had about the crime, but then I see he's reacting to something else.

We've been driving in circles around Washington Square Park—the most circuitous route I've ever seen anyone take to get to the Sixth Precinct—continuously passing the same joggers, dog walkers, and pedestrians hurrying from work. We're about to pass them once again when I notice what's caused Canavan to slam on the brakes: a group of students, ignoring the "Don't Walk" light, who march straight out into the middle of the street to cross to the college's main administration building.

If the detective hadn't braked in time, he'd have run right into them. Several other vehicles, including the free New York College trolley, have done the same. All of them are honking angrily, the taxi drivers shouting obscenities.

The students ignore them, marching up the curb and into the administration building, their expressions either stony-faced or tearstained.

"Kids today," Turner says, shaking his head in disgust. "They all think they're so entitled. Don't even have to obey traffic lights because Mommy and Daddy always told them how perfect they are, and their coaches all gave them awards for participating, not even winning. I should get out and write each of them a ticket for jaywalking. If I were still on patrol, I would."

"I bet you would," Canavan mutters.

"I know those kids," I say from the backseat.

"What?" Canavan says. "You know those kids? Are they retarded, or something?"

"Yes," I say. "I mean, yes, I know them, but no, they aren't retarded. Those are the RAs who got fired from Fischer Hall for partying with the prince."

Canavan whistles. "No wonder they look so pissed off."

"That's where the president's office is," I say, leaning down in the backseat to see if I can spot the top of the building. I don't know why. It's not like I'd be able to spy President Allington up there, through his plate-glass windows. His office is too high up, and he'd said he was leaving at five, anyway. "I bet they're going in there to demand their jobs back. It won't work, though. The office will be closed."

"Life is rough," Canavan says philosophically. "Especially when you're a kid who had everything one minute, then had it all taken away the next."

"Why don't we wait out here for 'em?" Turner looks excited. "Then we can snag 'em when they come out again, and question them."

"About the shocking 'homosexual affair of the flesh'?" Canavan asks. "Yes, Turner, why don't we do that? Then, after I've pistol-whipped you to death, no jury in the world would hold me responsible because they'd all agree that you're such an incompetent ass, it would be justifiable homicide."

"I can see that you two have some relationship issues you need to work out," I say, leaning forward in my seat. "Why don't you drop me at that corner over there and we'll take this up another time."

I point to a corner of the park where there happens to be a new bakery famous for its freshly made, warm-out-of-the-oven cookies, which it sells—and will deliver, free—with a container of milk. Cookies and milk seem like exactly the right thing to eat after so much talk about murder and attempted murder and affairs of the flesh.

"Keep your Spanx on, Wells," Canavan says. "I'm taking you home, like I promised your boyfriend. Just wanted to make sure the royal guard wasn't tailing us. Wouldn't like them to figure out where you live, now would we, in case they decide to shut you up next?"

I swallow and look behind us. We're not being followed by anyone, though, unless you count the goofy-looking New York College trolley, picking up and dropping off excited freshmen attending various late-afternoon orientation events.

"I'm not wearing Spanx" is all I can think of to say in reply to the detective. "That's insane. Who wears Spanx under stretch cords? They'd show a line across the thigh."

Detective Canavan only grunts in reply as he continues to drive the rest of the way around the park toward Cooper's brownstone. Turner, looking chagrined by his supervisor's rejection of his colorful suggestion, plays Angry Birds on his smartphone in silence. I'm the only one in the car who notices the blind man near the center of Washington Square, over by the fountain.

Unlike other blind men I've seen there in the past, however, this one isn't strumming a guitar for small change or using a German shepherd to guide him. This one is whipping a red-tipped white cane back and forth in front of him like it's a machete and he's Crocodile Dundee, mowing down jungle grass to make a path.

I lean forward to get a better look, not daring to believe my eyes, but they haven't deceived me.

It's Dave Fernandez, all right. He seems to be headed back toward Fischer Hall, a happy bounce in his step that matches the smile on his face. He appears mightily pleased with the way things are going (And why wouldn't he be? He just scored free room and board for a year in one of the most expensive places to live on earth), perfectly unaware that flocks of pigeons—and confused pedestrians—are scattering from the walkway in front of him in order to escape being struck by his cane.

I know it might be wrong, but I'm seized by a sudden urge to laugh. The fact that Dave can be so joyous—so fearless and lacking in self-pity—brings cheer into even my heart, which I've recently been told has become hardened from my job.

All I can think is if Dave Fernandez, who's been through so much pain and heartache, can navigate the crowded paths of Washington Square Park without being able to see, surely I can navigate the paths of my own life, murky as they've gotten lately.

But the sudden surge of optimism leaves me when Detective Canavan's Crown Vic pulls up in front of Cooper's pink brownstone and I see three familiar figures sitting on the stoop, waiting for me.

I thought of wearing white
But I really hate white
I thought of wearing puce
But who the hell wears puce?

"Marriage Song,"
written by Heather Wells

23

To give credit where it's due, Detective Canavan seems to be taking Cooper's request to protect me seriously. He pulls out his service revolver—though he doesn't hold it high enough for anyone outside the car to notice—and asks suspiciously, "You know any of those mutts on your front stoop, Wells?"

"I know *all* of them," I reply in a tired voice. "Unfortunately."

"What do you mean by 'unfortunately'?" Canavan asks. "Should I shoot them or not?"

"Well, it's up to you, but the two girls sitting there with what appears to be a gigantic wedding present between them are my future sisters-in-law," I say. "Although it might make things easier for me in the short term if you shot them, in the long term, it'll probably cause a lot of headaches, especially for you, since they don't look all that threatening. Of course, it depends on what's in the box."

"What about the big guy?"

Leaning against the doorframe with his massive arms folded across his chest is a large black man in a pair of clear-framed glasses. He's wearing a black knit watch cap and a blue Yankees jacket, despite the fact that it's close to eighty degrees outside. At his feet is a duffel bag large enough to hold a young child. He's assiduously avoiding eye contact with Cooper's sisters, sitting a few steps below him in light summer dresses and sandals.

"That's Virgin Hal," I say. "He's one of Cooper's friends. I have no idea what he's doing there, but please don't shoot him either. I imagine he's waiting for Cooper."

"Did you say *Virgin* Hal?" Turner asks, the word "virgin" having roused him from his smartphone. "The guy who looks like a linebacker is a *virgin?*"

"Apparently," I say. "But please forget I mentioned it. It's some kind of private joke. I've asked Cooper not to call him that, but the name's stuck, somehow. Can you unlock the door now? Whatever fresh hell this is that awaits me, I have to go deal with it."

Canavan lowers his old-school Smith & Wesson (it's sad that I now recognize the make and model of individual guns, but this is what comes from being engaged to a private investigator) and presses a button on his console, releasing the lock on my door.

"Using my keen powers of observation," Detective Canavan remarks, "for which, it should be noted, I am well known, I'm guessing that your boy Cartwright sent his pal Virgin Hal over to keep an eye on you until he's able to get home from wherever the hell he is, and keep you from kicking up more shit."

"That," I say, my fingers on the car handle, "is a ridiculous and sexist statement. Cooper isn't like that. He knows I can take care of myself. Hal's probably here to fix the Wi-Fi. It's been on the blink lately."

This is an outright lie. But I can't tell the detectives the real reason I suspect that Hal is on the front stoop, since it will only alarm them, and probably cause them to want to come into the house. This would be a disaster since there's no telling what level of contraband Cooper has holed up in there. While my fiancé swore to uphold the law when he passed the state private investigator exam, then got his license, at times he's been known to bend it a little. Okay, maybe a lot.

"Hal's a tech geek," I explain. "I bet Cooper called him to check his computer."

This is the biggest lie I've told yet.

"A six-foot-eight, three-hundred-pound tech geek," Canavan says drily. "Who happens to show up the day we found you being harassed by a billionaire oil sheikh's son, who I consider a suspect in a murder at your place of work. Sure, Wells. Anything you say."

Canavan's not falling for my fibs, but he's apparently too fed up to question me further.

"Well, it's been great spending time with you, as always,

Wells," he goes on. "See you at the wedding, if not sooner, when we bring you down to the station for questioning."

I've opened the car door and am getting out, but now I pause with one foot on the pavement and turn back to stare at him.

"The wedding?"

It's not that I don't like Detective John Canavan. But I purposely did not invite him to my wedding because every time I see his face, I'm reminded of multiple crime scenes from my past at which he was present, memories I don't particularly care to think about on the day on which I pledge eternal love to Cooper Cartwright.

"Sure," Canavan says, checking out his mustache in the rearview mirror. "The wife's excited about the invitation. She bought a new dress and everything. She's making me rent a tux, so the food at that reception of yours had better be good. We're talking steak, right? I'm not shelling out a hundred bucks for a tux to drive all the way into the city on a weekend and sit there and eat goddamned chicken, especially after everything you and I have been through togeth—"

"Don't worry," I say, from between gritted teeth. "The choices are prime rib, lobster tail, and salmon."

Furious, I slam the door before he can reply, then whirl around to stomp toward the front stoop of the pink brownstone Cooper and I are going to pledge to share together forever in one month. I could almost swear I hear Detective Canavan laughing behind me.

So, apparently, can the small party gathered on Cooper's stoop.

"Who's that?" Nicole, Cooper's youngest sister, pops up to ask, eyeing the Crown Vic as it begins to pull away. "Was that a *police car*?"

"Of course it wasn't, dummy," her twin sister, Jessica, says laconically. She stays exactly where she is, draped across several steps like a fashion model—or a jaguar—too lazy to move. "Police cars are black and white. Or blue and white. And they have the word 'police' written on them. Don't be such an idiot."

"It *looked* like a police car," Nicole says suspiciously, "painted *not* to look like one. And those guys in the front seat looked like undercover cops. Why were you riding around in a car with undercover cops, Heather? Is everything okay?"

I glance at Hal, who seems to have shrunk in on himself a little more every time either of the twentysomething twins said the word "cop." Cops are not well liked among many of Cooper's friends, for reasons I've always been too wise to ask about.

"I'm fine," I assure her. "Those guys just gave me a ride home from work."

Nicole looks surprised. "Don't you work a block from here? Tania pointed the building out once when we were down here shopping for the baby. She said it's that one with the blue-and-gold New York College flags in front of it. She said the cafeteria used to be a ballroom in the old days and was really nice until the college bought the building and did a renovation on it and now it's super crappy and filled with cockroaches and—"

"Oh my *God*," Jessica groans, throwing her head back so that her long, dark hair puddles onto the step behind her.

"Shut up, Nicole. Can we please go inside, where it's air-conditioned? I'm going to die, it's so hot out here. Plus, I have to pee like a racehorse. I'm not even kidding. I was about to go in the street between two parked cars before you pulled up."

Nicole looks nervously up at Virgin Hal, who hasn't said a word. "She was," she assures me, in a whisper. "But I told her it wouldn't be appropriate in front of *him*."

"I'm sure he wouldn't care," Jessica says with a shrug of her slim shoulders. "We're all human. And when you gotta go, you gotta go."

"Um," I say, regarding the odd threesome. "I'm not sure this is really the best time for a visit, you guys. I think Cooper's friend Vir—I mean, Hal, here, has a meeting with Cooper, so maybe it would be better if you girls came back some other time."

"Oh, Cooper isn't here," Nicole announces. Unlike her sister—though the girls are twins, they're far from identical—Nicole is heavyset, her hair dyed an unflattering auburn and twisted into Princess Leia buns pinned to the sides of her head, her summer dress rumpled and ill-fitting. In fact, it appears on closer inspection to be some kind of romper rather than a dress, a garment someone must have told her she looks good in.

Only what salesperson would be so cruel? Nicole looks like an upside-down ice cream cone. Being a big-boned gal myself, I know how difficult it can be sometimes to find stylish clothing that fits well, but I also know better than to buy something just because some salesperson who works on commission says it looks good on me.

"We've been calling and texting him," Nicole complains about her brother, "but he isn't picking up."

Hal uncrosses his ham-size arms to wave at me to get my attention.

"Hey, Heather," he says in a voice that's surprisingly soft for someone his size, though I know from hushed stories I've heard about him that Virgin Hal's shy demeanor is deceptive. Those arms have apparently crushed skulls like watermelons. "Cooper is going to be unavoidably detained. Nothing to worry about, but he asked me to stop by and check on a few things around the house."

As soon as Hal says the words "nothing to worry about," I know I need to start worrying. If Cooper isn't picking up when his sisters call—and he hasn't texted me back either—but he's sent Virgin Hal over to "check on a few things around the house," something is seriously wrong.

I also know Hal isn't going to tell me what it is. That would be breaking whatever absurd "gentleman's code" he and the rest of Cooper's friends have with one another. I'll have to wait until Cooper gets home to find out what's really going on.

"Well," I say tightly. "As you can see, ladies, this isn't the best time—"

"But you have to let us in," Nicole cries, reaching down to lift the enormous silver-wrapped box at her feet. "We brought your bridal-shower gift all the way down here!"

I glare at her. "I didn't have a bridal shower."

"I know," Nicole says. "You wouldn't let us give one for you, which was such a shame, because Mom really wanted to, and so did Tania. I don't necessarily believe in the institution of marriage because it's part of an outdated, patriarchal social system that for thousands of years only benefited men and wealthy women, but if you're going to do it, you should at least allow your loved ones to throw you a bridal shower. Especially if they want to say how sorry they are for ruining your wedding by inviting a lot of people you didn't necessarily want to attend the ceremony—"

"Speak for yourself," Jessica says, springing lightly to her feet. "I didn't have anything to do with that. That was all Nicole. I just really have to pee, so let me in."

I glance questioningly up at Hal, who nods and says in his whisper-soft baby voice, "It's all right, if you know them."

If I know them? What does *that* mean?

I look back at the girls, then say to them sternly as I climb the steps, pulling my keys from my purse, "All right, you two can come in. But just this one time. I know I'm marrying your brother, but that doesn't mean it's okay for you guys to drop in anytime you want. In the future, please call first. Cooper and I are private people with personal lives we'd like to keep that way—private."

"I'll bet you two keep it personal." Jessica shoots her sister a knowing look. "I told you. Now I know what to get you two for your wedding, a new spatula."

I knit my brows as I work the locks to the front door. "What are you talking about?"

"Come on," Jessica says. "*Fifty Shades of Grey?* Don't act like you haven't read it. Everyone's read it." She winks at Hal. "Am I right, big guy? We're definitely not eating pancakes in *their* kitchen."

Hal blinks down at her slowly. "I don't know what you're

talking about," he says, shouldering his enormous duffel bag. "The last book I read was *The Information* by James Gleick."

Jessica hoots at this. "A gentleman *and* a scholar," she says. "Me likee."

"I tried to call," Nicole says plaintively, following me into the house as soon as I've gotten all the locks undone and the door opened. "But you never picked up. I left a zillion messages. You never called me back."

"Things have been a little crazy," I say as I punch in the code to turn off the alarm. "It's check-in week at the dorm, and also—"

"I know," Nicole says. She's sticking beside me like glue, hauling her oversize wedding gift in both arms, so that all I can see of her above the sparkly silver bow are her Princess Leia buns and her eyes.

She isn't the only one sticking to me like glue. My dog, Lucy, is delighted that I'm home from work—and with company for her to sniff, no less!—and is leaping around, barking, her tongue lolling out.

"I know about your mom," Nicole says, trying to make herself heard above the barking. "Cooper already reamed me out about it. Heather, I'm so, so sorry. I didn't know. I mean, obviously, I *knew*—the whole world knows how your mom stole all the money you earned when you were a kid. But like, I never thought if I sent her an invitation to your wedding she'd actually *come*."

"What on earth did you think would happen?" I can't help snapping.

"I thought your mom would call you," Nicole cries. "In my precorps training institute for Teach for America—which, okay, I admit I didn't pass, but that isn't my fault, I have un-diagnosed hypoglycemia—they said in order to reach their full potential, it's important for individuals to *communicate*."

I turn to face Jessica in the cool foyer, which Cooper's grandfather had wallpapered in wide black-and-white stripes (to match the awnings over the windows outside) and that neither Cooper nor I have ever seen reason to redecorate. Jessica has already torn past us in her haste to find a bath-room, while Virgin Hal—mumbling an embarrassed "Excuse me"—squeezes by with his duffel bag in order to head to the basement, Lucy padding after him. She's always been par-ticularly fond of Hal, who has a soft spot for animals.

I don't bother asking why Hal's headed down there be-cause there's only one reason: the basement is where Cooper keeps his gun safe.

The only reason Virgin Hal is here and headed downstairs to the gun safe with a duffel bag is that . . . that . . .

I can't think straight because Nicole won't stop talking.

"So I thought if I could get you and your mom to talk it out, you would have a tearful reunion and make up after all these years of estrangement. I didn't think you would be so . . . so . . ."

"Angry?" I ask her. My head is pounding. "Bitter? Resent-ful? Or that my mom would be such a backstabbing, con-niving bitch?"

Tears begin to trickle from the eyes behind the silver bow. "Heather, I'm so sorry. I didn't know you were that mad at her. You never talk about your mom. I thought you were over it."

I tell myself to breathe. Everything is going to be fine.

Sure, I haven't heard from Cooper in hours, and he's sent one of his buddies here to protect me—and also go through his gun safe—but that doesn't mean anything is wrong.

Yeah, right. And I'm still number one on the record charts.

"Just because someone doesn't talk about something doesn't mean they're over it, Nicole," I say in the most even tone I can muster. "It might mean they've chosen to move on, but it doesn't mean they haven't been wounded, or that that wound, though partially healed, can't be ripped open again, very easily."

Nicole's face crumples. "Oh God. I'm so stupid."

The younger girl lets out a mournful cry, then turns to run away from me. Unfortunately, since she's hardly able to see where she's going thanks to the gigantic wedding gift in her arms, she runs down the hall farther into the house, and not toward the front door to leave.

Great. Now I've done it.

Sighing, I reach into my handbag and pull out my cell phone.

Coop, I text. *Hey, not to be a nag, but where are you? Both your sisters are here, and so is Virgin Hal. He says he's here to protect me, but it seems like he's hiding in the basement instead. Ha ha just kidding. OK maybe not. Love you. CALL ME. Heather.*

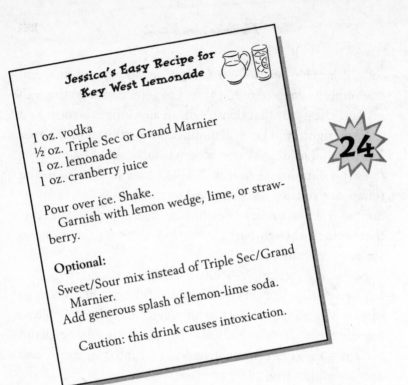

Jessica's Easy Recipe for Key West Lemonade

1 oz. vodka
½ oz. Triple Sec or Grand Marnier
1 oz. lemonade
1 oz. cranberry juice

Pour over ice. Shake.
    Garnish with lemon wedge, lime, or strawberry.

Optional:
Sweet/Sour mix instead of Triple Sec/Grand
    Marnier.
Add generous splash of lemon-lime soda.

Caution: this drink causes intoxication.

24

I find Nicole sitting at the huge wooden table in the atrium kitchen. She's slumped next to her gift, sobbing, her head dropped onto her folded arms.

"Nicole," I say, going to stand next to her. "Come on, it's okay. I didn't mean it. It's not that bad."

This is a lie. I did mean it, and it *is* that bad.

But I realize we're going to be part of the same family soon, so I'd better figure out a way to get along with her, or holiday dinners with the Cartwrights are going to be impossibly awkward.

Nicole doesn't reply. She simply continues to weep.

"Come on, Nicole," I repeat. "I'm angry, but not that angry."

"You *are* angry," Nicole sobs into her arms. "I've ruined everything. And now you aren't going to marry C-Cooper and become a C-Cartwright."

"Well, I was never going to become a Cartwright in the first place, but I'm still going to marry Cooper."

Nicole's head jerks up. She regards me with wide, tear-filled eyes.

"You're not taking Cooper's last name?" she asks in horror.

"Of course not," I say. "I'm Heather Wells, not Heather Cartwright."

"But—" Nicole sniffles noisily. There are no boxes of tissues in the kitchen, so I reach for a roll of paper towels and hand it to her. She tears a sheet from the roll, then noisily blows her nose. "But you realize Wells is your *father's* last name. You'll still be keeping some man's last name, only your father's instead of mine."

"Yes, I am aware of that." My feelings about Cooper's father are similar to my feelings about my mom, only maybe slightly less volatile. Only one of them is related to me, but both of them ripped me off. Cooper's dad did it by owning the record company for which I used to work, that's all. All record companies rip off their artists.

"But." Nicole blinks rapidly. "Why would you do that? Less than ten percent of women in this country keep their own names when they get married. And I thought you loved Cooper."

"I do," I say, pulling out a chair from beneath the table and sitting down beside her. "But I don't see why loving him means I should have to change my last name to his when we get married. I have a choice, and I choose not to. I like my name. Heather Wells is who I am. Maybe if we had kids, it would be different—"

I think, fleetingly, about the perfectly behaved ghost children I used to imagine Cooper and I would have one day: Jack, Charlotte, and Emily Wells-Cartwright, in their navy-blue-and-red-plaid school uniforms. Or maybe Cartwright-Wells. I'm not sure which sounds better. Since they're only ghost children, I have the luxury of never having to decide. That's the comforting thing about ghost children: they aren't real, so you never have to make the hard decisions, as opposed to real children, like the one growing in Lisa's belly.

"But we don't have kids," I finish with a shrug, "and I doubt we will anytime soon. So until we get to that road and have to cross it, I prefer to stay Heather Wells, and let the burden of carrying on the Cartwright name fall on Jordan and you and Jessica."

"That's my name, bitch," Jessica says affably, drifting into the kitchen like an overly tanned, raven-haired wraith. "Don't wear it out. Where do you keep your glasses?"

"Cupboard above the sink," I say, curious as to why she wants to know.

Jessica opens the cupboard. "Bingo. Ice in trays or ice maker?"

"Ice maker is in the bottom drawer of the fridge. There's a scoop. And please do make yourself at home, Jessica."

"Don't mind if I do." Now that she's relieved herself and reapplied her ink-black eyeliner—which had become a bit smeared in the heat outdoors—nothing seems to be bothering Jessica. Well, almost nothing. "What's with the water-works over there, Baby Huey?" Jessica is addressing her twin sister, Nicole.

"I've told you not to call me that." Nicole looks even more upset.

"Well, stop wearing rompers so you look like a baby duck in a gigantic diaper, and I will."

"My therapist says you're responsible for my low self-esteem," Nicole accuses her.

"Has your therapist ever seen the outfit you have on right now? Because it seriously explains a lot."

"Girls." I check my cell phone. Still no response from Cooper, which isn't like him. Unless he's driving or in a meeting with a client, he usually calls back within a half hour. "Remember when I mentioned outside that I have a personal life? Well, you two are seriously infringing on it right now."

"I'm sorry, Heather, but you have to let me apologize about the extra invitations I sent out," Nicole says. "Especially the one to your mom. Jessica, did you know Heather isn't even taking our last name after she and Cooper get married?"

Jessica lets out a whoop of sarcastic laughter as she scoops hefty amounts of ice into three tall drinking glasses. "Why would she? I'd rather be Jessica Wells than Jessica Cartwright. Why would anyone want to be related to *us*? Have you even seen the promos for *Jordan Loves Tania*? Jordan looks like the world's biggest douche bag in those white jeans. More like Jordan Cart*wrong* than Jordan Cart*wright*."

Nicole looks scandalized. "Mom's going to be really upset when she hears Heather's not taking our last name," she declares. "There've been Cartwrights dating all the way back to the *Mayflower*."

"Too bad it didn't sink," Jessica mutters, then asks in a louder voice, "How's Mom even going to know Heather isn't taking our last name? Unless some Baby Huey quacks about it."

Nicole looks prim. "She might notice at the wedding reception when the DJ says, 'Announcing Mr. Cooper Cartwright and Mrs. Heather Wells for their first dance as a married couple' instead of 'Mr. and Mrs. Cooper Cartwright.'"

"We're having a cover band," I say, "not a DJ. But we're having the lead singer say, 'Here's Cooper and Heather for their first dance as a married couple.' It's more intimate that way."

"Ha!" Jessica cries, her catlike eyes narrowing with delight. "She got you there, Nic. How come Heather isn't opening the tasteful gift you got her?"

"Oh." Nicole leaps up, her tears forgotten, and shoves the huge, ornately wrapped box at me. "Here, Heather. I know this can never make up for what I did, but I wanted you to know I'm not only sorry, I want to make amends. So I bought this with my own money, even though I'm unemployed, broke, and probably prediabetic. My parents didn't help pay for it at all, and neither did Jessica."

"I didn't help pick it out either," Jessica says. She's been digging around for something in her purse, an enormous white designer tote with metallic-gold accents. "Nicole did this one *all* on her own."

"Wow, Nicole," I say, reaching up to detach the large silver bow. "You didn't have to go to all this trouble." Obviously, I don't mean this.

"Actually I did," Nicole says. "It was wrong of me to call your wedding planner and give her all those extra names and addresses that I stole from your Rolodex and address book. Although, to be fair, I did it because there seem to be so many more guests on the groom's side than the bride's, which I felt was unfair, even though Cooper explained to me that's how you wanted it. And it was seriously unprofessional of your wedding planner to believe that it was okay with you, and not to call you and check to make sure it was okay before going ahead and sending the invitations out. If you think about it, there's something wrong with Perry. *I'd* make a better wedding planner than her. At least I have your best interest at heart."

"It's hard to dispute that," I admit, especially since the stupid woman still hasn't returned any of our calls. I've torn the wrapping paper from Nicole's gift and now I can see what it is she's gone to so much trouble to lug all the way from the penthouse apartment in which she lives with her sister and parents. "Oh. My. How thoughtful of you, Nicole."

"It's a juicer," Nicole says unnecessarily, since I can see perfectly well by the picture on the side of the box. "According to the personal shopper who picked it out, it's the top of the line. So now you and Cooper can start juicing things, like kale and celery and carrots and spinach. It's way healthier than the stuff you guys normally eat."

"Oh," I say, staring at the juicer. A juicer was not on the list of wedding gifts for which Cooper and I registered. I had not wanted to register for any wedding gifts at all, but Lisa, who'd been married in the spring, warned me that if we didn't register, we'd receive gifts anyway, gifts we did not want. Such as juicers. "How lovely, Nicole. Thank you."

Nicole beams happily. "I'm glad you like it. When you juice vegetables, as opposed to cooking them, more of the nutrients are absorbed into your system right away. In only a matter of weeks, you're going to begin to see a difference. You're going to lose weight, because you'll be too filled up from drinking all the healthy vegetable juice you'll be having to eat instead of all that nasty junk food you guys like, such as pizza and cookies, and your hair and skin are going to begin to glow."

"Wow." I can't think of anything else to say. I thought my skin was already glowing thanks to my exfoliating brush, but apparently I was mistaken. "That's so thoughtful of you, Nicole."

I want to punch her in the face, but I figure this will be even worse for Cartwright family relations than refusing to speak to her anymore, my previous plan for exacting revenge on her.

"Oh, I'm so happy you love it!" Nicole rushes over to throw her arms around my neck. She's crying again, but this time they're tears of joy.

I hug her back. What else can I do?

"Yeah," Jessica says in a sarcastic voice from behind us. "Just what you always wanted, huh, Heather?"

I hear the sound of ice being shaken in a glass. After Nicole lets go of me, I turn around to see that Jessica has pulled several bottles from her voluminous purse and poured their contents into the glasses she's set along the kitchen counter. Now she's shaking each individual glass with a salad plate over the top to keep the contents—which are very pink—from spilling out. A cocktail shaker would have been a more appropriate gift from Nicole—there is one on our registry—but apparently she did not consider that to be healthful enough.

"Jessica," I say curiously. "What are you doing?"

"Giving you a present you'll really appreciate," she says. "Key West lemonade. Vodka with triple sec, lemonade, and a little cranberry juice. I figured everyone could use a drink." She pauses her shaking to eye me. "Unless you'd like me to run down to the deli to buy some kale. We could juice that up really quick, if you'd prefer."

"No. It's okay. The lemonade sounds great."

Trust Jessica to drop by with a portable bar in her purse.

"Jess," Nicole says disapprovingly. "You know I don't drink hard alcohol. Why did you make one for me?"

"It's not for you, dummy," Jessica says. "It's for Rambo downstairs."

Jessica lifts two of the drinks like she's procuring one for herself and intending to take the other down to the basement for Hal.

I know this is a really bad idea, not only because it will freak out Hal, who has always seemed a bit uncomfortable—to say the least—around women, but also because of what I suspect she's going to find in the basement. Not that I think Jessica will disapprove. On the contrary, I'm pretty sure she will like it . . . so much that she'll probably snap photos and post them all over her many social media networking sites.

Then Cooper will be hauled up in front of whatever private eye board reviews these kinds of things and stripped of his license, and also probably sent to prison.

"You know what," I say, snatching both glasses from her hands. "Let me. You stay here and make one for Cooper. He should be here any minute."

Nicole brightens. "Really? You've heard from him?"

"And isn't he more of a scotch drinker?" Jessica asks. Sometimes, even as different as they are, the twins think uncannily alike.

"Oh, no, he just texted," I lie, moving quickly down the hall in the direction of the basement door. "He's on his way. And no, he loves fruity drinks."

If there's a hell I'm going straight to it for all the lies I've told in the past hour alone.

I have to nudge the basement door open with my foot because my hands are filled with sweaty-sided drinks, but I'm able to make it down the dark, narrow staircase unscathed. Cooper's brownstone was built around the same time as Fischer Hall, so it has many of the same odd features as the dorm, such as a basement that was originally used to store coal and ice and possibly even dead bodies—or at least hanging carcasses of meat—so it's dark and creepy down there, and has a tendency to flood because of an underground stream that runs beneath Fifth Avenue, Washington Square Park, and most of Greenwich Village.

Though most similar buildings have converted their basements into laundry rooms or at least parking garages (for which they charge shockingly high rent), Cooper's grandfather never bothered, nor has Cooper since he inherited the place, so it's continued to look like that malformed guy's cave from *The Hobbit* (which I've never seen or read, because it looks quite dull, but I've heard Gavin go on about it ad nauseam).

I find Hal sitting in a puddle of light at a worktable Cooper once purchased during a fit of HGTV-induced home-repair fervor. Only instead of fixing a broken lamp or sawing an unstable chair leg, Hal is loading .22-caliber bullets into a small blue-finished, rubber-gripped revolver. Before him are four or five open gun cases, each revealing other revolvers of various designs and finishes, along with a great many boxes of bullets.

I see that Cooper's gun safe is closed and locked, so I know none of the weapons came from there, and besides, only Cooper and I know the combination, which is Lucy's birthday. The gun cases all seemed to have come from Hal's duffel bag, which is lying on the floor beneath the worktable, right next to Lucy, who is studiously chewing on her left paw.

I'm not certain what to do. Hal hasn't yet noticed me on the stairs, so retreating is definitely an option. I could sneak back upstairs and tell Jessica and Nicole that there's a gas leak and they need to get out of the house, then call Canavan and ask him to get back here, pronto: there's a gun-hoarding madman in my basement.

But before I have a chance to do this, an ice cube in one of the drinks I'm holding shifts, making a loud tinkling noise, and Hal looks up, the lenses of his glasses flashing in the light from the work lamp. He's seen me.

"Why, hello, Hal," I say brightly. "Had a bad day? Violence is never the answer, you know. Let's have a nice refreshing drink and talk about it."

Hal smiles sweetly.

"These aren't for me," he says, gesturing to the gun cases. "Cooper asked me to bring them over."

"Oh?" I take a hesitant step or two down the stairs. "Is Cooper planning on arming a small militant group?"

Hal's smile broadens. "No," he says. "They're for you, actually."

There's the vow row
There's the mom bomb
There's the not now
That's the whole song

"The Whole Shebang,"
written by Heather Wells

25

I have to continue the rest of the way down the stairs and hurry to sit down at the stool opposite Hal's. Otherwise I'd have dropped both cocktails in shock. Once I'm safely seated, I take a long, restorative sip.

Jessica's right. Key West lemonades are quite refreshing.

"Excuse me, Hal," I say politely. "Did you say Cooper asked you to bring over all these guns for *me*?"

"Well, not to use all at once," Hal says, in his soft, breathy voice. "You're supposed to pick the one you feel most comfortable shooting. I was trying to remember the last time you were at the range. Didn't you like this twenty-two?"

I want to enjoy more of Jessica's drink, but guns and alcohol are a terrible combination, so I set both glasses to the far side of the worktable where I can look at them longingly.

"Hal," I say carefully. "Why did Cooper ask you to bring over such a large and varied selection of guns for me?"

"Did he not mention it to you?" Hal looks surprised. "He told me there's someone trying to kill you. Or at least, someone who's already killed one person where you work, and may come after you next. From what I understand . . ." Hal looks nervous. This is probably the longest conversation he's had with a member of the female sex since the last time he visited his mother. " . . . this kind of thing happens to you a lot."

"Okay," I say, after taking a deep breath. "I do get where Cooper is coming from. But I work in a seven-hundred-bed dorm, Hal. I mean, residence hall. I can't go around shooting a gun off in there. I might seriously injure—or kill—someone."

"Uh," Hal says. "That's sort of the point. The nice thing about these pistols is that they're for small-game hunting. Squirrels, rabbits, gophers, maybe a fox or coyote—varmints. You won't do much damage to varmints of the two-legged kind with one of these unless, of course, you're deliberately aiming at them, and they're standing very close to you."

I swallow. "Varmint of the two-legged kind" is a pretty good way to describe Hamad—or whoever it is that killed Jasmine and tried to kill Cameron Ripley.

Still.

"I do not need, nor did I ask for, a gun, Hal," I say, as politely as I can. "Not even one for small-game hunting. Where *is* Cooper, anyway?"

Virgin Hal looks uncomfortable as he sets aside the first pistol and opens the case for another. "He asked me not to tell you, because he doesn't want you to worry. But he said he'll be home soon, and in the meantime he asked me to stick around here to make sure you're all right, in case you have any visitors. Male visitors," he adds hastily, looking toward the ceiling. "I don't think he meant his sisters."

I latch on to only a single word Hal's uttered. "Worry? Why doesn't Cooper want me to worry about him? Is he in trouble, or something? I thought he was working on a simple case of insurance fraud."

"He is," Hal says quickly. "That's what I mean. Nothing to worry about."

So why am I only worrying more?

"Great," I mutter beneath my breath. "I'm the one Cooper's marrying, but he doesn't tell me anything. You, the arms dealer, he tells everything."

"I'm not an arms dealer." Hal looks hurt. "I would never sell any of these. I'm a collector. I only loan them to special friends. And don't you think it's better that someone like me has them than some mutt who's going to do something terrible with them?"

I narrow my eyes at him. "Wait a minute. Did you just say 'mutt'? Hal, are you a cop?"

"I . . . used to be," he says, with his head ducked. I can't see his eyes, because of the thick glasses, but he appears unhappy. "I don't really enjoy discussing those days. Could we please concentrate on selecting a weapon for you instead? It would make me very happy. You're a good shot, you know."

Now I widen my eyes at him. "I am?"

"I saw you at the practice range," he says, glancing up shyly. "You shot very accurately, even though you hadn't had much experience. Many women do, though." There's a hint of bitterness in his voice as he adds, "They tend to have a lighter touch on the grip than men, and more stability in the"—his gaze dips below my waist, and he clears his throat uncomfortably—"lower body area. A lower center of gravity helps with stance."

I have no idea how to respond to this. "Is that a fact?"

Hal is warming to his subject. "Oh, yes," he replies enthusiastically. "The only reason you don't see as many women as men in shooting competitions is because often the women who are the best shots are the ones least interested in pursuing shooting as a sport or hobby. They tend to be like you: they think guns are too violent, or too loud, or are only for criminals, or hunters. That kind of thing. It's a shame."

He sighs sadly, and it's evident in that moment why Hal is still a virgin (if his nickname is accurate): he simply hasn't found the right girl . . . or is too shy to have opened himself up this candidly in front of her.

"Really," is all I can think of to say.

I remember the few times I'd reluctantly allowed Cooper to drag me to the shooting range where he and his friends go to practice firing their weapons (something he feels he's required to do as a licensed gun owner in the state of New York, and also, I suppose, as someone in his line of work). The men had far outnumbered the women there, but there'd definitely been a few women.

One of them had been a bleached blonde wearing head-to-toe pink: pink stilettos, pink minidress, pink hair band, and even pink shooting gloves (to protect her manicure) to go with her pink-handled Ruger. She had fired a perfect heart shape (in bullet holes) around the center of her target from fifty feet away, then lowered her pink-tinted eye protectors, nodded with satisfaction, and walked out, swinging her pink Hello Kitty plastic gun case.

That was the only part of my trip to the gun range that I'd enjoyed. I'd mentioned to Cooper that I'd go with him more often if I could have an outfit color-coordinated with my gun, like the pink lady, but I'd been kidding.

So it isn't completely out of the blue that Cooper has sent Hal over on a mission not only to protect me, but to offer me a weapon with which to protect myself.

Sadly, none of the pistols Hal has on offer are pink. I sigh. I have absolutely no intention of taking a gun to work, but I figure I might as well play along to keep Hal happy.

"Okay. Which one did you think I shot best with?"

Hal looks pleased, and shows me. Once I'm holding the smooth handle in my hand, I remember.

"It's basically a target pistol," Hal explains. "Not at all what I or anyone else would recommend as a gun for personal safety. But you seemed to feel comfortable with it—at least, you hit the target pretty much dead to center every time—and at close range it will definitely maim someone, so that's all that matters."

"How nice," I say.

"Also, it will easily fit in your purse or a deep pocket," Hal goes on, missing my sarcasm. "It only holds nine rounds, but you won't need more than that. The key is to shoot and get out. Never let anyone take the gun off you. Unless they're a police officer, of course, in which case you have to surrender it, but then you'll go to jail because you don't have a license to own a gun, let alone carry it around the streets of New York City. Otherwise, though, never ever give up your weapon, no matter what."

"Okay," I say weakly. Simply holding a weapon outside a shooting range makes me feel a little sick. How does Cooper wear one every day? Maybe Hal is right, and I'm one of those women who is a good shot but simply doesn't like guns. "Are you sure I'm in enough danger to need this?"

"Well, Cooper seems to think so. And if he thinks so, it must be true."

It's kind of funny that just as Hal says this, Lucy, who's been lying worshipfully at his feet, suddenly lifts her head, her ears perked up. A second later, she's barking excitedly and racing up the stairs to the first floor, her foxlike tail streaming behind her.

This can only mean one thing, as confirmed when Jessica's strident voice shouts down the stairs, "Heather! You'd better get up here. Cooper's home. And you're not going to believe this."

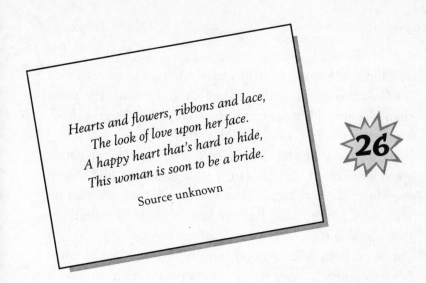

Hearts and flowers, ribbons and lace,
The look of love upon her face.
A happy heart that's hard to hide,
This woman is soon to be a bride.

Source unknown

26

Jessica's right. I don't believe it.

Cooper's coming through the front door, supported around the waist by another one of his bosom pals, Sammy the Schnozz. This is because Cooper's right foot is swathed in a black-fabric-and-metal cast, from his bare toes all the way up to his knee.

When he turns around as Sammy closes the door behind them, I see that Cooper's lip is swollen to three times its normal size, and there's a mouse forming under his left eye as well.

"I'm all right," he says when he sees the horror on my face, and hears the gasps from his twin sisters. He gently fights off Lucy's excited leaps with the foot in the cast. "It's worse than it looks." He attempts a wink and a boyish grin. Both look painful. "You should see the other guy."

Now I know why he called everyone but me. He can barely speak because of the size of the gash in his lip. His speech is garbled, the way someone whose mouth has been shot up with novacaine sounds. I'd have known instantly something was wrong and rushed to him, just as I do now.

I wrap both arms around him, taking over for Sammy. It's only when Cooper winces that I realize he must have a cracked rib or two as well.

"My God," I say, my heart pounding against his. "What happened?"

Cooper kisses the top of my head and whispers, "It's a long story. I'm just glad you're safe. I heard about what happened to the reporter." His arms tighten around me. "Thank God it wasn't you."

But it *was* me. It was my fault, anyway.

And carrying around a gun isn't going to change that, or make it right, whatever Cooper might think.

Now obviously isn't the time to tell him this, however.

Nicole is even more upset about her big brother's condition than I am—or at least she's more dramatic about it. As soon as she sees his injuries, she shrieks, and flings herself at Cooper with as much passion as Lucy, only Nicole's tongue isn't hanging out and she isn't wagging her tail.

Unfortunately, Cooper can't nudge his sister away with his cast as easily as he was able to nudge the dog.

"Were you in a *car accident*?" Nicole wails. "Was anyone else hurt? Were there *fatalities*?"

"No one else was hurt," Sammy the Schnozz says, trying to take some semblance of control of the situation. "Some kid was texting and rear-ended him, is all. Kid is fine, Coop is fine. Give the man some room, okay, ladies, whaddaya say?"

Sammy, who is a pawnbroker, speaks with a strong New York accent and is easily able to command a room, a must when dealing with what are probably stolen goods and hysterical twentysomethings like Nicole.

"Of course," Nicole says, backing off immediately. "Is there anything we can do? Tea? Jessica, go make some tea."

"Tea?" Jessica looks at her sister as if she's gone insane. "When the hell has Cooper ever drunk tea? No one wants tea. How about a real drink? Anyone? I've got some Key West lemonade already poured."

"Lemonade," Cooper says. "Mmm."

I can tell that Cooper is on painkillers, and also that Sammy is lying. I know injuries sustained in an accident from a fistfight when I see one. At Fischer Hall, roommate conflicts between girls result in nasty notes left on refrigerators and bathroom mirrors and social media pages. Roommate conflicts between boys result in fat lips and bruises exactly like the one blooming under Cooper's eye.

What happened to his foot, I can't even begin to imagine, but I know it's not from any fender bender. This is bad. Really bad.

I don't know how bad until Cooper looks down at me, smiles crookedly (thank God he still seems to have all his teeth), and says, "Sure, I'll take a lemonade, Jess. And sorry I didn't call, honey. I was a little tied up."

He giggles. Cooper, who never giggles.

"But Heather," I hear Nicole protest. "You told me Cooper *did* call—"

"Shut up, Nicole," I snap. Her eyes widen with hurt feelings, but I'm in no mood to apologize. I'm too busy checking her brother's wrists for rope burns, thinking he must literally have been tied up to be giggling like that at his own joke. I don't notice anything unusual, however. Just his poor, battered, gorgeous face.

"Have I told you lately how much I love you?" Cooper asks, nuzzling my ear. "You're so beautiful. The most beautiful girl in the world." It's hard to make out what he's saying because of his fat lip, but the gist is there.

"Oh my God," Jessica says with a horse laugh. "Screw the drinks. What's he on? I want some."

Unnerved, I say firmly, "No drinks. In fact, girls, I think it's time you both went home. I need to get Cooper to bed."

Nicole is still looking hurt. "But he's our brother. We want to help."

"No need. I've got him," Virgin Hal says with a sigh, stepping forward from the hallway where he's been lurking. He crosses toward us with so much deliberation that I realize he's been waiting for this: he's known all along that Cooper was hurt, and hadn't told me.

I'm furious.

"Oh, hey, Hal," Cooper says, delighted to see him. "How's it going?"

"Better for you right now than me, old friend," Hal says,

and bends down to lift my fiancé as gently as if he's lifting a child. Then he begins to carry Cooper up the stairs—not without some groaning on Cooper's part, as his cracked ribs are pressed the wrong way, and some grunting on Hal's part. Huge as Hal is, Cooper isn't exactly a small guy.

"What floor, Heather?" Hal asks, his voice strained.

"Second is fine," I say, though Cooper has been spending all his time in my apartment on the third floor since we got engaged. It would serve both of them right if I made them go up another floor. "There's a bedroom on the left."

"Thank God," Hal says, staggering a little.

Nicole and Jessica stand at the bottom of the stairwell in the foyer, craning their necks to watch Hal carry their brother up the steps. It's an impressive sight, and for once the two of them have been stunned into blessed silence.

Sammy the Schnozz, meanwhile, pulls a messy wad of official-looking forms from the pocket of his khaki pants and hands them to me.

"These are from the hospital," he says somewhat apologetically. "It's a simple fracture of the right tibia, they said. In English that means he has a broken ankle. A broken rib too. His face is just bruised. He should be fine in time for the wedding, I swear."

"What *really* happened to him?" I demand. "I know it wasn't a car accident, Sammy. And don't say he came by that shiner while investigating a case of insurance fraud, either."

Sammy glances at Nicole and Jessica. "Uh. Yeah. I better let him explain that to you."

Stupid guy code.

"Anyway, he's got an appointment to see the doctor again

on Monday," Sammy goes on rapidly, perhaps after seeing my face. "Until then he's supposed to rest and take acetaminophen only, not aspirin, as it impedes healing or something? Who knew? There's a prescription for some stronger stuff in there too, though they doped him pretty good at the hospital. He'll probably need to take more later. Oh, and there's a prescription for crutches too. You'll need to pick some up for him. They were out of them at the hospital. They said there's a twenty-four-hour medical supply place over in Chelsea."

Sammy clears his throat uncomfortably. He's a skinny guy in a short-sleeved dress shirt and a straw fedora, with the longest nose I've ever seen. "And may I just say," he adds, "I'm real sorry about this, Heather. But in our line of work, you know, it happens."

"Our line of work?"

I look down at the myriad forms, some yellow, some white, some pink. Since Cooper and I aren't married yet, I haven't been able to put him on my New York College health insurance plan, which is excellent. Being self-employed, Cooper is also self-insured, by some plan I believe he found in his favorite reference guide, the phone book. It is the worst insurance in the entire country. I know, because as his bookkeeper, I'm the one who's had to deal with the company.

You should see the other guy, Cooper had said. If the other guy is worse off, we might be sued. The police might show up to investigate, or the guy's friends might show up first, to finish the job. Maybe that's why Cooper's asked Hal to come over with all his guns . . .

"Heather, Jessica and I have talked about it, and we've

decided we'll go," Nicole says suddenly, tugging on my shirt sleeve.

I blink at her, startled. "I'm sorry, what?"

"We'll go get the prescriptions filled, the pills and the crutches," Nicole says, speaking to me slowly, as if I'm a child. "And then we'll leave, I swear, if that's what you want us to do."

"And I swear I won't take any of Cooper's pills," Jessica adds. "Even though I have nothing to do this weekend, so they'd be excellent for recreational purposes. But I'm really trying to cut down on my recreational drug use and go entirely herbal. And cut down on my alcohol intake, too, of course."

I look from Sammy to the wad of forms in my hands to the twins. Suddenly I want to cry. Not from feelings of depression, but from gratitude, and, yes, even love. I may not have a family—one I like, anyway—but I seem to have friends.

"You'd do that?" I ask, my voice breaking a little.

Nicole's jaw drops in shock. "Heather, yes. Of course!"

"Duh, Heather," Jessica says, rolling her eyes. "We're your bridesmaids, remember?"

"Which reminds me, you have your final fitting tomorrow." Nicole bites her lower lip, then releases it, and asks in a rush, "You still want us to be there, right? *Both* of us?"

I'd forgotten all about the fitting. At this point I can no more imagine squeezing in time for a fitting than I can remember the dress I chose so many months ago—but really it was only last May, right after Cooper proposed, when we'd been planning on an elopement.

But I do know one thing.

I say to the twins, tears filling my eyes, "Of course I want you there. Both of you."

I surreptitiously check the sidewalk before allowing them to leave, making sure it's free of lurking white Escalades, then triple lock the door behind the twins and turn to demand of Sammy, "All right, who was it who did that to Cooper? Tell me the truth. Was it a guy named Hamad?"

"Hamad?" Sammy looks confused.

"Sammy, don't play dumb with me. I know this fight Cooper got into had something to do with me, or Hal wouldn't be here, insisting I carry a gun to work tomorrow. So tell it to me straight. Was it more than one guy? Were they foreign? Were they driving an Escalade?"

Sammy looks even more confused. "There was only one guy, and he wasn't in an Escalade. His name was Ricardo."

I stare at Sammy, dumbfounded. Now I'm the one who's confused.

"Ricardo?" I echo. I'm certain I haven't heard him correctly. "Ricardo is my mother's boyfriend. Or ex-boyfriend, I guess. She says they've had a falling out . . ."

"Exactly," Sammy says. "But not to worry. From what I understand, Coop took care of that creep good. When this Ricardo jokester is released from the hospital, where he's currently being treated for the broken nose and pelvis Cooper gave 'im, he'll be taken straight to the Tombs, then on to Rikers, where scum like him belongs. Coop, he knows how to handle his business, you know what I mean?"

I murmur, "Yeah, I know what you mean," because I can't think of anything else to say.

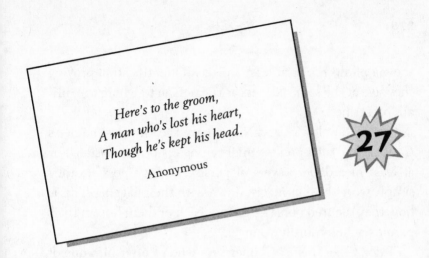

Here's to the groom,
A man who's lost his heart,
Though he's kept his head.

Anonymous

27

Cooper and I are finally alone in his former bedroom—unless one counts Lucy, passed out in her dog bed on the floor, and Owen, the cat, perched on top of Cooper's old chest of drawers, staring at us with slitted yellow eyes.

The painkillers they'd given him in the hospital are finally wearing off, but Cooper is reluctant to take the ones Nicole and Jessica went to so much trouble to get. Pharmacists no longer hand bottles of controlled substances over to just anyone, it turns out. They will only give them to the person to whom they are prescribed, and that person must show a photo ID, or at least a piece of identification proving they live at the same address as the person to whom the pills are prescribed.

Fortunately Jessica and Nicole have the same last name as Cooper, and also possess mighty powers of persuasion—or at least incredible powers of persistence. It's possible they simply wore the pharmacist down with their nagging. This is how they secured ponies—one for each of them—from their parents at an absurdly young age.

"I don't like them," Cooper says when I offer him one of the pills. "They make my head feel fuzzy."

This comes out sounding like "Day bake by hade beel bunny," because of his mouth injury.

"I don't care," I inform him. "You need sleep, in order to heal. It's called pain management. If you don't take a pill now, you're going to wake up screaming in agony in a few hours."

"Wow," Cooper says, obediently accepting the pill, along with a glass of water (into which I've inserted a straw for his sipping convenience). "Has anyone ever told you that you have a terrible bedside manner? I'm glad I was never a soldier gassed in the front lines of the Great War, and you were never my nurse."

"I never would have volunteered to be a nurse in the Great War," I say, taking the water glass away from him when he's swallowed the pill and setting it on the bedside table. "I would have volunteered to be a sharpshooter, and apparently excelled at it, according to Hal."

Hal, who's announced he's staying the night—and possibly the next few nights—is sleeping in Cooper's office downstairs. The contents of his duffel bag turned out to include several changes of clothes, a toothbrush, and the book he's currently reading, as well as multiple firearms.

I offered him the guest room instead of the couch—which folds out but isn't as comfortable as a bed—but he thanked me politely and said he preferred Cooper's couch. Cooper later informed me this is because his office has the best view of the street, so Hal can see anyone who might come up the front steps.

"Wouldn't it make more sense for an intruder try to break in through the back?" I asked.

Cooper shook his head. "That's what the alarm is for. Hal's worried about someone disguised as a pizza delivery-man walking up to the front door and knocking. Only none of us ordered pizza, and pizza's not what's in the box."

"Now you guys are being ridiculous," I said, rolling my eyes.

"Are we?" Cooper asked. "You said that blogger ate a lot of pizza, and look what happened to him. Maybe that's how his attacker got in."

There's not going to be any convincing Cooper that anyone could easily have snuck up behind Cameron Ripley and strangled him—he sits with his back to the door of the *Express*'s office, typing with earbuds in his ears—so I let it drop. Let Hal stare at the front porch for mysterious assassins disguised as pizza deliverymen who are allegedly coming after me. I have bigger fish to fry.

"So is Hal here," I finally ask Cooper, when his lids have become droopy from the painkiller and I know I'm likely to get the truth from him, "because you're worried about what's going at my place of work, or because you're worried about what's going on with my mom?"

Cooper shakes his head in bafflement. He wasn't wrong about the pills making him fuzzy-headed. "What do you mean?"

"There's no use pretending anymore," I say, reaching out to lightly run a finger down his cheek. It's already rough with razor stubble, and likely to get rougher as the days go by. With a broken ankle, cracked rib, and fat lip, he won't be bothering to shave. "I know you weren't in a car wreck. Sammy the Schnozz squealed."

"See if I ever do him another favor," Cooper says after a beat, with genuine bitterness. "You just can't trust people anymore, Heather."

"No, you can't, can you? Cooper, I believe I asked you to leave the thing with my mother alone."

"And I believe I told you that as a licensed private investigator, I couldn't. Heather, don't you get it? I couldn't *not* follow her."

"And look where it got you!" I've sat down on the bed beside him. Now I spread my hands to indicate his bandaged ankle and ribs. "This is what she does. She ruins everything she touches."

He captures one of my outspread hands, then kisses the back of it very gently so as not to hurt his badly bruised lips.

"Not everything," he says, with a lopsided smile. "Not you. Not this time. I didn't let her."

"Oh, right," I say, sarcastically. "So this time instead of hurting me, she hurts you. That's so much better, Coop."

"Come on, Heather. You think this is bad? Believe me, I've had much worse. In a couple of weeks, there won't be a scratch on me. And this had nothing to do with your mom—"

"Oh, right!" I cry again.

"Okay, well, maybe a little. She hangs out with some rough customers, your mother."

I shudder, then lay my head on his shoulder—carefully, so as not to disturb his rib—wrapping one arm around him. "Why do you think I told you to leave it alone? My God, Cooper, you could have been killed."

He grins crookedly, then winces. "Glad to hear you have so much faith in my abilities."

"I'm serious. Ricardo was never the nicest guy."

"Sorry to disappoint you, Heather, but I don't meet a lot of nice guys in my line of work. I'm not exactly a librarian."

"Yeah, but do librarians hang out with mobsters? Because I'm pretty sure Ricardo owed money to the Mob."

"Well, that could explain why he was so interested in your mom. She clearly has a lot of cash to spend. I started tailing her when she came out of your dad's apartment building this afternoon. She headed straight to Fifth Avenue to hit all the usual suspects—Tiffany's, Bergdorf's, Van Cleef and Arpels. It wasn't until we got to Prada that I realized I wasn't the only one tailing her."

I lifted my head from his shoulder. "You mean Ricardo—?"

"Caught him behind her just as she was exiting the store. I recognized him right away. He's aged a bit, but not that much. Plus, he's a pretty crummy tail. He had on a trench coat and fedora, pulled down low over his face, for Christ's sakes. Who wears an outfit like that when it's eighty degrees outside? The guy's clearly an amateur."

"So what did you do?" I ask.

"I said, 'Hey, Ricardo, long time no see,' and the guy's so

freaked out, he pulls a knife on me. I had no choice but to disarm him."

I gasp and sit up. "Cooper! Are you crazy? You could have been stabbed."

"There were ladies present, including your mother," he says, indignantly. "What was I supposed to do? As soon as she recognized Ricardo, your mom started screaming like she'd seen the antichrist. And even then, it took store security forever to figure out what was going on and call the cops. By the time they arrived, old Ricardo and I were already out on the sidewalk. He tried to push me under a cab—"

"Where was my mom?" I interrupt.

"Disappeared," Cooper says. "Didn't see her again once the cops peeled Ricardo and me apart."

I press my lips together, thinking dark thoughts about my mother, who hadn't even had the decency to stick around to help my fiancé while he was being half beaten to death by her ex—even if Cooper had eventually turned things around, and ended up winning the fight.

"Anyway, it just goes to show," Cooper says, playing with a long strand of my hair, "things aren't always what they seem."

"What do you mean? I think things are *exactly* the way they seem. My mother is a no good dirty—"

"Oh, Heather." Cooper cuts me off, shaking his head, then winces when the pain stops him. "So beautiful, yet so cold. I mean it just goes to show that your mother's motives for showing up here the other night may not have been entirely duplicitous. Judging by the size of the knife that guy pulled on me, I think she had reason to believe she was in trouble—real trouble—and needed our help, but she didn't know quite how to ask for it, especially after the way she's treated you all these years."

After this speech—which is a bit hard to understand thanks to his busted lip—Cooper reaches for the water glass, and takes a long drink through the straw.

"Why *would* I help her?" I demand. "Especially now! What has she ever done for me . . . or you? Except nearly get you killed today."

"I brought that on myself," he says, when his mouth is less dry, one of the side effects listed on the pill bottle. "As you pointed out, I should have left well enough alone. But . . . well, it's not in my nature. Let's face it, though: it's not in your nature, either, Heather. That's why we make such a perfect pair. We're lucky to have found each another. I feel sorry sometimes for people like your mom. Maybe her problem isn't that she's a dirty, no good whatever-you-were-going-to-call-her. It's that she was never lucky enough to find her soul mate, like we were."

I frown, even though I know there might be something to what he's saying. Still, this isn't something a girl likes to admit . . . especially since I can't help thinking back to Detective Canavan's unpleasant assertion that I'm a shitkicker. That makes Cooper one, too. So we're a couple of shitkickers in love?

How romantic.

"What about my poor dad?" I ask. "If my mom's taken off with Ricardo's money—and knowing her, you can bet that's what this is all about—then she's putting Dad in danger, staying with him." I snap my fingers. "This completely explains why she didn't want to stay in a hotel! She knew if she used a credit card, Ricardo could find her. Not that he didn't manage to find her anyway. Oh, this is a nightmare." I groan and cover my eyes.

"It's not as bad as all that," Cooper says. "Ricardo's going to be in the Tombs until at least tomorrow morning. Then if he can't make bail—which I doubt he will, since he resisted arrest, and you know how fondly judges look upon that— he'll be shipped off to Rikers. So wherever your mom's taken off to, she's got a good head start on him. And your dad's fine. He just ordered in Chinese food."

"Wait." I drop my hands away from my face in order to stare at him. "How do you know that?"

Sheepishly, Cooper holds up his cell phone. There's a text on it from someone called Kenny.

"You're having my dad's apartment building staked out?" I cry.

"Of course not," he says, as if this would be completely unreasonable. "I just bribed the doorman to keep me up-dated on your dad's activities."

"Oh," I say in mock relief. "That's so much better."

"See," Cooper says. "This is why I never wanted you to know the details of what I do for a living, because it's not pleasant. I spy on people. I'm always going to spy on people, even when I get beat up for doing it, and even when I'm not getting paid to do it. I *like* spying on people. It's what I do, Heather. And if you're going to be married to me, you're going to have to get used to it."

I lean back against the pillows and eye him, taking in the stubborn slant of his jaw, and the challenging gleam in his eye. "Gosh. You mean you wouldn't quit detecting if I asked you to?"

"No. Would you quit writing songs and working in the dorm if I asked you to?"

"No. Not unless you had some sort of fatal disease and you wanted me to come with you to the south of France to enjoy your last few months of life."

"Oh," he says, his features relaxing. "Well, that would be a different story. I would completely quit detecting to nurse you through a fatal disease, especially in the south of France."

I reach out to brush back a dark strand of hair that's fallen across his forehead. "I had no idea being a private detective was so . . . complicated. From your billing, it certainly looks boring."

"It usually is," Cooper says. "But like I said . . . things aren't always what they seem."

"Yes, I can see that now." I kiss the place on his forehead where the strand of hair had lain. "Well, enough about fatal diseases. Is there anything I can do to make you feel better right now?"

One of Cooper's dark eyebrows lifts. "I don't know. What did you have in mind?"

"I'm not sure," I say, my hand creeping beneath the sheet. "Where does it hurt?"

"Well," he admits. "Kind of *everywhere.*"

"What about here?" I ask, raising an eyebrow of my own.

He inhales. "I might need a little attention in that area. You did say something earlier about a finger sandwich, if I recall."

"Yeah," I say. "I'm not so sure you want one of those. I looked it up a little while ago. That's when a girl has sex with two guys at once. I could call Hal up here, if you—"

"I very definitely," Cooper says, "do *not* want a finger sandwich, ever."

"Message received," I say, flipping back the sheet. "Let's see what I can do to change your mind about my nursing abilities."

I did change his mind, thoroughly.

Students Allegedly Made Homeless by College Administration

College officials are declining to comment on the fact that nine resident assistants—more than half the staff—have been fired from their positions at Fischer Hall for "behavior not tolerated by this institution" and told to find alternative housing by Sunday.

The "behavior" in which the RAs are alleged to have been engaging is one most New York College students have engaged in at one time or another: partying.

These nine RAs, however, were allegedly partying with the prince of Qalif, and also with underage residents from their floors. Alcohol is said to have been present at this party in large quantities.

The morning after the party, a fellow Fischer Hall RA, Jasmine Albright, was found dead in her room in Fischer Hall. Cause of death has not yet been released by the medical examiner, but sources tell the *Express* that the student was not seen drinking at the party.

A petition has already been started by some of the RAs' freshmen residents in order to "save" the RAs' jobs.

"I love my RA," says freshman Lindsay Chu, "and I don't think it's fair that she got fired for something everyone else was doing too. And it isn't her fault that that a girl died. Everyone drinks. Who cares?"

So far the petition has over fifty signatures. None of the Fischer Hall RAs were available for comment.

New York College Express,
your daily student news blog

28

Cooper is still asleep when I leave for Fischer Hall the next day. The pills—and no doubt exhaustion, since it turns out I possess surprisingly excellent nursing skills—have finally knocked him out. I post a long list of instructions for Hal on the door to the refrigerator, which he eyes nervously.

"I think Coop wanted me to go with you," Hal says. "You know, to protect you from the crazy person who's killing people where you work, and from your mom's boyfriend too."

I laugh humorlessly. I know things must be pretty bad if Virgin Hal would rather hang out with me, a lady, than Cooper. Cooper's not exactly someone who enjoys spending time in bed . . . unless I'm there with him, of course.

"I think my mom's boyfriend is more interested in going after her than me, Hal," I say. "Besides, it will look weird if I have a bodyguard following me around the residence hall. And someone has to stay here and help Cooper. He's got a broken rib on top of a fractured ankle. He can't use the crutches yet. Who's going to bring him breakfast and make sure he takes his pills?"

The answer to this question should be me, but no way am I calling in sick to stay home to play nursemaid to my injured fiancé, even if he did do something incredibly brave and noble. I have a meeting with Rashid and Ameera at nine, and I'm not missing it, though I plan to come home right after.

Of course, I'll have to rush out again straightaway, since I have my final wedding gown fitting at noon. No way can I miss that appointment the way I did the one with our wedding planner.

"Well," Hal says, dubiously eyeing the list I've left, which says *Bring Cooper breakfast* as the first item, with *Order egg, cheese, and ham breakfast sandwich from deli (for delivery)* beneath it, and the number for the deli under that. Attached to it is a ten-dollar bill (I've included money for Hal's breakfast, and a deli menu), and then, beneath that, because I'm not sure Hal knows, I've written, *Deli guy is our friend. He will not hurt us. Do not shoot him.*

"I don't know," Hal says, slowly, still staring at the list.

"Look," I say. It's nearly nine. "Have Cooper call me when he wakes up."

I'm almost out the door before Hal calls me back. "Heather! You forgot something."

I hurry back only to have him slip the .22 into my purse. Its weight makes the bag considerably heavier.

"It's loaded," Hal says, looking furtively up and down the street. The sky is overcast, for a change, and thankfully there aren't many people around. "The safety is on. Remember what I said. Never, ever give up your weapon, no matter what. Not for any reason. Have you read *The Onion Field*?"

Oddly, I have. It's a fact-based novel Cooper keeps around the house and which I've flipped through (unlike *The Hobbit*). That's because it's based on a true incident in which a police officer in California surrendered his gun to a criminal who was holding the officer's partner hostage. The criminal then shot the officer's partner with the gun. The case caused police departments across the country to enforce a strict new rule: No officer is to surrender his weapon under any circumstances whatsoever.

Although the incident had to have occurred before Hal was born, the fact that he keeps insisting I not give up my weapon, no matter what, gives me sudden insight into why he's no longer on the force, and also why he himself owns so many weapons. He must have been put into a similar situation as the officer in the onion field, and broken the rule, with similarly tragic consequences.

"I have read it, Hal," I say gently, instead of what I want to say, which is, *Get this thing out of my purse.* "I'll be sure not to let anyone else get their hands on my weapon."

"Good. If you won't let me protect you," Hal says, his eyes looking oddly bright behind the thick lenses of his glasses, "at least protect yourself. You know it's what Cooper would want."

"Yes," I say. "I do. Thank you very much, Hal. And thank you for looking after Cooper."

Hal nods briskly, then quickly closes the door, probably so I won't see him looking misty-eyed. I'm glad, because I've grown a little misty-eyed, as well . . . which is absurd. Almost as absurd as the fact that I'm taking a target pistol to work. Fortunately, the bottom drawer to my desk locks. I'll put my purse in it—after I've removed all the files—and lock it in there. Explosives, fireworks, firearms, and ammunition are all prohibited in the residence halls, and subject to confiscation and disposal if found, according to *The New York College Housing and Residence Life Handbook.* I'm fairly certain this applies to employees as well as residents.

I noticed the night before when checking my e-mail that someone at the *Express*—not Cameron Ripley, obviously—had posted a story online about the RAs being fired. It had garnered a number of comments, most of them in favor of the RAs.

So I'm not surprised when I turn the corner and see student protesters marching in front of Fischer Hall, holding signs that say NEW YORK COLLEGE UNFAIR! and I LOVE MY RA! while chanting, "Hire back my RA!"

Most of the students are obviously freshmen. Freshmen, though adorable, are sometimes easily led, especially during the first few weeks of school, before they've become hardened and jaded, like me. That's why so many solicitors gravitate to the park in the autumnal months, offering free microwaves to kids who sign up for credit cards—carrying absurdly high interest rates—and passes to "rock concerts"—which turn out to be prayer meetings with a little live music thrown in.

"Heather!" One of the freshmen holding a sign rushes up to me. I recognize Kaileigh Harris. Two of her suite mates— but not Ameera, I notice—and Kaileigh's mother are trailing right behind her.

It's *way* too early for this.

"Heather," Kaileigh says, when she reaches me. "Did you hear what happened? They fired all the RAs!"

"Well," I say. "Not all of them. Only the ones who went to the prince's party."

"But it's not fair," Nishi, her suite mate, cries. "The RAs are students, just like us."

"Yeah," Chantelle, Kaileigh's other suite mate, says. "Why should they be punished when none of the rest of us got punished?"

No. Not this. Not before I've had coffee.

"You guys," I say. "I'm not saying I don't think the rest of you should be punished, because believe me, I do. But do you think it's possible there's more to the story"—like that a girl died, and the RAs covered up knowing at least a little about why—"and that maybe things aren't always what they seem?"

I'm consciously echoing Cooper's words from the night before.

"Oh, no," a fourth girl says, stomping up to me in her lime-green combat boots, her sign slung over one shoulder. "Things *are* exactly how they seem. We know *everything*. My RA, Megan, told me. The fact is that you, the administrators, don't care about us, the students, the people who pay your salary! Well, it's time we took charge. We want our RAs back! We. Want. Our. RAs. Back!"

Her chant is quickly picked up by the rest of the students, some of whom I now see are the fired RAs. Megan is one of them. She's giving me a slant-eyed look through her horn-rimmed glasses as she marches around in front of the hall.

I resolve to make sure Megan's final paycheck takes quite a circuitous route in getting to her, wherever Megan ends up after moving from the building.

"Ms. Wells," Mrs. Harris sidles up to me to say. She looks worried. I can hardly blame her. "Do you know anything about this?"

"I do," I say, forcing a smile onto my face. "Please don't worry about it, Mrs. Harris. We have some really great candidates in line to replace the RAs we've lost."

Well, one great candidate.

"We've already met him," Mrs. Harris says bleakly. Today she's dressed all in tones of lemon. How can she look so well put together so early in the morning? "Last night, while we were having dinner in the cafeteria, your assistant, whatever her name is, the one with the frizzy hair, was introducing him around. No offense, Ms. Wells, but are you aware he's *blind*? Our daughter's going from a dead RA to a blind one? Excuse me, but how is that going to work? What if there's a fire?"

I look upward at the overcast sky, fighting for patience.

"Well, Mrs. Harris," I say, after I've counted to three. "I'm sure if there's a fire, Dave will hear the alarm, smell the smoke, and get his residents to safety, *just like a sighted person*. Now, if you'll excuse me, I have to get to my office."

I storm past her, but I don't head for the office. I head for the cafeteria. I need that coffee and a bagel.

"Morning," Pete says glumly as I pass the security desk. He knows better than to speak to me too cheerfully in the A.M. He feels the same way about mornings.

"Are you seeing this?" I ask, pointing over my shoulder at the picketers. "Are you picking it up on your monitors?"

"Unfortunately," he replies, just as glumly. "They've been at it since eight. They've got a group of 'em protesting in front of the president's office as well. Some of 'em have got their parents driving in too, from what I hear."

I roll my eyes. "Shoot me." Then I remember what I have in my bag. "I mean . . . never mind."

Pete nods solemnly. He has a cup of coffee and a bagel on his desk, so he's already several steps ahead of me. "Just so you know, there's a bunch of 'em waiting outside your office. Couldn't get in because you changed the locks last night— good move, by the way—but all that seemed to do was raise their fighting spirit."

I say a curse word I normally reserve for when I've stubbed a toe or forgotten to order paper for the photocopier.

"I heard that!" Gavin's voice drifts out from behind the front desk. "That can only mean one thing. Heather Wells is in the house!"

"Shut up, Gavin," I say moodily, and continue toward the cafeteria.

"Is that any way to talk to your most devoted employee?" Gavin calls. "Hey, stop by the desk on your way back. I have a message here for you."

"Okay." I mutter the curse word again, this time under my breath.

Fortunately Magda has anticipated my needs, and has forced Jimmy to set a bagel aside for me, before the ravenous hordes of protesters could wipe him clean of baked goods.

"You poor thing," she says as Jimmy surrenders the bagel. This time he's too busy to toast it for me—a wave of freshmen leaving for an orientation trip to Central Park has come in ahead of me—so I'm forced to cut it in half myself with the large serrated knife left on the cutting board by the bagel basket for that purpose. "I heard about Cooper. How is he? How are *you*?"

Her question takes me by surprise. "How did you know about Cooper?"

"Bridesmaid hotline," she says, holding out her phone. "Nicole told me. All these people texting while driving. It should be against the law."

Of course. Nicole told her what she knew, which wasn't the truth . . .

"Cooper's doing as well as can be expected," I say as Magda

walks me toward the coffee dispenser. "And there *is* a law against texting while driving. But that isn't exactly what—"

"You know what I was thinking? If his foot isn't better in time for the wedding, he can use a—what are they called? Mr. Jazzy? Those little carts the very old people use at the grocery store."

"Jazzy power scooter?" I ask in horror.

"Yes." Magda claps her hands delightedly. "You will look so nice in your beautiful white dress and veil, sitting on his lap, as Cooper drives you around on the dance floor at that fancy hotel on his Mr. Jazzy."

My coffee-and-hot-cocoa drink secured, I say, "You always look on the bright side of things, don't you, Magda?"

"Well, I try," she admits with a modest shrug. "It's just my way."

"Cheers," I say, saluting her with my coffee mug. Then I head back to my office.

"Heather!" Gavin stops me. "Hells, woman. What is wrong with you? You walked right by without stopping to say hello or get the message Lisa left for you."

I take a fortifying sip of coffee. "Lisa left me a note? She isn't in the office?"

"Nah," Gavin says. As usual, since he's working the morning shift, he's in his pajamas, which today consist of blue New York College sweatpants, a Ramones T-shirt, and his usual Goofy slippers. "She and Cory left about a half hour ago. She said she has a doctor's appointment. Good thing too, she looked pretty sick. Probably all these damned RAs." He looks disapproving. "They're making me sick too.

She stopped to write this for you, though, before she left."

Gavin slides a sealed envelope toward me. I set my bagel and coffee drink on the counter, tear open the envelope, and find a folded note, written on New York College stationery, in Lisa's distinctive, loopy handwriting.

– **New York College** –

Heather,

Sorry to leave you in a lurch like this, especially with the RAs acting so nuts, but I called my doctor last night like you said to, and she was able to squeeze me in for an appt. first thing this morning. I should be back by 11:00 a.m., noon at the latest. I haven't forgotten your fitting, don't worry! Thanks, you're the best!

Lisa

P.S. I told Cory. You were right, he's over the moon! And now, I have to admit, so am I!

Smiling, I refold the note, slip it back into the envelope, and stick the envelope into my purse.

"What's so funny?" Gavin asks.

"What?" I ask, trying to wipe the grin off my face. "Nothing. Mind your own business. Have you finished the mail forwarding from yesterday? Because that pile over there doesn't look like it's getting any smaller to me."

"Damn, woman!" Gavin cries. "Why you gots to be that way?"

"I'm not paying you to work on your screenplay, Gavin," I say, pointing at his laptop, which is sitting open in front of him. "Do the mail. And why are those flowers from Prince Rashid still back there?"

Gavin looks over his shoulder. "Those are the ones for that girl in fourteen-twelve. I've left her like four notices. She says she doesn't want them. So can I give them to Jamie? *Please?*"

"No, you may not," I say. "Items left at the desk are not yours for regifting. Get to work on that mail."

But Gavin can see that I'm still smiling. I'm finding it impossible not to.

"Seriously," he calls as I walk away from the desk. "What did the note say? Obviously it was good news. But what kind of good news could Lisa possibly have had on *today* of all days?"

"Not good news," I call to him over my shoulder. "The *best* news."

"We're all getting raises?" Gavin shouts, in a hopeful tone.

"You wish!" I shout back at him. "Get to work."

I realize it's a little premature—okay, a lot premature—

but I'm picturing all the fun Lisa and I are going to have with her baby in the office (I was serious about making a little cradle for it in one of the file cabinet drawers). It's going to be especially fun for me because it's not *my* baby, so I don't have to worry about changing diapers or sleepless nights or paying for college or it growing up to be a serial killer. I'm thinking about names—I wonder how Lisa will feel about Charlotte or Emily if it's a girl?—when I turn the corner to the residence hall director's office and see all the people lined up outside it.

Weirdly, the door to the office is propped open—as it usually is when I'm at my desk—only I'm not at my desk, and I had the lock to the office door changed the night before.

So who's in there?

Prince of Qalif Held to Different Disciplinary Standard

Sources tell the Express that although Rascally Rashid, the prince of Qalif, has thrown a number of large parties in his room(s) at which alcohol has been present, he has received no disciplinary sanctions, while nine resident assistants in Fischer Hall have lost their positions.

"Of course they haven't done anything to him," says a student and resident of the building (who wishes to remain anonymous for fear of reprisals). "His father donated half a billion dollars to the college. He can do whatever he wants."

New York College administrators have declined to comment.

New York College Express, your daily student news blog

29

Look," Sarah is saying to Howard Chen, Kyle Cheeseman, and the rest of the RAs gathered around my desk, where she's sitting behind the still-enormous—and even more fragrant—flower arrangement Rashid sent me. "Lisa isn't here, all right? I don't know where she is or when she's coming in, but—"

She breaks off, seeing me walk through the door.

"Oh, thank God," she says, and rises from my office chair, looking relieved. "There you are. I thought you'd never get here. These . . . *people* . . . want to talk to you."

Sarah hesitates before saying the word "people" as if she'd have preferred to use a different word, but chooses the high road out of professionalism. Apparently, her patience has been worn thin.

I can't say I blame her. The office is a zoo. Not only is it packed with dissatisfied RAs, but Carl, the building engineer, is back on his ladder, drilling the ceiling again, this time near Sarah's desk—which is why she'd abandoned it for mine. Prince Rashid is there too, sitting on the visitors' couch, right on time for his appointment with me . . .

But he's brought along both his bodyguards, including Hamad, who are standing stiffly on either side of him, their expressions stony-faced.

Odd how State Department special agents go missing right when you need them.

"What's with this letter?" Jasmine Tsai demands, waving a piece of paper in my face. All I can see is that it's written on formal New York College letterhead. The paper has a watermark. We can't afford paper like that in this office. Our budget isn't big enough.

Jasmine Tsai isn't the only one waving a letter.

"Miss Wells," Hamad says woodenly, holding the letter I sent to Rashid the day before. "May we speak to you about this?"

"Yes, you absolutely may," I say, moving into the seat Sarah's rapidly vacated and placing my bagel and coffee drink on my desk. I have the feeling it's going to be a long time until I'm going to enjoy them. "At nine o'clock, when the prince's appointment begins."

Hamad looks toward the ceiling . . . at Carl, who is pulling wiring through one of the ceiling tiles he's removed and paying rapt attention to all the drama going on below him while pretending to be working.

"No, Miss Wells," Hamad says in a tired voice. *"Now."*

"I don't mind waiting," Rashid says, from the couch. He's practically hidden by the shadows of his protectors. "I'm happy to meet with Miss Wells."

"The prince of Qalif shouldn't have to—"

"Be held to a different disciplinary standard than the rest of the residents in the building?" I shake my head. "I don't think so." I'm stalling for time. Ameera hasn't shown up yet for her appointment. But it's still only three minutes to nine.

"Discipline?" Hamad's face looks like it's going to melt off, he's getting so hot under the collar. "You dare to suggest a prince of the royal blood will be disciplined by—"

"I need the free room and board I was promised!" Howard Chen yells, unable to contain himself a second longer. "My parents can't afford to send both me and my brother to school at the same time unless I have free room and board!"

"How could you and Lisa let this happen?" Kyle Cheeseman screams at me. "I thought you guys liked us!"

"Lisa and I didn't let this happen," I say. "All of *you* let this happen when you exercised such poor judgment by going to a party in the residence hall where you work. Just what, exactly, were you thinking? There was alcohol at that party, being served to *minors*. You're RAs, remember? You're supposed to bust parties like that. Then you lied to Lisa the next day about why you felt sick." I make quotation marks in the air with my fingers when I say the word "sick."

"When Lisa told you that she felt sick—which she genuinely was—you dummies let her believe you had the flu. But you didn't, did you? What you actually were was hungover. How long did you think it was going to take for her to find out? You do know there are monitors all over the fifteenth-floor hallway, to help protect our VIR?"

I don't wait for any of them to speak. I don't feel like listening to anything they have to say.

"So it's not *my* fault you lost your free room and board," I go on. "It's *your* fault. You broke the rules of the employment contract *you* signed, not to mention all rules of human decency, when none of you mentioned that Jasmine Albright had been at the prince's party, even after you found out she'd died the next morning. Clearly you knew what you'd done was wrong because you tried to cover your asses. Didn't you?"

All of the RAs look at one another. I can see the naked panic on their faces.

"I'm sorry," I say. "I didn't quite hear you. I said, *didn't you?*"

"This isn't fair." Stephanie Moody is the first one to speak. "*I* didn't even see Jaz at the party. And I didn't find out she was dead until Lisa told us at that staff meeting."

"Oh, shut up, Steph," Christopher Mintz snaps. "You're such a brownnoser."

"I don't think any of you understand," Howard says, with mounting hysteria. "If I don't get free room and board, I'm probably going to have to take out a student loan."

"Howard," I say, "well over two-thirds of students in this country will graduate this year holding a student loan of some kind, probably way more than whatever yours is going to be. I'm sure the financial aid office will be more than happy to help work something out with you. With all of you, as a matter of fact."

"It is now nine o'clock," Hamad, the more loquacious of the prince's bodyguards, points out, holding up his diamond-encrusted watch. It probably cost more than the entire work-study-student budget the housing department was allotted. "May we please have our appointment, Miss Wells?"

"No," I say. "I'm not ready yet. And even when I am, you aren't invited to the meeting, Hamad."

He looks furious. "Then we're leaving." Hamad utters a few words of Arabic to the prince.

Rashid looks as if he's seen enough anyway and has grown bored. He stands.

This is a disaster. Where is Ameera? Maybe I should call her room to make sure she's coming.

"Disciplinary action will ensue if you fail to attend this meeting, Rashid," I say quickly. "It's better if you stay and talk to me."

"You're not even the one in charge here," Hamad says, with a sneer. "It's the Oriental lady. Where is she?"

"Asian," I say. "Lisa's Asian-American. Rugs are Oriental, not people. And she isn't here right now."

"But my parents," Howard is saying. I notice he's wearing his Harvard hoodie again, like a reminder of his alleged failure. "They're going to kill me."

"*My* parents are going to kill Phillip Allington," Jasmine Tsai declares. "They're on their way into the city right now to demand a meeting with him over our unfair treatment. We're not going down without a fight."

"I noticed," Sarah says drily. "Which one of you leaked the president's letter to the *Express*? Because that was superclassy. By which I mean not classy at all."

The RAs raise their voices in unanimous protest. Rashid, looking disgusted, turns to leave . . . then freezes. I soon see why. A familiar (if somewhat ghostly pale, though still very beautiful) face has appeared in the doorway.

It's Ameera, fashionably late for her nine o'clock meeting with me.

She looks frightened. Well, the wording in my letter *had* been strong. And, of course, the RAs are being extremely loud. One thing about RAs is that they don't have problems expressing their feelings.

"Come in, Ameera," I shout. I have to shout to be heard over the RAs voices and also Carl's drilling.

Rashid steps quickly out of her way. As he turns, I see that his face has gone almost as pale as hers. He can't seem to take his eyes off her.

Ameera steps across the threshold, looking shy (and thin) as a young doe. She's wearing a white print sundress, brown leather sandals, and no jewelry except for the gold pendant with interlocking rings she'd been wearing the last time I saw her. She looks around the office uncertainly, but finally focuses her attention on me, since I'm the person behind the most centrally located desk.

"I got a letter," she says in her polite, British-accented voice. I can hardly hear her above the din, she's speaking so softly. "You wanted to see me?"

Rashid hasn't budged from the doorway. He's still staring at her. Even his normally voiceless bodyguard looks uncomfortable. He lays a hand on the prince's shoulder and says softly, "Your Highness? I think we should go now."

But Rashid ignores him, staring at the girl.

"I do want to see you," I say. "You and the prince, whom I think you know. Am I right about that?"

Ameera barely glances at Rashid. "We've met," she says, in the same shy voice.

"So you wouldn't mind talking with me for a couple of minutes," I say, getting up to unlock the door to Lisa's office with my master key. "In here, privately, both of you."

It's Rashid who responds first.

"Of course," he says eagerly. "I'll be happy to." He barrels across the office, elbowing through the clusters of RAs, practically knocking Carl's ladder over in his haste to get into Lisa's empty office to meet with Ameera alone—well, not quite alone, since I'll be there.

But he's apparently willing to take whatever he can get, as I'd suspected when I'd heard from Mrs. Harris how desperate he was for a few minutes of the girl's company.

"Your Highness," Hamad cries, attempting to follow the boy. "No!"

I hold out a hand to halt the bodyguard.

"I'm sorry," I say. "This is a residence hall judicial meeting. It's private. Only Rashid and Ameera may attend. You'll have to wait outside."

Hamad was traveling so quickly to protect his prince that he walks straight into my hand. I don't know if touching an unmarried woman is against Qalifi law, but the bodyguard sure acts like it is. He leaps back about three feet, looking shocked.

"No," Hamad practically spits. "You cannot! You *cannot . . .*" Then he seems to remember himself, and declares, "You cannot meet with the prince alone! It is not done."

"Hamad," the prince calls from Lisa's office. His voice is steady and self-assured. "It's fine. I'll be all right. Do as Miss Wells says, and wait outside."

Hamad looks more enraged than I've ever seen him. His dark-eyed gaze is practically crackling with fire. I reach instinctively for my purse handles. Of course I have no intention of going for the pistol Hal insisted I bring to work with me . . . but suddenly I'm awfully glad he did.

"All right," Hamad says, throwing himself down upon the couch Rashid has recently vacated, with the ill grace of an angry child who's been given a time-out. "I will wait. But for five minutes *only.*"

"I can't imagine it will take longer than that," I say, relaxing my grip—but only a little—on my purse handles. "Ameera?" I look questioningly at the girl. "Will you come with me?"

Ameera is holding her shoulders so tensely, you'd think she was going to her execution, not a meeting in the residence hall director's office with the young heir to the throne of Qalif.

Still, she doesn't demur. She nods, and says faintly, "I will," and walks into Lisa's office like Joan of Arc on her way to the stake.

Now that I have the two residents I've most wanted to question since Jasmine's death exactly where I want them, I turn to the RAs in the outer office and say, "As you can see, I'm about to have a very important meeting. I understand how frustrated and upset all of you are, but you're not going to accomplish anything hanging around here. Lisa's not going to be back until noon. I suggest you go visit President Allington's office now that it's open. One word of advice before you go, though."

I pause to take a sip of my coffee—thank goodness I've fortified it with extra whipped cream, because I really need it.

"One thing I've noticed is that not a single one of you has said the words 'I'm sorry.' When you get over to the president's office, if you do manage to get an appointment with him or any other administrator, that's something you might want to consider doing—taking some responsibility for your actions. A girl died, you know. I'm not saying her death was your fault, or even that she died as a result of the party, but the whole reason residence halls exist is to help students transition safely into adult life. The whole reason RA jobs exist is to *assist* them in doing that."

I take a deep breath. I have their full attention—even Hamad's. It's a bit like when I used to perform onstage, only instead of touching the audience's hearts with a tender love ballad, I'm giving the RAs the speech they should have had *before* they were hired. Unfortunately, Simon Hague, the director of Wasser Hall, hired them, and he knows as little about responsibility as I do about nursing—real nursing, not below-the-sheets nursing.

"But you guys not only failed to do your job, the night of the party you actually encouraged young people to behave irresponsibly. So a nice 'I'm sorry for violating New York College student code and setting a terrible example' might go a long way with some of the people you talk to today. It might have gone a long way with me, or with Sarah, or even Lisa, if you'd also said, 'I'm sorry for deeply disappointing you guys after all the hard work you did training us and making our rooms so nice before we moved in.' It definitely would have gone a long way with me if you'd said you were sorry for making Lisa cry, because you did: you made Lisa cry. For that alone, I have no more time for any of you. So get out of my building."

All of the RAs blink at me in astonishment. I don't think any of these particular students have ever been rebuked by an adult in their lives. Because these are the type of kids who, in the words of Detective Canavan's irrepressible probie, always got awards simply for participating.

Well, not anymore. New York College may not be perfect, but over on this side of the park, we do things the right way, not the easy way.

I'm gratified to see that a few of the RAs—even the boys—have tears in their eyes.

None of them leaves, however. They stand in the office in awkward silence.

"I'm sorry," I say. "Did I not make myself clear? That last part wasn't an invitation. It was an order. Get. Out."

Carl nods. "Clear enough for me," he says, and begins packing up his drill bits.

"You c-can't tell us what to do," Howard Chen says, sticking out his chin. He's one of the RAs who's crying. "You're not the hall director."

"No," I say. "But she's not here right now, so I'm in charge. And you don't work here anymore, and you never will again. So sayonara."

"Come on, buddy," Joshua Dungarden says, slapping Howard on the shoulder. "Don't worry about it. I called my dad, and he's on his way into the city. He's friends with the dean of the law school. He'll get this bitch fired, and we'll get hired back."

Bitch? Could he be referring to me?

Carl's drill begins to whirl dangerously as he turns it toward Joshua. Since he's standing on the ladder, the bit is eye level. "Pardon me, young man. What did you call her?"

"Uh," Joshua says, swallowing. "Nothing."

Quickly, the RAs begin to file out. Only three of them—the two other Jasmines and Joshua Dungarden—murmur "I'm sorry" as they leave, and Joshua only says it out of fear of Carl, so it doesn't count. Howard Chen gives me a look of such burning hatred that it could almost have come from Hamad.

Only Carl's departure is at all affable.

"Well, that was interesting," he says to me as he leaves, ladder and toolbox in hand. "Hope we can do it again sometime. Have a nice meeting!"

Fired Fischer Hall RA Staff a Bunch of "Pussies" Says Tom Snelling

"I'm sorry, but they are," says the director of Waverly Hall, the building that houses the Greek fraternities. "They had it easy. All they had to do was be on duty a couple nights a month and not drink while they were doing it, and they blew it. Wait, are you recording this? You little pissant, give me that!"

This is the only comment any administrator at New York College has been willing to give the Express thus far.

As always, we will be delivering the story as it unfolds!

New York College Express,
your daily student news blog

Sarah," I say, shouldering my handbag and heading into Lisa's office. "If anyone comes in looking for me—"

"You're in a meeting," she finishes for me from behind her desk. "I get it."

Her eyes are wide, her gaze darting from me to Hamad to Rashid's other bodyguard, who's taken a watchful position by the main office door.

I don't blame Sarah for being nervous. I'm counting at least three firearms—all illegal by college housing standards, some illegal by New York State licensing standards—in this room alone . . . the guns in the bodyguards' shoulder holsters, and the target pistol in my purse.

Sarah doesn't know about my gun, of course, but she knows about the ones in the bodyguards' shoulder holsters. Who knows what other heat they're packing in ankle holsters, however, or wherever else bodyguards from the kingdom of Qalif might hide weapons? Not to mention whatever the special agents down the hall are carrying, in the conference room that's been converted into a special office for security monitoring.

Fischer Hall probably hasn't seen this many sidearms since it was a speakeasy and allegedly served bootleg gin to card-carrying members, which it supposedly did from a secret passageway in the second-floor library (long since converted to student rooms) back in the 1920s.

"Thanks, Sarah," I say, slipping through the door to Lisa's office. "And take messages if anyone calls, okay?"

"Got it," Sarah says. "That was quite a speech, by the way. Thanks. Though I think you're probably going to get fired for it, if Joshua Dungarden's dad has his way."

I shrug. "Then I can just take another week off for my honeymoon."

I don't mean it, of course. If I get fired, I'll fight it tooth and nail. How else will I ever be able to afford a college degree without my tuition remission?

Rashid and Ameera are sitting about as far apart as they can be in Lisa's tiny office without one of them being outside it. Ameera seems to be hugging the file cabinet where I plan to keep Baby Wu—although I guess Lisa's baby will probably take Cory's last name, which is Esposito. Emily Esposito. Hmm, that name might not work—while Rashid is over by the windows, his dark hair being ruffled by the air-conditioning unit.

Except that I got the sense, as I walked in, that the chairs weren't *always* spaced that far apart. I can't explain it, but as I ease the door open to make room for myself and my voluminous bag—well, I guess I'm a little more voluminous than my bag—I sense a rustle of some kind—almost like two bodies coming apart—and then what can only be the sound of chair legs scooting on carpeting.

Lisa's door opens *in* to her office, and both visitors' chairs are kept *behind* the door. By the time I let myself in and close the door, Rashid and Ameera are sitting conspicuously far apart. There's no denying what I heard, though.

Judging by their body language, they could not be less interested in each other. Rashid is flipping through a copy of *The New York College Housing and Residence Life Handbook* as if it is the most engrossing thing he has ever read, and Ameera's legs are crossed and twisted toward the office wall, her arms folded, and a finger inserted into her mouth so she can chew on what's looking like an already ragged set of nails.

Both their faces, however, are scarlet beneath their similarly olive skin tones, and Ameera's hair looks as if it's had some fingers run through it recently—and not her own, since she'd have been more careful not to pull out the tortoise-shell barrette which now hangs forlornly along one side of her head.

I don't comment on the very obvious fact that these two have been making out in Lisa's office while I was reading the RAs the riot act, however. This is, after all, the girl

Mrs. Harris kept insisting to me was a "slut." Though I've dealt with actual "sluts" before—or rather, girls (and boys) who've brought so many strangers back to their rooms for sex that we've had to cut off their guest privileges, as they were infringing on their roommates' rights for a safe living environment—and Ameera in no way seems to fit the bill.

But, as Cooper said last night, things aren't always what they seem.

"Hi, you two," I say, placing my bag on Lisa's desk and sinking into her chair. It's incredibly uncomfortable. Lisa has what she calls an "Asian butt," which she's explained is "no butt." To combat this, she's made me purchase all manners of padding for her office chair from the supply catalog.

I have plenty of natural padding on my size-twelve white-girl butt, so all of Lisa's cushions make it quite difficult for me to sit in her chair without towering over everyone like that blond lady knight on *Game of Thrones*.

"So," I say, looking down on Rashid and Ameera like I'm sitting on a draft horse. "Thanks for coming. I'm sorry for dragging you both down here so early in the morning, and I'm also sorry too for that outburst you must have heard out there—"

"Please," Rashid interrupts with a charming smile. He closes the student handbook to show that I have his full attention. "Don't concern yourself about that. I'm sorry about the difficult time you must be going through right now. I'm so glad to see that you received my flowers."

"Yes," I say. "Thank you for those. They're very beautiful. I noticed that you also sent some to Ameera."

Rashid throws a look at the girl that I recognize. It's the

same one he wore in the outer office that day he'd heard her roommate say that Ameera was ill, an expression of worried concern that you rarely see on boys' faces unless they're speaking about . . .

. . . well, about a girl they love.

"I did," he says. "She had quite a shock. I don't think she's picked them up from the desk, though."

"She hasn't," I say. "Ameera, do you want to tell me why you didn't pick up the flowers Rashid sent you?"

"Please," Rashid says with a smile. "I told you. My name is Shiraz in this country. Because I'm chilled, like the—"

"Fine wine," I say, gritting my teeth. "Yes, I know, we got it. Ameera? The flowers? What's wrong with them?"

Ameera squirms uncomfortably in her chair, removing her finger from her mouth and giving me a shy smile.

"I never received a notice about a flower delivery. Is that why I'm here? I can go get them now, if that's all this is about. I didn't know it was against the rules not to pick up flowers."

She's a good liar. I might believe her if I didn't know Gavin had already talked to her about the flowers.

"This isn't about the flowers, Ameera," I say, "and you know it. It's about your roommate Kaileigh."

The smile vanishes. She looks genuinely shocked—and worried . . . more worried than the statement warrants. Where before her cheeks had been flushed with color from whatever she and Rashid had been doing behind the door, suddenly they're pale again.

"Kaileigh? What's the matter with her?" Ameera asks, her

fingers now going to clutch her chair seat. "I saw her in the room a little while ago, and she was fine—"

Ameera glances at Rashid, who meets her gaze, then does something that completely and utterly surprises me:

He reaches out across the distance between their two chairs for her hand . . .

. . . and she releases her seat and takes it, clutching his fingers so tightly, and gazing at him so deeply, that I'm certain in that moment that she loves him every bit as much as he loves her, and I love Cooper.

It's not the kind of look you can mistake.

"Of course Kaileigh's all right," I say, bewildered. I'd been about to introduce the topic of Kaileigh's mother's complaint—Ameera's failure to spend a single night in her own bed for most of orientation week. I'm fairly certain I now know in whose bed Ameera has been sleeping. "Why wouldn't she be?"

"I don't understand," Rashid says, still holding tightly to Ameera's hand. There's something protective, but also possessive, about his grip on her. "If Ameera's roommate is all right, then why are the two of us here?"

"Why don't you tell *me* why the two of you are here, Rashid? And *don't* ask me again to call you Shiraz," I add quickly as he opens his mouth. "I'm sorry, but that name is ridiculous. I don't believe any of your true friends really call you that—and it's obvious you two are a little more than friends."

Ameera stares at me with wide, frightened eyes. Rashid's gaze flies immediately to the grate above Lisa's doorway. His expression has gone as wary as hers. Only now does he drop Ameera's hand, and then it's to raise a finger to his lips.

"Shhh." He points to the grate.

I look at the grate, then back at him, and nod that I understand—though of course I don't, not really. Now the expression on Ameera's face is one of absolute terror.

Rashid gets up from his chair and pulls the blinds on both of Lisa's windows so that no one walking by on the street can see us. I reach over to Lisa's computer and turn on her Patsy Cline playlist, loud—Patsy, we've discovered, makes excellent ambient background noise so that anyone who might be eavesdropping in the outer office can't hear a thing that's being discussed in the inner sanctum. The only problem is that sometimes we forget to turn her on.

Not this time, however.

"Okay," I say to them, keeping my voice low. "I get it. You two are dating, and it's bad form for the prince of Qalif to have a commoner as a girlfriend, right? But why did you get so worried when I asked you about your roommate, Ameera? Is it because you thought the same thing might have happened to her that happened to your RA, Jasmine?"

Rashid has sunk back into his chair—but not before moving it next to Ameera's so he could put a comforting arm around the girl's trembling shoulders.

"No, Miss Wells," he whispers. "You don't understand. Ameera is not my girlfriend. She is my wife."

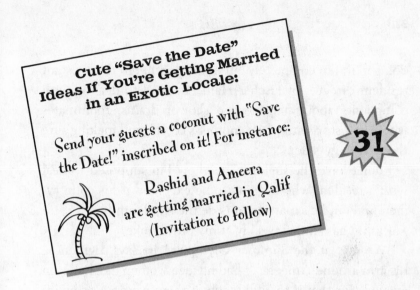

Cute "Save the Date"
Ideas If You're Getting Married
in an Exotic Locale:

Send your guests a coconut with "Save the Date!" inscribed on it! For instance:

Rashid and Ameera
are getting married in Qalif
(Invitation to follow)

31

In my country," Rashid explains, "for me to marry a woman who is not a member of the royal family is a sin punishable by death. Stoning for her. Beheading for me."

"Oh," I say. Good Lord. I've never thought of my future in-laws as particularly warm, but at least they don't want to execute me. "Well, as long as you both die, and they keep it fair between the sexes."

I'm being flippant, but I don't really feel that way. I'm horrified . . . horrified for them, and horrified at myself. My butt may more than fill Lisa's chair, but I don't know what I'm doing in it. I'm completely out of my depth. I'm the assistant resident director of Fischer Hall! I'm used to dealing with complaints about hair-clogged shower drains, roommates who won't stop eating one another's cereal, and making sure the payroll gets done.

I don't have the slightest idea how I'm supposed to deal with a resident who is going to be executed if his country-men find out he's married outside the royal family.

Rashid has smiled weakly at my pitiful joke.

"We met at the Summer Olympics," he says, tightening his arm around Ameera. "I had no idea women like her even existed—or that if they did, one of them would ever be in-terested in an idiot like me."

"Don't," Ameera says, reaching up to stroke his face. She still looks frightened, but not as much now that Rashid is beside her. "Don't speak about yourself that way. You're not an idiot."

"I am," the prince informs me. "She's the smart one. Per-fect test scores! She's here on a full scholarship, can you be-lieve it? But for some reason she likes me."

"Everyone likes you," Ameera says warmly.

"Not my father," Rashid says, with a scowl. "He thinks I'm a wastrel because I'm not interested in his missiles and defense systems. But when I told him I wanted to give up tennis and go to college in the States, he was overjoyed. He moved heaven and earth to get me into this school. The only thing I didn't tell him was why it was so important that I go to New York College, of all places—that I was following my strong, beautiful, intelligent wife there. She wants to be a pediatrician—"

Ameera laid a hand on his chest and said, blushing, "Darling, stop it."

"I won't. I wish I could tell everyone in the world about how wonderful you are. But for now I'll have to settle for Miss Wells."

"So all the partying?" I ask. "The Shiraz thing? It's an act to cover up the truth?"

"Of course." Rashid regards me as if I really am the dumb blonde I'm occasionally told I look like. "Ameera and I don't even drink. Our religion forbids it. But I can't let anyone find out the truth, or it could endanger our lives."

"But you're not even a resident of Qalif," I say to Ameera. "Aren't you British?"

She nods.

"No one can drag a British citizen to a foreign country and stone her, no matter who she's married to. Not without facing some really severe consequences. And you." I look at Rashid. "There's no way a father would have his own son beheaded."

Rashid looks at me sadly. "My father had his own sister shot in the middle of a public square when she tried to flee Qalif with a commoner with whom she'd fallen in love. He had the commoner beheaded. The charge was fornication. You can look it up if you don't believe me, it was only a few years ago."

"It's one of the many human rights violations for which Rashid's father has been criticized," Ameera says, just as sadly. "It's why some of the faculty members of this college didn't want to take the money he donated."

"Oh God." I sink my head into my hands. I need to think. This is all happening too fast, and I've only drunk half my coffee.

"That's why we've tried to keep this a secret, Miss Wells," Rashid says gently. "We don't want to endanger anyone else by dragging them into it. I love the country in which I was born, but some parts of it are ugly . . . very ugly. If I live long enough to rule Qalif someday, I hope to change the ugly things. But I honestly don't know if that will ever happen."

"*Worry*," Patsy Cline wails over Lisa's computer speakers. "*Why would I let myself worry?*"

Easy for her to say.

"Okay," I say, lifting my head. "Okay. So who else knows you two are married? Does the State Department know? Special Agent Lancaster?"

Rashid and Ameera look at each other blankly. "No," Rashid says. "I certainly hope not."

"For obvious reasons," Ameera says, "we've told as few people as possible, and I've tried to keep people from suspecting we're even acquainted by not being seen alone with him, and not accepting expensive gifts from him—for example, large floral arrangements." She nudges Rashid reproachfully in the knee.

"You don't have to go that far," he protests. "I got flowers for the two ladies in this office as well."

"My family doesn't even know," Ameera says.

"They don't?" I'm shocked. "What's the point of even getting married, then, if it's going to put you both in so much danger?"

The young couple exchange knowing glances, the way people who share a secret often do.

"Because we love each other, of course," Rashid says simply.

"So your family doesn't know, Ameera," I say, frustrated.

"And obviously Rashid's doesn't know. Your roommates don't know." Obviously, or Kaileigh would have figured out where Ameera was going every night. "Who *does* know?"

"Well, you, now," Rashid says. He glances once more, at the grate. "And Hamad and Habib, of course."

"Your *bodyguards* know?"

"Of course," Rashid says, as if I'm a fool not to have guessed this. "They know everything about me."

"But don't you think that's risky?" I ask, thinking of Hamad's burning gaze, and the iron grip in which he'd held my wrist the day before. "Isn't there a chance they might tell your father?"

Anger flashes across Rashid's face. "Of course not," he says. "My men are completely loyal to me. They would die for me! They might *literally* have to die for me one day if our secret gets out and my father sends his own men to kidnap us and take us back to Qalif for punishment—"

"Do you think your men would kill for you?" I interrupt.

"Of course they would," Rashid replies, without hesitation.

"Did one of them kill Jasmine Albright?" I ask. "Is that why she's dead? Was she about to reveal your secret to the world?"

Rashid and Ameera exchange glances again, but this time those glances aren't knowing. They're bewildered.

"Did she see something the night of your party—maybe the two of you kissing, or something—and take a photo of it?" I press on. "Did one of your bodyguards go into her room and steal her cell phone and suffocate her to death in order to save your life, Rashid, and your bride's?"

Ameera's face disintegrates into tears at the same time

that Rashid stands up, so swiftly that he knocks over the chair in which he's been sitting.

"No!" he cries. No amount of Patsy Cline is going to drown out his angry voice. "How dare you? How dare you even suggest such a thing?"

A second later, there's pounding on the door to Lisa's office, and someone is trying to turn the knob, but thankfully the door is locked.

"Your Highness!" Hamad shouts. "Your Highness, open the door. Your Highness, what's wrong? Are you all right?"

I stare up at Rashid, breathing almost as heavily as he is.

"Someone suffocated Jasmine to death, Rashid," I whisper. "Someone held a hand over her mouth and nose until she died from lack of oxygen. She was leaking things about you to the *Express*, the student news blog. She was at your party, and she saw something, and someone killed her a little while later to keep her quiet about it. What did she see? *What did she see?*"

Rashid swings around to look at Ameera, who has tears streaming down her face. She's shaking her head, mouthing the word "No. No, no, no."

"Your Highness!" Hamad shouts again, beating on the door.

"I'm all right," Rashid calls to his bodyguard. "Stand down." To Ameera, he whispers, "What could she have seen?"

Ameera shakes her head, pressing a hand to the two rings she wears on the chain around her neck . . . rings I now realize, belatedly, are her and Rashid's wedding rings. She wears them over her heart.

"*Nothing*, Rashid," she whispers back. "I've been playing

that night over and over in my head, ever since I saw her body. And there's *nothing*. We never even looked at each other at that party. We were so safe. I stayed on one side of the room, and you stayed on the other. It wasn't until after—after everyone left—that we—that we—"

She breaks off, sobbing, and Rashid wraps his arms around her, then looks at me, his expression desperate.

"She's right," he says. "Whatever it was the girl photographed at my party—if there *was* a photo—it wasn't us. We're careful in public. The parties are so my father won't suspect. I have to maintain my image—Rascally Rashid." He gives a single, bitter laugh. "I can never let him know who I really am—a married man."

A married man—married to the Fischer Hall "slut."

Cooper was right. Things aren't always what they seem.

"But if Jasmine wasn't killed because of something to do with you," I say bewilderedly to Rashid, "what *was* she killed for? It had to have been something that happened at your party."

Rashid has sat down again, this time to cradle a sobbing Ameera in his arms. He doesn't seem particularly interested in my questions. I guess I wouldn't be either if I were a boy and the girl I loved had been ignoring me for days and was now suddenly weeping against my chest.

"How should I know?" he asks. "Why don't you ask one of your precious RAs? They were all there. Maybe one of them saw something. I had no idea the girl was even murdered. I thought she died of asthma."

"*I* thought she was murdered," Ameera sobs. "I took one

look at her face and all I could think was, 'That's going to be me someday. Someone's going to sneak into my room and do that to me in my sleep one night—' "

"Shhh," Rashid says, burying his face in her hair. "No, they aren't, not if you spend every night with me. You know you're safe with me, you silly thing. Stop sleeping in your room with those terrible roommates of yours, and sleep with me, where you belong . . ."

He continues murmuring to her, but I've stopped listening.

Something that Rashid has said has caused my blood to run cold. Suddenly I realize that Cooper's wise words from last night aren't entirely true after all. Sometimes things are *exactly* as they seem.

It just takes a while to figure it out.

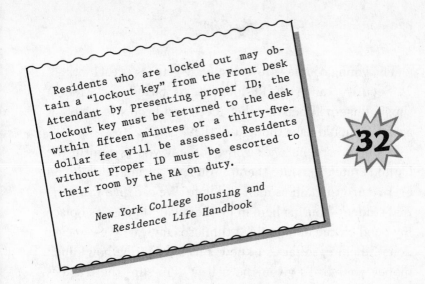

32

You two," I say, pointing vaguely in Rashid and Ameera's direction as I rise distractedly from Lisa's chair. "Stay here. Don't go anywhere. We're going to notify the State Department about your situation."

Rashid lifts his head from Ameera's hair. *"What?"*

"No," Ameera cries in a panic-stricken voice. "You can't!"

"Relax," I say, lifting my purse. "They probably already know you two are an item. There are security cameras on the fifteenth-floor pointing toward your door, Rashid. I'm sure they've got plenty of shots of Ameera slinking in and out of there this past week."

The young couple throw desperate glances at each other.

"Security cameras," Rashid repeats bitterly as Ameera slips a fingernail between her teeth and begins to nibble it again. "I should have thought of that."

"Don't worry, no one's going to deny you asylum in the United States," I assure them. "You face certain death if you ever return to Qalif as man and wife. We can give you married student–housing here in Fischer Hall." I pause as I place my hand on the doorknob. "I think so, anyway. We've never done it before, so far as I know, but considering how much money your dad's given the college, I'm sure the trustees will make an exception.

"Besides," I add, "it's hardly in your father's best interest to go around executing young lovers in the age of social media networking. Can you imagine what people would say about Qalif on Twitter if they beheaded you, Rashid, and stoned you to death, Ameera?" I shake my head. "Trust me, your father will back off when blogs like the *Express* get hold of this."

"Miss Wells," Rashid says as I open the office door. "I really don't think my father is the type of man who cares what anyone says on Twitter."

"Tell that to the guy who used to govern Egypt."

I stick my head out the door and into the main office. Both of the prince's bodyguards tense when they notice me. I'm surprised to see that Dave Fernandez is sitting beside Sarah's desk, engrossed in conversation with her.

"Oh," I say. "Hey, Dave. It's me, Heather Wells."

"Hello, Heather." He climbs to his feet, cane in hand, smiling broadly. "I hope you don't mind my stopping by. Lisa let me know that the room won't be available for a while, but I like Fischer Hall so much, I can't seem to stay away."

He likes *Fischer Hall* so much. Right. And his increasingly frequent visits have nothing to do with Sarah, whom I notice surreptitiously checking her reflection in a pocket mirror she keeps in a desk drawer, which is sweet, given that Dave is blind. It's funny how hard it is to break our old habits.

Like failing to see what's staring us straight in our faces, even if we possess 20/20 vision.

"No problem, Dave," I say. "Visit Fischer Hall all you want."

"Hey, guys," I say to Hamad and Habib, who've both come to crowd around the door. "The prince and Ameera are ready to tell the State Department the truth about—" I wink broadly at both bodyguards. "*You know.* Sarah, can you call Special Agent Lancaster in the surveillance room down the hall? I think he's going to be the best person to handle this."

"Sure, Heather," Sarah says, and picks up her office phone to dial the extension.

Both bodyguards look shocked.

"Wait," Hamad says, flinging a hand toward Sarah to stop her. "Do not make this call!"

"Uh." Sarah stares at him blankly. "I already have them on the line—"

Hamad rushes forward, snatches the handset from her, then slams it back down onto the receiver with enough violence that I'm certain I hear plastic crack.

"How dare you?" Hamad seethes at me. Then he pushes me aside—not hard enough to cause me to fall down, since, as Hal mentioned, my center of gravity is quite low—and

rushes toward Lisa's office door, behind which the prince
and Ameera are still huddled.

"Your Highness?" Hamad asks. "Are you all right?"

"Of course we're all right," I hear Rashid say. "Thank you,
Hamad. Do you think you could find some water, though,
for Ameera? She's feeling a bit under the weather."

"I'll get it," Dave volunteers. He walks unerringly in the
direction of the office watercooler, finds it by whacking it
with the tip of his cane until it makes a telltale bubbling
sound, leans down to fill a paper cup with cool water, then
brings it back an instant later. "Will this do?"

Habib looks at him in astonishment.

"It will do very nicely," he says. "Thank you, sir." Then he
takes the water into Lisa's office, where Hamad and Rashid
are consulting in hushed voices.

Sarah stares up at Dave worshipfully. "We have work-
study-student office hours available this semester, don't we,
Heather?" she asks. "To help out processing service requests
and stuff. Maybe we could hire Dave to fill some of them."

"Maybe." I roll my eyes. It's okay, because neither of them
notices. One is too busy staring at the other, and the other
can't see.

"Did someone from this office just call me? Is something
wrong?"

Special Agent Lancaster is standing in the doorway to
the outer office, panting a little. He's clearly run from the
conference room, where the surveillance cameras have
been set up. He's got his firearm in one hand, and a half-
eaten jelly donut in the other. He's also forgotten his suit
jacket, his tie, and the fact that his shirt is untucked and

that he's got a paper napkin pressed into his shirt collar to keep errant jelly donut guts from getting on the front of his pure-white shirt.

"Yes," I say. "We did just call you. But no, nothing's wrong, so you can put that away."

I point at the gun, which Lancaster seems for the first time to notice he's holding. He looks embarrassed, stuffs the jelly donut in his mouth, and holsters the gun, then begins tucking in his shirt.

"The prince has something he wants to tell you." I point at the half-open door to Lisa's office. "It's pretty big news, so you might want to call for reinforcements."

Lancaster nods, then reaches for his cell phone, dialing one-handed while ripping the paper napkin from his collar. "It's not about the girl, is it?" he asks with his mouth full.

"The dead one? No," I say. "But there *is* a girl involved."

He looks up, sharply. "The British one?"

It's my turn to nod. "I thought you guys might have noticed her."

"She turns up a lot on the monitors. What about her?"

"You'll never guess, so I won't hold you in suspense. They're married."

He utters a curse word that blisters even my hardened ears.

"Wow," I say. "I'll be sure to pass on your congratulations to the happy couple."

"Sorry," he says, and lowers his head to his phone again. "This has to be why the other girl—the RA—was murdered. Why the reporter was attacked too. The RA must have found out those two were married, and was going to leak the story."

"Maybe," I say noncommittally. "She was going to leak

something, but we can't know for sure it was that, can we? Not until we find her phone. And her murderer too, of course. How did you know Jasmine was murdered? That hasn't been released to the public."

He gives me a sarcastic look. "I work for the government, Ms. Wells. Besides, I've been talking to that friend of yours, Eva." He'd pronounced it the way Eva does, the Russian way, without the long *E*, so I know that, though his tone is dismissive, the dismissiveness is feigned—they know each other well . . . especially since the skin around his neckline, no longer hidden by the napkin, is turning pink. "We've chatted a couple of times. Strictly work-related, of course."

"Of course." Although I can't imagine the Eva I know letting any relationship with a guy she's really attracted to remain "strictly work-related" for long.

"Anyway," he says as he texts, "when Rashid's father finds out the kid's married a commoner, it's going to be the shit storm to end all shit storms. And we're the ones who are going to have to clean up the debris." He points at me, then himself.

I remember Detective Canavan's accusation that I'm a shitkicker. Now, apparently, I'm also someone who clears away debris from storms composed of—what else?—shit.

"Great," I say with mock cheer. "And it's all going to happen here, in Fischer Hall." I glance over at Sarah and give her a big smile. "Did you hear that, Sarah?"

Sarah shakes her head. All her attention's been focused on Dave. "I'm sorry, Heather, what?"

"Never mind," I say to her. "I'm going to the desk for a few minutes to check on some things. Hold down the fort for me back here, okay?"

Sarah throws me a dazzling smile. "Of course!"

"See you later, Heather," Dave calls sunnily, waving in my general direction.

"Not if I see you first," I say, waving back, before realizing how completely asinine it was of me to say such a thing, since *obviously* I'm going to see him first, and he's going to see me never. Fortunately he doesn't seem to have noticed my gaffe, as he's turned back toward Sarah, still smiling, to continue their discussion on his cat, or the problems with nuclear proliferation in undeveloped countries, or whatever it is they're talking about.

I take myself and my handbag up to the front desk, where I'm unsurprised to find Gavin working on his screenplay instead of the mail forwarding, though he at least hastily closes his laptop and swings his slippered feet down from the desk when he sees me.

"I just needed to finish this one scene where the zombies eat my protagonist's parents' brains," he says. "I got a sudden burst of inspiration. Please don't yell at me for not doing the mail forwarding. I'm an artist, I'm fragile."

"I don't care about the mail forwarding right now. I need to talk to you."

I open the door to the desk area and slip through it, placing my bag on a stack of *New York Times* whose owners have yet to come to the desk to ask for them.

"This looks serious," Gavin says, spinning around on his elevated reception chair. "Please, lovely lady, have a seat. Let's discourse. What's troubling you?"

He gestures toward the shelf next to the backs of the mailboxes. I sit down on it, cross my legs, and say, "Remember the night of the prince's party, the one you said you were working during?"

"Jamie and I split the shift," he says, nodding while he strokes the few dark wisps of the goatee he's apparently trying to grow. "But yes, I recall it. Why?"

"Who was the RA on duty that night?"

Gavin leans forward to retrieve the duty log. I require the desk attendants to record every communication of note that takes place during their shifts. Only through organization have I kept Fischer Hall from descending into madness.

"That would have been"—Gavin runs his finger down the log entries for that night—"Howard Chen. Oh, yeah, right, remember? He was still on duty the next morning, when you made me call him to go up to Jasmine's room with Sarah. He did not like that too much."

"So I recall your saying. You also said something about him not liking it too much when you called him for a couple of lockouts."

Gavin nods. "Yeah. Because he was so hungover. He bitched me out. He wanted me to give the keys to the residents anyway, even though they didn't have ID, because he didn't want to get out of bed." His eyebrows gather. "Wait a minute, am I in some kind of trouble? Because I *didn't* give those residents their keys. I made Howard get the hell out of bed and get down here for the floor masters to let those residents in. He's a lying little punk if he's saying otherwise—"

"No, Gavin, you aren't in trouble," I assure him. "I'm only double-checking something. Can I see the sign-out log for the floor masters, please?"

He shrugs and says, "Sure," putting away the duty binder and then walking over to the key cabinet.

Extra copies of keys to every resident's room are kept in a large metal cabinet behind the desk, as well as master keys that fit into the lock of every room on each floor. While residents who have misplaced their room keys are allowed (three times per semester without charge, with a show of their student ID) to check out spares, only RAs are permitted to use the floor masters to escort a resident who's forgotten his or her keys *and* ID.

To be escorted to one's room by a sleepy RA on duty (who's had to stumble all the way down to the front desk in the middle of the night to get the master key to your floor simply because you've lost your ID) is a serious embarrassment, and tends to happen only when students are extremely drunk or in some other way distressed, which is why we don't allow the front desk attendants to simply hand them a spare key. We require an RA to speak with them, to make sure they don't require medical care, and of course make sure they really are residents by forcing them to recite their student ID codes from memory. Additionally, the lockout is recorded on the student's registration card. If such infractions become a habit, the lock to the door of the student's room is changed as a safety precaution, and the student is billed for it.

Lockouts and lock changes seem to make up a good 25 percent of my job some days.

I run my finger down the floor master checkout log for the night of the party after which Jasmine died. Sure enough, there's a note in Jamie's handwriting that the master key to the fourteenth floor had been checked out at 2:45 A.M.

That's going to be me someday, Ameera had wept. *Someone's going to sneak into my room and do that to me in my sleep one night.*

The initials of the person who'd checked out the fourteenth floor master key are *HC.*

I feel the same chill sweep over me that I'd felt in Lisa's office.

No, I tell myself. It's not possible. Jasmine and Howard were friends. They went to that party together. I saw them myself in the fifteenth-floor hallway on the video monitor. They were laughing, having fun.

Then I remember Howard's desperation in the office, the tears in his eyes as he asked how his parents were going to pay for both him and his brother to go to college at the same time.

Was it possible the murder of Jasmine Albright had nothing whatsoever to do with Prince Rashid and his secret bride, and instead had to do with a boy, distraught over losing a lucrative student employment contract—as Howard must surely have known he would, if word got out that he'd been at an alcohol-fueled rager while serving as the RA on duty?

Was *that* the photo that Jasmine had snapped on her phone, and threatened to Tweet? Howard Chen, drunk while on duty?

But that's ridiculous. No one would kill for such a reason. Except . . . people had killed over much less.

Who benefits?

Howard.

Eva would never have detected the tooth marks on the

back of Jasmine's lips if I hadn't found out about the party and asked her to take a second look.

Detective Canavan had said whoever had nearly succeeded in strangling Cameron had known what he was doing, and knew something about human anatomy.

Howard's major is premed.

"Gavin," I say in a tight voice. I so want it to not be true. "How many residents have checked into the fourteenth floor so far?"

Gavin pulls out my check-in binder and flips to the fourteenth floor. "Not that many. It's mostly upperclassmen, so we probably won't get the rest until this weekend. So far it's only the girls in fourteen-twelve. And Jasmine, of course, but she's—"

"Never mind that," I say. "Check the registration cards of the girls in fourteen-twelve. See if any of them had a lockout the night of the party."

"*All* of them?" Gavin asks dubiously. Looking up one registration card is a pain in the ass. Four is beyond tedium.

"All of them," I say.

"Okay."

He sighs, and gets to work. Nothing at the desk is computerized, a result of New York College's outdated conviction that if it supplied the residence hall public areas with computers, the student workers would immediately steal them and/or spend their shifts looking at pornography, when in fact what I know from experience they'd most likely do is spend their shifts writing screenplays.

It can't be Howard, I tell myself as I wait, idly flipping

through a copy of *Cosmo* I find at the top of the mail for-warding pile. Howard spent the entire time after the discov-ery of Jasmine's body vomiting down the trash chute. What cold-blooded murderer does that?

One who regrets his actions, but can't go back and change them.

How had Howard known I'd been at the student center, talking to Cameron Ripley?

Oh *God*. That's right. Howard had run into me and Lisa as we were returning from the meeting with President Al-lington. He'd been trailing along behind the campus tour Jasmine Tsai was giving her residents. Howard could easily have left the tour and followed me to the student center—I'd never have noticed, I was on the phone with Cooper—then walked into Cameron's office after I left, and—

Well, we know what followed. At that time Howard didn't know all the RAs who'd gone to the party were getting fired. He'd thought he still had a job to save.

Cooper was right. I was lucky to have escaped Cameron's office with my life.

My cell phone rings. I reach—very carefully—into my bag to retrieve it. It's Cooper.

"Hi, honey," I say in as normal a tone as I can muster considering I've just realized how close I came to being killed by a deeply disturbed homicidal maniac in my own place of work—and not even the one I *thought* was a homi-cidal maniac, a different one altogether. "How are you feeling?"

"I'm good," he says. His voice sounds sexily sleep-roughened. "But I'd be better if you were here, in bed with me, so we could play nurse and patient some more. That's a very good game."

"I know, I enjoyed it too. Sorry I had to go, but my shift at the hospital was over. I'll be back in a little while to check on you and give you your next injection."

I notice Gavin giving me an odd look from over the tops of the registration card boxes, so I get up and walk toward the front desk window for more privacy.

"I believe I'm the one who gave *you* the injection," Cooper says with a happy growl.

"You certainly did."

I notice out the window, which faces Washington Square Park, that Howard Chen, Joshua Dungarden, and several of the other ex-RAs are returning to the building from wherever it is they've been. Howard in particular does not look happy. He's lagging a little behind the others, staring at his own feet. Apparently, their attempts to get their jobs back from either the president or Joshua Dungarden's father's friend who works in the law school have not gone well.

"Cooper," I say as the RAs stop to talk to the residents protesting on their behalf in front of Fischer Hall. "I have to finish up something here at work. I'll talk to you as soon as I'm done, okay?"

"You sound weird," Cooper says. "Is everything all right?"

"It will be," I say. "I think. In a little while. I'll call you back." I hang up.

"What was *that* about?" Gavin asks curiously.

"None of your business," I say. "What have you found out?"

"Only that none of the girls in fourteen-twelve has had any lockouts whatsoever."

"What?" I leave the window to go to the desk to see for myself, but he's right. The back of each girl's registration card, where lockouts are listed, is clean.

There's only one reason Howard Chen could have checked out the master key to the fourteenth floor at a quarter to three in the morning the night Jasmine Albright died.

And that was to kill her.

Fischer Hall Cafeteria
Worker Shocked

Fischer Hall cafeteria cashier Madga Diego (voted "Most Popular Employee" on the New York College campus) has stated that she is "shocked" that New York College housing and residence life staff (as well as the president's office) has chosen to terminate the employment contracts of over half the RA staff of Fischer Hall, giving them less than a week to find alternative housing before classes begin and leaving the residents of nine floors of one of the most popular dorms on campus without effective leadership or guidance as they enter the fall semester.

"Poor little movie stars," Ms. Diego told this reporter. "I am shocked. I will no longer see their little faces here in my dining hall. Honey, take a napkin with that, you are spilling it on the floor."

The RAs were fired for allegedly attending a party at which alcohol was allegedly served, something every college student around this globe has done at one time or another, usually without ill consequence.

The *Express* will continue covering this news story until some kind of comment is given by some member of this administration.

New York College Express,
your daily student news blog

Evidence. That's what I need. Canavan will laugh at me if I go to him with what I have so far.

Simply finding Howard's fingerprints in Jasmine's room won't convict him, because they were friends, and she probably invited him into her room a number of times before the night of her murder. If his fingerprints are in the *Express* offices, though . . .

Wait, he'll probably say he volunteered there, or something. That won't convict him either, though the security tape from outside the offices of the *Express* just after Cameron's attempted murder probably could, providing the footage is clear enough to see Howard's face.

And what are the chances it is? No one's arrested him so far. He probably had his hoodie pulled over his head.

I need more.

"Gavin," I say. "I need you to do something for me. It's really important, but it also might be a little dangerous, and technically also a little bit illegal."

Gavin rises from the reception chair, planting both Goofy slippers firmly on the floor. "I'm in."

"I haven't even told you what it is yet."

"Doesn't matter," Gavin says. "I've told you before, I'm your servant until the day I die. Or the day you die. Which will probably come before I die since you're so much older than I am, but on that day I shall weep copiously until I have tears to weep no more."

I want to roll my eyes at his theatrics, but they're kind of cute and happen to suit my purposes at the moment.

"Okay," I say. "I want you to use my master key to let yourself into Howard Chen's room—it's okay, he's outside right now—then stand there and listen for a ring tone. If you hear it, grab the phone, come back downstairs, and give it to me. Do you think you can handle that?"

Gavin yawns. "Child's play."

"Good." I unhook the building's master key—there are only four copies; mine, Lisa's, Carl's, and Julio's—from my key chain and hand it to him. "Hurry. Room fifteen-fourteen. If there's no ring tone in five minutes, come back down, unless I call you sooner on your own smartphone. That will mean that Howard's on his way up, and you need to get the hell out of there. Got it?"

"Got it." Gavin is already running for the elevator. Meanwhile, I've taken my emergency phone list from my pocket. Jasmine Albright's number is the first one listed on it, since her last name came first on this semester's crew of RAs.

Funny how she'd sneered at my emergency phone list, I think, and now it just might help catch her murderer.

I figure I'll give Gavin a minute to catch the elevator, then key into Howard's room before I dial. Howard is still outside with the other fired RAs, talking to the protesting freshmen. This is going to work. It's going to work fine.

Of course, it's likely Howard's destroyed Jasmine's phone. What kind of fool would keep such an incriminating piece of evidence?

Then again, Howard hasn't shown many signs of intelligence so far. Funny how med students—and even doctors—can be so bright about some things and so dumb about others.

"Excuse me." An impossibly young-looking girl approaches the desk, speaking in a voice so low it's practically a whisper.

"Yes?" I say to her.

"I heard a rumor you guys give away"—her voice drops even lower, so low I have to lean forward to hear her—"free toilet paper here. Is that true?"

"The rumors are true," I say, and hand her two rolls from the shelf beneath the phone. "Enjoy."

The girl's face brightens as if I've handed her rolls of twenty-dollar bills. "Oh, *thank you*," she cries, and rushes off.

Considering how much her family is paying in tuition, you wouldn't think free toilet paper would make her so delighted. But I'm glad to have brightened someone's day.

I'm sure Gavin couldn't have gotten to Howard's room yet, but I pick up the desk phone and dial Jasmine's number anyway. It rings four times before her voice mail picks up.

"Hey, you've reached Jazz." She sounds confident and happy. Obviously she couldn't have known at the time she was recording this message what kind of fate was awaiting her. *"You know what to do."*

Beep.

I hang up and dial again. Please, I pray as I do so. Please let Gavin pick up. I know there's no such thing as closure. But please help us find the person who did this to Jasmine, so we can keep him from ever doing it to anyone else again.

"Hey," Pete calls, from across the lobby at the security desk. "What are you doing over there, Heather?"

"Oh, filling in for Gavin for a few minutes while he gets something to eat," I say, dialing again.

Pete looks around the empty lobby. "I didn't see him go into the caf."

"No," I say casually. "He went up to his room. He has some special cereal he likes."

What am I doing? I ask myself as Jasmine's phone rings in my ear. I'm even lying to my closest friends and coworkers now. I've gone insane.

This probably has to do with what happened yesterday, the thing with Cooper and my mother and Ricardo. That's what Lisa would say anyway, if she were here. That I should go see a therapist, because I have issues. Mommy issues. It always goes back to our mothers. Isn't that what shrinks are always supposed to say?

"Who are you on the phone with?" Pete wants to know.

"Oh, no one," I say, hanging up. "Wrong number."

A second later, I pick up and dial one last time. Come on, Gavin, I pray. Great. Now I'm praying to Gavin. *Pick up. Pick up. Pick—*

"Hells, woman." Gavin's voice fills my ear. "You didn't tell me this was *Jasmine's* phone! Am I speaking into a *dead girl's* phone? It's pink and has unicorn stickers all over it. I hope ironically. Anyway, it says 'Jazz' on it in purple sparkles."

I close my eyes. Thank you, God.

"Gavin," I say, opening my eyes again. "Where was it?"

"Under his damn pillow," Gavin says. He sounds manic with excitement. "This guy is a *freak*. Who keeps a dead girl's phone under his damn pillow? I am so putting this into my screenplay. Hell, I am starting a *new* screenplay just so I can put this in it. You should see this shit. This guy is

Hannibal Lecter the Second. How did he pass the test to become an RA? *I'd* make a better RA than this guy. Who hired him?"

I wince. *Simon Hague*, I want to reply, but I'm too professional.

"Can I have some trash bags, please?" a voice at my elbow asks.

I duck to grab some from beneath the counter.

"Gavin," I whisper urgently into the phone, "please do as I asked. Leave Howard's room now, and come back down here with that phone *immediately*."

"Oh, hells no, I'm not leaving," Gavin says. "This is research, dude. I have never seen anyone who makes his bed so damned tight. You could bounce quarters off this shit. This guy's mom must have warped his brain to make him so anal."

Mommy issues.

"Gavin." My throat has gone dry. That's because as I've straightened up to hand over the trash bags, I see the face of the person who's asked for them.

It's Howard Chen.

He looks as shocked as I feel. His lips are parted in confusion, his eyes wide, his fingers, on the trash bags I've just handed him, white-knuckled.

"Did I hear you tell *Gavin* to leave my room?" Howard asks. "And to come back down here with a phone?"

"No," I say quickly, giving a completely fake laugh. "Of course not. Why would Gavin be in your room, Howard? He's in his own room, on a break, and he's taking way too long, which is why I'm telling him to get off the phone and get back down here."

"Uh-oh," Gavin says in my ear. "Got it. He's back. Getting out of here, quick."

There's a click. Gavin's hung up.

"Okay, Gavin," I say, pretending Gavin's still on the line. "No, I don't care if you're talking to your mom, I want you back down here now. I have work to do and need to get back to my office."

I slam down the handset and roll my eyes at Howard. "God. Gavin's so annoying sometimes, right? So, you're going to start moving out, huh, Howard? Is that why you need trash bags? Getting rid of old stuff?"

Howard isn't falling for my act.

"I know what I heard," he says in a voice without a hint of humor—much like his face. "You said, 'leave Howard's room now, and come back down here with that phone.'"

"Now, why would Gavin be in your room, Howard?" I ask, walking over to the pile of newspapers on which I've left my purse. My heart has begun thumping a little erratically. Earlier, I had absolutely no intention of taking out the gun Hal insisted I bring to work.

Now I'm even more determined not to. What I need is my cell phone, so that I can discreetly text Pete over at the security desk and have him call 911, as well as Dr. Flynn over at psych services and also campus security.

Howard Chen may indeed be the "lying little punk" Gavin recently accused him of being, and he's also no doubt a murderer.

But he's also a student at this college, and a deeply disturbed one at that, who needs our help.

Instead of answering, Howard simply stares at me, his eyes narrowing. The hand on the trash bags is no longer white-knuckled.

This is a good sign. Maybe I'm getting through to him.

"That doesn't even make any sense," I say, taking my purse with me as I stroll casually back to the area of the desk where the reception phone sits. I have the best chance of surreptitiously slipping out my personal phone there, without his noticing.

"Why don't you just go on up to your room and check if you're so worried about people invading your personal space," I say to him, confident that Gavin's long gone from Howard's room by now. "I'm sure you'll find it exactly the way you left it."

"No, I won't," Howard says. He's released the trash bags completely, and slipped both hands into the deep pockets of his hoodie.

"Howard," I say. I've dug my smartphone from the pocket in which I keep it. "I think you're being a little paranoid. Maybe this whole thing with the president's office is getting to you. I swear to you it's going to work out, though."

Pete, I'm texting as I speak. *Howard Chen killed Jasmine. Call 911/Psych/Security. But do not alarm him! Dangerous!*

I add a frowny face for emphasis and hit send.

"It's not going to work out," Howard says emotionlessly.

"Hey," Gavin says, panting as he throws open the door to the desk and jogs in. "Sorry that took me so long. Thanks for the break, Heather. I was starving."

Howard stares at him, dead-eyed. "I thought you were calling your mother."

Gavin darts a quick glance at me. "Oh, yeah. I grabbed something to eat while I was returning her call."

"Well, I'm glad you got that straightened out," I say in a briskly businesslike tone, darting a glance over Howard's shoulder at Pete. He's received my text, thrown me a wide-eyed, startled glance, and begun pointing questioningly at Howard, who fortunately doesn't notice since his back is to the hefty security officer.

"Yes," I say, nodding energetically. "We definitely have it all straightened out now."

Pete's nodding and giving me the thumbs-up as he reaches for the phone on the wall behind him.

"I don't think we do have this all straightened out, Heather," Howard says somberly, and draws his smartphone from the pocket of his hoodie. He pushes a button on it.

My heart gives another staggered leap. I don't know quite what I'm expecting—maybe for the package room to explode—but it certainly isn't what occurs, which is that Gavin's pajama bottoms begin playing Miley Cyrus's "Party in the U.S.A."

"Oh, shit," Gavin says, looking down at his pants pocket. The material of his pajamas is so thin, I can see a bright pink phone flashing in his front pocket as the ring tone continues to sound.

Howard holds his smartphone toward me so that I'm able to see the name on the screen of the person he'd dialed.

Jasmine Albright—Emergency Contact.

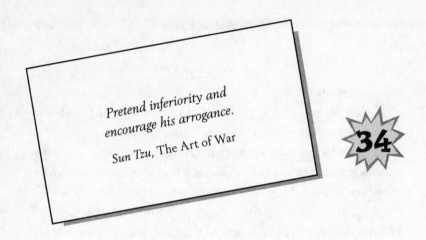

Pretend inferiority and encourage his arrogance.

Sun Tzu, The Art of War

34

What was that you were saying about how Gavin didn't go into my room?"

Howard's lower chin has begun to tremble, the way it did in the hall director's office right before he'd started to cry.

Only this time he doesn't look like he's about to cry. He looks furious.

"Howard," I say. I've dropped the act. I'm sincerely frightened over what he might do next. We've just proven that he's killed one person, and probably tried to kill at least one other. There's no telling what he might do next. "Howard,

I'm sorry. We did it because we're worried about you. We care about you, and we want to get you the help you need."

"Don't you get it? It's too late for *help*."

On the word "help," Howard hurls his cell phone across the lobby. It whizzes so close to a kid who's strolling into the building, carrying his skateboard, it almost hits him in the face. Instead, it smashes against one of the marble walls near the ornately carved fireplace, which hasn't been lit since I've worked at Fischer Hall.

"Hey, man," the kid with the skateboard says, giving Howard a dirty look. "What are you trying to do, kill someone?"

Gavin and I exchange wide-eyed glances. Um, yes, actually.

Kyle Cheeseman and Joshua Dungarden enter the building from the protest just in time to see the projectile go flying. Both of them gawk at Howard as well.

"What's the matter, dude?" Joshua asks, seeing his friend's face, as well as the expressions on ours, not to mention Pete, who is standing, rigid, behind the security desk. It takes an emergency of some momentousness to cause Pete to stand.

Howard shrugs off the gentle hand Joshua's laid upon his shoulder.

"I'm not going to jail!" he screams.

Then he runs past his startled friends, as well as the skateboarder and Pete, before the security guard can react. Instead of dashing outside, he heads through the lobby straight into the cafeteria, which I can tell from the busy hum emanating from its open doors has become crowded with late-rising Friday-morning diners.

"Shit," I say, grabbing my purse and tearing out from behind the front desk. "Shit, shit, shit, shit."

"Heather," Gavin cries. "Wait. What do you want me to do?"

"Stay there," I shout, trying to remember from the crisis management seminars I attended over the summer what one is supposed to do in situations like this. The only thing I can recall is a video from Homeland Security that instructed us that, if attacked in our workplace by gunmen, we're supposed to run, then hide, then, as a last resort, throw a pair of scissors at the attackers.

Tom Snelling and I had laughed until we cried at the idea of throwing a pair of scissors at an armed gunman, particularly the one in the video, who was dressed in full body armor. We'd been asked by Simon Hague, who'd been running the seminar, to leave until we could compose ourselves. We'd gone out for gelato and then shopping for shoes to match my wedding gown. (I'd asked Tom if he wanted to be an honorary bridesmaid, but he'd refused on the grounds of preferring to work behind the scenes to "beautify" me.)

The information from the seminar isn't very useful in a situation concerning an unarmed, clearly deranged student, even if he has already killed one person, attempted to kill another, and seems ready to kill himself.

I call over my shoulder, "Keep people from going into the dining hall!"

I don't stick around to see how Gavin processes this information. I follow Pete as he sprints into the cafeteria, shouting into his radio, "We've got a ten-fifty in progress at Fischer Hall, I repeat, a ten-fifty who is a danger to himself and probably others. Send units immediately."

"What's a ten-fifty?" I ask him.

"Disorderly person," he says. We've stopped in the middle of the cafeteria, where there are quite a few empty tables, but even more that are crowded with freshmen in their pajamas enjoying healthful egg-white omelets. I immediately recognize Kaileigh, who's apparently taking a break from her busy protesting schedule to have breakfast with her mother and a balding man who can only be her father.

Kaileigh ducks her head when I attempt to make eye contact, however, and pretends not to know who I am as she heads toward the bagel bar. I am now apparently one of the Evil Administrators, and the Enemy.

Great.

Everyone else in the dining hall seems to be staring at us, however (except Mrs. Harris, who is engrossed in what appears to be a frittata). The security guard and the girl with the big purse who've come running in for no evident reason are the source of a great deal of interest and whispered speculation.

"I don't really know how else to classify him," Pete is going on. "Disorderly seems good. I could have said it was an assault, but he hasn't really assaulted anyone . . . today, anyway."

I feel that Pete is overthinking things. "Do you see him anywhere?"

I'm scanning the tables, the bagel bar, the fresh-fruit spa water bar, and the hot food line. There are people everywhere, but none of them is Howard.

"No. Do you?"

"I'm guessing he ducked through the kitchen doors and out the back exit."

"Crap," Pete says with a sigh as he begins trundling toward the kitchen door. "Why do they always have to run? I hate running."

"*Mi amor.*" Magda approaches us, having abandoned her post by the ID scanner. "Heather. What are you two doing in here? And why do you look so sweaty?"

"Did a kid just run through here?" Pete asks. "Asian kid in a hoodie?"

Magda shrugs. "I don't know, I was busy, the guy is here." She points at "the guy," who turns out to be the snack-cake deliveryman. He is stuffing fresh delicious fruit pies and chocolate cakes into the snack rack. I try not to let this distract me, but register it for later, since I still have some declining dollars left on my ID card. "I didn't see anything. What did this boy do? Try to sneak into the building? Is he a deliveryman? Is he from Charlie Mom's? Is he trying to put menus under all the doors again?"

"No, Magda," I say. "He lives here. He's troubled. We want to help him."

Actually, he's a murderer and we want to incarcerate him, but it would probably be a violation of his student right to privacy to share this in front of the table of sleepy freshmen girls who are sitting nearby.

"Oh, poor little movie star," Magda says, looking sad. "If I see him, I'll let you know."

"We saw him," one of the first-year girls chimes in. She has red hair and freckles. "In the Harvard hoodie? He ran over there." She points in the direction of the door to the kitchen.

Pete sighs. "I knew it. He ran. Okay, I'll go. You stay here,

Heather, in case he circles back this way. Also in case the cops show up. Tell them where I am." He hustles off—speed-walking more than running—the leather of his duty belt creaking.

"Cops?" The freshmen girls look thrilled and frightened at the same time. "What'd this guy do? Did he *rape* someone?"

"No," I assure them, though of course the truth is going to come out soon enough. "The police want to ask him some questions, is all."

"Oh." The girls look disappointed, until Red Hair and Freckles points again. "There he is! He didn't go through the door! He was hiding!"

Unbelievably, when I glance in the direction she's pointing, I see that she's correct. Howard is slinking out from beneath a cafeteria table, his gaze on the door through which Pete's just left. Looking relieved, Howard is straightening up and tugging on his hoodie. He begins sauntering back toward the lobby, apparently considering only the security guard a threat to his freedom.

Well, he's in for a surprise.

"You!" Magda says, pointing at him with one long, metallic-gold nail. "Stop and talk to this lady." The fingernail turns toward me.

Howard freezes, his eyes widening in surprise. All his attention had been concentrated on Pete. Apparently, he hadn't even realized I was in the room until just now.

The entire cafeteria falls silent, including everyone working behind the steam tables. No serving forks scrape. Not even a coffee cup rattles as it returns to a tray.

"Howard," I say, moving toward him. "I'm not here to hurt

you—" I add this as he takes a step back for every one I take forward. "But I'm not going to allow you to leave either. You need help, and we're going to make sure you get it. That's why we're here."

"That's not why you're here," Howard says in a voice that shakes. "I know why you're here. To take me to jail. Well, I don't need that kind of help!"

He whirls around and tears off in the direction of the hot food line, colliding with the fresh-fruit spa water bar on his way, which he destroys—on purpose to keep me and who-ever else might be in pursuit—by overturning, one by one, first the watermelon water dispenser, then the honeydew (both flavors of the day).

The oversize glass watercoolers go crashing to the floor, sending gallons of water, sharp splinters of glass, ice, and chunks of melon everywhere.

The silence in the cafeteria is broken. Magda screams. So do the first-year girls at Red Hair and Freckles's table. By now everyone in the cafeteria is aware that there's a madman on the loose. They do exactly as we were instructed to do by the crisis management video from Homeland Security: they run, streaming through the open doors to the lobby.

All except for the few people who have the misfortune to be behind the water bar. That includes everyone standing in line for hot food. They scatter as they see Howard coming, some ducking beneath the counter and joining Jimmy, who's waved for them to join him in the kitchen, and others making a run around Howard for the lobby, only to find themselves slipping and falling on the spilled water and melon, cutting themselves painfully on the broken glass.

Magda, who's bravely remained behind, rushes forward to help them up, with napkins for them to press against the wounds.

Unfortunately, Howard seems focused on a single area of the dining hall, and one resident standing beside it can seem to neither run nor hide. Kaileigh Harris is frozen in place at the bagel bar, a newly toasted English muffin in one hand (I got the last bagel) and a butter knife in the other, staring wide-eyed at Howard as he lurches toward her.

My heart sinks. Oh, no. Not Kaileigh. Anyone but Kaileigh.

For a second Howard comes so close to her, it seems as if he means to snatch her muffin. Kaileigh, who obviously doesn't understand what's going on (who would?), drops the butter knife and holds the English muffin toward him, as if to say, *Here. Is this what you want? Take it.* It's a little like watching a child fall into the gorilla pen at the zoo, then seeing the child offer the enraged gorilla his balloon.

Bread isn't what Howard wants. He slaps the toast from Kaileigh's hand, reaches past her, and grabs the large serrated knife sitting on the cutting board behind her.

Oh God, no, I think as from somewhere in the cafeteria, I hear Kaileigh's mother scream in a voice that sounds as if it's been ripped from the depths of her soul, *"Kaileigh!"*

It's too late though. Kaileigh turns huge, frightened eyes in the direction of her mother's voice. I see her lips murmur the word "Mom?"

A second later, Howard has one arm around her narrow waist, and the edges of the serrated knife at her throat.

35

I love him.
Does he love me?
Enough to last an eternity?
In thirty days, we'll pledge our troth
Unless something happens
To call it off

"Wedding Jitters,"
written by Heather Wells

I'll kill her!" Howard shouts at everyone around him, which, it turns out, is only me and Kaileigh. Everyone else has run away, or is keeping a wide, respectful distance.

"Please don't," I say to him softly.

I have melon stuck to the bottom of my shoe because I've raced through the broken watercoolers. I'm standing only ten feet away from him. I can see each tear as it slides down Kaileigh's cheek.

"I'll slit her carotid artery and she'll bleed out before you can get her to a hospital," Howard says. "Your common carotid is the artery in your throat that you check for your pulse. If it's slit, all your blood pulses out, and you die. Is that what you want? For this girl to die right here in front of you?"

Everyone except for Kaileigh's mother, who is sobbing, is absolutely silent. My heart is pounding so hard, I'm positive I'm not the only one who can hear it.

"No, Howard," I say. "None of us wants that. There's no need for anyone to get hurt here—"

"What about me?" Howard demands. Kaileigh's not the only one who's crying. He is too. "Doesn't anyone care about me? *I* got hurt."

"Who hurt you, Howard?" I ask. I've got to keep him talking so he won't hear what I hear, the sound of sirens in the distance. They've been growing louder every second. I hope Howard doesn't notice them.

Or the fact that I'm slowly undoing the buckle on my purse.

"All of you," he says. "But especially Jasmine. She had a photo—"

"Of you at Prince Rashid's party?" I ask.

"She thought it was funny," Howard says. "She was going to Tweet it. The RA on duty, partying with a prince. I tried to explain to her—I tried to get her to delete it, but she wouldn't. I told her I could lose my job. I could lose my housing."

His voice breaks.

"But then I did anyway. Stupid. So stupid. My parents are so mad at me. They told me I'm a joke."

"Oh, Howard," I say. "I'm so sorry."

I've slipped my hand into my purse. I can feel the cool, smooth metal groove of the pistol against my fingers.

"All because Jasmine didn't care," he goes on. "She thought it made a funny story for that stupid blog. Jasmine came from a rich family. She didn't need the RA job. It was all a joke to her. *I* was a joke to her. But I'm not a joke."

He presses the knife closer to Kaileigh's throat, and I see the girl flinch in pain, though she's otherwise paralyzed with fear.

"I may not have gotten into Harvard," Howard sobs, "but I am no one's joke!"

"No, Howard," I say. "You're no one's joke. I agree that the way Jasmine treated you was really unfair. I wish you'd come and talked to us about it, but it's not too late. Why don't you let Kaileigh go so you and I can talk now?"

I'm a pretty good actress. You have to be in order to convince stadiums filled with tweens and teens that the song you're singing is going out only to them, or that your heart truly was broken by the boy in the lyrics you're crooning.

Over the years since I've stopped performing, I think my acting skills have only gotten better, more subtle, especially since I've taken the job at Fischer Hall. Every day I have to convince parents that I truly do feel the pain of their precious son who simply must have a room facing south or he'll never make good grades because of a lack of sunlight, or their sweet daughter who needs a single because her PMS is so chronic, she could never possibly get along with a roommate. Every day, I pretend to like students I cannot abide, and supervisors I heartily wish I'd never met.

But somehow my acting skills fail me today—either that, or Howard's guilt over his crimes has given him hypersensitive powers of perception.

"No," he says, his voice a high-pitched whine. "You're trying to trick me, just like Jasmine."

He backs away, dragging a now openly weeping Kaileigh with him.

"I'm not, Howard," I insist. "Let Kaileigh go, and you'll see. I'm on your side. If you release Kaileigh, you and I can go somewhere quiet, and we can talk about what Jasmine did to you, and come to some kind of arrangement about your housing situation. I swear it. You know me, Howard. You know I wouldn't lie to you about this. Just put the knife down and let her go."

Can I really do this? I ask myself as my fingers close around the handle of the pistol Hal gave me and I steady my index finger along the barrel of the gun. Cooper told me to keep my finger there, and never to curl it around the trigger, until I'm ready to release the safety and fire.

But can I fire on this boy, and do it quickly enough so he doesn't have a chance to cut Kaileigh more deeply than he already has—I can see the serrated points of the knife sinking into the soft skin of her throat—and also not hit her anywhere vital? He's using her as a shield, probably fully aware that an NYPD SWAT team will be showing up soon. He's backed them both up so that his spine is against the metal steam tables where hot food is served. No way SWAT will be able to get to him from behind, even if they could sneak up on him without his noticing.

I don't see any alternative. Blood is beginning to trickle down Kaileigh's neck, splashing onto the stylish white lawn blouse she's wearing. I no longer hear the sirens behind me, which means the police are here, parked outside the building, and probably lining up outside the cafeteria with their own pistols drawn. The minute Howard sees them, he's going to panic.

I could wait for Dr. Flynn, and whatever hostage negotiator the police are undoubtedly going to bring in, but I'm not sure I have that much time. One motion of that knife—which I know is sharp, because I used it earlier this morning to slice through my own breakfast—and Kaileigh will be dead.

Kaileigh Harris is my resident. Protecting her is my responsibility. Howard already took the life of one Fischer Hall resident, and attempted to take the life of another student.

I won't allow him to take the life of another.

I shoulder my bag and flick off the safety of the pistol Hal assured me was so good for picking off varmints, but not so good for hitting threats of the two-legged variety.

"Howard," I say. "I'm going to ask you one last time. Let her go."

"I told you," Howard says tiredly. "I don't believe—"

I pull the pistol from my bag with both hands, aim, and fire in one smooth motion.

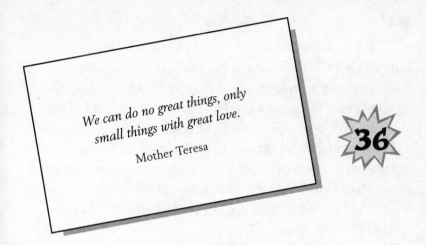

We can do no great things, only
small things with great love.

Mother Teresa

36

The bullet lodges itself neatly into the back of Howard's hand, the one holding the knife.

Fortunately, instead of raking the knife across Kaileigh's throat, Howard's hand jerks upward and out from the force of the bullet, and the knife clatters harmlessly to the floor. Hal had the foresight to load the pistol with small-caliber hollow-point ammunition, so that instead of traveling through Howard's hand and into Kaileigh's neck, the bullet stays in Howard's flesh, expanding upon entering its target. Not at all appropriate for squirrel hunting, but highly effective for stopping mentally unstable boys holding young women hostage at serrated knifepoint.

"Ow!" Howard screams, waving his smoking hand in the air. "Ow! Why did you do that? That really hurt!"

I lower the gun, my hands shaking uncontrollably.

Howard doesn't know how lucky he is. I was aiming for the center of his head, the largest part of his body not covered by part of Kaileigh's. It was a perfect target.

Thank God I missed.

The next thing I know, SWAT officers from the Sixth Precinct are swarming the Fischer Hall cafeteria screaming, "Freeze! NYPD! Everyone down on the floor!"

Both Howard and I are pressed to the floor by police officers dressed all in Kevlar and holding assault rifles. Howard is quickly arrested and taken away. Mr. and Mrs. Harris fall upon Kaileigh, who is shaken up but unhurt, except for a superficial cut on her neck. They shower her with kisses and promises that they will never, ever leave her side again.

It's not until much later, as I'm sitting at a table in the cafeteria—where I've been commanded to stay by the unit supervisor—picking pieces of honeydew out of my hair, that Detective Canavan saunters over and sits down beside me.

He has a mug of steaming coffee for himself in one hand and another mug piled high with whipped cream in the other. He slides the mug piled high with whipped cream toward me.

"So, Wells," he says. "What's this I hear about you shooting the perp in the hand with an unregistered and unlicensed target pistol?"

"It's not true." Magda is sitting beside me, helping to pick

pieces of melon from my hair, one of the unfortunate consequences of having been forced to lie on the cafeteria floor for
so long. "I didn't see a gun. And no one can find a gun. So,
there is no gun. Is there, Heather?"

"It's not true," I say, taking a sip from the mug Canavan
has slid my way. It's coffee mixed with a generous portion
of hot cocoa. In fact, it would be more accurate to call it hot
cocoa with a splash of coffee. How did he remember? "What
would a girl like me be doing with a gun, anyway? Hey—"
I jerk the mug away from my lips. "Is there *alcohol* in this?"

Canavan shrugs. "There might be a little whiskey. In my
personal experience, it's the only thing that works on the
shakes."

I glance down at my fingers, which are still trembling. I
quickly pull both my hands beneath the table.

"I didn't think anyone had noticed," I murmur, staring
down at the whipped cream floating on the top of my drink.

"No one has, I don't think," Canavan says. "Takes someone
who's been in your same shoes to see it." He doesn't mention
the details—who he shot when he was in my shoes, or how
it turned out. He doesn't have to. "The boy'll be all right—
fit enough to stand trial, anyway, for murdering the first girl
and attempting to murder the reporter and the other girl,
today. He won't lose the hand either."

"That's good," I murmur, remembering Howard's scream
as the bullet entered his skin. *Why did you do that? That
really hurt!*

Canavan curls a lip, amused by my expression. "You really
need to toughen up a little, Wells, if you're serious about
getting a degree in criminology. All these mutts have a sob

story about why they did the things they did, and a lot of them are pretty good. Hit you right here." He points to his heart. "On the other hand, there are millions of other people out there in the world with stories that are equally heartbreaking, and guess what? They *didn't* solve their problems by sticking their hands over a girl's face to suffocate her, or by trying to choke some other guy to death with his earbuds. So don't let 'em get to you. Now. Where's the gun?"

I raise my eyes, widening them innocently the way Howard had. "Gun? I don't know what you're talking about, Detective."

"Cut the crap, Wells. Someone shot that kid. To get off a shot like that, and without injuring a hair on that girl's head, would take a pretty decent marksman."

"Or markswoman," I point out. "Women are actually thought to be better shots than men, overall, because they have lighter grips and lower centers of gravity, and so a firmer stance."

Canavan stares at me with something akin to horror. "Who the hell told you that?"

"Oh, I don't know," I say. "I read it on the Internet. Why, is it not true?"

"Not in my experience," he says. "My wife and daughters won't go anywhere near the range, and God knows I've been trying to get them to for the past twenty years."

"Lack of interest," I say, "and lack of skill are two entirely different things."

"Did you shoot the damned kid or not, Wells? Hostage says you did."

I've long since disposed of the evidence. It's amazing what a girl can do if she's resourceful enough, has worked in the same building long enough, and knows enough people in the right places. Oh, and is getting married in a month, and leaving for her honeymoon in Venice, and doesn't want to deal with the hassle of an unlawful-use or possession-of-firearm charge that might keep her from traveling outside the country.

"I have no idea what you're talking about, Detective," I say sweetly.

"Neither do I," Magda says. "I was there, and I saw the whole thing. I don't know where the shot came from. Somewhere over there, maybe." She points in the direction of the snack-cake rack. "Oh, he's gone. Well, it could have been him. You know, that little girl was hysterical. Who knows what she saw?"

She finds another piece of melon in my hair and drops it onto the table.

Detective Canavan looks dissatisfied. "Right," he says. "Why don't I believe you two?"

I shrug. "This job has hardened you," I say. "You really should think about retiring. Maybe let a younger detective take over for you. Maybe even me, someday."

"God help this city if that ever happens," Canavan mutters. He scoots his chair from the table and says, as he leaves, "Use bar soap and water on your hands, none of that anti-bacterial stuff. That's the best way to remove gunpowder residue. And for God's sake, go home to that boyfriend of yours. And finish that." He points at the mug in front of me. "That's an order."

"She can't go home," Magda says matter-of-factly as she begins to braid my hair. I'm afraid to look at what she's styling it into. "She has her final fitting for her wedding gown. It's in half an hour."

I groan. I'd forgotten all about it.

"Oh God," I say. "I think I'm going to have to postpone that."

"No," Magda says, smacking me lightly on top of the head. "You can't do that! It's important! You have to look your best for the big day. You can't disappoint Cooper. Besides, we're all coming, to see how the dress has turned out."

I groan again, and reach for the drink Canavan has doctored. "Magda, no. It's all the way uptown and I'm just not feeling up to riding the subway right now. I'm too, uh, beautiful—"

"Jesus, Mary, and Joseph," Canavan says disgustedly. He turns and whistles at a uniformed officer walking by. "You. Sullivan. C'mere."

The officer hurries over. "Sir?"

"You got a patrol car, right?"

"Yes, sir."

"Drive these two ladies uptown," he says.

Officer Sullivan looks down at us in confusion. "Sir?"

"They've got a very important appointment," Canavan explains tersely. "Use your lights and siren. They can't be late."

Sullivan looks even more confused. "I'm sorry, sir, which precinct am I taking them to uptown?"

"No precinct," Canavan roars. "They've got a wedding-dress-fitting appointment. Now go!"

Which is how, forty-five minutes later, Magda and I find ourselves outside the boutique at which I bought my wedding dress, thanking Officer Sullivan and his partner, who both seem highly amused by the unusual mission.

"Next time I have an emergency," Magda coos across the sidewalk, blowing them kisses, "I'm only calling you two!"

"You do that," Officer Sullivan says, and smiles as he waves back. There are probably worse ways a police officer can spend a morning than transporting two blondes in the back of his cruiser.

Before I touch the door to the boutique, it's yanked open, and Nicole Cartwright is standing there wearing a butter-yellow jumpsuit and a stricken expression on her face.

"Where have you been?" she demands. "You're late."

"Only a little late," I say. "There was traffic by the Pan Am Building."

"You couldn't have called?" Nicole demands. "It never occurred to you that things might have gotten a little hectic here too?"

"At the bridal shop?" Magda looks at me, her drawn-on eyebrows raised. "What happened? Has someone had diarrhea in the sink like in that movie about the bridesmaids?"

"Oh my God, Huey, chill." Jessica suddenly appears in the doorway, a glass of champagne in one hand and her cell phone in the other. "Quit blocking the doorway and let them in."

"I've told you to stop calling me—"

The door is torn open from behind Jessica, and suddenly Cooper appears on crutches, his face dark with beard scruff, not to mention new purple bruises that are only now beginning to show.

"Where is she?" he demands, squinting in the sunlight. Then he sees me and, despite the obvious pain he's in, begins to hobble toward me. "Don't you ever—"

I have no idea what kind of threat he's about to deliver, because I run toward him to wrap both arms around his neck and kiss him on the mouth, forgetting all about his bruised lips. He appears to forget about them too, and his cracked ribs as well, pulling me tight against his heart and filling me with the crisp clean Cooper-ish scent of him.

"What are you doing here?" I whisper, when he finally releases me—which he has to do, since he needs at least one arm to balance on his crutches. "You're supposed to be home, resting."

"You think I could stay in bed after hearing you *shot* someone?" he whispers back, his blue eyes looking a little moist. "And then went to try on *wedding dresses*? You crazy kook."

"Just one wedding dress," I say. "And you can't see me in it. It's bad luck."

"I think we've had all the bad luck any two human beings are allowed in one lifetime. It's time our luck changes for the better."

I kiss him on the nose, the one part of his face that escaped his encounter with Ricardo. "Then don't look at me in my dress until the big day."

The one arm he's kept around me tightens. "Deal. And don't you shoot anyone else until the big day. Unless they deserve it, like I hear the kid today did."

I squeeze him back. "Deal."

"Wow, Heather, I love your hair like that," Jessica says as Cooper and I enter the shop, reaching up to touch the French braid Magda's given me. "That's a good look for you. Anyway, don't listen to Nicole, it's not that big a deal."

"What's not that big a deal?" I ask. The owner of the shop, Lizzie Nichols, gives me a warm greeting, pours glasses of champagne for both Magda and me, then goes to make sure everything is ready in my dressing room, including the vintage wedding gown I've purchased from her, which she's been busy adjusting to my exact measurements. I'm not too surprised to see that Hal has accompanied Cooper to the shop and has taken up residency on a pink fainting couch beside a shabby-chic ivory-colored coffee table, looking completely uncomfortable and out of place.

I *am* a little surprised to see that in a gingham fabric armchair not too far from him sits Sammy the Schnozz, looking much more at ease, scrolling through messages on his smartphone (being a pawnbroker is a full-time business, after all).

What surprises me even more is when I hear a delicate cough from behind me, and I turn around.

It's my mother.

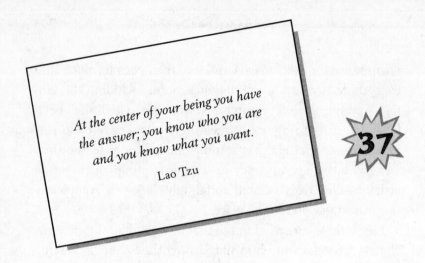

At the center of your being you have the answer; you know who you are and you know what you want.

Lao Tzu

37

R eally?" I ask in disbelief.

Because I haven't been through enough in one day? I've had one resident reveal he's put his and another resident's lives at risk by entering into a marriage forbidden by his criminally despotic father.

I've had to shoot another resident because he took a student hostage at knifepoint.

And now *this*?

I'm ready to turn around and walk straight out of the shop, champagne glass still in hand, when my father, of all people, stops me by blocking the door with his body.

"Just listen to what your mother has to say, Heather." His voice registers weary resignation.

"Why?" I demand flatly. "I'm tired. I have watermelon in my hair. I want to try on my wedding dress and then go have a nice lunch with my friends, like a normal person. I don't want to listen to any more bullshit excuses from anyone, Dad, *especially* Mom. Honestly, I can't take it anymore."

"Darling, I know," my mother says, moving toward me. She's wearing a long dove-gray tunic over soft, draping gray trousers and enough silver jewelry to choke a horse. Every time she moves, the chains around her neck and bangles at her wrists tinkle musically, exactly as they had the night she'd invited herself over to Cooper's brownstone. "I'm so, so sorry about what happened to Cooper—not to mention what I understand you went through this morning. But what happened with Cooper . . . that was my fault, and I couldn't be more sorry."

My eyes fill with tears—and ridiculously, almost more than anything else today, this is what enrages me the most. Why do I feel like crying over something this stupid woman has said?

"You're sorry for *that*?" I demand. "Not that you shouldn't be . . . you should. But out of everything, *that's* what you're sorry for? You aren't even responsible for that. Ricardo did that, not you."

"Yes, yes," my mother says. "But I should have known better than to think he wouldn't find me here, even if I did try to keep a low profile. You don't need this on top of all the other stresses you have."

By "this" she appears to mean Cooper's injuries. She gestures toward him as she says it, the bangles on her wrists tinkling.

I stare at her. I'm not the only one. All of my bridesmaids, and Cooper and his friends, are staring at her, too.

The urge to weep has left me.

"What stresses?" I ask my mother. "You mean wedding stresses?"

"Well, those," she says, "and everything else your father's told me about. I mean, my God, Heather, giving up your music? Working in a dorm? Do you think this is the life I'd hoped you'd have? Of course not."

I feel as if the ground beneath me is moving—like a subway train is passing beneath us. But there's no subway station nearby. What I'm feeling is a seismic shift in my emotions. A therapist would probably call it a breakthrough.

"What's so wrong with my life?" I demand. "I'm surrounded here in this shop with people who love me."

Well, except for Patty. Where *is* she? On the other hand, dancers are notoriously late for everything, and pregnant dancers are even worse.

"I do something I love for a living," I go on, "that helps others and gives me meaning in my life. I'm also going to school and studying to get a degree in something I believe in, something that I hope will make a difference in the world someday. I'm marrying the man I love, who loves me back—"

I throw a smile at Cooper, who smiles back so encouragingly as he leans on his crutches between his two sisters that I can feel his love radiating through me. It more than makes up for the love this woman has withheld from me.

"We're going to start a life together," I say to my mother.

"It may not be the kind of life you'd want, Mom, but it's exactly what I want. So why exactly did you have to come here now and try to mess it up?"

My mother blinks back at me, as well as at all my friends, who are glaring at her with what I can only call extreme hostility. Magda looks ready to grab the nearest champagne bottle and smash it over Mom's head, and I can't help noticing that Hal has one hand inside his duffel bag, which of course he's brought with him, sitting at his feet. Even Jessica has folded her rail-thin arms across her chest and narrowed her heavily lined eyes at my mother, like she's waiting for the signal for the bitch slapping to begin, and Nicole has both her plump hands squeezed into indignant fists. Sammy the Schnozz has actually looked up from his cell phone, shocked into paying attention to something other than falling gold prices.

In the ensuing silence, Lizzie Nichols, has come back into the waiting area.

"Well," she says brightly. "Everything's ready if you'd like to try on your dress now, Heath . . ."

Her voice trails off as she senses the tension in the room.

"Or maybe," she says, slowly backing away, as if from a coiled rattlesnake, "you and your family need a few more minutes. Why don't I come back later?"

She gives a bright smile and hurries away as quickly as her stylish, but extremely narrow, pencil skirt will allow.

My father breaks the silence.

"I think what Heather is looking for," he says to my mother, "is an apology. Not only for what happened to Cooper, but for . . . well, everything."

My mother nods. Now she's the one who appears resigned.

"I can see that," she says with a sigh. "I do have a way of mucking things up, don't I? But contrary to popular opinion, I didn't come here to try to mess up your life, Heather. Not on purpose, anyway." She walks toward the coffee table Hal is sitting beside and removes one of her jangly silver bracelets, dropping it onto the glass table cover. "I actually came here with the intention of trying to set things right between us." Another bracelet joins the first. "But as usual, what I wanted to say to you didn't come out the right way. I've always had problems expressing myself—unlike you. And then, of course, there's what happened to Cooper. I know you don't want anything more to do with me. That's probably better for everyone concerned. Ricardo will be making bail soon, and I wouldn't want to put any of you in danger by letting you know where you can find me, in case he asks."

She scoops off a few of the silver necklaces and drops them beside the bracelets. They make a surprisingly solid thunk on the glass.

"So trust me," Mom goes on. "I won't bother you again, Heather. The truth is, I never did get the hang of this mothering thing. Not everyone has the maternal instinct, you know. I read in a magazine once that some female mammals abandon their young in the wild. They simply can't be bothered. It's not the fault of the offspring. It's a faulty gene in the mother. The mothering gene, it's called. They lack it. I think I do too. In other words, Heather—" She pulls out both her long, sparkly chandelier earrings and lays them beside the rest of her jewelry on the coffee table. "It was never you, darling. It was me."

I stare at her bewilderedly. "I know that, Mom," I say. "Why are you taking off all your jewelry?"

"Oh." She looks down at the pile as if realizing for the first time it's there. "Call it a wedding present, if you like."

"Mom." I'm not angry at her anymore. How can I be, when I have such a rich life, and hers is so pathetic? Plus I've said everything I needed to say to her. I'm feeling pretty good. "I don't want your old jewelry."

"Oh," she says lightly. "I think you do. Consider it your 'something borrowed.'"

She steps forward to give me a quick hug. Now that all her necklaces and bracelets are gone, she doesn't jingle when she walks.

I don't want to hug her back, but there's something about being hugged by your mother that makes it impossible to not at least raise your arms and put them around her. The scent of her Chanel is as familiar to me, in a way, as the scent of Cooper's shampoo and laundry detergent. And also as comforting, even though she completely betrayed me once.

But it turns out you can't help loving your mother, no matter how hard you try.

"Good-bye, darling," she says, and turns and walks swiftly from the shop before I can say another word. My father doesn't attempt to bar her way.

"What the hell," Jessica demands, after downing the remains of her champagne, "was that all about?"

"I haven't the faintest idea," I say.

Sammy the Schnozz has begun lifting pieces of the jewelry from the coffee table. Of course he has a loupe, the magnifying eyepiece used to closely examine gems and precious metals. He's pulled one from his pocket and is studying her bracelets and chains with a jeweler's concentration.

"She feels bad, Heather," my father says. "She wanted to make amends."

Cooper laughs out loud at this.

"She does," my father insists. "She understands she won't be welcome at the wedding—and obviously can't attend because Ricardo will be hunting her—but if you can make a place for her in your heart, Heather—"

There will always be a place for her in my heart, I think. In my life? I'm not so sure.

Sammy the Schnozz whistles, slowly and appreciatively.

"What is it?" I ask him.

He lowers the loupe and looks at me solemnly. "Your mother may lack the maternal instinct, but she sure knows a thing or two about jewelry. These are platinum. All of them. Solid platinum."

I glance at Cooper, then back at Sammy the Schnozz. "No. No, they're not. They're silver. No one walks around wearing that much—"

"Platinum? No one I know. Pirates, maybe. Who else wears their fortune around their necks?"

"Or someone else's fortune," Cooper says, looking down at all the softly gleaming metal on the table.

I shake my head, hardly able to comprehend what I'm seeing.

"No," I say again, shaking my head. "No, she wouldn't do that. She wouldn't have stolen all my money only to give it back."

Sammy has his smartphone out and is working the calculator. "She didn't," he says. "Platinum is selling high these days, but what you'd get if you sold this by weight"—his fingers fly over the keyboard—"is only about a quarter of a million dollars."

I glance at Cooper, who returns my stunned gaze. "*Only* a quarter of a million dollars," I say to him.

"Not nearly what she owes you," he says. "But a start." A grin begins to spread across his face. He holds out one arm, and I step into his embrace. "We could definitely upgrade the honeymoon."

"Or," I say, "we could turn the basement into a nice apartment, and then rent it out and make a healthy return on our investment."

"So practical," Cooper says, kissing me. "Such an amazing head for money."

"And she's got really good aim," Virgin Hal adds shyly.

"Don't forget," my father, the convict, hastens to add, "whatever you do, you'll have to pay taxes on the sale of the jewelry."

"Thanks for the reminder, Dad," I say, looking up from Cooper's chest. "Did you know anything about this?"

"Well," Dad says, looking a little sheepish. "I can't say I'm entirely surprised. I knew your mother wanted to make amends, and I knew she and Ricardo had split up, judging from some phone conversations I've heard her making. I knew she took something of his, and he wanted it back—"

"No wonder she said to consider it something borrowed!" Magda cries, pointing at the jewelry. "She stole it!"

"From *my* manager, who stole it from me first. That jewelry is mine," I declare. "It's the only restitution I'm going to get."

"Damn straight," Cooper says, nodding at Hal. "Confiscate it, in the name of the law. Heather's law," he adds, winking at me.

"I'll be happy to," Hal says, and sweeps the jewelry into his duffel bag.

"How are we doing out here?" Lizzie, the proprietor of the salon, pops her head back into the waiting room. "Are we feeling ready to try on a wedding dress now?"

"You know what?" I say, turning to her. "I absolutely am."

"Well, then," she says, looking pleased. "Follow me."

And so I do.

The pleasure of your company is
requested at the marriage of
Heather Marie Wells
to
Cooper Arthur Cartwright
Saturday, the 28th of September
at half past two in the afternoon
The Grand Ballroom
The Plaza
Fifth Avenue at Central Park South
New York, New York

38

I stand at the back of the room, nervously twisting the ribbons on the end of my bouquet. Cooper and I chose Gerber daisies for our wedding because they're a nice cheerful flower for fall, and they aren't fussy in the same way we aren't fussy.

But the place where we've chosen to get married certainly is fussy.

"I think this is all a little too fancy," I say to Patty as she adjusts the bow on the sash on the side of my dress. It's shaped a little bit like a Gerber daisy, or at least a large, white silk rose. "Do you think this is too fancy? Cooper and I should have eloped. I knew we should have eloped."

"Hush," Patty says softly. "The Plaza Hotel is not too fancy for you. It isn't fancy *enough* for you. You should be getting married in the White House rose garden in this dress." She takes a step back and looks at me. "Seriously, this dress is perfect on you. You look like a modest, virginal Marilyn Monroe. You know, if President Kennedy had married her instead of Jackie."

"Modest and virginal wasn't exactly the look I was going for," I say, turning to look at myself in the mirror.

"Undercover bombshell," Patty says, adjusting my veil, which is really a confection of net, flowers, and a couple of feathers sticking out of the loose bun my long hair has been pulled into. "Tea length is perfect on you. Now go out there and knock Cooper dead."

"Please," I say queasily. "Don't use that phrase."

"Ooo." Patty winces. "Sorry. I forgot about his near brush with death last month. *Both* of your near brushes with death. Okay, let's go out there and not cause Cooper any bodily harm with your beauty, but make him remember all over again why he fell in love with you . . . your wit, beauty, and charm."

I take a deep breath and give myself one last glance in the mirror. I look nothing like my usual self. I've been up since dawn dealing with last-minute minicrises, such as Cooper's lost cummerbund, and a bomb scare at the Plaza that threatened to shut down the entire wedding (until we learned it was a "prank" by Cooper's younger brother, Jordan, who'd now been demoted from best man to the role of guest-book attendant. Frank, Patty's husband, was now best man, with Sammy the Schnozz and Hal as ushers).

Then I'd had to rush off to have my hair professionally styled and makeup professionally applied, all the while fighting butterflies in my stomach. I'm secretly convinced that somehow, Cooper and I are never going to end up as husband and wife, even though we've got the license.

Patty's right. I do look somewhat virginal in my white dress, cinched in tightly at the waist, then cascading outward to the knee like a bell of silk and tulle. But a virgin with a mischievous twinkle in her blue eyes and naughty twist to her red lips. How had the makeup artist done that? And why can't I accomplish it on a daily basis?

"Heather?" My father is calling from the outer room. "Are you ready? Perry says the music is starting, and we need to get to our places."

Perry. I so wish I could fire her for being so snooty. Well, I'll never see her again after today. You only get married once!

Oh God, please let me only get married once.

I turn around and hurry toward my father.

"Oh my," he says. "Don't you look pretty."

Dad's never been that liberal with the compliments, or the emotions.

My bridesmaids are more gushy when they see me.

"Heather!" Magda cries. "You look like an angel. A real angel from the top of a Christmas tree."

"That dress kicks ass," Jessica says, appraising me. "Seriously. You could kick someone's ass in that dress, and not rip it, that skirt is so full. I'm glad you didn't go for a mermaid, mermaid skirts suck. You can't kick ass in them at all."

Only Nicole is pouting, as usual. "I still think you should have gone for a long dress," she says. "When else are you going to get to wear a long dress but on your wedding day?"

"Don't be stupid, Huey. How's she going to run from a bad guy in a long dress?" Jessica asks. "She'd trip."

"There won't be any bad guys here today," I say, trying to believe it. "Not with all the cops we've got out there." And the fact that Ricardo is still sitting in Rikers, awaiting extradition back to Argentina, having turned out to have a few outstanding warrants there. "And you guys look *amazing.*"

They do. I let them select whatever they wanted to wear, so long as it was a dress matching the colors of the Gerber daisies in the floral arrangement I'd picked out.

Magda chose, as one would expect, a shimmering, Barbie-like one-shouldered evening gown in shocking pink. Patty is looking as cool and collected as a heavily pregnant woman can in rust. Jessica is seductive in a slinky lipstick-red number that clings to her slim body like a second skin, and Nicole— clearly with some guidance from her sister—looks sunny in a yellow Empire-waisted gown that is, as she so dearly wished for me, full length, but flattering on her.

"Ladies." Perry, the scarily busy wedding planner who refused to return our calls for so much of the time we were actually planning our wedding, appears at the one moment we actually need her least. She taps her headset imperiously. "It's time."

She propels Nicole out the door. Jessica turns to me.

"Are you sure you don't want an antianxiety med?" she asks, tapping her purse. "I have a ton. Half will take the edge right off, trust me."

I smile at her. "I think I'm going to be okay." I'm lying. I think I'm going to throw up, to be honest.

"Okay," Jessica says dubiously. "Well, you know where they are if you change your mind." She sets down her purse and starts toward the door. "If any are missing, I'll know," she adds darkly, giving Perry the stink eye. "I counted them earlier."

Perry purses her lips disapprovingly and points at me and my dad. "You two," she snaps. "You're on."

My dad looks down at me. "Ready?"

I don't have butterflies. I have bulls, ramming their way through my small intestines. Why am I so nervous? I'm marrying the man I love.

In front of four hundred—no, more—people, in the Grand Ballroom of the Plaza Hotel.

Why, oh, why, did we agree to do this? We were happy as we were. Marriage is going to ruin it. I'm going to trip. I'm going to mess up. I'm going to—

"Heather," my father says to me sternly. "You used to do this before every single performance. But everyone always loved you. So wipe that terrified look off your face and smile. Everyone out there is pulling for you and Cooper. There's nothing but love for you out there."

I blink up at my dad. I'm not entirely sure what he's talking about—he was barely even around when I was performing.

But he's right. No one is here to see me fail. They're here because they support the love Cooper and I have for each other.

And if I do trip, what's the worst that can happen?

I'll get back up again, like I always have.

"Okay, Dad," I say, and slip my hand through the crook of his arm.

The Grand Ballroom is even grander—and larger—than I remember it from last night's rehearsal, especially when it's filled with hundreds of chairs, and those chairs are filled with hundreds of people, most of whom I don't recognize. My heart begins beating so quickly when I see them, I'm certain it's going to burst. The music is beautiful, but it can't drown out the sound of my pulse.

Still, the girls look lovely as they move slowly down the aisle. Not slowly enough, however. Before I know it, the music changes, and it's my turn. Everyone is standing.

No, no, don't stand. Turn around. Sit down. Don't look at me. Nothing to see here, folks. Go home.

But no one's listening. Everyone's looking at me, and smiling too, and whispering to one another. What are they whispering about? Me. They're whispering about me? Shut up! Stop talking about me. I hope they're saying nice things. They must be because they're smiling. Where's Cooper? Where's Cooper? Where's—

Oh, there he is. I see him. He's only a tiny blob because the aisle is so long, but he has to be the tall man in the tuxedo standing so proudly at the end of the aisle, without crutches or even a cane because the doctor declared him such a speedy healer. To be honest, he's still limping a little, but he's sworn to take it easy for the—

What's that flash? Oh, I see. Some of the people are taking

photos with their phones. The flashes dazzle my eyes. My God, I can't see. No, wait; I can. I can see. I'm starting to recognize people in the seats. There's Detective Canavan. He looks incredibly uncomfortable in his tuxedo, but quite distinguished as well. The excited-looking woman beside him in the new dress, taking all the photos, must be his wife. I'm glad, actually, that Nicole invited them.

Okay, maybe not so glad that she invited Carl, who's sitting in front of them and is toasting me with a cocktail he's already secured from the bar, but whatever. Julio and his wife look so pleased to be here (without actually being drunk before the reception's even started).

And there's Sarah, from the office in Fischer Hall. What's she doing here? Oh, right, I invited her. Who's that next to her?

Oh, Dave Fernandez, that's right, she asked if she could bring a plus one. Dave moved into Jasmine Albright's room after we finished removing all her belongings, and is proving to be an amazing asset to the staff. The other day, while I was talking to him at the front desk while he was putting braille stickers on the mailboxes, a group of freshmen boys walked by wearing backpacks, and Dave called out to them, "Hey, are you going to share those with me?"

"Share what?" the boys asked.

"Those beers you have in your backpacks," Dave said.

I made the boys unzip their backpacks. Somehow they'd gotten hold of three twelve-packs of bottled Budweiser. I confiscated the beer, then asked Dave how he'd known. He'd cocked his head at me as if I were crazy.

"I could hear them," he said. "Couldn't you?"

Sitting in front of Sarah and Dave are Muffy Fowler and her date—I have no idea who that guy is. He looks rich, though. Which would explain why Muffy looks so happy.

Beside them is Tom Snelling with his partner, Steven, the New York College basketball coach. Tom looks extremely handsome in his cream-colored tuxedo. He catches my eye and lays a hand upon his heart and mouths the famous line "You complete me."

In front of Tom is Eva from the medical examiner's office and . . . oh my God, Special Agent Lancaster. He looks incredibly hot—I can see that Tom thinks so too, since he's taking a huge amount of photos of him, though he's trying to be subtle about it. It's all right, though. Special Agent Lancaster is doing us a solid, arranging for both Prince Rashid and his new bride to receive asylum in the United States.

The fallout from Qalif hasn't been subtle, though it's been kept very hushed up in the press. No more leaks to the *Express*, though Cameron Ripley's been released from the hospital and has returned to his position as editor. He's been occupying himself with stories on the no-confidence vote on President Allington (not that this will have any effect whatsoever on the way things are run around the school). He's also apparently trained his baby rat to do tricks, including to come when called.

What Cameron—and the other members of the press—doesn't know is that Rashid's father pulled his $500 million donation to New York College in a rage as soon as he found out what Rashid had done—married a girl of his own choosing, and one of "common" blood, at that. The general sheikh cut off not only New York College, but Rashid, without a cent. The Escalade, the home theater, the lunches at Nobu—all gone, in the blink of an eye.

But Rashid, as far as I can tell, has never been happier. He's gotten to keep his room and his bodyguard detail, of course—courtesy of the U.S. government—because his father also vowed to send armed assassins to America to kill Ameera, and make the prince a widower, and thus eliminate the problem.

Rashid's mother, on the other hand—the first and oldest of the general sheikh's nine wives—vowed to do the opposite: welcome her son and his new bride back to Qalif whenever they wish to come, and to support them in any way she can. She's even opened a Twitter account—the first royal woman ever to do so in Qalif—in order to publicly vent her dissatisfaction with the way her husband is handling the situation. Rashid told me the other day, with a smile, "Spring is coming to Qalif. It may take a little while. But it's coming."

Ameera's moved into the prince's room, so Kaileigh got what her mother most wanted for her in the world:

A single.

Well, a single within a suite, since she still lives with Chantelle and Nishi.

The only person who hasn't gotten what he wanted out of Rashid's coming to New York College is President Allington. His half billion is gone, vanished somehow—*poof!*—because it turns out the sheikh's donation was only ever *promised*, never actually sent.

The worst part is, the president already spent it on plans to build a new state-of-the-art fitness center for his beloved basketball team.

Sure, he would have had to tear down a few buildings to do it, but those buildings didn't matter, as they served simply to house a few faculty members, boring old professors who'd done nothing with their lives but teach and win Pulitzer and Nobel prizes. So who cares?

Now all those professors are writing scathing op-ed pieces about the president in the papers every Sunday.

President Allington has decided to start spending weekends in the Hamptons, where no one he knows reads the New York papers.

I spy Lisa and Cory a few rows ahead of Eva and Special Agent Lancaster. Lisa is so excited to see me, she waves excitedly, and I can't help waving back, some of the butterflies beginning to disappear.

Dad's right. These people *are* my friends. They do want what's best for me, just as I want what's best for them. Now that the excitement over the RAs has died down—the rest of them moved out without incident once Howard was arrested, and new ones, handpicked by Lisa, were hired to replace them—things at the office have settled into a smooth routine, with one exception: Lisa's been bringing birthing videos to work from the hospital where she's chosen to give birth, for us to watch during downtime.

They truly are disgusting. No horror film can compare. Lisa says she can't understand why any hospital would give videos like this to expectant mothers. My retinas are forever scarred. We passed the videos on to Gavin, who is determined to find a way to work the scenes into his zombie film.

Gavin is sitting behind Lisa, not far from Pete (who can't take his eyes off Magda), and I can see that he's appointed himself our wedding videographer, to the annoyance of Cooper's father, who's paid for an official videographer, something we tried to stop, since I don't want a video of our wedding being shown on Cartwright Television (they televise a sort of lame *Where Are They Now?* rip-off). Tania—oh, there's Tania, looking so pretty in pink beside Jordan, uck, that jerk—warned me that the last thing I'd want is my nice wedding ruined by having footage of it broadcast on TV for everyone to see.

Cooper says not to worry, that he's got "someone on it," whatever that means. I suppose it means there's going to be an "accidental" fire in the videographer's studio, knowing the kind of "someone" Cooper is likely referring to.

Jamie, Gavin's girlfriend, looks almost as annoyed as Mr. Cartwright, but only because Gavin is blocking her view of the proceedings. Patricia, Cooper's mom, looks drunk, but it's two o'clock on a Saturday afternoon, so that's to be expected.

Only when Dad and I finally reach the end of the aisle, and I'm able to look into Cooper's eyes, do the butterflies in my stomach vanish completely. His face is filled with pride, love, and admiration for me. He can barely contain his happy grin as he moves to offer his arm in place of my father's.

"Take care of her," Dad says to Cooper, patting my fingers.

"I'll try," Cooper says. "She's pretty good at taking care of herself, though."

"So I've noticed," Dad says with a roll of his eyes, and shuffles off to his seat.

The officiant smiles kindly at us and tells our guests to sit down, and during all the shuffling, Cooper grins at me and says, "Nice dress."

"I hope you like it."

"It could be lower cut," he says, looking down the demure lace front of the dress at my cleavage. "I can barely see anything."

I roll my eyes, knowing he's teasing. "You've seen it all a million times."

"But I like seeing it *all* the time," he says, wiggling his eyebrows lasciviously.

"This is the Plaza, show some class, you dirty dog."

"Dearly beloved," the officiant begins. "We are gathered here today . . ."

The ceremony passes in a blur. I stand in my unfamiliarly high heels, feeling like a jangly cluster of nerves and excitement, hardly knowing what I'm saying. I repeat the words the officiant tells me to repeat, unable to look away from Cooper's face, the same way he's unable to look from mine. We're both smiling like idiots. It's a very good thing we both vetoed the idea of exchanging our own vows. We'd never have remembered them. I can't even remember what day it is.

As Patty comes up to take the bouquet from me when it's time to exchange the rings, she whispers, "You've almost made it. Two more minutes. Hang in there."

I can't believe it. It seems like mere seconds later that I've slid a ring on Cooper's finger and he's sliding a ring on mine—only mine, unlike the simple white-gold bands we'd picked out for each other, is inlaid with diamonds.

"What . . . ?" I look up at him, stunned, but he's repeating the words the officiant is feeding him. A sly smile has spread across his face, because he's managed to outwit me. We're supposed to be saving the money from the sale of my mom's jewelry so that we can renovate the basement.

Although I suppose it's all right that he's spent a *little* of it on something frivolous that we don't need. The diamond band certainly seems to go very nicely with my sapphire engagement ring.

"I, Cooper Arthur Cartwright," Cooper is saying, in a voice that suddenly sounds a little choked with tears, "take you, Heather Marie Wells, to be to be my lawful wedded wife, to have and to hold from this day forward, for better or for worse, for richer, for poorer, in sickness and in health, to love and to cherish, from this day forward until death do us part."

Is he *crying*? But Cooper never cries. Well, except during movies where animals die—

And then the officiant is pronouncing us husband and wife, and telling Cooper he can kiss me, and Cooper is dragging me somewhat urgently toward him and kissing me very emphatically on the lips.

My bright red lipstick is going to get all over him, I think, and as soon as he releases me, I see that it has.

But Cooper doesn't care, he looks deliriously happy. Why does he look so happy?

And then it hits me. It's over. Everyone is standing and

clapping and cheering. Even Nicole is clapping, and crying, while laughing at the same time, and Nicole hates everything.

We've done it. Cooper and I have done it. And neither of us tripped, or was shot, or knocked unconscious, or choked, or cut with a knife.

It's incredible. But it's true.

I turn to Cooper, who's slipped an arm around my waist.

"We did it," I say breathlessly. "We actually did it."

"Of course we did it," he says, kissing me again, this time more tenderly. "What did you expect?"

"I don't mean that," I say, looking around at the faces of all our friends and family. "Or rather, I do, but I mean . . . I think we might actually have changed our luck."

"Heather, don't you know? We've always had good luck. We found each other, didn't we?"

I smile at him, realizing he's right. Once again, I'm the one who wasn't seeing things clearly . . . they weren't at all the way they seemed. I slip my hand into his and allow him to lead me down the aisle, while everyone continues to applaud and cheer.

"What do we do now?" I ask him, forgetting the details of Perry's carefully mapped-out plan for the afternoon. Sign the wedding license? Give the officiant his fee? Sit for photos? Cocktail hour? Sit-down supper? Dancing? Cake?

"Now?" Cooper looks back at me with a joyous grin. "Now we live happily ever after."